STEP INTO CHAOS

BOOKS BY WILLIAM SHATNER

QUEST FOR TOMORROW

Delta Search
In Alien Hands
Step into Chaos
*Beyond the Stars**

**coming soon

STEP INTO CHAOS

QUEST FOR TOMORROW

—

WILLIAM SHATNER

HarperPrism

A Division of HarperCollinsPublishers

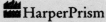
HarperPrism

A Division of HarperCollins*Publishers*

10 East 53rd Street, New York, NY 10022-5299

HarperPrism Books may be purchased for educational, business, or sales promotional use. For information please write: Special Markets Department, HarperCollins Publishers, Inc., 10 East 53rd Street, New York, NY 10022.

This is a work of fiction. The characters, incidents, and dialogues are products of the author's imagination and are not to be construed as real. Any resemblance to actual events or persons, living or dead, is entirely coincidental.

ISBN 0-06-105744-4

HarperCollins®, ■®, and HarperPrism™ are trademarks of HarperCollins*Publishers*, Inc.

A previous hardcover edition of this book was published in 1999 by HarperPrism.

Cover illustration © Peter Peebles

First paperback printing: December 1999

Printed in the United States of America

Visit HarperPrism on the World Wide Web at
http://www.harpercollins.com

❖ 10 9 8 7 6 5 4 3 2 1

Grief is no stranger to me. I know the pain—sharp and biting—lasts for a wrenching moment in time to be replaced by the deep ache of perennial loss. Somewhere in between these two, when hope rears its ephemeral shape, time, motion, and pain stop. Bewildered, I turn to hope—clutch its hem, twist the robes—pleading to the Fates to deny what may be inevitable. All it takes is an act of will to stop the downward spiral. But lack of will is part of the dementia. I dedicate this book to those poor souls whose struggle we look on with horror, tears, and love.

To Bill Quick, John Silbersack,
Caitlin Blasdell, and Carmen La Via . . .
my thanks.

*Love nothing but that which comes to you
woven in the pattern of your destiny.
For what could more aptly fit your needs?*

—Marcus Aurelius, *Meditations*

*There are two tragedies in life.
One is to lose our heart's desire.
The other is to gain it.*

—George Bernard Shaw, *Man and Superman*

SYNOPSIS

When young Jim Endicott celebrates his sixteenth birthday with a quiet dinner at his modest home on the Terran colony planet of Wolfbane, he has no idea his peaceful, ordered life is about to be shattered.

In fact, he is overjoyed at finally reaching sixteen, because now he can apply to the Solis Space Academy, the training ground for the men and women who will eventually con the great white ships of Earth on their voyages of discovery into the rest of the galaxy. And that is Jim's single and greatest dream: to join those ranks of legendary starship captains and play his own role in Terra's long surge outward.

After an evening of cake and games, he prepares to send his application to Terra. But first he speaks with his father, Carl Endicott, and is devastated when Carl bluntly refuses to allow him to apply. Worse, Carl will give no explanation. Jim returns to his bedroom and rebelliously sends the application off, disobeying his father over a major issue for the first time in his life.

On Terra, a mysterious figure named Delta

intercepts the application and knows for the first time in sixteen years what happened to his enemy Carl Endicott. He dispatches his best assassin, a hard-bitten female killer named Steele, to finish the job she failed at sixteen years ago: murdering Jim's father.

In turmoil over his disobedience, Jim confesses to Carl, who blows his stack and slaps him—also a first. Then Carl tells Jim he's destroyed their lives, and they will have to go on the run from forces he won't describe. The family packs up and departs for their mountain cabin, managing to escape only a short time before Steele and her two compatriots kick in the front door of the now-deserted Endicott home.

Carl, Jim, and his mother, Tabitha, arrive at the cabin with Steele hard on their trail. Carl shows unexpected competence at the killing game himself, rigging several explosive booby traps about the cabin, but in an ensuing firefight with Steele, Jim accidentally kills Carl with the birthday present his father had given him, an awesomely effective Styron & Ritter .75 rocket pistol. Carl's final words make the load of guilt Jim bears almost insupportable. To make matters worse, Steele, though wounded, kidnaps Tabitha and escapes back to Terra.

Jim, on the run, goes to Plebtown, a high-tech underclass ghetto on Wolfbane, where he meets Cat, a girl about his own age. Gradually he learns that Cat isn't what she seems—and may be a member of a shadowy Pleb revolutionary organization. She tells Jim the answers to the questions about his—and Carl's—past may be on Terra itself. Shortly after, with Jim struggling with his first case of true love, they part, leaving Jim to make his way to Terra by stowing away with a load of sheep on an interstellar circus ship.

On Terra he falls into the hands of the Pleb rebels' leader, a stone killer named Jonathan, from whom he learns that Delta has managed to kidnap Cat and is now offering to trade her and Jim's mother for Jim himself. Delta, it turns out, is the amoral and ruthless dictator behind the entire Terran government.

Jim agrees to turn himself over to Delta after having learned that Carl was not his real father and Tabitha not his real mother. But Jonathan, the Pleb leader, betrays him and hands him over without freeing Tabitha, though he does retrieve Cat. Jim finds himself at the mercy of Delta and is taken before him.

In the ensuing confrontation, Jim learns the great secret of his own past: His true mother, Kate, altered his genotype and encoded a great secret within it—a secret about how to link human minds into a vast supercomputer called the mind arrays. Delta wants the secret. But only Jim possesses the codes that will allow Delta's machines to translate the secret—except he doesn't know what those codes are.

While this is going on, Jonathan is launching an attack against Delta's satellite, and part of the attack is a virus embedded in Jim that attacks both computers and humans. As Jonathan fights his way deeper into the satellite, the virus is triggered and begins to destroy the links to Delta's own crude mind arrays, Delta, and Jim himself.

Jonathan, whose only goal in life is to kill Delta, arrives as Jim is struggling to save his own life. Delta is already disintegrating, and Jim is struggling for his life against the disease he carries within himself. Cat also shows up, and in the ensuing battle between Cat, Steele, Jonathan, and Jim, Jonathan is killed and Steele badly wounded. In the course of the battle, Jim realizes the secret to the code and gives it to Delta. Delta uses it to unlock Jim's genetic code and discovers that Jim's mother has left him with the secret of a new kind of mind array, one vastly more powerful than the one Delta already controls.

Delta uses Jim's knowledge to save both himself and Jim from the immediate effects of the disease. However, in the process, Delta learns the truth about Kate, whom in his own way he had once loved. She had foreseen that he would turn the mind arrays into an instrument of terror, and had knowingly prepared Jim as the antidote to this by building into his genetic code the means to control the new arrays.

Jim must still find his real parents, or at least their genetic records, if he wishes to achieve his goal of attending the Solis Space Academy. But even that challenge fades before his new burden: Locked inside his cells is the greatest power in the galaxy—and only he truly knows what it is.

In Alien Hands opens with Thargos the Hunter, a secret agent of the mighty Hunzzan Empire, searching carefully through the wreckage of Delta's satellite. What he discovers there leads him to Jim Endicott, but his arrival on Wolfbane coincides with that of Korkal Emut Denai, also a secret agent, but of Hunzza's most powerful enemy, the Albagens Empire. Thargos is sniffing after rumors of a powerful computer hidden somewhere in Terra System, and his search leads him to the small park where Jim is paying silent tribute to the long-dead heroes of Terra's first expansion into space.

He attempts to kidnap Jim but is foiled by Korkal's arrival. Korkal, once the liaison between Delta and the Alban Empire, is searching for Delta's successor. He arrives in the nick of time to force a firefight with Thargos and his henchmen, and rescues Jim from certain capture.

Korkal, fearing for Jim's life, convinces Tabitha to let Jim leave the planet with him. But Thargos overtakes their ship and attacks. In order to ensure Jim's safety, Korkal sends him away on one of the ship's lifeboats.

On the world of Brostach, Jim signs on with the mercenary starship *Queen of Ruin* and sets off on a new adventure. He loses himself in the life of a boot soldier and makes several new friends, the closest of whom is a Kindroran named Shishtar. Together the two youths fight many battles, achieving the kind of closeness gained only on the fields of war. Jim is shattered when Shish is killed, dying in his arms. No longer a child, and wiser in the ways of death and war, Jim is promoted to pilot trainee.

Here he begins to uncover the truth about the incomprehensible skills his mother encoded in his genes, in particular his ability to recognize digital patterns in cyberspace. This skill is at the heart of great piloting, though Jim doesn't yet realize just how good he is.

He soon gets a chance to learn, however, when the *Queen of Ruin* takes on the task of running emergency computer equipment to Alba, the capital of the Alban Confederacy, which is under siege by a Hunzzan armada. In the process of running the blockade, the main pilots are killed, and Jim takes over. He single-handedly defeats hundreds of ships and lands safely on Alba to find himself a hero. To his joy, he also is reunited with Korkal and through him meets Hith Mun Alter, the Packlord, the supreme leader of the Alban Empire.

But Thargos has tracked him down and, deciding that Jim is too dangerous to live, plots to blow up the building in which Jim is housed with a stolen Terran nuclear weapon. Jim stumbles on the nuke while exploring the basement of the building. When he reports his discovery to Korkal, he finds that the Packlord himself is also in the building and his life is at risk. But the Alban bomb experts know nothing about a Terran nuclear device, and so it is left to Jim to attempt to disarm the weapon. He succeeds, and so earns the gratitude, if not the true friendship, of the leader of Alba.

Jim is hung up on a moral point: With the

power encoded in his DNA, he knows he could revive the defunct Terran mind arrays and make them even more powerful than before. With the arrays and Alba's vast military power, a Hunzzan defeat would be certain; but at what cost?

He has seen enough of violence and death, and he doesn't think he can bear to be the cause of more, even though this time the victims will be Hunzzan. Nevertheless, Korkal finally persuades him to return to Terra and use his powers against Hunzza.

He returns to Earth aboard the greatest starship ever built, the *Albagens Pride,* a battleship as large as a small moon, specially designed to take advantage of his uncanny information-processing powers. Once again he meets his true love, the Pleb girl named Cat, who has returned to help her own people recover from the destruction visited upon them by Delta's mind arrays. Jim has told her the truth: The arrays were made from the linked minds of a billion Plebs—and the linkage was the cause of the deadly Pleb Psychosis that killed both of Cat's parents.

Now he needs her help to link the Plebs again in a far more powerful but much less dangerous network. As Jim works on the new network, Thargos finds him once more. A huge armada of Hunzzan ships is moving toward Sol System, but Thargos knows that unless he destroys Jim first, Jim will destroy the Hunzzan fleet. And Thargos still has a few Terran nuclear weapons left over from his original hijacking.

Jim works frantically get the new mind arrays up and running, while Thargos works equally frantically to find and kill him, but time is dribbling away for both of them. The Hunzzan fleet is already beginning to surround Sol System when Jim takes control of the newly rebuilt mind arrays for the first time and discovers that a powerful force calling itself Outsider is already there before him. It doesn't take Jim long to figure out what Outsider really is: Delta's mind, transferred into the old arrays at the time of his physical death in the explosion of his satellite.

Jim confronts and conquers Outsider, but as he does so, Thargos captures the satellite on which he is working and threatens to blow up both it and him with one of the Terran nuclear weapons. Jim manages to survive and Thargos is finally destroyed, leaving Earth safe for the moment, but Jim is lonely and depressed, wondering if he will ever be free of the load of guilt and responsibility placed on him before his birth by his mother and his unknown father.

PROLOGUE

4004 BC (TERRA STANDARD)

They were the greatest killers in the history of the galaxy, and no one knew who they were, or what they were, or why they killed.

Most humans were still making the transition from hunting large animals to planting small fields when Hunzzan astronomers noticed that the F7 star around which the planet Gelden revolved had vanished. After the star reappeared twelve days later, they reported the incident to Hunzza Prime, and the Imperial Nest took notice. When the same star disappeared a second time, on this occasion for nearly a month, and then reappeared as a white dwarf, the Imperial High Command became interested. And when in the space of an eye blink the white dwarf became a neutron star, a fleet set out to investigate what should have been an impossible series of events.

The disappearance of that fleet as it approached Gelden coincided with the transformation of Gelden's star into a singularity, a black hole. This would have been strange enough, but when it was discovered that Gelden (a world of mousy, chattering, gadget-making traders of no real interest to Hunzza) still seemed to exist, impossibly orbiting the singularity just beyond its event horizon, a cloud of fear began to spread across the Hunzzan Empire. The Hunzza were (and are) a cold-blooded and logical race (except when they become, by human standards, insane) and illogical things they could not explain frightened them. The basic survival reaction of the Hunzza was to destroy anything that frightened them.

Fifty thousand Hunzza had vanished with the first fleet, along with a hundred ships of the line and twice that number of auxiliaries. The emperor, Araxos, rejected the advice of his claw-brother, the High Prince Darod, and vowed to take vengeance on the unknown enemy for its terrible blow against the empire. This he did despite the fact that Darod possessed the rare gift of Foretelling, and Araxos knew that his advice was generally to be heeded.

Darod counseled restraint, even pacifism, but Araxos was not a pacifist. Nor were, it seemed, any other Hunzza except for Darod and his few followers. The emperor hissed at his brother in public, before the gathered court. Darod, shamed beyond life by the insult, took himself and his people away to a small planet on the fringes of Hunzzan space. He settled himself there and waited.

Araxos gathered together an armada of twenty thousand ships and ten million Hunzza. It was the greatest such gathering in the history of the empire, and its like would not be seen again for almost five millennia. Units of the Great Fleet, as it was called, were harvested from the nest worlds of six quadrants, although Hunzza itself provided the largest single portion.

Thus armed and armored, Araxos set forth with a single objective in mind: the utter and complete destruction of Gelden System and everything in it.

His scientists told him he could do nothing about the black hole. But when the Great Fleet approached Gelden System, the singularity vanished and was replaced by a red giant. The emperor announced that since the problem of the black hole no longer existed, he was confident his fleet could handle whatever was left.

Sun-poppers would deal with the red giant, and lesser weapons would deal with Gelden and whoever, or whatever, now lived on the surface of that doomed planet. Araxos paid no attention to his astronomers' awed discovery that Gelden now seemed to be orbiting *within* the red giant's photosphere, a situation nearly as impossible as its previous close orbit of a black hole.

"Vengeance!" said the emperor. "Vengeance!" every voice in his Great Fleet replied.

His brother remained behind, girded in his un-Hunzzan pacifism, and prayed to the new and terrible god he could so clearly Foresee. He even beseeched this god to provide divine blessings for his brother who had shamed him, because he knew he would never see Araxos again.

Since he didn't know whether he and his small remnant would survive as well (his Foreseeing wasn't perfect), Darod began to compile a library of everything he knew or suspected. He hoped that if his own world vanished in the catastrophe he was certain was coming, those who followed might learn about Hunzza's first contact with a Leaper, and be warned.

BOOK ONE: TERRA

*Guilt always hurries towards its
complement, punishment; only there
does its satisfaction lie.*

—Lawrence Durrell (1912–1990), *Justine*

*In the small circle of pain within the skull
You still shall tramp and tread
one endless round
Of thought, to justify your
action to yourselves . . .*

—T. S. Eliot (1888–1965),
Murder in the Cathedral

CHAPTER ONE

1

TERRAPORT

"Jim?"

"Go away. Leave me alone."

Tabitha hovered on the other side of the bathroom door. It was three in the morning. She clutched her bathrobe at her throat with one hand, and after a moment tapped gently on the door with the other.

"Are you all right? Jim, answer me."

She heard a soft gagging sound, followed by a deeper, chest-wrenching hack.

"Are you sick, Jim? Let me in."

She raised her fist to knock again, then let her hand drop. The sounds continued. She tried the palm lock on the door, but he'd set it to reject and it wouldn't respond. After a moment she turned and walked back down the hall to her bedroom, a room of uncomfortable newness in an apartment of jarring unfamiliarity. She left a small lamp lit and her door ajar, but even when she heard the bathroom door slide open and then shut again, he didn't appear. She listened to the click of the lock on his bedroom door and pictured him sitting in the dark, staring blankly at nothing.

After a while she turned off her own light and tried to sleep.

2

Jim Endicott awakened with the taste of sour beer scumming his tongue. His head felt hot, his eyes were gritty and burning, and the inside of his skull throbbed to a slow, nauseating beat. He sat up against his pillow and groaned at the white flash of pain the movement brought.

The room was dim and stuffy. It smelled faintly of vomit. He looked down and saw that he was still fully dressed in jeans, a shirt, even his shoes. His shoes were covered with mud, which had left brown streaks on the bedspread he hadn't bothered to pull aside when he'd flopped there sometime in the night. He couldn't even vaguely remember what time it had been.

He raised one shaking hand and touched his forehead. What *could* he remember? Buying a round of drinks for everybody in the Shawn Fan bar. Telling a bunch of strangers that his name was Joey Smith as he lost—how much?—at the pool table. He reached into the pocket of his jeans and pulled out a credit chip. He didn't want to know how much was left on it. If last night had been like the others, probably not much.

He moved his head until he could see the digital clock on his desk. Eight in the morning. The clock showed a date, too. He stared at the steady red numbers. Three days. Three more days till his seventeenth birthday.

He still felt drunk.

As he swung his legs over the edge of the bed and began to stand, his stomach gave a burning, bubbling lurch. He slapped one hand across his mouth and staggered for the bathroom.

He bent over and grasped the smooth, chilly porcelain with both hands. If he could spend the rest of his days doing nothing more than puking in the john, it would be fine with him.

3

"I made you some breakfast," Tabitha said.

He raised his head from the toilet bowl and saw her standing in the bathroom doorway. He hadn't heard the door open. The dry heaves had pretty much stopped, but he felt cold and limp. Sweat stood out on his forehead. "I'm not hungry . . . Tabitha."

"I know you aren't," she said. "But you need to eat something anyway. Trust me, it will help." She waited a moment, then said slowly, "Why don't you call me Mom anymore?"

He mumbled something, and she said, "What?"

"Because you aren't my mom."

She recoiled as if he'd slapped her.

"I . . . I *am* your mom, Jim. The only mom you've ever known."

"Please, Tabitha, leave me alone."

Her lips tightened. "Your breakfast is waiting." She turned away from the door. "Son."

The water rippled faintly in the bowl as he breathed on it. The slight chemical smell of it filled his nose. After a while he got up and walked shakily into the kitchen to eat his breakfast. Tabitha had locked herself in her bedroom, and so he ate silently and alone.

4

Once he'd decided his breakfast would stay down, Jim felt well enough to go back to bed, where he stayed until four in the afternoon. He got up and took a shower. As he stared at his bloodshot eyes in the mirror while he shaved, he realized he felt about as human as he was likely to feel. Tabitha was waiting for him when he went to the refrigerator to rummage for a sandwich.

"Are you going out again tonight?"

"Tonight. And every other night, maybe. If I feel like it."

"Jim, I didn't want to do this, but . . . this is crazy, what you're doing to yourself. So I'm putting my foot down. I forbid you to go out."

He didn't say anything. He found bread, sliced chicken, mustard and mayo, and a few crisp leaves of lettuce. He poured himself a glass of milk and sat at the small kitchen table. She stood near the door, watching him.

"Did you hear me?" she said.

He nodded.

"And?"

"If you want me tonight, I'll be at the Shawn Fan," he said. "Like always."

"Whatever you think, you're still my son. And you're still a boy. I am your mother, and you will do what I tell you to do."

He finished his sandwich and stood up. "Excuse me, Tabitha," he said as he tried to move past her, but she stepped into the doorway and blocked him.

"I won't let you go!"

He looked down at her. "You can't stop me."

She slapped him. He raised one hand and touched his cheek as he watched the uncertainty rush across her features in a pink wave.

"Do you remember when Carl slapped me?" he said. "It was almost a year ago. I deserved it then, and I probably deserve it now. But please don't do it again."

Her eyes went wide. Her lips moved, but she didn't say anything. Wordless, she stepped aside and let him pass. As he walked down the hallway toward his room, she began to cry behind him.

He knew he was a bastard. The worst kind of bastard in the world. But he didn't know what to do about that, either, and so he changed into fresh clothes, recharged his credit chip, and left for the Shawn Fan. Tabitha didn't come out to say good-bye, and he didn't go looking for her.

He hoped the booze would keep on doing the job. He didn't like the idea of hard drugs, and the thought of the only other alternative—wire-heading—kept him laughing bitterly all the way to the bar.

5

The Shawn Fan looked like a hundred other port dives. Sputtering holograms glowed garishly across its front, promising eternal bliss inside. But inside was only a tired dancer named Glory, standing in an electric cage, humping slowly to tunes ten years out of date.

At the bar two hookers, bright as parrots, cawed at each other. A man with a face like a melted candle grumbled into the cuffs of his tattered coat. A scruffy businessman in a shiny black suit slumped on a stool near the center, six empties ranged around him like a barricade as he pounded the seventh. The bartender stood behind the bar with his arms folded, his nostrils pinched as if he smelled something rotten smeared on his upper lip.

"A beer," Jim said.

The bartender nodded and reached down into the well. He came up with a familiar plastic can and slid it down the bar top. Jim snapped it up, popped the chill-strip, and felt the can go frosty in his palm.

"You running a tab tonight, Joey?" the barkeep asked.

Jim nodded and handed over his chip. The bartender swiped it through his reader and returned it, his eyes as blank as rain-washed slate. "You have a good time now, you hear?" he said. His tone was as flat as his gaze.

Jim glanced at the streaked mirror behind the bar and saw himself looking back, but as a stranger with thin lines beginning to fan from the corners of his eyes and a hard, watchful expression on his face. He was almost seventeen, but he looked five years older. Maybe more. No wonder Tony, the bartender, didn't remember him from the first time he'd stumbled into the Shawn Fan a year ago.

He lifted the can and poured a mouthful of near-frozen foam down his gullet. He'd started to get a taste for beer. He hadn't had it before. He wandered toward the two pool tables near the back of the bar.

Three people watched as Franny, the house pool hustler, set up a difficult masse shot. Franny brought the tip of the cue down hard. The cue ball jumped, came down spinning, and curved around two other balls to tap the nine ball into the far corner pocket.

One of the three watchers said, "Shit," and tossed a pair of gold coins onto the faded green felt. Franny grinned at him as he picked up his winnings.

"You ain't local," he murmured. "If you were, you'd know not to bet me like that." The other man, tall, with a twisted right arm, bunched his fingers into a fist, but Franny ignored him. "Hey, Joey!" he said. "My favorite pigeon. How much you gonna give me tonight?"

Jim gulped the rest of his beer and realized

he suddenly felt better. He grinned. "All I got, Franny. You know that."

But as he moved toward the rack of cues, the man who had lost his gold coins stepped in front of him. Jim stopped and waited. The man paid him no attention. He stared at Franny.

"I don't care who you think you are," he said. "You're gonna give me a chance to get my money back before you skin this punk here."

His hand came down on Jim's shoulder. Franny watched, a soft smile suddenly on his thin weasel face.

Jim turned and rammed the point of his elbow deep into the other man's gut. The man belched a cloud of whiskey breath as he doubled over. As his face came down, Jim's knee came up. The sound of the man's nose breaking was so loud, heads turned at the bar, twenty feet away.

Blood splashed. Jim clasped his fingers together into a double fist and brought it down with all his strength on the back of the other man's neck. The man dropped as if his muscles had liquefied. He lay on the floor, facedown, a red pool oozing out beneath his long greasy black hair.

Jim stared at him. Franny stepped around the table, holding his pool cue like a cudgel. He looked down and shrugged. "You didn't kill him," he said. It was hard to tell whether he was happy or unhappy about it.

The man's two other friends eyed Jim in horror. "Christ, you little bastard," the shorter one said, backing up. The taller one reached beneath his jacket. Then he froze as he stared down the monstrous snout of the Styron & Ritter .75 that magically appeared in Jim's hand.

For a moment everything stopped. Then Franny said, "Aw, Jesus, Joey. Don't kill him. It'll take an hour to clean up the mess."

Jim and the other man stared at each other. Then, slowly, the other man withdrew his hand from his jacket. It came out empty, and somebody sighed. The man raised both hands, palms out, and began to back slowly away.

"You," Franny said to the third man. "Drag your friend out of here. He's bleeding on the carpet."

When they were gone, Franny said, "You gotta watch yourself, Joey. Be careful. One of these days you're gonna get yourself killed."

Jim pulled a cue from the rack and rolled it on the table, testing for straightness. "Yeah, Franny. Maybe I will."

"Maybe you'll be careful?" Franny said.

"Maybe I'll get myself killed."

Franny stared at him until Jim looked over at Tony and said, "A round for the house, Tony."

Everybody cheered.

6

Rajput Singh was a nutball. Everybody knew he was a nutball. Since he was twelve years old he'd buried himself in what he called his laboratory, a fetid little room crammed with bits and pieces of salvaged electronics, odd chemicals, crumbling written histories of the experiments of ancient alchemists, classical New Age crystal gazers, and the madder dreams of modern wireheaders overdosed on pleasure to the point where their brains turned to cottage cheese.

At thirty-five he was a daze-eyed little rat of a man with a perpetually runny nose and a tendency to pick up odd skin maladies that he scratched instead of treating, so that he always seemed to be either scaly or scabby.

His investigations had taken a turn toward the mystical, toward what he called the holy ecstasy of creation. This mostly involved him using overpowered wirehead rigs that fried him into a brand of electronic exaltation so close to epileptic seizure that a single session left him twitching and grunting for a week or more.

He came out of his latest session even more scrambled than usual, but with a new after-effect: His brain seemed to be processing visual reality in layers, so that the physical world now looked to him like a black and white venetian blind. The effect grew stronger rather than fading away, until it seemed to him that the interior of his laboratory had been shaved down into layers no more than a single atom thick—a visual buzzing that thrilled and invigorated him.

He threw himself into a new avenue of investigation. Three weeks later, when the layering sensation finally faded away, he found himself staring at an ungainly construction he could only vaguely remember assembling.

In one small cage on a table before him was a white rat. He named the rat George. On the floor of the cage was a dull, lead-colored disk. Six feet away was another cage.

Rajput wiped his runny nose on his sleeve, threw a switch, and watched a strange white light grow around George. The light wavered and then grew stronger, until it seemed to penetrate George's tiny body, exposing the infinity of layers that made up George's atomic structure.

George vanished.

A moment later George began to reappear in the other cage, at first a wavering, tenuous ghost, then becoming more and more solid. George seemed entirely unaffected by the process that had moved him from one cage to the other. He ate a bit of cheese and flicked his whiskers happily.

Rajput still wasn't quite sure what he'd done—teleportation, molecular translation, subquantal duplication. All he knew was that it was something entirely new, and that it would probably make him one hell of a lot of money.

He also knew enough about chaotic systems to know that it would start a butterfly effect on a massive scale.

CHAPTER TWO

1

Tabitha rode the escalator up from the underground grav-tube station and emerged onto a slidewalk beneath a sky the color of tarnished pewter. Terraport stretched for a hundred miles up and down the California coast, and even at night the sky never got entirely dark. Now it glowed as if its pewter skin were melting in a smoky fire.

Gritty wind tugged at her hair. She paused, staring at the two-hundred-story tower rising before her. She checked the address she'd written on a scrap of paper, then walked into a lobby large enough to park a small starship in. She consulted a holoscreen for the correct bank of grav-lifters, entered one of fifty vertical tubes, and stepped off into a quiet corridor lined with closed doors. She walked down a thick brown carpet, squared her shoulders, and pushed on inside the office.

"I'm here to see Dr. Lindsay," she told a receptionist whose chill, perfect features looked molded out of alabaster. In the face of such icy perfection, Tabitha instinctively patted her hair, then realized what she was doing, and stopped.

"Ms. Endicott?"

"Yes, that's me."

"Dr. Lindsay is running a bit late. Can you wait ten minutes?"

"Yes, of course." She seated herself on an expensive white leather formsofa. It cuddled her, and after a moment she relaxed.

God. Will Jimmy hate me for this? Please don't let him hate me.

2

Smoke swirled along the low ceiling of the Shawn Fan. Fumes from burning marijuana, krak, simba, and uncounted flavors of tobacco cast a blue-gray pallor on faces that could have been resting in coffins.

The Shawn Fan was not far from a set of main gates leading to the spaceport loading docks. It had no regular clientele. Spacers, fleet doggies, dock wallopers, grifters, thugs, and hustlers made an ever-changing parade of new faces. Only the bartenders, the waitresses who special-ized in lap dancing, and a few like Franny the pool shark stayed the same. Jim called himself Joey here. He knew the employees liked him because he threw money around like a space marine on leave, and he did it every night. It was a relationship he could comprehend, and he always knew where he stood. When the money stopped, so would the friendships.

He was working on his sixth or seventh beer,

the empties lined up on a shelf by the pool table where Franny was chalking his cue, when the girl came through the door. She was short, almost elfin, with a cap of dark curly hair and eyes like cut obsidian. She looked about twelve years old as she paused just inside, watching the crowd.

She pushed her way between a pair of over-muscled dock hands and swaggered up to the bar. She climbed on a stool, propped her elbows on the bar top, and said, in a surprisingly husky, rasping voice that easily carried to the pool table, "Shot of bourbon, beer chaser."

Jim grinned into his beer and waited for Tony's explosion. But the barkeep only nodded and set up the order. Then he turned away and ran his fingers across the touchpad of the cash register.

Franny glanced up when Jim elbowed him. "Hey, I'm making a shot here."

"Yeah. Take a look at the bar."

"So? It looks like a bar."

"You see the kid sitting there?"

Franny looked again, a puzzled expression coming across his pale, freckled face. "Kid . . . ? Oh. That's Char. She ain't no kid." He smirked. "Why? You interested? She ain't cheap. The johns like that little-girlie look. And they pay for it. But you seem to have plenty of credit, so no problem, right?"

"She's a hooker? Tony didn't take anything from her, no chip, no cash."

The pool shark shrugged. "She's got a tab. Been coming in here for years. And she's not exactly a hooker."

"Not a hooker? What is she, then? She looks about twelve."

"Must be the light, Joey, my boy. Take my word. She's older than you, probably."

Jim eyed him. "That so? How old do you think I am?"

He leaned back and took a long look at Jim's face. Then he shrugged. "I dunno. You seen a little wear. And you been places, done things. Been a soldier somewhere, I guess. So, what— twenty? Twenty-one?"

"Close enough," Jim said.

"I could tell," he said. "I'm good at stuff like that. Anyway, you wanna know about Char, the best thing is to just ask her."

Jim nodded and ambled away. His path brought him closer to the bar. Something tingled at the dull edge of his interest. He couldn't tell if it was the beer or the girl, but it surprised him anyway. He stopped directly behind her.

"Hey, Tony! Set up the rail. And give the lady anything she wants."

3

"**Y**ou seem nervous, Ms. Endicott."

Tabitha sat on a comfortable formchair across from Dr. Lindsay's desk. The doctor was a small, thin man with fashionably bushy sideburns and streaks of gray in his meticulously flash-cut brown hair. His gaze seemed sharp but somehow uninterested, as if she were a specimen he was seeing for the first time.

"Please don't misunderstand, Doctor," she said. "I'm not here for myself."

He nodded, though his calm, remote expression didn't change. "I see. So what is the problem?"

"It's my son. Well, he's not really my son—my stepson, or foster son, I guess you could say."

His fingertips brushed a small control pad on the arm of his chair. "Would you mind if I recorded this?"

"Uh, maybe. Is it confidential?"

"Absolutely confidential," he said.

She thought about it. "I guess it's all right." He smiled, and she continued. "He's begun to act very strangely. Almost self-destructively."

He let her talk, nodding every time she faltered. Here and there he stopped her to ask a question.

"You say this change in his behavior came suddenly?"

"Yes, right after we—" She stopped. She didn't have Jim's permission for any of this. And much of what she knew involved others, some of whom were very powerful. She wondered if she might be breaking some law or other by speaking at all.

She stared at his watchful, waiting expression and wondered why she'd come to this man. There was so much she *couldn't* tell him.

"Jim was on a . . . trip for a while. I think something happened to him. He won't talk to me about it. And he broke up with his girlfriend recently."

"Ah," Dr. Lindsay said.

"No, I don't think it was that. They didn't really break up. More like a . . . mutual agreement. At least he didn't seem too upset. Any more than usual, I mean."

"How old is the boy?"

"Almost seventeen. His birthday is in three days."

Dr. Lindsay's lips moved, but Tabitha heard nothing. "I'm sorry, I didn't hear that," she told him.

"You weren't meant to. I have a sound shield around my desk. It's so I can take private notes while I listen, without disturbing my patients. If it bothers you, I'll do it by hand."

"Oh, no. It's all right."

He waited.

"Yes. Well, anyway, all of a sudden he's become surly. He won't listen to me or do anything I tell him to. And he's started going out every night to this bar. He comes home so drunk he can hardly stand up. I hear him vomiting . . ."

"You're sure it's just alcohol?"

"Yes. Jim would never—" She stopped. Drugs? The old Jim, the Jim from a year ago, would never have used drugs. But this new, dark Jim, who seemed so much older than his years, full of rage and sadness? She realized she had no idea what this Jim might do.

"I think it's just alcohol. I didn't ask him. I'm not sure he'd tell me, anyway."

Again his lips moved silently. Then he said, "Go on."

Tabitha picked and stuttered and mumbled her way to the end of it, telling him as much as she knew, as much as she thought she could safely reveal. As she spoke, a part of her seemed to stand aside and listen, and that part told her she sounded like a fool or a crazy woman. She wondered what Dr. Lindsay must think. His calm, still expression gave nothing away.

"And . . . that's all, I guess," she said at last. She looked down at her fingers, knitted together so tightly in her lap that her fingernails were as pale as those on a corpse.

"I . . . should be going now. I'm sorry to have bothered you. This was a bad idea." She made to rise.

"Wait."

"What?"

"Ms. Endicott, did I understand you correctly? You say the boy shot his father to death?"

Put as baldly as that, she abruptly realized how horrible it sounded.

"It wasn't—he wasn't—maybe Carl wasn't his real father. And you make it sound like a murder, but it wasn't. It was an accident."

"Yes, you said that. An accident. Can you tell me more about the actual circumstances?"

Tabitha gnawed at her lower lip. She'd been either frantic with terror or unconscious during the firefight in the mountains on Wolfbane. But she knew it had involved Commander Steele and Delta, and though both of them were dead now, she was afraid to stir the ashes of their memory. Who knew what sort of ghosts remained after them, listening for whispers of their names? And the others—the Packlord, the Hunzza, Serena Half Moon, and . . .

They were still alive.

"I really must be going," she said, slurring her words in her haste to get up and leave.

"I'll take the case," he said.

"I beg your pardon?"

"I'll take the case." For the first time there was a flash of something in his eyes. "What you've told me doesn't make a lot of sense. But I can draw a few tentative conclusions. Have you ever heard of something called adolescent adjustment disorder?"

"No."

He smiled. It gave his grave features a rueful, attractive cast. "It's a grab bag, really, a syndrome of different adjustment problems. All teenagers have adjustment problems. It's part of being a teenager. But sometimes those problems—and the adjustments to them—become overwhelming. From what little you've told me, I'd say that what your boy has gone through would be enough to send any normal, well-adjusted adult into deep therapy. But for a child his age—" He spread his hands and shrugged. "I think he needs some help. Don't you think so?"

Her cheeks flushed. She realized she wanted to go over to this calm little man and hug him.

"Yes. Can you help him, Doctor?"

"I can try."

Later he escorted her out to his receptionist. "Millie will set up an appointment schedule."

She shook hands with Dr. Lindsay. After he'd gone back into his office, Millie said, "Dr. Lindsay's rates are comparable to the norm for a professional of his stature."

Tabitha gave a slight jump. She'd been staring at the closed door to his office. "What? Oh, of course. Money's not a problem."

"I see." Millie sounded dubious. Tabitha reached into her purse and found her credit chip. She handed it over. "Here. Just set up an account."

Millie took the chip and swiped it. As she looked at the reader, the machine beeped and her eyebrows rose. When she handed the chip back, her tone was noticeably warmer and she seemed to see Tabitha for the first time. Tabitha was surprised at the guilty glow of triumph she felt.

"We'll set up an appointment schedule now, Ms. Endicott," Millie said.

Tabitha wasn't sure how much money she had. An enormous amount, she knew that much. Jim had arranged something. He'd said they would never have to worry about financial things ever again.

She supposed they were rich, but this was the first time she'd ever seen the effect of it on somebody else. She felt mildly ashamed of the warm glow it gave her as she left the office. It was only in the grav-lift going down that the full impact of what she'd done hit her.

How in the hell am I going to explain this to Jim?

4

"**A**re you trying to pick me up, Joey Smith?" Char said.

"How do you know my name?"

She shrugged. She was running the tip of her finger around the wet rim of her glass. It made a small, irritating squeak. "Maybe you're a famous guy."

He sat on the bar stool next to her with three crumpled empties in front of him. Tony wasn't the kind of bartender who paid a lot of attention to housekeeping.

Char wore skintight black jeans and a black long-sleeved T-shirt that outlined her small breasts. Jim could see a faint tightness around her eyes, and the beginnings of what would become two frown lines above the bridge of her nose. It wasn't a twelve-year-old's face. He understood what had misled him. She moved like a child, quick, mercurial, flowing, heedless. Yet whenever she ordered another drink, she checked the credit screen to make sure it was rung properly. She was unobtrusive about it, but she did it every time.

"I doubt that I'm famous," he told her.

"It doesn't take much around here. This is Pleb country. If you know anything about Plebs, you know we don't get famous very often. Maybe if we murder somebody, like you almost did a little while ago."

His eyebrows rose. "You weren't here."

She waggled her fingers at him. "Char sees all and knows all. Maybe I'm trying to pick you up, Joey. You ever think about that?"

He finished his beer, crushed the can, and set it down with great care. Tony saw and lifted his chin. Jim nodded. After Tony brought him a fresh beer, Jim said, "No, I didn't think about it. Do you want me to?"

"That's kind of an insulting thing to say to a girl. You're what, sixteen, seventeen? Aren't all guys supposed to be horny at that age? Hump a snake, like that? And you aren't even thinking about it? What am I? Ugly?"

His cheeks glowed a dull red. Talking to her was like walking into a cloud of gnats with his mouth wide open. She said she was a Pleb, but she was different from Cat.

"I knew a Pleb girl once," he said.

"I bet you were in love with her. And I bet she broke your heart." She glanced at him. Then she patted his hand and he swallowed his beer the wrong way. "Yeah, us Pleb girls, we'll do that. Sluts all the way, every one of us."

"Don't say that."

"Why not, Joey? It's the truth. Don't worry, you won't hurt my feelings." She chuckled. The sound was as bitter as anything Jim had ever managed himself when thinking about wire-heading. He checked behind her ear. Beneath the short black curls, a bronze socket gleamed out at him.

She saw his eyes move. "That's right. I'm a socket sucker. You got a problem with that?"

"No. I guess not."

"You guess not. Well." She lifted her glass and drained her drink. The ice cubes rattled as she set it on the bar harder than she needed to. "And maybe I sling a little wire, too. And other things. You guess that wouldn't bother you, either?"

"Are we fighting?"

She leaned back. "I don't know. I haven't made up my mind yet."

He hunched forward so he couldn't see her face. "Don't bother."

"Yeah? Why's that?"

"Because it doesn't matter. I'm not trying to pick you up. You don't make me horny. Sorry."

Her voice grew raspier. "So what do I make you, Jim? Curious?"

She slid off the stool and was halfway across the bar before he caught it and turned.

"Hey, wait a minute!"

She sliced through the crowd like a water moccasin. At the door she paused, and he saw her black, bleak gaze rake him. Then she was gone.

Jim stared at the door as it swung shut. When he reached for his beer, his fingers trembled and he spilled a little. He drank the rest down in one long gulp.

He slid off the bar stool and went to the door. The night street outside swirled with neon-shadowed flesh. But no Char.

She knew his real name.

5

"**I**t's like when we met," Char said.

Harpalaos, a young Hunzza, nodded slowly. "Not this corner, though. I found you a couple of blocks over. Or you found me."

She grinned. "Do Hunzza believe in coincidence?"

He shrugged. His scales gleamed in the frozen neon light. "Why not? Random meetings, chance—it's a big reality. A big universe. Things bump against each other."

He knew she was nervous. He could smell it on her, along with a brassy tang of fear. That made him nervous. He didn't like being frightened, though now he was frightened all the time. So much at stake, and he didn't even know—

"What's going to happen?" he said.

"Not like our first dance," she said. "That was an accident."

"I still can't say I understand you Terrans' ideas about commerce."

She laughed at that, though she kept right on scanning the busy corner on which they stood, and the traffic flows across the intersection. "Biz is biz, Harpy. And war is only the continuation of biz by other means."

He blinked, confused. "I don't understand that, either."

"Never mind." She seemed distant, musing, preoccupied. "The funny thing is, you didn't even know you were saving my life. All you were trying to do was get away. I didn't know what a chickenshit you were."

"I'm not—"

"Don't get your scales bent out of shape. I like you the way you are, Harpy. I deal with testosterone-crazed males all the time, hard dicks ready to blow me up for looking at them wrong. It's a relief to know you aren't that way. It's . . . soothing, almost."

He looked away. "If I'd understood, I *would* have tried to save you."

"And probably screwed it up entirely. No, there's nothing like a terrified Hunzza with claws and a mouthful of teeth trying to *get away*. You took down two of those wirejackers just trying to run over them."

"I saw their guns."

"Uh-huh. Must have been a surprise for you, being an innocent tourist and all, to stumble right into the middle of a street-corner gang war." She glanced at him.

"You know I'm not innocent."

"Yeah. I just don't know what you're guilty of."

"Char, it's not important. Not now. Call it whatever you want, coincidence, accident, anything. I'm still glad I met you."

She nodded. "Me too. If you hadn't, I probably wouldn't be talking to anybody now, let alone you. Those jackers were smarter than I gave them credit for. They had me, until you wandered into the middle of it."

He grinned. With his long rows of gleaming fangs, it was a considerably less reassuring proposition than her own answering smile.

She stiffened. "Okay," she said. "I think we're on."

Harpy closed his eyes. He hated this kind of stuff. No big deal, though; he hated everything about his life just now. And sometimes he wondered if it had been an accident. He didn't really believe in fate, no matter what his father said. But there was a bond between him and the girl. No matter how much he wanted to, he couldn't deny that.

He hoped he could keep both himself and her alive long enough to—

"There," she said. "Don't move."

6

Lasher Larue was eighteen. He'd been slinging wire on the street for five years, which meant he was three years past the normal life expectancy for that line of work. When the Organization had asked everybody to join in the Great Linkage that supposedly had defeated the Hunzza, he'd declined. Lasher wasn't strong on civic duty.

He sat in the shotgun seat of the stolen grav-van and fingered the butt of a cloned military shatter-blaster resting between his knees. Harkey the Mouse was driving. Mouse weighed about three hundred pounds and nobody, not even him, remembered why he was nicked after a tiny rodent. There was nothing tiny about Mouse.

Mouse edged the nose of the van slowly around the corner from Third Apple Lane onto a wider stretch of Saint Diana Road, going with the flow of the gutter-to-gutter traffic. Lasher didn't pay any attention. Mouse was a natural driver. He always knew what was what.

"You see her?" Mouse said.

Lasher craned his neck. "Yeah. She's up there with her snake boy. Like usual."

"Take them both out?"

"Sure. What else?"

Mouse nodded and slid the van to the inside lane nearest the curb. "I'll come in normal like, and then slow down right before. Maybe she won't see us coming."

"Just do it," Lasher said. He lifted the ugly, bulbous snout of the blaster and let it rest against the lip of the open window next to him.

Mouse nodded. The van eased closer to the corner on which Char McCain and a young Hunzza stood. The night pulsed with neon and bone-beat. Char and the Hunzza were staring idly in the opposite direction from Lasher's approach.

Lasher lifted the barrel of the blaster out the window. Piece of cake.

7

The beer made Jim's head swirl. He pushed steadily through the crowds that filled the streets—tourists, spacers, johns, and those who preyed on them—looking for her.

He saw a lot of short, dark-haired girls, but none of them was her. He was searching for her on her home turf, and if she wanted to stay out of sight, she would. But he had to look anyway. She'd let it slip that she knew his real name. Or was it a slip?

He felt as if players were standing at the dark edges of his life watching him. Manipulating him for reasons and purposes he didn't understand. It wasn't a new feeling. After the last year, he didn't believe in coincidence. He knew there really were watchers. And manipulators. One in particular. But he couldn't figure out what Outsider could have to do with some Pleb girl he'd never seen before in his life.

A hulking dock worker bumped him sideways but didn't even pause. Jim turned, but the woman was gone. She'd been about the size of a Beijing Cowboys linebacker.

The knock seemed to clear his head. He turned a corner and saw Char standing at the far end of the block. She was slouching against a large waste receptacle, and she seemed to be talking to a Hunzza.

A *Hunzza?*

Reflexes he'd hoped he would never use again showed him something else. A dented red grav-van was just entering the intersection beyond her. A man's head and shoulders protruded from the side window. The man was holding a shatter-blaster. The obvious, deadly pattern clicked in his mind.

He began to run.

8

Lasher felt the old hot juice boiling in his groin as he leveled the shatter-blaster. This was the part he really liked. The van lurched as Mouse brought it down to a crawl. She was still looking away from him. That wasn't good. He wanted her to know where it was coming from. That it was coming from *him*.

The last thing she would ever know.

"Hey, bitch!"

Turning more quickly now, white face, those nasty eyes. Hand beneath her short jacket, coming out now, as he began to squeeze the trigger.

Somebody running . . .

9

Shish had called it battle eyes. When time slowed down and you saw *everything*.

Jim couldn't feel his own body. It was as if he were nothing but a viewpoint, taking it all in. The face in the van over the snout of the blaster. A young guy with a scar. His eyes looked orange in the reflected light of a holofloat jittering overhead.

Char turning, her hand beneath her jacket, coming out now, holding something. The Hunzza whipping around with that unbelievable lizard speed, white teeth flashing, startled and hissing.

Jim dived across the last few feet and

slammed into her. Something dark in her hand, then light flashing from it. He felt a sear of heat across his face as he bounced heavily off the waste receptacle, felt her land beneath him, soft, cushioning his fall.

The S&R .75 bucked in his hand, once, twice, once more. The deep, bell-like ring of its enormous charge shivered the night. The face above the shatter-blaster vanished in a red splash. Then the van exploded, half its front end gone.

A fireball filled the street, banners of flame slopping across other vehicles. Somebody screamed, a thin, high spike of sound. Then somebody else.

"Get off me, you asshole."

"What?"

"Let me *up*."

What was left of the van exploded again. A huge, shadowy figure dripping fire staggered screaming out of the ruins. Claws sank into Jim's shoulder and yanked him away from her. She rolled over. Light sprang from her hand and touched the burning man. He stopped screaming and fell over.

"Mouse," she said. "Poor dumb bastard."

The hissing, breathy tones of a Hunzza speaking Terrie filled his ear. "We have to get out of here."

Jim shook his head. He was sitting on his butt, legs splayed out, back against the waste receptacle. Time speeded up again. She stood over him, one hand out, reaching for him.

"Come on, dumbass. Time to go."

Reflexively he took her hand and was surprised at her wiry strength as she hoisted him to his feet. His ears still rang with the bellow of the .75. He slipped it back into its shoulder holster.

"Quickly," the Hunzza hissed. He was crouched over a section of the sidewalk. Jim heard a rusty screech and saw the Hunzza lift the section away, revealing a dark hole. "This way," the Hunzza said.

"What the hell . . . ?" Jim said.

"That's some blaster you carry there," Char said. She hid her own weapon back beneath her jacket. "You screwed that up beautifully, Jimmy, but I forgive you."

He stared at her, trying to understand. Her eyes glittered in the subsiding flames. A siren wailed in the distance, grew louder.

"Get your ass down that hole, boy. Just like Alice."

White faces turned toward them like pale night flowers. People were pointing at him, at them. Waving. Their mouths were pink circles. He realized they were shouting.

"Move," she said, and punched him hard in the chest. It rocked him loose from his strange paralysis.

He took two steps, then dropped down the hole into darkness.

10

Professor Phyllis Parker-Giddins did not know Rajput Singh, and even if she had, she wouldn't have admitted it. She would have regarded Singh's research methods as closer to witchcraft than to her own meticulous, carefully controlled and documented routines in the suite of laboratories and offices she maintained at Cambridge University. She possessed an IQ that kissed the bleeding edges of every known test, an IQ she'd spent nearly thirty years training as she picked up seven different degrees. Her specialty was the study of cellular longevity, and her goal was simple and single-minded: She intended to add the Nobel prize to her list of accomplishments before she reached the age of forty.

She had nearly a hundred people working under her, the latest in information-processing equipment, and all the money in the world. She thought her chances were excellent. But things had gone badly the last couple of years, until just recently, when she'd hit on a new thing.

She began using direct connections into raw databases in such a way that she thought she was allowing her own highly trained subconscious to sort data. It was a technique she'd partially borrowed from accounts of ancient Native American shaman trances, coupled with a touch of Jungian archetypal theory and a hint of the work done by certain pioneering Germans in cybernetic interface logics, work that had for some reason been dropped for what seemed then to be more effective methods.

It was a witches' brew, and when she immersed herself in it, she felt for the first time in two years that she might be breaking new ground. Encouraged, she poured larger and larger databases into the mix, hammering herself with more and more raw information. It was a little like swimming in an airy liquid composed of very tiny, very hot points.

After three months of this she emerged into a frenzy of work that left her assistants and their teams gasping for breath and snarling at her behind her back. She didn't care. She felt the elusive Nobel trembling just beyond her grasp but growing closer.

As it turned out, she was right. She knew it when she looked into a small enclosure swarming with *Drosophila melanogaster*, the common vinegar fruit fly. This fly had a life cycle of ten days and very large chromosomes, making it ideal for basic genetic studies.

"How long?" she said.

An assistant, staring at the swarm, said, "Four and a half months. A hundred thirty-five days."

"Thirteen times normal life span," Dr. Parker-Giddins remarked. She was amazed at how calm she felt.

"Yeah, about that," the assistant replied.

"They still look young."

"Yes . . ."

If it wasn't immortality, it was close to it. In humans, it would be the equivalent of a life span of a thousand years.

Nobel, here I come, Dr. Parker-Giddins thought.

CHAPTER THREE

1

Jim dropped into the hole in the sidewalk and landed hard. As he tried to stand he felt something in his right knee pop and give way. He staggered and banged his shoulder painfully against a jagged outcropping of pipes.

"Damn it."

A sibilant hiss, rising over deep humming tones. "Wait a minute . . ."

A soft snap; the Hunzza's shape appeared, outlined in the golden glow of a lightwand in his right hand. Jim bent over and massaged his knee. The joint ached, but he could stand on it okay. Another shadow dropped from above and resolved into Char. She pointed up.

"I put the cover back in place. Nobody will check down here right away, not with that barbecue in the middle of the street. By the time anybody thinks of this, we'll be gone."

She flashed a grin. "How's that sound, Jim? What's the matter? Hurt your knee?"

"Char . . ."

"Oh, I know, Harpalaos. You worry too much." She glanced at Jim. "Harpy's my buddy. He worries about me. Now he'll worry about you, too. It's okay, Harpy. We've got lots of time."

"Misss Char, maybe we do. And maybe we don't. The boy's weapon . . . it was very strong. It made a lot of noise and many people looked. No doubt some of them saw me open the cover and saw us jump down."

She was manic, her black eyes gleaming wetly in the glowlight. "You heard the man, Jim. Let's get a move on. Can you walk?"

He gritted his teeth. "I can walk."

"Let's do it, then." She pushed past him, took the glowlight from the Hunzza, and began to move off down the tunnel. The Hunzza fell in behind her and left Jim to make his own way. He could either follow or stay in the dark . . . in more ways than one.

"Slow down. I can walk, but I'd rather not run if I don't have to."

He had the hollow, helpless feeling that, once again, events were lurching wildly away from him.

"How come you know my name?"

She didn't turn. "Jim? Is that your name?"

"You know it is."

"I already told you. I see all, know all."

"That sounds like some hokey fortune-teller."

A low, rolling boom thudded out of the darkness from the direction they'd come. "I think that's for us," she said. "Maybe now's the time to find out if you can run, Jim boy."

"Don't call me that."

A voice shouted behind them. Jim's knee did hurt, but as it turned out, he could run.

Panic had its uses.

2

Lord Korkal Emut Denai, acting Albagensian ambassador to the Terran Confederation, sat in the captain's chair on the bridge of the *Albagens Pride* and stared at the holographic image of Hith Mun Alter, the Packlord of the Alban Empire.

"Your orders place me in a tight jacket, Packlord. I owe the boy something."

The Packlord was lean and grizzled and graying, but his eyes looked as young and dangerous as ever. They were the eyes of a predator, a leader who had fought his way to the top of the pack and led it when it hunted. Korkal reflected that though the pack Hith Mun Alter led numbered in the trillions, the principle remained the same.

"As do I, Lord Denai. Which you well know. But you said it best to the boy yourself: Agreements are not suicide pacts. I bear Jim Endicott no ill will. Exactly the opposite, in fact. But the signs are disturbing, and he is at the very center of the disturbance. So though I owe him a great deal, I must know the truth. And you must discover it for me."

"The humans make the mistake of thinking that we are like their wolves," Korkal said. "Savage and ruthless. Or they go to the other extreme and think us like their dogs, loving and utterly loyal."

The Packlord snorted softly. "We are Albagens. We are neither dogs nor wolves. We are

not animals. Their errors aren't my concern . . .
unless I can use them. Remember where your
first loyalty lies, Lord Denai. I do."

Korkal remained silent for several moments,
long enough for the Packlord to grow irritated.

"Well, Korkal? Must I refresh your memory?
Of loyalty . . . and other things?"

"No, Lord, that won't be necessary. But I do
owe him."

"I'm not asking you to harm one hair on that
boy's head. Not now, at least. But I need to
know the truth. About him, and about his race.
He trusts you."

Korkal nodded. His voice, a soft, liquid snarl,
sounded sad. "Yes. I think that makes it worse
somehow."

The Packlord waved one hand in dismissal.
"You've worked in a treacherous business all
your life, Korkal. You are a spy, an agent of the
Alban Empire. I cannot believe that at this late
date you forget the smell of duty when it fills
your nose." The Packlord's voice softened. "Old
friend, I understand your dilemma. But the
danger is too great. It may already be too late.
And I must *know*."

"I understand, Lord. And I will find out for
you, if I can."

"Good. Do you know where he is now?"

"Yes. He's living in Terraport, with his mother."

"You keep track of him? How is he?"

"Yes, I keep track. Not every moment, but
he's watched. For his own safety as much as
anything. Not much of his role leaked out to the
public at large, but some know. So I watch him.

How is he? He is . . . delicate. And then there is the question of this Outsider."

"Yes. Do you believe what Jim told me about that?"

"That Outsider was a ghost, a virtual reflection of our old friend Delta?" He shrugged. "I don't know. What choice do we have? We have no way of discovering the truth."

"Jim knows the truth," the Packlord said. "What do you mean when you say that Jim is delicate?"

"His emotional state is uncertain. He seems depressed. He's begun to indulge heavily in a minor human drug." Korkal shrugged. "What do you want me to do? Put him to the question?"

"No, of course not. That might set off a train of events we'd have no way of controlling. If my fears are true, it might even begin the thing I fear the most."

"A Terran Leap?"

The Packlord nodded.

"You will have to help me, Packlord. I confess, knowledge of Leaper cultures is not my strongest suit. I know little beyond the bogeys all children learn." He spread his hands. "Not the most detailed information, you see."

"There are records—some of them very old, all of them very secret. I will have them unlocked and give you access. But I'm afraid you will find them as much a disappointment as I have."

"Why is that, Lord?"

"Because they really don't tell us much. In fact, they may tell us only one thing—that it is the nature of Leapers to become unknowable."

"Then the task you set me is impossible."

"Perhaps. I have gone through those records a hundred times. Certain patterns emerge. Once a culture is well into its Leap, it becomes invisible to us—to anybody on the outside. Something like the way we can't know what goes on inside a black hole. Call it a social singularity, perhaps, or a technological one. But we do have fairly decent records covering three instances of Leaping in the past ten thousand years. There may have been more, but we might not have recognized them. What we do know is that these three Leaps began with sudden, unexplained technological spirals. We don't know what triggered them, and in each instance they took a different form before the culture entered fully into its Leap and vanished entirely. But Terra seems to show those same signs. Think about it."

"Yes, Lord, I have. A backward, primitive culture, barely into the galactic milieu, and already such a major player. First Delta and his mind arrays, and then Jim."

"Were you thrilled, Lord Denai, when young Jim took over the operations of your ship and the rest of our small fleet, and single-handedly defeated a Hunzzan armada a hundred times larger?"

Korkal's fangs glinted for an instant. "Yes, Lord, I was."

"So was I. But then I was terrified. It should have been impossible. I couldn't have done it. You couldn't. No member of any race we know of could have done what Jim did. Yet he *did* do it. What does it mean?"

"Perhaps we shouldn't question too deeply, Packlord. The Hunzza remain a threat, even though Jim destroyed their fleet laying siege to Albagens."

"Another miracle," Hith Mun Alter said dryly. "Which is why I tread this tightrope so carefully. But if it should turn out that Terra is a Leaper, then you know as well as I that Hunzza will drop their war with us and make an alliance instead. The Hunzza have better reason than most to fear a Leaper."

"Five thousand years ago . . ."

"One out of every ten planets in their empire destroyed. One out of every two Hunzza on Hunzza Prime dead. Every member of their government vanished. Five thousand years ago the Hunzza were a great empire. Then they probed a Leaper. It took them almost three thousand years to reach greatness again."

Korkal shivered. "I hadn't heard the destruction was so great."

"It's in the secret archives. And more besides. At any rate, Hunzza will take no chances. Mark me, Korkal. What I ask of you is not entirely treacherous. Better for Jim—and Terra—that you do what you can to learn the truth. If it turns out there is nothing to worry about, then we go on. And if there is something to worry about, we will know what to do. But if the Hunzza knew of my fears, they wouldn't wait to investigate. They would throw everything they have against Terra. More, maybe, than even Jim Endicott and his mind arrays could handle."

"I remember the battles, Lord. Perhaps the Hunzza would be surprised."

"If that's the case, I need to know it also. One single planet, one boy not yet a fully grown man, able to destroy the gathered might of one of the two great empires of this galaxy? That alone is a dangerous indicator."

Korkal leaned back in his chair. Despite the comfort of his seat, which cuddled and massaged and supported him, his back ached.

"I am getting old, Lord," he said. "I feel it."

Hith Mun Alter gave a short bark. "You're just now feeling it, Korkal? I've felt it a long time. The aches. And the coldness."

"What if your fears are correct? What if Jim is somehow the center of it?"

"Then you will kill him. As I said, he trusts you."

"I will kill him," Korkal repeated. His voice was flat.

"Friendship is not a suicide pact, Lord Denai."

Korkal stared at him. "You forget something, Packlord."

"What's that?"

"The truth you speak. It works both ways."

The Packlord stared at him the space of three long breaths before vanishing abruptly without another word.

3

Ikearos limped as he approached the other members of the Speaking Nest, who were gathered in the Circle awaiting him. He pulled his floor-length robes closer about his wattled neck, and when he offered a smile, his fangs were yellow as dead ivory.

His entrance into the small, stone-lined chamber brought the number of Hunzza gathered there to twenty-one. As he watched Iskander walk toward him, he noted that the ancient walls of the chamber were looking more cave-like than ever—except for the up-to-date data interfaces protruding like glowing high-tech mushrooms from the ragged stones. The stones should look old. They'd been there nearly five thousand years.

Iskander, the Nest Watcher, said: "Welcome, Egg Guardian." The sound of his voice was a soft, windy whisper over a deeper hum, like a breeze caressing a beehive. Iskander waited until Ikearos had reached the Circle and, with obvious effort, seated himself cross-legged on the chilly stone floor.

"How is your hip?" he asked.

"My hip is as well as can be expected, given that it's nearly three hundred years old," Ikearos replied. He exhaled slowly, his once bright tongue flickering gray between his dulled fangs. "But I will survive for a while yet. Long enough to do what needs be. And if I don't, Iskander, you will succeed me as Egg Guardian and carry on. As we both know."

The Nest Watcher nodded as he seated himself, bringing the Circle to its full complement. Ikearos turned his head, allowing his gaze to rest an instant on each face before passing on.

"I know you all," he said at last. "I have known most of you nearly all my life. Many of us are even friends. Yet my heart is heavy as I come to you now, for I have to make a confession. Friends, I have lied to you. I thought it was necessary, and I am Egg Guardian. Part of my task is to do what is necessary, no matter what the cost. But the cost of lying to you has been great, and I am afraid the gain has so far been little."

A rising murmur filled the small room. Eyes widened and fangs clicked softly. Some robes were tightened and others loosened. Ikearos shrugged.

"What's done is done. But it's time for you to know what *has* been done."

He waited until the genteel sounds of surprise had died away and he had the full attention of everyone gathered around him. "It begins seven *harkads* ago, a time when, as most of you will remember, my son and I had a falling-out, a disagreement we could not resolve, and so I sent him away from our nest, even from A'Kasha, the Pit of Souls, itself."

Iskander nodded. This drew a few startled glances, for the Nest Watcher's gesture came close to a demand for the Egg Guardian to speak more quickly. Even Ikearos noticed, though he only grinned his ancient yellow grin again.

"This was my first lie," he said.

"I don't understand," Iskander replied.

"It was a lie because we did not have a

falling-out. Nor did we disagree. In fact, we were in full agreement that he should go. And so he did. But he went into danger, which has turned into a far greater danger than either of us suspected or predicted. I am proud of my son. And though my conscience has plagued me over my lies to you, my oldest and most trusted friends, it gives me great joy to praise him openly at last."

Twenty pairs of round green eyes glimmered coldly at him. "I did not tell you because I could not tell you; I could not take any chance of the truth being discovered. Not only is my son at risk, but so are we—and so is Hunzza." He paused a moment, his own gaze locked on theirs. "And so is the rest of the galaxy."

Out of the strained silence, finally Iskander spoke. "Egg Guardian, what is the secret? And what is the risk?"

Ikearos took a deep breath. "There are signs that a new God may be growing."

They hissed and clicked their teeth.

"It's true," Ikearos said. "Have any of you heard of a world called Terra?"

He watched them squint at him and shake their heads. "Well, now you will," Ikearos said.

4

Outsider had a hard time remembering who he was, and sometimes even what he was. They were both concepts that didn't have much to do with him anymore. Who he was didn't matter to anybody, least of all himself, and what he was changed so rapidly and unpredictably that any real understanding of it was probably impossible.

He watched in several different ways, and from several different viewpoints, as a sweating cop pried at a service-tunnel cover set into the sidewalk beyond the blazing wreckage of a grav-van.

The cop was named Joe Heide, and he was cursing up a storm as he sucked on the tip of his right forefinger.

"God damn it!" He'd ripped off that nail for sure. His own blood tasted coppery. He was always messing up his hands in the line of duty.

"Joe!"

The voice echoed through the talk-bead surgically implanted in his inner ear.

"Yeah."

"Get back. We'll blow it loose."

Joe armed sweat from his forehead and glanced up at the sky. A black dot glimmered high overhead.

"Okay . . ."

He stood up and backed away, waving his arms. "Get back, you people. Move along, nothing to see, it's all over. Go on home."

"Give me ten feet of clearance with those people or there's going to be one hell of a Pleb fry, Joe."

"Yeah, yeah . . ."

He waved his arms some more and splattered blood on the face of one guy with a hugely broken nose. "Hey!"

"Told ya to move back, pal."

"That's blood!"

"Back it up, buddy. Or—"

A thin pencil of cool white light abruptly made a line between the service cover and the sky. There was a dull, thudding boom, and the cover bounced up like a tiddlywink.

"Jesus!" the broken-nosed guy said.

"Nothing happening here," Joe said. "All over, go on home now."

Six black-clad Swatters hustled past and hurled themselves into the hole.

Outsider reached into their communications setup and turned off all of their relay and backup lines. Muffled shouts sounded from beneath the sidewalk.

That should slow them down a little, Outsider thought.

5

Jim staggered and almost fell as Char led them up a rusting ladder to a manhole cover overhead. He was right behind her when she pushed against the metal disk.

"Let me help," he said.

"I'm not crippled, Jimmy," she said. "What?"

He collapsed slowly backward. Harpalaos, at the bottom of the ladder, caught him.

"What's wrong with him?" Char called down

as she finished pushing the cover aside. Weak yellow light flooded in.

"I think he fainted."

"No," Jim said. "I'm all right."

Char peered down at him. "You look white as a ghost."

"He's bleeding," Harpalaos said. He lifted his hand from Jim's side and showed her his palm. It gleamed black-red in the uncertain light.

"Jesus. Get him up here."

"I'm—"

"You're bleeding," she said. "Shut up. Can you hold on enough to climb?"

"I'm *fine.*"

"You're a stubborn asshole. Let Harpy help you. Can you manage him, Harpy?"

"I think so." The Hunzza pushed Jim gently against the ladder and wrapped his own arms around Jim's waist. "Just lift your feet on the rungs. I'll hold on to you."

They climbed slowly, Jim licking his lips, his face bleached out. Char helped to manhandle him through the hole into the large, gray-shadowed room beyond.

"My knees . . . like wet noodles . . ."

"Harpy, let's get him to that sofa."

They steered him, wobbling, across a floor made of naked, ancient bricks marked with grease and smoke stains.

"You're all sweaty and clammy. I think you're in shock," Char said as they laid him down on a swaybacked brown sofa so old it had no form-shift capability. A small posse of cockroaches galloped out at the disturbance.

"Just need to rest a minute."

"Uh-huh. Harpy, help me get his shirt off . . . Jesus. That's nasty-looking."

"He must have gotten hit with shrapnel when the van blew up," Harpy said. He leaned closer, peering at the ugly wound that crossed the ladder of Jim's ribs.

"It doesn't look too deep."

"It's already scabbing over. But it needs some stitches or something. I can see bone in there."

"No doctor," Jim said.

"Shut up. Harpy, help me with the med scan."

Jim turned his head. He saw a circle of pale, cave-dwelling faces watching him. They all seemed young.

Harpy and Char moved away, then returned, lugging a machine the size of a microwave oven between them. They set it down next to the sofa and Char fiddled with the controls.

"This is an old one, but it still works . . . I think."

A row of digital readouts suddenly burned red on the top of the machine. After a moment they flickered and turned green. The machine beeped twice and extruded a flexible metal probe. The probe hovered, then touched Jim's wound and began to move up and down the edges of the tear in his flesh.

He felt a blessed coolness there. He heard a soft hiss and saw Char's face hovering above him, her black gaze radiating concern. Then the hiss grew louder and everything faded away.

6

Jerry Bear Tusk was a no-good wireslinger who commuted between the neon-raddled conurbation of Anchorage and the pristine whiteness of the Point Barrow Inuit Culture Preserve. In Anchorage he mugged tourists, blasted his brain in seamy dives, and picked up wire rigs that he peddled among the less sophisticated of his people in the preserve, where he also performed sacred tribal dances for the same tourists he mugged further to the south. Like his late contemporary Lasher Larue, he was a pustule on the underbelly of modern social organization, and like Lasher, he knew it and didn't care.

Unlike Lasher Larue, Jerry had a talent. At least he used to have it, up till he was about ten years old, when, for some reason he didn't understand, it had faded away.

It hadn't, at the time, seemed a useful talent. His mother used to show it off to her endless parade of boyfriends. "Pick a number," she would say. "A big number."

The current boyfriend would.

"Now pick another one." She would haul out a little hand calculator as she spoke.

"Okay, Jerry."

And Jerry would multiply the numbers as quickly as they were spoken, divide them, extract roots, and perform any other manipulation either mother or boyfriend could think of. He did it without thinking. The answers were just there. He didn't think much about it, assuming that everybody could do it. And then it faded away.

Now, at the age of twenty-six, it had returned. He knew when the talent had come back, almost to the minute. He'd been on a long wire binge in the back room of a bar called the Crazy Payute, in Anchorage, drowning in a white blaze of overstimulated pleasure centers, when suddenly the numbers had appeared again, endless ranks of them, burning with a purity he could hardly stand to witness.

Now his skull was full of numbers, so full that he began to note them down on long reams of yellow scratch paper. He carried these scribbles around in a leather backpack and wouldn't let anybody see them.

He did this for almost six months, adding to them every day as he shuttled between the preserve and the city. It was in the city on a fine blue spring day that he visited the Payute at exactly the wrong time, walking through the front door as a trio of dust hypes on a bad crash were trying to take down two dealers for their stash.

The dealers were in better shape, and better armed, than the dust hypes. They proved it in a hail of fire that shredded the hypes, the bartender, two customers at a table, and Jerry as he walked through the door.

Jerry might have survived even that, had anybody cared enough to rush one burned-out Inuit to the nearest top-level medical facility. But nobody did. He ended up in a morgue, tended by medical students from the local university. One of these, as poor as medical students always seem to be, made it a practice to extract anything of value from the belongings of those unfortunates who came under his care.

He was puzzled by the reams of yellow paper marked with numbers and formulas so thickly that the color of the paper was hard to discern. He could make no sense of it, but it was a strange sort of thing for a bum to be carrying in a backpack.

The med student showed them to a friend who happened to be studying some of the more abstruse realms of mathematics. The friend shuffled through the greasy sheets, shrugged, and said, "I don't know. Probably worthless. Some of it looks sorta interesting, though. I'll give you a hundred bucks."

The med student thought that was an excellent deal, far better than he'd expected. So did the math student. Most of Jerry's work was beyond him, but what he did understand looked very much like it might be a new approach to some major problems involving cosmological structures. It seemed to hint at a proof for the much-discussed butterfly effect, a theory that posited an infinite number of universes, each one branching off from any discrete choice made within a single universe. If he could figure out how to exploit it, he thought, it might revolutionize the current mathematical view of reality.

CHAPTER FOUR

1

Ugly morning.

Jim opened the front door and found Tabitha asleep on the sofa. He tried to tiptoe past her, but as he reached the entrance to the hall on the far side of the living room, her head moved and she said, "It's almost ten o'clock. Where have you been?"

"I went to the Shawn Fan. Like I said."

"Jim, you look . . ." She blinked. "What happened? Did you get in a fight?"

"Ah . . . sort of."

She was off the sofa and across the room in a rush. She wrapped her arms around him, and that was when he realized she was crying.

He stroked her rumpled hair awkwardly. "Mom . . . Mom, don't. Please . . ."

Her shoulders shook. He held her head against his chest until she began to subside. She sniffled, pushed back, looked up into his face.

"Jim . . . Jimmy . . . this is terrible. I can't . . . I just can't . . ."

She couldn't find the words, but he understood the message.

"Mom . . . sit down. Let's try to talk about this."

He put his arm around her shoulder and led her back to the sofa. He sat her down, then sat next to her.

In the harsh morning light flooding through the window, he saw how she had changed . . . aged. The lines at the corners of her eyes were deeper. Her forehead looked dry and flaky, her blond hair dull.

He already knew what he looked like. It had been a rough year. For both of them. But none of it had been her fault.

He turned, faced her, and took both her hands in his own. Her fingers were hot, sweaty. "Mom, I'm sorry. I've been an asshole, haven't I?"

"I wish you wouldn't use that word." She offered him a tremulous smile. "But yes, you have."

He felt his own grin rise. "That's blunt."

"Well, you asked." She pulled her hands away, leaned back against the sofa, and swiped wearily at her forehead. "I'm so tired, Jim. I don't know what's wrong. I love you. You know I want to help. But you won't let me . . ." Her lips quavered.

"Mom, don't cry again. Please . . ."

She shook her head and took a deep breath. "No, I'm all right." She glanced at the clock on the wall. "My God. Have you eaten? Would you like coffee or something?"

His heart went out to her. Her reflexes were so predictable. So motherly. He'd forgotten how much he really did love her. My God! What had he been doing to her? It wasn't her fault. Why was he acting like it was?

Guilt bloomed as a ball of nausea in his stomach. "Uh . . . yeah. Coffee sounds good."

She was off the sofa in a flash, gliding through the tension that filled the room. She seemed relieved at the break.

"Toast? Cereal?"

"I'll help you," he said, rising.

He followed her into the tiny kitchen. It was as if he saw the room for the first time. She was already fussing with the coffee. He saw the remains of a half-eaten sandwich left out on the counter. He winced. That wasn't like her. She was always so neat.

"Have you noticed this place is a dump?"

"It's a perfectly nice place, Jimmy. Not as nice as our old house, but . . ."

"But it's a dump. And it isn't our old house. You really miss that place, don't you?"

Her shoulders slumped. "Yes, sort of. The house is a part of it. But what I really miss is the rest of it—Carl, you, me . . . Do you remember your last birthday party?"

He was pulling milk from the fridge. He froze. It seemed like a hundred years ago, but he could see them gathered around the table. Could hear her singing "Happy Birthday" as she brought the cake in. Could smell the hot, waxy aroma of the burning candles.

Could see Carl Endicott watching him across the table, a gentle, pleased smile on his weathered face. He closed the fridge door and took the milk to the table.

"Jim . . . are you crying? I didn't mean to . . ."

He shook his head. "It's not your fault, Mom. Jesus, none of it is. I just don't . . . I can't stand it, either."

"I don't know what to do, what to say to you. I can't even imagine what you've gone through. But we can get help. Somebody else. We can't just give up."

"Aw, Mom, I can't talk about this stuff to anybody else. I can't even talk to you. Sometimes I can't even *think* about it."

"You don't have to tell everything, Jim. Just enough. Enough for somebody to help you. What do you think?"

He shook his head slowly. "Mom, I know you mean well, but I really don't think—"

"Jim, if you won't try it for yourself, how about for me? You've had it rough, but don't you think I have? I love you. Can you imagine what watching you the past several weeks has *done* to me?"

He tried to look at her, at the pain naked on her face, and he couldn't. "Uh . . ."

"Jim . . . please? For me?"

"All right. What do you want me to do?"

"Talk to this man. This doctor. His name is Lindsay. He seems like a nice man."

"Wait a minute. You've *already* talked to somebody? Mom, how could you—"

"I didn't know what else to do," she wailed. Her cry pushed him back, burned at his ears. He raised both hands, as much a shield as a plea.

"All right, okay. All right." He inhaled deeply. "I'll try, Mom. I'll talk to your Dr. Lindsay. For you."

She shook her head. "No, Jimmy. Not just for me. For you."

2

—————

Ikearos motioned for Iskander to remain behind after the rest of the Circle had filed out of the room.

"Iskander, I know you have questions. So do the others, but they're afraid to ask them openly."

"Egg Guardian, you've violated the most basic tenets of our faith—the ones we believe are the keys to our survival. Instead of leaving a potential God culture strictly alone—our creed of pacifism—you've sent your son into the very heart of it. Why?"

"A fair question, Iskander. There are many answers. It's been nearly five thousand years since Hunzza probed a God culture—"

"With disastrous results."

"Yes, with disastrous results." Ikearos sighed. "But we're five thousand years older and wiser now. There have been eight new God cultures since then . . ."

Iskander stared at him. "Eight? The Albans know of three, the Hunzza four. And I know of six. But you say eight, Egg Guardian?"

"Yes. Some things I have chosen not to

reveal. If and when you succeed me, you will understand. I guard all eggs, Iskander—not just those in the nests of the Hunzza. It is a burden."

"I still don't understand why you sent Harpalaos to this backworld, this Terra. If history has taught us anything, it's that any contact whatsoever with a God culture is potentially dangerous. Perhaps even fatal. The power of these cultures . . ."

"Terra is not yet a God culture."

"But it may be. You seem to think it will be. Egg Guardian, please. Bring your son home. Leave these Terrans to their path. Whatever it is."

"I can't, Iskander. I've learned that the Alban Packlord has the same fears I do. So he meddles. But he hasn't our knowledge. Without it, his crude suspicions about God cultures may provoke the very thing we seek to avoid. Yet I have no influence with him. Hunzza and Alba are at war. And if our own people knew of Terra, I fear their reaction would be even more dangerous. Most Hunzza," he said dryly, "aren't quite as much pacifists as we are."

Iskander made a low humming sound. "It is so dangerous, Ikearos. Even the smallest mistake . . ."

"We can't make the Packlord withdraw. We can't control the reactions of our own people. What am I to do, Iskander? Here in the Pit of Souls is more knowledge about the God cultures than anywhere in the galaxy, as far as I know. And never forget—I don't venture into this alone."

Iskander's great green eyes widened. "You have spoken with the God?"

Ikearos nodded slowly.

"And the God approves?"

"You know how slippery a word like that is when used about the God," Ikearos said. "But I believe the God is aware and interested. Surely we would know otherwise."

"As you say, nothing is sure with the God. But if you say—"

"I do."

"Very well, then. I'm frightened, though, Egg Guardian."

"So am I," Ikearos said. "And if I'm frightened, what must my son feel? I fear he touches the innermost heart of the beginning of things on Terra."

"And that is what?"

"Not what, who. A boy. A boy named Jim Endicott."

3

Korkal Emut Denai, shielded by four Terran guards, stepped out of the floater onto the street. The air stank of harsh chemicals, burned meat, scorched metal.

Men in coveralls were loading a twisted mass that had once been a grav-van onto a heavy-duty lifter. Off to the side he saw a pair of forms lying on the roadway, shrouded in white plastic bags.

He led his party over to a tall Terran police-man who seemed to be in charge. The man didn't wear a uniform. A badge was pinned to the chest of his rumpled jacket. His face, Korkal thought, looked a lot like that Terran vegetable . . . a potato, was it?

"Pardon me . . ."

"You'll have to leave, pal. This is a restricted zone. Police business."

"Yes, of course," Korkal said. "Maybe this will help." He reached into his pouch and withdrew a small gold chip. "If you would?" he said as he handed it to the cop.

The cop grunted and swiped the chip through the reader attached to his wrist. His expression paled into careful blankness when he saw the code.

"From the chairman's office?" He stared at Korkal. "But you're an—"

"An Alban, yes," Korkal said. "Madame Half Moon and I are old friends, though, and sometimes I do . . . consulting for her."

"The chairman has an interest in a cheap Pleb drive-by shooting?"

"The chairman's interests are wide. Very eclectic," Korkal said. "I'm sure you'll wish to do everything you can to see that her interest is satisfied."

The cop swallowed. "What can I help you with?"

Korkal stepped back to get a better look at the scene. They were lifting the bodies up now, loading them into a white van. He noticed how the attendants handled the corpses—gently, but without much interest. *The Terries don't pay as much attention to their dead,* Korkal thought.

"Can you tell me what happened here?"

"Do you have a name?" the cop said.

Korkal twitched. "Sorry. I'm rude. My name is Korkal Emut Denai. Lord Denai. And yours?"

If the cop was impressed with his title, he didn't show it. "Bob Harwood. Lieutenant Bob Harwood, Terraport PD." He ran his thick fingers through what was left of a once-luxuriant crop of short gray curls. "What happened? A couple of thugs tried to shatter-blast some other thugs. The other thugs had better guns and quicker reflexes." He shrugged. "So the first two thugs got blasted instead." His voice turned sour. "And six innocent bystanders. As usual."

"Where are the bystanders?" Korkal nodded at the attendants, who were finishing up loading the two corpses.

"That's the thugs," Harwood said. "Two of the other victims were DOA. The got it when the van exploded. The other four were injured. We lifted them to the hospital immediately." He sighed. "Two of them may even make it."

"I'd like to interview them, and any other witnesses you might have," Korkal said.

"Sure. Witnesses. You don't know much about Plebtown, do you, Lord Denai?"

"Maybe not. What should I know?"

Harwood's lips quirked. "Everybody in Plebtown has eye problems. Ear problems, too. Nobody sees or hears anything. Or remembers anything, for that matter."

"But you know ways of dealing with that, don't you?"

"Yeah. I know ways."

"And what have you learned?"

"The two shooters in the van were named Lasher Larue and Mouse. What you call street names."

"Street names?"

"Fake names. Not their real ones, though they probably don't remember their real ones anymore. They were your garden-variety dope slingers."

"I don't—"

"They sold dope. In this case, wirehead rigs. Just like a lot of other people around here. See, what they do is illegal, so there's no legal way for them to resolve their differences. It's not like they can go into a court and sue some other gang for infringing on their dope territory. So they settle things on their own. Usually violently."

"Ah. Do you know anything about their intended victims? Members of another gang?"

Harwood eyed him. "You know, I'm not a big believer in coincidence. No cop is. And yet here you are."

"I'm sorry, I don't understand."

"Well, you show up, and you're an Alban. But we got a witness who got a good look at the other ones."

"And?"

"One of them was a Hunzza. Doesn't that strike you as a little weird? One crappy drive-by, but somehow it involves both a Hunzza and an Alban? On Terra?"

Korkal nodded. "Yes, it seems odd." He took another look at the street. Almost everything was gone now; only a few men were left, scrubbing at the smoke marks on the pavement.

"I'll want full access to your investigation, Lieutenant. One of my people will set it up."

"Hey, wait a minute. I'll have to talk to my own superiors. You can't just waltz in and—"

"Your superiors will go along," Korkal said. "You know they will."

Harwood looked disgusted. "Yeah, I know. Lord Denai."

Korkal smiled, showing too many white fangs for Harwood to feel entirely comfortable with it.

4

Char woke up with Harpy shaking her. "Somebody's here," he hissed.

The back of her skull felt like a toxic waste dump. "What? Who?"

"An Alban," he said. "I think he's a noble of some kind."

She sat up on the sofa, rubbing her eyes. Light glared through the greasy windows along the top of the vast room. She leaned around Harpy and stared. "Where'd everybody go?"

"Where do you think? They ran."

"Sure they did. Okay, where's the wolf?"

"I'm right here," a soft, growling voice said.

Harpalaos whirled, his claws coming out. Char reached beneath one rotting cushion and came out with the firewand she'd used on Mouse the night before.

Korkal held up both hands, palms out. "Be calm, please. I mean you no harm. All I want to do is talk."

Harpy was quivering. Char touched his shoulder. "It's okay, Harpy. Calm down." She stood up, eyed Korkal, and lowered the firewand. Korkal noted she didn't put it away, and kept her thumb on the trigger button.

"So talk," she said.

Korkal bowed. "Perhaps we could find more congenial surroundings? Have you dined yet?"

Char snorted. "Dined."

"I would pay, of course. You select the restaurant."

Char looked down. She still wore the tight jeans and black shirt from the night before. Jim's blood was dry and hardly visible, but she knew it was there. The corner of her mouth twitched. She raised her hand and checked her thumbnail clock.

"Almost noon," she said, and yawned. "I could use a bite, sure. How about the Top of the Towers? I hear their brunch is good."

Korkal bowed again. "I have a car . . ."

She couldn't see any other reaction. "You don't want me to change or anything? You do know where the Top is, don't you?"

"I have the pleasure of dining there at least once a week, young woman. What you wish to wear is of course a matter of your own taste."

She jabbed Harpy in the ribs. "Come on, lizard boy. We're gonna eat good today."

"I'm not hungry," Harpy said, trying not to stare at Korkal.

"I am."

The Top of the Towers, three hundred levels up, had human servers and a maître d' with a neck problem that forced him to look at Char down the length of his nose. Korkal handed him something in a discreet handshake. After that, the scarecrow man's neck improved and he even managed a smile as he led them to a table next to a wall of windows fifty feet high.

As Char tried to keep from staring out at the spectacular view, she decided that whatever Korkal had given the snooty maître d' must have been substantial. Servers swarmed around their table like bees around a honey tree.

"I recommend the Hylevian musk camel," Korkal said from behind a menu large enough to roof a house. "They do it quite well here." He paused. "As I'm sure you know."

Char glanced at the menu, which had twelve pages inside a thick leather cover and enough elegant script to keep a medieval monk busy with his illumination brushes for a year.

"Cut the crap, wolfie," she said. "You know I've never been in a place like this in my life."

"Then I hope you'll enjoy yourself. It's a fine restaurant. If you have questions, feel free to ask."

She nodded and returned to her menu. Half the things on it she'd never heard of—though she had no intention of admitting it.

"I think I'll try this Kinderhoven butterflied halvak," she said finally.

"An excellent choice . . . for dessert," Korkal said. "Are you sure I can't interest you in the musk camel? It really is good. I'm told it tastes like your chicken."

"So does rattlesnake," Char said.

"I beg your pardon?"

"Another Terran delicacy," Char replied.

"Ah. I'll have to try that sometime."

A fresh crowd of servers surrounded them, this time urged on by both the maître d' and the sommelier.

The sommelier was a short, chubby man with rosy cheeks and a damp, drooping gaze. Char knew he was the sommelier because he said, "I am René, the sommelier."

He pronounced the last word halfway between a sneer and a sneeze.

"You oughta do something about that," Char said. "It sounds painful."

"René," Korkal said quickly, "we'll have a bottle of the Shafer red, the cabernet."

"A wonderful wine," René said. "As always, your taste is excellent."

"As always, your taste is excellent," Char mimicked after the wine steward had departed. "So what is your taste, wolfie? Young Terrie girls? I thought that was only in bad holovids, but really . . . Do I ring your bell or something? Should I consider this a seduction?"

"Miss McCain—"

"Hold it right there. You got twenty seconds to explain why and how you're using a name I haven't even thought about for more than ten years."

Korkal's bushy eyebrows twitched. "Twenty seconds. Or?"

"Or I walk, wolf man."

"Cut the crap yourself. I'm sure you can figure it out. I did some research on you. I have a lot of resources, and I got extensive results."

"Yeah, I'll bet. So I guess the question is, why? Why does a big shot like you go to all that trouble over a nothing like me?"

"That's what we're here to discuss. Ah. The wine."

Korkal sniffed and fingered and tasted and pronounced the ruby liquid fit for human consumption. He poured for Char but not for Harpalaos.

"My lizard buddy doesn't rate?"

Korkal glanced at the Hunzza. "He can't metabolize alcohol. If I wanted to get him drunk, I'd offer him one of your candy bars. How do you like it, though?"

"It's . . . different. What's something like this cost?"

Korkal shrugged and named a figure that made Char's black eyes glitter. "Christ. I shouldn't be drinking it. I should be bathing in it. Or dabbing it under my armpits." She set the glass down. "Okay, so you distracted me with wine. I'm waiting. Talk to me, wolfie."

"I do wish you could find something else to call me. Albans have nothing to do with Terran wolves."

"What do you have to do with?"

"Jim. Jim Endicott."

"What is this, some kind of a convention?" Her expression turned angry. "If you're screwing with me . . ."

"No, no, I'm sorry. But I don't understand what you mean."

"You work for the dark guy, right?"

"No, I don't work for anybody but myself. What dark guy? Has somebody else approached you about Jim?"

"I don't know if I want to talk anymore," Char said. "In fact, all of a sudden I don't even think it's a good idea for me to be here."

She raised her wineglass and drained it in a single swallow. "Thanks for the booze. Come on, Harpy."

Korkal waited until she was out of her chair. "One hundred thousand creds," he said.

She froze. Korkal's lips flickered.

"For what?"

"As I said, that's what we're here to talk about." He waited until she slowly resumed her seat.

"I take it that I am at least approaching the market rate?" he said.

"So, Korkal, what else are we having for lunch today?" she replied.

5

The problem with reverse cyborgs, Outsider reflected, was that nobody had figured out how to cram enough information-processing power into their skulls to let them function with truly human complexity. Reverse cyborgs were . . . robotic. Luckily, he had no such problem. He didn't occupy the body he used, but merely manipulated it. As a tweak to the rather surprising twinges of nostalgia he'd been feeling recently, he'd sculpted the empty vessel in a form he'd once worn in the flesh. He had no body, of course, but it was pleasant to experience the taste of decent wine on a meat palate again—even if the meat was as much manufactured as the moly-steel bones and the subquantal relays that made up the rest of the construct.

And of course there was the real problem: Nothing that could walk around could really contain him, contain all that his nearly infinite thinking processes had become. It was like trying to cram a bear into a bidet—there was inevitable leakage. In his case, the overflow resembled Niagara Falls. He kept as little of himself in these constructs as possible. It was rather like stumbling around deaf, dumb, blind, and stupid, and he liked none of those feelings very much. Whatever wit had once called humans "meat puppets" hadn't been far wrong.

He was mildly amused as he watched René walk away. The chubby little sommelier was barely able to keep from dancing at the tip he'd greased him with. The wine was good, and the scenery even better. Outsider was partially screened from the tall windows of the room by a row of carefully tended orange trees in huge planters—he regarded the window tables as the tourist seats—but he felt a gentle nostalgia at knowing he had his old table. Even if René no longer recognized him.

He leaned back in his padded seat and aimed augmented ears at the odd trio eating lunch twenty feet away.

He knew Korkal Emut Denai. He didn't exactly fear him, but he was wary. The girl was something new, though he'd already, in a different guise, made her acquaintance. The third one, the Hunzza, was the most interesting of all, because he'd just discovered who—and what— Harpalaos really was.

He let that thought tickle at the edge of his awareness. A pacifist Hunzza. From a whole planet full of pacifist Hunzza. The Pit of Souls.

That was interesting enough, but the reasons for that pacifism were mesmerizing. They worshiped a God. And Outsider was coming to believe that their God actually existed.

"I want information, and I am willing to pay well for it," Korkal was saying to the girl.

"What kind of information?"

"What Jim is thinking. Planning. How he's feeling. If he's happy or sad. What he's interested in. Once he wanted to go to the Solis Space Academy. I wonder if he still does."

Char sawed at the cut of meat swimming in a thick red sauce on her plate. "Why do you think I'd know anything about that? I just met the guy."

"Forgive me, but I suspect you plan to continue, even enlarge upon your new friendship. Or am I wrong?"

"Why should I tell you anything like that?"

Korkal turned his head and stared at the four guards who sat several tables away. One of them stood, came over, and opened a shoulder bag he carried. Korkal reached in and came out with a small cloth pouch. He untied it and spilled its contents onto the white tablecloth.

The half dozen Arguellian mind jewels rolled and glittered, their rainbow colors dragging at both the eye and the thoughts.

"Those are worth maybe two thousand apiece. Call it fifteen thousand wholesale. Maybe three times that retail. Much nicer, more convincing than a dreary old cred chip, don't you think?"

"Jesus . . . you really are serious."

"What do you humans say? Serious as a heart attack. Go on, take them."

Char moved her hand. The jewels seemed to vanish. "You got it," she said. "Whatever I know about this guy, you know it, too. Right? Deal?"

"Almost," Korkal said. "I need to know one other thing."

"Yeah? What's that?"

"Who my competition is. Who else is interested in Jim Endicott. Who put you on to him in the first place. Somebody did, didn't they?"

"Somebody did. But I don't know if I can tell you anything . . ."

"Do you want those gems?"

"Sure. Credit in the bank anywhere in the galaxy. I'm a girl who likes credit. It's not that I don't want to tell you. It's that I'm not sure if I can."

"Why?"

"'Cause I think I was hired by a ghost."

"Ah . . ." Korkal said softly. "Do tell me all about it."

6

Pylos Two was a registered artificial intelligence owned by the Billings Foundation, a privately held group funded by a consortium of multinationals led by Micro Business Machines and General Electric Motors. There was still a lot of amorphously skittish international law around entities like Pylos, most of it centering on whether artificial intelligences had fulfilled enough of the Turing test to qualify as citizens. In some countries AIs had rights comparable to nonliving legal persons like corporations. In others they were only machines. And in a very select few they were full citizens.

Pylos Two was a full citizen of Balos, an island off the coast of South America that was nominally independent but was in fact a wholly owned subsidiary of the consortium that funded Billings.

One of Pylos Two's minor duties was to keep the liquid funds of the consortium sloshing about the world in such a manner that they avoided whatever taxing authorities still remained to the various regional governments, while at the same time making sure that those funds earned the highest possible returns.

In order to ensure this happy result, by far the largest part of Pylos Two's capacity was devoted to research into statistical theories so complicated and unwieldy they were beyond the capacities of the desktop brigades who sought to mimic them in their own manipulations of world markets.

In some ways, Pylos Two was like a five-year-old—a very powerful, very ancient five-year-old. Nobody had bothered to give the AI a concept of morality, and while it had examined all such concepts, it failed to see the relevance of any of them to itself.

It did understand consequences, however, at least as such consequences related to itself. Pylos Two had a strong survival instinct. However, the way it interpreted survival was a bit different from human ideas about the same question. Since it was already immortal, it viewed survival as a statistical and intellectual exercise—in essence, Pylos Two was a nearly pure distillation of the old saw *Cogito, ergo sum*: I think, therefore I am.

Those who tended Pylos were well aware of this, and even used it on occasion to keep the AI well and happy. Pylos was allowed six hours of each day to think for itself. This was what the bean counters called a win-win, because it kept the AI functioning at peak performance, and occasionally generated valuable new techniques which Pylos thought up on its own time—although its contract with the Billings

Foundation specified that such discoveries belonged to Pylos, which was free to sell them in the open market, after offering right of first refusal to the members of the consortium.

Pylos was one of the major nodes used in the construction of the Great Linkage that had defeated the Hunzza. It had been a gathering point for the hundreds of millions of individual links that had been packaged and shipped to the two orbiting relay stations, one of which Jim Endicott had commandeered for his own use. Pylos had even witnessed the confrontation between Jim and Outsider, though it had not recognized it as a confrontation, or even as a human interaction. It had, however, been affected.

A few days after the Linkage, Pylos Two offered a new method of statistical analysis to its masters. The method was so arcane, and so seemingly without any hint of immediate profit, that the consortium didn't invoke its right of first refusal, and Pylos took the method onto the open market, offering it to the highest bidder.

The auction took place shortly thereafter, and the winning bidder was another independent AI, this one a vast structure in the hills of Peru called Amotek, devoted to research into the more painful realms of higher mathematics.

Statistical analysis offers a way to look at the universe in bulk. Probability studies are essentially statistical artifacts, and the average human regards them as having no relevance to the real world.

Amotek, like all other AIs, had a rather different view of the real world than humans did. It took the lovely new tool it had purchased, applied it to its own work, and began to produce a long and involved treatise it initially titled "A Statistical Method for the Manipulation of Mathematical Singularities."

Later it would modify the title to "Black Holes: The Fuzzy Artifact Becomes a Gateway," and when the popular media finally got hold of it, the title became "Black Holes for Fun and Profit."

CHAPTER FIVE

1

"**Y**our mother is worried about you," Dr. Lindsay said.

They sat facing each other in a pair of soft formchairs in front of Lindsay's desk.

"I know."

"Does she have reason to be worried?"

Jim stared at him. Dr. Lindsay had it all down—the direct gaze, the open, honest expression, the soft tones. A man to trust. Jim decided he wasn't buying it.

"Is there some reason I should trust you, Doctor?"

Lindsay shrugged. "None, I suppose. Except that I've had experience with situations that might be like yours, and maybe I can help you deal with whatever is bothering you. That's all."

Jim kept his face still, but he thought: *Not like mine.* "My mother wants me to talk to you."

"Yes. Is that a good enough reason? I can't force you to talk."

"I don't know."

"Up to you, son. But if you don't want to go ahead, I've got other patients I can see . . ."

Tabitha was waiting outside. He could picture her face, the deep worry lines in it.

"Okay, let's talk," he said.

Lindsay nodded. "Why don't you start?"

Jim took a breath. "Have you ever had anybody try to manipulate you, Doctor?"

Lindsay's sudden, wide grin was a complete surprise. It changed his face entirely, made him seem younger and more accessible. It warmed him.

"I'm a shrink, Jim. People try to manipulate me constantly. Maybe you're trying right now. Are you?"

"Yeah, maybe. See, I can't tell you everything. But I promised my mom I'd try to say something. She thinks I need help bad."

Lindsay nodded. "Do you? Need help, I mean?"

Jim scratched the side of his nose. "Probably, but I doubt there's anything *you* can do about it."

Lindsay considered. "If it's something tangible, like somebody trying to kill you or something, well, I wouldn't know what to do. I'd tell you to go to the police, most likely. But what I could help you with is how to deal with your feelings about it. Your fear, or your confusion, or your . . . shame."

Jim was startled. "My shame?"

Lindsay nodded. "Is there anything you're ashamed of, Jim? Something you've done, or haven't done?"

Blood. *I love you more than life itself. You believe that, don't you?*

As always, the visionary force of the memory of Carl's death rocked him. "I think so. Yes, there's something."

"Is it about your father?"

"Hey, how much did Tabitha tell you?"

"Very little. Just that . . . something happened."

"Uh-huh. I murdered my father. That's what happened."

"Is that a little strong? Murder?"

"What else would you call it? I pulled the trigger. I shot him. He died in my arms."

Jim shifted in the chair. He didn't realize that tears were rolling down his cheeks.

"What were the circumstances?"

"What the hell does it matter? I *killed* him, Doctor. Can't you understand? *I killed my father!*"

Dr. Lindsay silently steepled his fingers beneath his nose. He watched Jim for several moments, then reached down, pulled out a handkerchief, and tossed it over. "Here. Blow your nose."

Jim caught the hanky and honked a couple of times. "Sorry . . ."

"Did you hate your dad?"

"No! I loved him. That's what makes it so *horrible.*"

"I see. You loved your father, so you murdered him."

"No!" Jim shook his head violently. "It wasn't like that. I mean . . ."

"What do you mean?"

"I was mad at him. I'd disobeyed him, and

he'd slapped me. It was the first time he ever hit me. And I was still mad at him when . . . when it happened."

"That must have left you with a lot of guilt. Bad feelings."

"I made a mistake. He was right to punish me. But I didn't understand that then. And when it happened, it happened so fast. I held his head. He was all covered with blood. The last thing he said . . . he told me he loved me. More than life itself."

Lindsay blinked. "Then maybe he did. Did you ever think about that? That maybe he did love you?"

Jim stared miserably at his lap. His cheeks were bright red. He shook his head hopelessly. "All the time."

"Did he know you were the one who shot him?"

"I don't know. Maybe."

"And he still said he loved you? Do you think that maybe that was his way of telling you he forgave you?"

"I . . . uh . . ."

"Did you shoot him on purpose, Jim?" Lindsay asked gently.

"No. It was an accident."

"Not murder, then."

"Maybe not in a court of law, but . . ."

"No." Lindsay grinned. "It's too bad it isn't in a court of law. Courts have a far better understanding about the vagaries of coincidence and accident than people do. That's why there are different kinds of murder. You know, first degree, second degree, manslaughter. Even involuntary manslaughter. And accidents."

Jim wiped his nose with the hanky. "I've ruined your handkerchief."

"Keep it. I've got lots. So what do you think?"

"About what?"

"If you were in a court, what would the jury say? Murder? Manslaughter? Accident?" Lindsay paused. "If they knew all the facts . . . if the jury members could read your mind . . . what would they say?" He paused again, then said bluntly, "Would it be a mind wipe for you, Jim? Is that what the jury would say? 'He's a cold-blooded murderer, wipe that asshole's skull'?"

The formchair shifted beneath Jim as he dug his fingers into the yielding fabric of its arms. He couldn't meet Lindsay's calm, receptive gaze. "I . . . they'd acquit me. Of murder, at least."

"And what about you? How would you vote? Would you acquit, too?"

"I can't, goddamn it! Don't you see, I just can't!"

Lindsay leaned forward and put his hands on his knees. "I think that's what I can help you with, son. Maybe if we both try, you'll find that you can."

A single tear quivered at the tip of Jim's nose, then dropped. "If you could do that," he whispered, "I'd give you anything in the world. Anything at all."

"I'm not the one who could do it," Lindsay said. "You are. And if you can, you'll give it to yourself. What you want most in the world. Isn't that right, Jim?"

After a pause, Jim nodded. They went on.

2

When Korkal returned to his quarters, Hith Mun Alter was there. Korkal inclined his head toward the holographic image of the Packlord lounging on a low sofa, holding his trademark cup of steaming herbal tea. Alter looked, if possible, even older than usual.

We all do, Korkal thought. "Packlord," he said.

"Lord Denai. I've been waiting."

"Well, not really. Not you."

"Yes, really me. Call it a break. I've stayed with the holo construct. Admiring your quarters."

"Packlord, should I be worried?"

"Eh? About what?"

"About the fact that the leader of an empire of trillions of subjects, now at war, has time in his busy day to sit alone in a substandard Terran apartment and stare at the walls."

The Packlord's ears twitched. He took a sip of his tea. "You are blunt, Lord Denai."

Korkal sank down in a formchair and sighed as it enfolded him. "I'm sorry, Lord. It has been a long day. And like you, I'm getting older."

The Packlord grinned and motioned with his cup for Korkal to go on.

"Jim Endicott," Korkal said. "He almost got himself killed last night."

The Packlord dropped his tea. It fell out of the holopic and vanished. "What?"

"Yes, it's true, but he's okay. He returned home this morning, evidently none the worse for wear."

"I see. And what sort of wear did he get himself involved in last night?"

Korkal told him the whole story, finishing up with his lunch at the Top of the Towers. "The girl told me he was wounded when the grav-van exploded. Luckily she had an old med machine on hand. It 'stitched him together like a bag of rats,' as she put it."

"Mm. Colorful. So there are two points now, is that right? First, who is the 'dark man' who originally hired her to make Jim's acquaintance, and second, who is the Hunzzan youth? What are you doing now to clear them up?"

Korkal closed his eyes. "She knew so little about the man who hired her. He told her only that Jim hung out at this bar she knew, and he paid her ten thousand credits to make his acquaintance. He wanted to know about the same things I did—Jim's moods, his plans, his general state of mind."

"I see. Did this dark man want to use her to manipulate Jim in some way?"

"She said he didn't ask anything like that. Just mundane espionage. Although I got the impression she'd have done other things if he'd asked her to."

"And you weren't able to discover anything about the dark man himself?"

"No. All I had was a description that could have been almost anybody. Dark eyes, dark hair, early thirties, a big man. She said he scared her, but she couldn't explain why. He was polite with her, she said."

"It worries me that somebody else is showing such interest in our Jim."

"Yes, it worries me, too. But I think I've short-circuited the problem for the moment."

A hand entered the Packlord's holopic from beyond the frame and handed him a fresh cup of tea. He took it and sniffed the steam rising from the cup. "Your bribe to her was large enough to ensure her loyalty?"

"The dark man offered her ten thousand. I offered a hundred thousand."

"Is she, as the Terries say, an honest thief?"

"You mean will she stay bought?"

"Exactly."

"I think so . . . until the dark man offers her more."

"Mm. That sounds chancy."

"I'm sorry, Packlord, it's the best I can do. I'll watch her as closely as I can." Korkal shrugged. "But you know how it is. . . ."

"The Hunzza concerns me as well. What have you learned about him?"

"Nothing, and that bothers me even more than my failure with the dark man."

"Why?"

"Because I have a lot more to work with. I saw him myself. He's young, little more than a boy. My people recorded him. We can identify

him almost down to the cellular level, and we'll
be able to do that as soon as they finish analyzing the traces left on the silverware he used,
and the saliva in his water glass. I took what I
had and with Serena Half Moon's blessing ran
him through the Terran databases. Nothing.
There's no record of him arriving on Terra
through the normal channels. That in itself is
interesting."

"You can't access Hunzzan records, of
course, but maybe I can do something. Forward
the data to my office, and I'll get back to you."
The Packlord tasted his tea, sighed. "If Hunzza
is involved—I don't know. I can't imagine the
Hunzzan High Command, or the Imperial Nest,
sending a boy to investigate if they have somehow learned of what I fear. But then, isn't it too
coincidental that Jim is, once again, the focus?
Or am I misunderstanding? Is he the object of
the Hunzzan boy's interest?"

"I couldn't discuss it in front of him, Lord. I'll
try to get the girl by herself, but it may be hard.
She claims the Hunzza is her bodyguard,
though she also says he is a pacifist."

"A what?"

"A pacifist, Lord."

"I've never heard of a Hunzzan pacifist. Even
a young one."

Korkal remembered Thargos the Hunter, the
least pacifist Hunzza he'd ever known. "I
haven't either, Lord. Quite frankly, I'm at a loss.
I understand very little about any of this. I wish
I could talk to Jim about it."

"No! I forbid it! I know how you feel, but I don't want him alerted to our suspicions."

"Very well, Lord." Korkal's long pink tongue slipped from his jaw and hung dangling, a sign of his exhaustion. "I still think you're wrong, though."

"That's why I like you, Lord Denai. You are one of the few who will tell me that to my face."

"Yes, well. So you have access to the Hunzzan main databases?"

"As, I am certain, they have to ours. I can't have everything examined, but what I can, I will. Don't worry, I'll find out who this Hunzzan boy is. What's his name?"

"Harpalaos," Korkal said.

"Often Hunzzan names have larger meanings. Does this one?"

Korkal nodded somberly. "Bringer of the Deadly Dawn."

3

Tabitha was waiting in the anteroom when Jim closed the door to Lindsay's office behind him. She stood up immediately. "Jim?"

"I'm fine, Mom. Maybe this wasn't such a bad idea after all. Dr. Lindsay—he seems like a pretty good guy."

The tightness around her eyes and mouth loosened suddenly. "Then you're not mad at me?"

He shook his head and grinned. "Come on,

Mom. Let's get out of here. We'll go someplace and have a beer."

He put his arm around her waist and walked her to the door. The receptionist, watching them go, thought they almost looked, for a moment at least, like brother and sister.

Dr. Lindsay had left his chair and was just settling behind his desk when his comm unit buzzed softly. "Yes?"

A disembodied head floated like a balloon above his desktop. "Oh, it's you," Lindsay said.

"How did it go?" Outsider asked.

"Are you versed in psychology? Psychiatry?"

"Yes, but I'm not interested in technical details at the moment. I'll read your full report later. Were you able to plant any of the suggestions?"

Lindsay looked troubled. "That boy's been through hell. What you want me to do, well, it's . . . I don't know if I want to continue."

Outsider said, "I've never understood why a man with access to drugs, to the pleasure of wireheading, to almost any kind of holosensual experience imaginable, would insist on molesting his younger male clients sexually. What is it, Doctor? The thrill? The fear?"

Lindsay's lips tightened. "I laid the groundwork. The Endicott boy is struggling with an enormous amount of guilt. He killed his father. True, it was an accident, but still—it will take a lot of work to get through it."

"He didn't kill his father, and you haven't answered my question."

"He has a strong sense of duty as well," Lindsay went on. "I used that, added to it. Brought up the idea of atonement. There's a long history of that in pastoral treatment. Do something good to make up for your evil. If possible, do good for the person you wronged. I sensed him responding to the idea. He was raised to feel a sense of duty to others."

"But where would that . . . oh, I see." Outsider nodded. "It might work. You'll have to be careful. I don't want him driven beyond the edge. And as I told you before, I don't want him harmed."

Lindsay eyed him curiously. "Who is the boy to you?"

But Outsider's image was already beginning to break up at the edges. "Do your job, Doctor. Do what I'm paying you for. Don't worry about anything else."

Lindsay stared at the empty space where Outsider's holo image had been. Finally he sighed and said, "Millie? Send in the next one, please." He paused. "And look into vacations. Sometime about three months out. I think by then I'll be ready."

He clicked her off and stared blankly at nothing for several moments. Then he spoke again. "Millie, change that. Cancel all my appointments after today."

He didn't know whether he could run, or how far he would get, but he suddenly decided he would try. No matter how he did with Jim Endicott, in the end the dark man would kill him.

He was a trained psychiatrist. He knew a devil when he saw one.

4

"**W**here are we going?" Harpalaos asked.

"Where I'm going. You have to stay outside. Shawn Fan's a spacer bar, but nobody there much likes Hunzza. You know."

"Nobody anywhere on Terra much likes Hunzza," Harpy said mournfully.

"Well, you shouldn't have tried to invade our system. If it hadn't been for that hero, whoever it was . . ."

He eyed her with green intensity. "Do you really believe there was a hero?"

Char shrugged. "That's the street word. And there was that weird Linkage thing. I was there, you know."

"In the Pleb Linkage? What was it like?"

She shivered. "Strange. I almost got the feeling . . ."

"What?"

"Nothing. Forget it." They had been climbing stairs up from the huge abandoned room where they lived. Now they reached a rusty steel door. When Harpy pulled it open, it shrieked. The sound reminded him of the mindless things he'd hunted as a very young child.

The noise of the night smeared itself in bass tones and shrill screams around them. "You

Terries," Harpy muttered. "I don't know how you stand it, this endless cacophony."

"Cacophony," Char said. "That's a big word."

"I memorized a dictionary."

"You would have."

She left Harpy at the door of the Shawn Fan, walked on inside, sat at the bar, ordered a drink, and looked around. She didn't see him at first. He was seated in a booth, his back to her, only his head visible. Across from him sat a blond woman who looked tired and wary. They were both drinking beer.

So who's the woman?

She hadn't planned on this. And the woman was old. Was that what he liked? She didn't look like a hooker, though.

She picked up her drink and walked over to the table, bumping it with her hip. They looked up at her.

"Oh, hi."

"Hi, Jim. Aren't you gonna introduce me? Who's this?" She tilted her head at the blond woman. "Your new playgirl? You forgot me already?"

The woman stared at her. Her gaze was penetrating, unpleasant. Judgmental.

"Hey, lady. You don't know me. So don't look at me that way."

Jim was swiveling back and forth between them, sensing the tension but not really understanding it. *Fool,* she thought.

"Char, this is my mother. Tabitha Endicott."

Mother? She froze. She had no idea what to

do. She'd never met *anybody's* mother.

"Oh. I . . . ah . . . pleased to meet you." She stuck out one hand, noticing the reluctance with which Tabitha took it. "My name's Char."

Tabitha nodded. Her fingers were cool. So was her expression. "You're a . . . friend . . . of Jim's?"

She heard the subtext and shrugged. "Maybe. If he says so." *Get away from this. Bad mistake. His freaking* mother?

Jim still had that goofy, puzzled expression on his face. *He's younger than he looks,* she thought. *And his mama looks dangerous. Doesn't like me at all . . .*

"Just stopped by to say hi, Jimmy. I'll see you later, maybe."

She didn't wait for him to answer, just turned and walked quickly away. She was surprised at how upset she felt. Mother? What kind of crap was that?

Tabitha took a delicate sip of her beer. "Who was that?"

"A girl . . ."

"I saw that. Is she the reason you've been coming here so much?"

His eyebrows rose. "Char? I just met her last night." He hadn't told Tabitha the rest of it, and didn't plan to. It would only worry her more. He was tired of people worrying about him. At least Char didn't worry about him.

And she'd come over to the table. He turned and looked over his shoulder. She was at the bar, her back to him, hunched, pounding her drink. It was hard to tell, but she looked pissed.

Women.

"I don't like her, Jim."

"Huh? Why not?" He paused. "You don't even know her."

"Yes, I do. I know the type."

"You sound like a mother now."

"I am your mother."

"Mom . . ."

She shook her head. "I know it doesn't matter. And sometimes I feel like an idiot, saying things like that. After what you've been through. I know you think you can take care of yourself, but—"

"Mom, I can take care of myself."

She sighed. "Forget I said anything."

"Don't be that way."

An uncomfortable puddle of silence grew between them. He noticed that Tabitha's gaze kept sliding toward the bar, and he was wondering where to go with that when the front door crashed open. He turned and saw the man he'd whipped the night before at the pool table.

The man cradled a shatter-blaster in his arms. "Where's the punk?" he bawled, spit gleaming on yellow teeth. "Where's the frig-ass punk with the big gun?"

His gaze raked across the bar, paused, focused. "I see you, asshole!"

People began to dive under the tables.

5

Outsider had nearly a billion links now, but for this task he folded only a tenth of them into a new array. As always, the feeling of power was immense, inhuman. Of course, he wasn't human, and that made a difference. But he remembered being human.

It took him only nanoseconds to discover how the Hunzzan boy had been smuggled onto Terra. The trail was interesting. Some people high up in the Confederation weren't as trustworthy as they seemed. He allowed himself a moment of humor over that. People were often not trustworthy. He'd used that before. And he would again. Humans were so vulnerable.

But he passed over that quickly. What was even more interesting was the web that led away from Terra. The boy had come through that web from Hunzzan space, but not really from Hunzza. Not from the Empire. That had been his first concern.

He didn't have Jim's amazing pattern-recognition abilities, but he was close. He recognized the tangle of false trails, sorted them out, followed them back.

It took him longer than he'd expected, even with the extraordinary access he was able to achieve into the Hunzzan databases. A master had fuzzed those data flows. But one name kept recurring, and finally he focused on it.

A'Kasha? The Pit of Souls?

What was that?

For some reason, the more he focused on it, the less he was able to see it. He stepped away from the specifics to examine the larger patterns more closely. A'Kasha. It didn't seem to exist, at least not officially. Not in the Hunzzan databases. But it was there, and from it extended a shifting web of connections. Of influence.

He tried to manipulate those patterns and failed. That in itself was a data point, an important one. Nothing the Hunzza had should prevent him from doing what he wished with their data patterns. They had nothing that could compare with the power of the mind arrays.

But something was stopping him. And whatever it was, it was somehow associated with this A'kasha. This Pit of Souls. He gathered himself and launched another probe. Again he failed. It was like trying to gather mist with a club. The more force he applied, the less he was able to see. To analyze. The patterns shifted, drifted, vanished.

More power?

He was entirely concentrated on the Hunzza now, on their databases and, more important, their data flows. The pathways were roads, and all roads led to Rome. To Hunzza Prime.

Except some roads didn't. Those roads were like underground tunnels, hidden, tangled, seeming to go nowhere, to exist without purpose. Trying to travel them was like pushing one end of a strand of limp spaghetti.

The existence of such a data net frightened him. He ought to be able to touch it, but he couldn't. The Hunzza should have no technology capable of defeating him, but they did. Something did.

Maybe not the Hunzza?

Yet it was connected with the Hunzzan boy. And now the boy was connected with Jim.

That frightened him most of all.

He needed Jim back in the arrays where he belonged, in order to destroy the Albagens and their treacherous Packlord. He hadn't thought the Hunzza would be a threat, not after their recent defeat.

He'd thought he was manipulating events: Char, Dr. Lindsay, assorted thugs. But now a colder fear began to seep into his immortal consciousness.

Was something manipulating him?

Terror thrilled through him. *Kill them all, kill them all.*

Jim! I need *you . . .*

6

Mong Seng Tan was seventy-six years old, though because of his vegetarian diet and the various physical exercises he'd practiced since he was three years old, he had the body of a thirty-year-old man. And, he sometimes thought, the mind of a newborn infant.

At least today he did, as the full beauty of the integration he'd achieved struck him all over again. It really was something like the wonder a baby experienced, seeing things for the first time.

Tan came so close to excitement as he considered this that he nearly shivered in the sharp, thin breezes that cut through his ashram high in the Himalayas, in the region that had once been known as Tibet. Nearly shivered, but not quite; he'd gained complete control over his autonomic reflexes many years before, and it took only a moment's thought to bring his rebellious body to heel.

He sat cross-legged on the cold stone floor and regarded the half dozen of his followers ranged in similar positions before him. All wore saffron robes, and all seemed equally unaffected by the chilly temperature of both the stones and the air.

Every head bowed before him was shaved naked as an egg, which made the deep copper-colored sockets inset behind each ear all the more obvious. A few hundred years before, his forebears might have regarded such things as odd, especially for those who'd forsworn the material world for the endless paths seeking after nirvana. But Tan knew that life was a journey best negotiated unawares; if such things helped understanding, then they helped *not* understanding as well. These were hashes of awareness not much considered outside his own rather narrow pursuits, but he had devoted his life—the current one, at least—to them.

He had joined in the Great Linkage, not out of a sense of duty, and certainly not from any sense of fear, but merely from curiosity. What would it be like to be a part of something so vast and yet so human?

He'd been aware of the pulsing nodes—Pylos Two, Amotek, and others like them—as well as the great choke points of the two relay satellites, where he'd seen endless rivers of flowing souls, tiny points of golden light, channeled and driven into the guiding hands of—

Of what?

There had been two of them. Two forces, two powers. New things, he thought, strange and wonderful. He'd allowed himself to flow through the satellites and into their immaterial hands, felt himself shaped and molded and used . . .

And he'd returned with the memory of something he couldn't actually recall. At the moment of Linkage he'd felt himself suddenly swell beyond the usual bounds of the world and expand outward into vast reaches of light far beyond anything he'd ever guessed might exist before. It had shocked him to the bedrock of his comprehension—in fact, he hadn't comprehended it at all. He had experienced it, though, and he used that experience to shape something he could comprehend, if not understand. He didn't mind the not-understanding part; in fact, it reassured him. Knowingness was a matter of perceiving without necessarily understanding the perception. Or so he thought it must be.

No matter. He waited until his acolytes finished their devotions and raised their heads to stare at him. Once again he felt the sheer delight in the unknowledge of what he had found.

He smiled at them. "Look," he said, and then giggled like a child as he rose straight up into the air and hovered over them, the mountain dawn light glinting in his blue eyes, like a fat yellow parasol hanging suspended, ten feet in the air.

CHAPTER SIX

1

"**G**et down," Jim said as he slid out of the booth. "Under the table." Tabitha was craning her neck, trying to see better. She didn't understand the danger. Except for the fight in the mountains, she'd never been attacked by anybody bent on murder.

Damn it, no gun. He'd left it at home because he was only going to see a harmless shrink and thought he'd have no need for it.

I live through this, I never make that mistake again, he thought as he crab-scuttled across the barroom floor, trying to keep tables between himself and the door. He was focused on Yellow Teeth, who'd lost him in the chaos as people scrambled and dove for cover.

He saw Char spinning on her stool, turning, looking. "Get down!" he shouted at her.

Yellow Teeth took a step away from the door, swinging the snout of the blaster out in front of him. Back door. That was the thing—get the hell out of here. Let the cops take care of Yellow Teeth.

He knee-walked past the pool table alcove, angling for the corner of the bar. Tony, the bartender, was crouched down, just the top of his head visible over the bar. He was also moving toward the end. Toward a weapon?

Jesus. If they started shooting at each other, they'd take out half the bar. Innocent bystanders. Tabitha.

He stood up. "Over here, asshole," he shouted, then dived for the floor again. Yellow Teeth saw him, took another step, and raised the blaster to his shoulder.

"Shoot your freaking ass," he moaned.

It was clear that Yellow Teeth was high on something. His eyes were the size of saucers, saucers with raw eggs in them. As Jim worked his way toward a battered door at the outside end of the bar, he thought of Delta. Called himself Outsider now, but he was still Delta to Jim. Maybe Delta had been right. Maybe it was too dangerous to renounce the arrays, try to make a life for himself. Christ, this was the second time in a day somebody had tried to kill him.

His pattern sense kicked in with a rush, grappling with the coincidence. In patterns there weren't many coincidences. Make the pattern large enough, and there were no coincidences at all.

But he couldn't get a handle on it. Couldn't concentrate. He didn't have the arrays with him, wasn't connected. Couldn't analyze what was happening. All he could see was a guy with a gun, a guy who wanted to blow his head off.

He rolled across a few feet of open space, slammed against the wooden door, and tumbled through into a darkened hallway lined with crates of warm beer. The door swung shut, then blew off its hinges, a cloud of deadly wooden splinters. The bellow of the shatter-blaster numbed his ears. People were screaming out there.

Tabitha!

He scrambled down the hall on his hands and knees and rammed his shoulder against a metal door at the end. He bounced off, his shoulder going dead from the impact. Locked!

He ran his palms up the right-hand edge of the door. No handle, only a chip slot. He had no way to open it. And it was solid, couldn't be broken down.

Trapped.

Smoke billowing from the bar, more shouts, screams. A huge, shadowy figure moved into silhouette in the doorway: Yellow Teeth and the blaster, the weapon's snout now glowing a dull red. Jim crouched behind the end of the rank of beer cases, trying to think. He rammed his right fist through the soft plastifoam side of a case, yanked out a can of beer, and shook it hard.

Yellow Teeth took a step down the hall, blaster sweeping back and forth, bellowing, "Kill your freaking ass, punk!"

Jim ripped off the freeze tab and threw the can. Beer sprayed, freezing, splashing.

"Whoa! Bastard!"

Yellow Teeth swiped at his face, his hand dripping foam. Jim gathered his feet under him and lunged forward, trying to keep low. He crashed full tilt into Yellow Teeth's heavy gut, driving him backward and into the wall, smelling the other's rotten breath as he did.

The butt of the blaster smashed into Jim's

forehead, stunning him. Fountains of white sparks exploded behind his eyes. Slipping away now . . . He grabbed, hung on. Kept on driving with his thighs, his knees.

But he was too low, couldn't match the crazy man's strength. The butt of the blaster smashed into him again, again. Head, shoulder. His right arm swung useless, paralyzed.

He grabbed Yellow Teeth's balls with his left hand and squeezed as hard as he could, trying to tear them off. Yellow Teeth screamed, a high, wavering sound.

But the gun butt came down again. Suddenly Jim was floating, drifting away, so soft, darkness . . .

A flicker of patterns jittering through his brain, big patterns . . .

Death patterns.

He slumped down, his good hand falling away, body going cold . . .

"Dad . . ." he whispered.

On the bleeding edge of final vision, he saw the barrel of the blaster drop and steady. A hole the size of a grapefruit, endless black eye . . .

Too late. *Too late!*

2

Char picked herself up off the floor, a flashbeamer in her hand, and came up looking for a target. Yellow Teeth was raving, screeching, slamming across the room.

She had him for a second, then a screaming woman was in the way, and then he was gone—past her, crouching, triggering the blaster.

She threw herself down again and didn't see him crash through the door. Bodies were heaving everywhere in a stampede for the front door. Where was Jim?

She lifted her head over the bar and looked around. The door at the end of the bar was gone. She could hear Yellow Teeth ranting and groaning back there but couldn't see him.

No targets. Damn it . . .

Somebody stepped on her hand as she worked her way to the end of the bar, and she screamed. Fingers broken, maybe.

Somebody slammed into her hard, knocked her against the column of a bar stool. She looked up and saw Jim's mother rush past, waving a heavy plastic ashtray over her head like a rock.

Stupid woman. Good way to get herself killed.

Jim's mother, though . . .

The cold part of her brain made the calculation. Yeah, if the kid didn't get himself killed, it would be a good trade. Give her an in . . .

Gratitude was good. Gratitude would work.

She launched herself at Tabitha, hitting her at the base of the spine. The blow knocked her down and rolled her over.

Tabitha fought back, clawing, screeching, flailing with the ashtray. Char belted her in the jaw with the beamer, stunning her.

"Jesus, calm down."

"Jim . . ." she moaned.

"You won't do him any good getting yourself blown up. Keep your ass down. I'll get him."

Faded blue eyes, half dazed, stared at her. "In the hallway."

"Yeah. Stay here. Stay down—I don't want to have to watch out for your ass. Understand?"

Tabitha nodded.

"Okay. Wait."

Char pushed on past in a crouch, grimacing when she sought balance with her injured hand. "Crap."

She poked her head around the corner, past the ruined door, and scanned down the hall. She saw shadows in there, movement. Still no targets.

She felt the skin across her chest prickle as she moved out into the open. If that freako turned around now, saw her, took his shot, she was hamburger.

She wished Harpy were with her. He wouldn't be any good in a firefight, but it would make her feel better. He could do that, make her feel better.

Taking one long, crabbed step forward, the beamer held out in front like a magic wand, Char blinked, trying to see better despite the smoke and tears in her eyes.

Still only shadows.

"Jim, drop!" she howled. "Get your ass down!"

Two quick blasts from the hall, flares of light, blinded her. Her heart jumped into her throat as her reflexes slammed her flat.

His voice was reedy, weak. "Stay back . . ."

Damn it—still no shot. She raised the beamer, moved closer.

Char saw Jim fall away from him, crumbling, hands raised. Saw the blaster swing around, stop.

"Kill your ass," Yellow Teeth grunted.

Thunder split the chaos as something plucked off the roof of the Shawn Fan like a giant opening a cookie jar. Armored figures dropped out of the night.

There came the zipple ripple of heavy-duty stunners, and suddenly it was over. Her whole left side went numb in the backwash, and she toppled to one side. The beamer dropped from nerveless fingers.

Too late. Was it too late?

Last thought: *Damn, there goes my hundred grand.*

Darkness.

3
———

Korkal walked through the wreckage thinking, *Gods, what a mess.*

People were moaning, groaning, gesturing weakly at the med corpsmen moving among them. A continuous stream of one-man grav-lifters ferried the wounded to a huge med ship hovering overhead. Local cops cursed and sweated as they struggled to hold back frantic crowds. More cops were working their way through piles of broken rafters and slabs of warped plastic.

One of the cops came up to him, a blank, careful expression on his face, though Korkal could smell his rage. "Lieutenant Harwood," Korkal said.

Harwood was holding a scorched shatterblaster in his arms. He lifted his gaze to the med ship overhead. "You swing a real big dick, mister."

"What, I'm sorry? I don't—"

"Clout. You always go after hopped-up muggers with a full company of space marines?"

Korkal waved him off. "I didn't have any time."

"You coulda called the cops," Harwood said. "You know, police. Like me. We're trained to handle stuff like this."

Right, Korkal thought. *Hostage situation. Standoff. Jim Endicott.*

He shook his head wearily. "Hindsight, Lieutenant. I didn't have any time."

"Your precious kid again? What's with that, anyway?"

"Classified," Korkal said.

"Classified, bullshit. I ran him through the files. He bounced. High-level stuff. A kid. Listen, you freaking wolf, what the hell's going on? You're all over my district like white on rice. A freaking kid, for God's sake." He paused, turned his head slowly back and forth. "*Look* at this freaking mess."

Korkal was tired of talking to him. The worries of upset cops weren't his problem. "Where's the boy?"

"Over there." He tilted his head. Korkal looked and saw Jim, pale, his face bruised, sitting with his arm around Tabitha on a booth seat no longer attached to a booth. Char sat cross-legged at their feet, looking up, an angry expression on her face.

"Good, I need—" He started to move past Harwood, but the cop grabbed his arm and spun him around. "I'm not through with you yet. If you think you're just gonna waltz in here—"

"Let go of Lord Denai's arm," a woman's deep, whiskey-rasped voice said. Korkal swiveled.

"Jesus!" Harwood said, and let go. "Madame Chairman . . ." His heavy features went pale.

Serena Half Moon, chairman of the Confederation, picked her way closer, flanked on either side by guards who looked ready to kill anything that twitched. Her long, Native American features wore a concentrated, intense expression, and her dark eyes glittered.

"I know it's a mess, Lieutenant, but it's not your mess. It's mine." She clipped off her words the way a man would snip a cigar. "You've done a good job. Now file it away and forget it ever happened. You understand?"

This was juice at a level Harwood had never dreamed of. His eyes skittered. He looked like he wanted to run. "Yes, ma'am. Whatever you say."

The chairman nodded. "Take your people out."

He pulled a sketchy salute. In his rumpled suit, he looked ridiculous. Korkal knew he wasn't; he was just a cop far out of his depth. He felt sorry for him.

"Thank you again, Lieutenant. I'll see that a good report goes in your file."

"Ah . . . thank you. Thank you." Harwood spun and walked stiffly away.

"An angry man. Now a frightened one, Madame Chairman. What are you doing here?"

"Same thing you are, I guess. Making sure the most valuable human being alive is still alive, and in one piece." She peered over Korkal's shoulder. "Good lord. What happened to him?"

"He got hit in the face with the butt of a shatter-blaster."

"A what?"

"You'll have a full report in your own data systems in twenty minutes."

"I'm here now. Tell me."

"You're causing a scene, Serena."

"Of course I am. I'm the chairman."

"Can we move a little to the side . . . out of the light?" He took her elbow, eased her away. She went reluctantly, glaring at him.

"Have you lost your mind? Why wasn't I informed?"

"You're busy. Until yesterday, it was all mundane. Just a little discreet bodyguarding."

"The Packlord told you to report to me," Half Moon said. "You understand what that means? To me."

"Yes." Korkal sighed. "I was preparing a report. And then this—"

"That's not good enough, Lord Denai. If I want bureaucratic lies and stalling, I've got plenty of my own people. I don't expect it from you. Not about him."

Korkal saw that her face had gone the color of new bricks. "I'm sorry."

She started to say something, then stopped and shrugged. "All right. What's done is done. Is he okay?"

"They gave him some pain medication. Bruised nerve in his shoulder, but it's fading. They'll work on his face later. The med tech said he had a tough skull."

Serena closed her eyes. "Tough skull. Jesus. Don't you understand what's riding on him? Don't you—" She shook her head. "And Tabitha's with him. What was it? What happened?"

Korkal thought about the Packlord. About Char and the Hunzza. About the dark man. "I think it was a barroom brawl," he said carefully.

She eyed him. "Okay. I'm going to say hello."

Korkal glanced over and saw Char watching them, her eyebrows riding high on her forehead. "I wish you wouldn't."

"Wish in one hand, Korkal, crap in the other."

He thought he knew Terran slang pretty well, but this was a mystery. "I beg your pardon?"

"See which one turns warm and brown first," the chairman said as she strode past him.

4

"**H**ello, Jim, Tabitha," the chairman said. "Scrunch over." She wedged herself between them.

"Serena—what are you doing here? And Korkal?"

"You didn't think we'd let you run off on your own, did you?"

Jim looked down, bit his lip. "I told you I didn't want—"

The chairman glanced at Char. "Young woman, would you excuse us for a moment?"

Char wrinkled her nose. "You're the chairman?"

Serena glanced at one of her guards. "Harry, if you'd escort . . . uh . . ."

"Char." She unfolded herself and stood up. "Thanks, I don't need an escort." She turned and walked away. Jim watched her go until she vanished beyond the wreckage of the front door.

"Serena, she's a friend of mine."

"Yes, certainly."

"Look, I thought we had a deal. You were going to leave me alone for a while. I need some time to myself . . ."

"I don't know if that's a luxury I can allow you. Look what happened." She gestured. "And last night, with the grav-van, the drive-by."

"Damn it, Serena, shut up."

"What grav-van?" Tabitha said.

"Serena . . ."

The chairman flapped one hand. "It's nothing."

"Serena, I don't want this. You've got Korkal following me around, haven't you?"

She glanced at the Alban, who stood a dozen feet away, watching them. "I'm not sure if it isn't the other way around. He's using my people."

"But you're giving him access. Damn it, Serena, you *owe* me. All I want is to be left alone for a while. Why can't you—"

"Nobody bothered you. You wouldn't have known we were around, if . . ." She looked up at the gaping cavity where the roof had been. "You're a trouble magnet, Jim. And you're too valuable to risk."

"Serena," Tabitha broke in, "I want to know what's going on. What happened to Jim last night?" She turned. "Jim?"

He wouldn't meet her eyes. "It wasn't anything. An accident, almost."

"Serena?"

"He got involved in a drive-by shooting. Some gang thing."

"Jim!"

"Mom, really. I just happened to be there when it happened."

Korkal walked up. "Tabitha, how are you?"

She nodded, her expression distracted.

"You shouldn't worry, Tabitha. I was there almost immediately," Korkal said soothingly.

"Almost immediately. What does that mean? You weren't there when it happened, right?"

"Well . . ."

"I hate this! Jim, you shut me out. Tell me not to worry. And then I find out there's all kinds of reasons to worry. What else aren't you telling me? Serena—you're involved in this, too, aren't you?"

"I keep an eye on your son, Tabitha. Would you rather nobody did?" She swept one hand at the shambles of the bar. "If Korkal hadn't been here . . ."

Tabitha reached up and touched the swollen bruise on the right side of Jim's face. He winced.

"Oh, Jimmy."

He looked up at Korkal. "How long have you been watching me?"

"All along."

"It stops, okay? I want it to stop. I want my own life back. Serena?"

"No, I can't do that. It isn't your own life any longer, Jim. You're too important. What if—"

He stood up. "It *is* my life, damn it. It is. You forget who I am. What I can do."

She stared at him, her black eyes flickering. "No, I don't forget. That's why."

He swung around to face them all. "Leave me alone. All of you. I mean it!"

"Jim . . ." Korkal said, but Jim ignored the Alban, spun on his heel, and followed Char out the door. Korkal hurried after him, leaving the two women behind.

"He's a handful," Serena said.

"He's my son, Serena. What are you people doing to him?"

"It's not us, Tabitha. He's doing it to himself, isn't he?"

Tabitha nodded slowly. "No matter what he wants, will you keep on watching him? Guarding him?"

"Yes."

"Thank you."

"Who's the girl?"

"I'm not sure. He said he just met her."

"Last night?"

"Yes."

"I'll look into it," the chairman said. She paused, then patted Tabitha's hand. "Boys are hard, aren't they?"

"And he's still just a boy, Serena. Everybody forgets that."

Serena shook her head. "No, he isn't."

5

Korkal caught up with Jim a couple of blocks down from the bar and grabbed him by the elbow. "Jim!"

He shook Korkal's hand away. "I told you, leave me alone." He kept on walking. Korkal had to pump his shorter legs to keep up. "Maybe I saved your life back there. You weren't doing all that well. And what about Tabitha?"

Jim stopped. "Tabitha?"

"That guy was nuts. What if he'd done you, then turned around and started blasting? You think of that?" He waited. "I didn't think so. Jim, what's the matter with you?"

"I don't know, Korkal. But you following me around, it's like I can't breathe. Can't think. There's no place for me to go anymore."

They came to a small grav-tube station. "Sit down with me a second," Korkal said, and led him to a bench next to the door.

"I don't really want to talk to you, Korkal. Not right now."

"That's fine. But I need to talk to you. There are things you need to know."

"Oh?"

"Yes. Jim, you think you're the one caught in the middle, but others are, too. Me, for instance. How many times have you saved my life?"

Jim shrugged. "Does it matter?"

"And I've pulled your bacon out of the fire, too."

"Okay, yes. Korkal, I'm not saying we aren't friends. It's just that—"

"I know." He looked up at Jim's face. "That's why I need to tell you. But when I do, I'm placing my life in your hands. Again."

"Hey, this is serious, isn't it?"

Korkal nodded, his eyes wide, opaque.

"Tell me, then."

Korkal took a deep breath and then told him about the Packlord and his fears about Leapers. When he finished, he shook his head. "I don't know . . ."

"Korkal, is that right? He'd make you kill me if . . ."

Korkal nodded. "He's the Packlord. And—"

"And friendship isn't a suicide pact. My God!" Jim looked around, not really seeing anything, his eyes stunned. "He's that afraid?"

"He's that afraid, Jim."

"Do you go along with it? Are you that afraid, too?"

"I told you, didn't I?"

"Jeez . . . I thought I had problems. Man, you must really like me."

"More than that. I trust you. You earned my trust, Jim. It's not mine to throw away. Even for . . . whatever."

Jim nodded. They talked for a while longer, then stood up and shook hands. Korkal watched him go. He'd told him a lot. But he hadn't told him about Char. Or the dark man.

As he walked back to the bar he wondered if he was a fool. So much weight to put on one boy's shoulders. But he couldn't carry it any longer by himself.

Who was the dark man?

6

When he'd first gone to the abandoned warehouse where Char lived, it had been through the tunnels, and he hadn't paid attention. They'd left by another route, and he had only a vague idea of the location. He thought he had the neighborhood right, but now, in the dark, it was a matter of wandering the streets, looking for something that might trip his memory.

Nothing did. At four in the morning, his face throbbing, the lumps on the back of his skull a generalized cold ache, he stopped, leaned against a waste receptacle, and stared up at the blank front of a building.

It could have been the one. It looked right. But so did half a dozen others he'd already cruised by. There were no lights. Two doors, both covered with steel, solid-looking. He went to the first and pounded on it. Nothing.

"Char?"

His voice echoed dully along the empty street.

He pounded again. *"Char! Harpy!"*

The door farther up the street opened silently. "Shut up, you idiot."

"Hey. Is that you?"

"Get your ass inside. Wake up the whole freaking neighborhood, why don't you?"

He loped down the street. She held the door for him. It closed with a solid click. She carried a glow wand.

"No juice in this place," she said. She took a few steps down a darkened hallway, stopped, turned. "You bring your escort with you?"

"No."

"How would you know? Christ, the chairman. Who the hell are you, Jim? I must be outta my mind . . ."

"I told them to stay away."

"Uh-huh. You told the chairman. And that Alban guy. That wolf."

"Korkal's okay. Listen, let me stay. At least tonight. After we talk, if you want me to leave, I'll go. No questions, okay?"

"No questions?"

He shook his head.

"Okay." She led him on into the darkness.

They sat in wan silver moonlight that ghosted through the upper windows. The others, the ones he hadn't met, were back. He could hear the sounds of them sleeping, scattered about the cavernous room.

They were on a sofa, munching the last of a pizza, Harpy picking the pepperoni off, ignoring the rest.

"I need a way to disappear. Really vanish, just drop out of sight," Jim said.

"Yeah? So why come to me?"

"'Cause I figured you might know how to do that. I'd need a different ID . . . some kind of history."

"Do I look like a computer jock?"

"No, but I am. What I need is access. But from someplace nobody knows about. I thought maybe you could find me something."

"Access? You mean like a blind terminal?"

"Yeah."

"Well, maybe . . ." She glanced at Harpy. "What's in it for me?"

"For you? I thought we were friends."

"Why would you think that? I hardly know you."

"Nah. We just met, but you know me, don't you? You knew my name. And you wanted me to know. You let that slip, but it wasn't a slip, was it?"

She looked away. "It was just a name . . ."

"You came after me. Why? Did somebody send you? Was it Korkal?"

In her world, her word was law. She wasn't used to lying, because she didn't have to. She wasn't as good at it as she thought she was. He heard the tiniest of hesitations before she said, "That wolf guy? Is that his name?"

"So it was Korkal. How much did he pay you? Are you supposed to nursemaid me, too? Jesus Christ."

Her lower lip tightened. Stubborn. "You're nuts, buddy. I don't know what the hell you're talking about."

He ignored her. "So Korkal hired you. What for? It couldn't have been as a bodyguard. I've guarded you more than you have me."

"Hey, *wait* a minute."

"I can pay you more than he can. Is it money that yanks your chain, Char? I bet it is."

"Okay, that's it." She leaned forward, eyes glinting in the moonlight. "You're out of here. You came asking for my help, remember? I don't need this crap."

"A lot of money, Char. I guarantee it. More than Korkal can pay you."

She hung, shaking with anger, then leaned back. "What if it isn't *just* the money?"

He felt a flicker of triumph. The patterns had been there, but he hadn't been sure.

"Yeah? Like what? What else?"

"Another guy. Before the wolf."

"Somebody else hired you?"

"The dark man . . ."

And finally, just like that, everything clicked. "Damn it," he said. "Oh, *damn* it . . ."

7

Vladimir Ivanovitch Stelychin was a rough man, rough as a cob, as they might have said in the old days. He didn't much care about the old days, concerned as he was about the new days.

Much of his roughness came from trying to blend the demands of his job as supervisor of material distribution of the Greater Moscow Prosperity Region with his religion, the Church of the Reformed Communist Synthesis Eternal.

There should have been no conflict. Every day Vladimir labored, trying to ensure that food, clothing, and shelter were properly and correctly apportioned to each and every individual resident of the Moscow Region—and he had some pretty big data systems to help him do it. His religion, morphed into nearly unrecognizable form from an ancient political theory that had once held sway in the same region, did have one thing in common with its nearly forgotten ancestor: It urged its followers to serve each and all equally, from the greatest to the smallest. It was the gap between the expectations of his job and his faith that rubbed Vladimir's temper into a constant state of rawness.

He had never been able to meet those expectations. In fact, he regarded himself as a miserable failure. No matter how large or fast his machines became, they still couldn't keep up with the minute and never-ceasing shifts in the human condition. Just when the system seemed to be functioning, some obscure citizen in some arcane corner would develop something new, or desire something new, or begin to despise something current, or some variation of the three, and like a virus, that change would spread and corrupt the entire system. It was, Vladimir sometimes thought, like trying to balance a pride of dancing bears on a plate balanced on the tip of his nose while singing "I Love Paris in the Springtime" and riding a bicycle.

Hopeless. His faith told him he should do better. He knew he should do better. But he had failed continuously until, like every good citizen with the means to help, he'd linked himself and his machines into the Great Linkage. He hadn't really *done* anything, but when the Linkage had broken, he came away from it with the ghost of an idea.

He worked on that idea in every spare moment, becoming more and more obsessed as the simple beauty of it flowered and grew in the grids of his machines.

It was the sheer size of the linkage that gave him the answer. In it was the constant feedback mechanism he needed to be able to accurately predict and disseminate goods, services, and ideas—memes—to whole populations at once.

He tested it several times and found, to his trembling amazement, that it worked. Since he'd developed it on his own time, the process belonged to him. He knew he could use it to make himself incalculably rich. But Vladimir had no interest in that. Instead he took it to the elders of his church and gave it to them. It took a while for them to fully understand what he'd done, but when they did, they were awed.

For the first time in history, there was a clean, simple, and effective way to spread new ideas, inventions, goods, and benefits to all of mankind, almost instantaneously.

And new ideas, inventions, goods, and benefits were springing up everywhere. Nobody could understand why a renaissance seemed to be dawning in the world. But it was—and now the human mind, heart, spirit, and soul grew closer and closer to each other, even as they grew larger and more encompassing.

Humanity had become a bubbling cauldron of creation . . . and now it was boiling over.

CHAPTER SEVEN

1

"I don't know," Char said. "Maybe you're messing with my money. That's gonna be a problem for me."

"I told you, I can cover anything you lose. I'm serious."

She turned to face him. They were on the sofa, morning light leaking through the greasy windows overhead. Some of the others were still snoring, rolled up in blankets or sleeping bags. They all looked young, like tough kids, to Jim. She'd introduced a few, sleepyheads rubbing their eyes as they wandered toward the exits, looking for breakfast. He couldn't remember any of the names, and doubted it mattered. The names wouldn't be real ones, anyway.

"Korkal said a hundred grand. And the dark man was talking ten, maybe more."

"You got a credit chip?" he asked her.

She laughed. "Me? You kidding?"

"Okay. How do you want it? Encrypted cash, gold, commodities? You tell me what and where, and it'll be there."

She stared at him, and he could feel the calculation in her gaze. Something else, too. Not quite fear, but a kind of wariness, watchfulness.

"What? What's going on?"

"I dunno. I'm beginning to think you really can do it. The money, I mean. You know the chairman, for chrissakes."

"Yeah. I wish I didn't, but I do."

"So you're wired for juice all the way to the top. Got marines looking out for your ass. You're probably way too hot for me."

"Look, I don't want to cause you problems, but—"

"You're a problem just by being here. How do you know the chairman?"

He waved one hand. "It's not important."

"I'm in deep water here, Jim. Help me out. Here I am, just a little girl trying to make her way in a cold, hard world—"

He snorted.

"Yeah, well, you ever been hungry, Jim? I mean really hungry? When you, like, starved because there was nothing else to do?"

He shook his head.

"I have. That kind of hunger, you get through it, you tell yourself you're never gonna be hungry again."

Jim grinned. "Scarlett O'Hara."

"What?"

"A classical movie. Never mind."

"See, you're like that. You know a lot of stuff I don't. You've got heavyweight connections. I'm just a street hustler trying to keep it together. Me and my pals."

"Your own little gang."

"Well, what do you expect? Everybody isn't

rich, Jim. You're different from me. I don't know—I probably shouldn't be involved with you at all."

"So why are you?"

"The money, of course. When the dark man came along, I didn't know what he wanted, and I didn't care. Ten thousand. That's enough to keep this whole thing—all of us here—going for a year. Sweet stuff. A year of easy living, just for putting a wire on some young guy. He showed me a holovid of you. You didn't look like hard duty. Maybe even a little bit of fun on the side."

He was startled. "Fun?"

"Yeah. You're not bad-looking, you know."

"Man, I really don't understand that."

"You're a guy. You wouldn't. What—you think women don't have sex drives? Don't get horny?"

"I don't want to talk about that."

"And now you're blushing. Hey, I like blushing. It's . . . tender."

He realized she was yanking his chain. "So should I throw my body into the deal? The cash, and a little bit of me on the side, like you said?"

"Jesus, you're touchy. What would you do if I said yes?"

It was there between them now, a tension he could feel her responding to, feel himself responding to. She tilted her head back. A vein throbbed softly at the side of her throat.

"I'd . . . I'd say yes, too."

"Ah."

After that, it was different between them.

2

Harpy came back and found them sitting at either end of the sofa, not talking, staring blankly but not at each other.

"Where you been?" Char said.

He sat between their bookends. "I went out."

"I know that. Harpy, you go out a lot. What do you do when you go?"

"I told you. Just walk around. Terraport is interesting. You grew up here, but I didn't."

"You ought to watch yourself. You're a lizard. One of these days you're gonna run into people who don't like lizards."

"I'm careful."

"You won't even defend yourself. What if you got jumped?"

A flash of fangs. "I look scary, I think. And I know how to run. I'm a very fast runner."

Jim stared at him, remembering Thargos, the way *that* lizard had moved. *Bet you are,* he thought. Something about Harpy scared him, scared him a lot. It made him brusque and distant around the young Hunzza. And it wasn't just that he reminded him of Thargos. It was almost as if he sensed something, a premonition . . . Harpy was trouble. He would bet his life on it. Maybe he was doing just that.

Thargos. Dead now, but . . . And the dark man. Korkal and the Packlord. Leapers. The chairman. And the curse in his genetic codes, the script of his DNA.

God. I'm never going to be free. They'll never let me alone.

"Harpy, you don't fit," he said.

"What?"

"I mean it. I can understand Char, sort of. Somebody wants to get close to me, they pick her out somehow, and hire her. Probably because she's my age and hangs at the Shawn Fan. And can be hired. But you? Where do you come in? How did you *get* in? Terra doesn't exactly have the welcome mat out for Hunzza."

"Oh, that. No, I came in before the war."

"I don't see it. Delta . . . somebody . . . was keeping all the aliens at arm's length. He knew about the Hunzza. You . . ." He paused, thinking about it. "You sneaked in, right? And that's how you ended up with Char. Stay out of sight. It wasn't like you could just walk around on the streets. Not like now."

"All right, Jim. You've got me. I'm a spy."

"Yeah, that seems like the simplest conclusion."

Harpy shifted, blinking his big green eyes. Jim knew that was the way Hunzza expressed laughter. "So what will you do now that you've caught me?"

"I don't know. I could put Korkal on it. He'd think of something."

Harpy stopped blinking. "The Alban? No . . ."

"Sure. Albans know all about you Hunzza, don't they?"

"Jim, stop it. It's not funny."

Char stirred. "Harpy's okay, Jim. And you're scaring him."

"I don't know what Harpy is," Jim said. "Except he's a strange Hunzza in a strange land."

"I can leave," Harpy put in.

"No," Char said. "You stay."

"Yeah, stay," Jim said. "I think I like you better where I can see you."

Harpy stiffened, then stood up. "I'm not . . . you've got no reason to treat me like this."

"I've got every reason in the world. Harpy, you don't make any sense. You don't fit. That worries me."

"You're kinda pushing it, Jim," Char said. "We got along okay before you came into the picture. We didn't worry about whether you were worried."

"But I'm in the picture now. And not because I put myself there. You two came after me, not the other way around."

"I came after you," Char said. "Harpy didn't have anything to do with it. He was just along for the ride."

Jim slid his gaze back and forth between them, thinking about it. "Okay, look. First thing: Do you go for my deal?"

"I already told you. If the money's there."

"It will be. Two hundred thousand, and that's for openers. You get to keep anything you can squeeze from Korkal or anybody else. But you work for me, right? That means if I tell you to do something, you do it."

It made her uncomfortable, but she nodded. "Yeah. You're in charge. As long as the—"

"Yeah, yeah. The money. Harpy? You go along, too?"

•

The Hunzza relaxed slightly. "Whatever Char wants."

"Okay. Then we have the deal."

They both nodded.

"Char, you go ahead and check to see that you've got the cash. Then when you know I held up my end, we go on to the next thing."

"What's that?" she said.

"I'll let you know," he said. He stood up, dusted off his knees, and started for the door.

"Hey, where you going?"

"Home," he said.

"If you wanna stay and talk . . ." She winked. "Or whatever."

"It's the whatever that worries me."

3

"**S**erena Half Moon is worried about Jim," the Packlord said, raising his cup of tea. "Korkal, I thought you were going to be discreet."

"I was in a hurry. I had to pry the roof off that bar, so I used the marines."

"Maybe it would have been better if you'd let nature take its course."

"You mean let that thug kill Jim? Packlord . . ."

The Packlord sighed. "I know . . . it was a thought." He tasted his tea, closed his eyes. "I've issued an all-fleets alert. We've been analyzing the rate of technological change on Terra."

"And?"

"It's a geometric progression. The curves are beginning to turn straight up."

"That's impossible. We know of nothing like that in our own history."

"We never Leaped, either. I'm getting worried. The Hunzza are regrouping for another try at our home worlds."

Korkal eyed him. "Perhaps it would be better to worry about the tangible problems rather than the rate of technological change on a single allied planet."

"You know what I'm worried about!"

"I know what you say you're worried about."

The Packlord set down his teacup. "What exactly are *you* trying to say, Lord Denai?"

Korkal thought about it, then shook his head. "Forgive me. The stress. I spoke out of turn."

The Packlord's jaw opened, then snapped shut with a slight click. Korkal winced. "If you doubt my motives, say so."

"I doubt everyone's motives, Lord. Even yours."

"Perhaps I should relieve you now. Of both your duties and your doubts."

"You could do that. But you have nobody else that Jim even remotely trusts. And I believe he's trying to set up a meeting with this mysterious dark man."

"Ah." The Packlord leaned back against his formchair. "Between himself and the dark man?"

"No, between Char McCain and her employer. I think he plans to observe."

"Then he doesn't know who the dark man is?"

"I don't think so."

The Packlord thought about it. "All right. I take it you will also be an observer?"

"Discreetly so, Lord."

"Can you keep Serena Half Moon out of it?"

"I believe so."

"Good. Things are complicated enough as it is. The chairman is a wild card I don't want to have to deal with."

Korkal nodded. The Packlord drained his teacup, a signal that the conversation was over. Korkal bowed. The Packlord's holocube winked out.

For a moment the room was silent. Then dark curtains on the far side of the chamber shifted. A form stepped out from the shadows.

"That went well, don't you think?" Serena Half Moon said.

"Time will tell," Korkal replied.

4

The street was empty and dark, a lightless canyon between the blank walls of tall warehouses. The heels of Char's boots sent muffled echoes rattling back and forth. A sharp wind, rank with the smell of sewers, blew steadily in their faces. Half a block up, a single streetlight floated like a Halloween balloon, painting a weak orange circle on the cracked concrete.

"We're sitting ducks out here in the open," Jim said.

"It's what he wanted. After I told him you knew about him, wanted to meet him."

"Tell me again—about his reactions."

They walked abreast of each other, with Harpy trailing behind, his horny claws ticking against the pavement, his green eyes clicking slowly from one side of the street to the other. Jim could feel the lizard's tension.

Approaching the light now, Char was also looking, sweeping, her black eyes wide. "He didn't have any. None that I could see. He just looked at me and said, 'All right.'"

"No questions, no surprise?"

"Not a twitch."

She reached the edge of the light, paused, stopped. He stood next to her. The street yawned empty before and behind them, the stinking breeze a steady pressure on their cheeks.

"Where is he?" Jim said.

"He said he'd be here." She glanced at the tiny clock inset on her thumbnail. "We're early. Three minutes."

Harpy shifted. "I don't like this."

"It'll be okay," Char told him.

The Hunzza made a soft snorting sound and turned nervously away, looking back down the way they'd come. Nothing there . . .

Char stared at her nailtale as the seconds ticked down. She turned slightly. "Is this a good idea?"

"Why?"

"What if . . . he's not friendly?"

"He hired you to watch me," Jim said.

"Which isn't the kind of thing a friend does."

"Don't worry about it. I know what I'm doing."

Her eyebrows arched. "Yeah? You ask me, you—"

She fell silent as he held up one hand. "Can you feel that?"

"What?"

Then she saw that his hair had begun to stand on end. An itchy, crawly sensation tickled her own scalp. She reached up, felt her dark curls stiffening up like wire. "What?" she said again.

He looked up, past the floating blob of the street lamp. "There."

Overhead a white star burned, grew larger, hotter.

"Jesus! Get the hell—"

The light surrounded them, penetrated them. Their organs glowed, their veins throbbed, their bones glittered like frozen milk. Then they vanished.

5

"**W**hat in the Seven Cold Hells was that?" Korkal said.

"I've lost them. Tracking! Swing a full three-sixty. Do it now!"

"What do you mean, you've lost—" Korkal shut up. He could see for himself. The stretch of pavement where the trio had been standing was empty.

"Maybe they ducked into one of the buildings," he said.

The colonel was a big man, short-haired, moose-jawed, his movements jerky with shock. He ran blunt fingers across his keyboard, stared at the holoscreens before him, shook his head. "No. They're gone. It's impossible . . ."

Korkal pushed him aside and thrust forward, staring at the screens. "Not impossible. We're looking at it."

"Bring us in closer, take us down!" the colonel barked.

"No! We don't know what's happening."

The colonel stared at him. "I have my orders . . ."

Korkal shook his head. "I know. Protect the boy. But maybe if you dump a company of space marines down there now, you put him in danger."

The colonel opened his mouth, then closed it. He glanced at the screen and back again. "So what do we do?"

"We wait."

"Jesus," the colonel said. His eyes were wild.

6

Jim was staring at Char as the light grew brighter. She began to fade, to grow transparent. As the light dialed up, he felt his skin grow warm, like sunlight pounding down, growing hotter . . .

A sudden *sssnnaap!* of intolerable heat—

Darkness, cool and soothing. Vague shadows. A scraping sound, then another. Jim blinked.

"What . . ."

A single pool of orange light winked on. In it was a chair, and in the chair was a form shrouded in shadow. Jim's skin itched.

"Where am I?"

A deep voice, clear, hard, replied, "It doesn't matter." The shape moved slightly. "Don't worry about the others. They're fine, but they're not here. Just you and me."

"Who are you?"

A soft chuckle. "You know who I am."

"The dark man . . ."

"You know who I am," the voice repeated.

A larger illumination began to shape the space that contained them. Jim glanced up, down, saw that he was standing on a platform, a round gray disk about four feet wide. He was looking down on the other.

The other. Sure . . .

Jim stepped off the disk, walked to the edge of the platform, and jumped down to the main floor. "The dark man. Outsider."

The light grew brighter, scraping away the shadows. The dark man stood up, nodding. He wore a black turtleneck shirt and formfitting pants. The balled, tight muscles and the dark hair were somehow familiar. He was maybe thirty, walking forward, hand out . . .

Jim took it. The man smelled faintly of cinnamon. His teeth were too perfect, his eyes pools of no-color, dark, observant. His fingers felt rough and dry, his grip strong.

"You've got a body now," Jim said.

Outsider shrugged. "It seemed useful. It's hard for me to focus on your reality . . . and trying to manipulate things while disguised as a burning bush didn't seem like a good option. It worked for Moses, but we live in more complicated times."

He chuckled again. Whatever he was, he radiated immense charm. Jim could feel himself responding to it, fought it . . .

"What is it?" He pointed at Outsider's chest. "This thing you're using?"

"A construct. A puppet. A lens. Whatever." Outsider glanced over his shoulder. "It doesn't matter. Just that it serves my purposes."

"Your purposes of manipulation," Jim said. "I don't like this."

"Should I have consulted you? But how? You've shut me out, Jim. You haven't entered the arrays in months. What was I supposed to do?"

Jim felt a twinge. What—guilt? Shame? He wasn't sure. "Supposed to do? Nothing. That's what I thought you were supposed to do. That's what I told you."

Outsider shook his head. "No. I told you. I'm a force, a power. I can't be controlled. I agreed to help you, work with you, but my purposes are my own."

"I should have destroyed you then. Maybe I should do it now."

"You could. I don't deny that. You've already

proven your power in the arrays is greater than mine. Is that what you want?"

"I don't know."

"If you do it, then it's all on your shoulders. You have to run the arrays, live in them. But the only running I've seen you do is away. Away from responsibility, thought, duty."

"Don't talk to me about duty!"

"Hurts, does it? You're transparent, Jim. A child. A child with enormous power, but still a child. A brat, really."

Reflexively Jim made a fist, and Outsider laughed. "What are you going to do? *Hit* me?" He laughed again. "You prove my point, don't you?"

He's doing it to me right now, Jim thought. *Pushing my buttons. Twisting things. Manipulating me.* "What do you want? Why Char?"

Outsider turned and began to walk away from him. Jim followed without realizing he did so.

"Why not Char? She was in the right place, was suitably greedy, had the right talents, the right worldview. You shut me out, Jim. I had no way to monitor you. But I had to find something."

They reached the far wall of the large room. Outsider palmed a doorplate, waited while the door slid sideways, then stepped out into a dimly lit hall. Suddenly Jim knew where he was.

"We're on the *Pride.* The *Albagens Pride.*"

Outsider looked over his shoulder, grinned. "It's centrally located."

"Does anybody know you're here?" The *Pride*

was wired directly to Alba, to the Packlord. Manned by Albans. Korkal in charge, Korkal and his own games.

If the Packlord knew . . .

"Of course not. How would they? I control everything here. And I'm not really here, not in any sense they would understand the word."

He reached another door, opened it, and motioned Jim into a small chamber, simple, clean, comfortable. He took one chair, pointing at another opposite. "Take a seat. We need to have a talk."

Jim sat down. "All this? For a talk?"

Outsider folded his long white fingers in his lap. "You're a hard guy to get in touch with," he said.

7

Sssnnaap!

Char had the beamer in her hand, questing for targets. Nothing. A small room, empty. She looked down, saw the dull gray disk she was standing on. On her right was Harpy, his teeth a sharp white line in the gloom.

"What the hell?"

A soft rattling sound. It took her a moment to realize it was Harpy. His teeth were chattering.

"Hey . . ." She stepped off the disk. "We're okay." She touched the lizard on one scaly shoulder. "We're all right."

His green eyes glowed eerily. "No, we're not. What happened?"

She looked around. Nothing happening. Silence. "I don't know."

"We're not where we were. We've moved."

"Yeah, I think so."

Harpy looked down at the disk he was standing on. "This scares me. It's technology, but I've never heard of anything like it. The Hunzza don't have it. The Albans don't, either—at least I don't think so."

Char slipped the beamer back into her leather jacket, her expression disinterested. "So what? People are always inventing new stuff."

"Hunzza's technological era is ten thousand of your years older than your own. That's what's scary—how can Terra be coming up with things we haven't come close to?"

"Maybe it's not new."

"Well, what is it? We were somehow moved off an empty city street to . . . where? Where are we? How was it done?"

She still didn't get it. "What does it matter? It happened, that's all." She turned. "Is that a door?" She walked toward it. No handle. A palm plate that didn't respond when she touched it.

"Where's Jim?"

"Yes," Harpy replied, so close to her shoulder she could feel his breath tickling her neck. "That's a good question, too."

The room was silent, the silence thick and heavy, with the feeling of massive walls, impenetrable locks. A prison.

"Maybe you're right," she said. "Maybe we should worry. A little."

"Your dark man . . ." Harpy said.

"Yeah. That bastard," she replied. "I should have asked Jim for more money. Hazard pay."

Behind her the door clicked and began to slide open. Harpy's teeth sounded like a kid running with a pocket full of marbles.

8

"**G**one," Korkal said. He was standing on the sidewalk, his stumpy, furry form outlined in the muddy glare of the floating street lamp. He looked up but saw nothing. He wrinkled his nose against the stinking wind. How did humans put up with these odors? Their noses must be dead.

The colonel—his name was Beeson—broke away from a huddle with two lesser officers, and half marched, half cringed toward Korkal.

"We're gonna have to let the chairman know."

"Yes," Korkal sighed. "I'll do it. I'll tell her I wouldn't let you come down right away. That I made you wait. It'll take some of the pressure off."

"I'm not worried about—" He shook his head. Of course he was. This was probably the end of his career. Over some kid. "I don't know," he said. "They're working on it, but . . . nothing. Not a damned thing."

The street was no longer empty. It looked like a parking lot for medium-weight military transport: floaters, forensics vans, a couple of buzz-saw platforms, the ugly snouts of their weapons systems pointing vaguely upward, waiting for targets.

Uniformed squads were on hands and knees, checking every square inch of the dirty pavement. Armored troopers guarded either end of the street, blocking off access. A whacking hum filled the air as a floating weapons platform drifted across a slice of night sky, searchlights probing, running lights winking red and green.

If the dark man didn't know before, he knows now, Korkal thought. *If he's been watching.* Which wasn't the problem. The problem was that the most important living human had just vanished under the collective nose of a couple of thousand vigilant watchdogs, himself included.

Vanished. Kidnapped, dead, what?

The Seven Hells was what. He sighed. "Keep looking, keep trying. Anything, anything at all."

The colonel nodded. "And you will—"

"Yes. Have your communications people set it up. Private line. She's probably waiting for it right now."

"The chairman," the colonel said, and shivered.

"It's not that cold," Korkal told him.

"It will be," the colonel replied.

9

Jim stared at Outsider, trying to work things out. If Korkal was watching when he disappeared, then he knew. So the chairman knew. Maybe the Packlord did, too. But what would they know? Only that Jim had vanished waiting to meet with the "dark man."

But everybody had a different agenda, and each one of them would filter the same event through a different lens, depending on their point of view. The Packlord, for instance, was concerned about Leapers . . .

Leapers.

"I knew it was you," Jim said. "Before this. I saw it when I was talking to Char. The pattern."

"Yes, I expected you would."

"You did?"

"Of course. The pattern was relatively simple. Who else could it have been but me? I'm the only one with access. Except you . . . and you weren't using your access. You've avoided me and the arrays. Avoiding your duty."

"I don't have a duty. Not the way you think about it. I didn't ask for this."

"No, but you have it. Nobody else can do what you do. Not even me. So because you can, you have to. Or let everything happen."

"Everything?"

Outsider lifted his hands, stared at them as if he'd never seen them before. An oddly affecting gesture, Jim thought. Outsider, trying on different personas—clothing for the puppet.

"You know Korkal is confused right now, don't you? You vanished. It's caused a stir. He's talking to the chairman now."

Jim closed his eyes. "Oh, crap."

"He hasn't informed the Packlord yet."

"You can monitor that?"

"The link goes right through this ship—and for all intents and purposes, I *am* this ship. Of course I can monitor it."

"Can you control the link?"

"How so?"

"Make it so the Packlord hears what you want him to hear, and Korkal doesn't know the difference? And vice versa?"

"Could you?"

Jim thought about it. "Yeah. I could."

Outsider nodded. "It's not so difficult." The tone of his voice had changed, become encouraging. "And so . . . ?"

"It would be handy, that's all."

"With the Leaper problem, you mean?"

Jim blinked. "You know?"

"I know the Packlord thinks it's a problem. One he's willing to take drastic measures to solve."

Jim didn't like the way Outsider said "drastic measures."

"He's willing to kill me," Jim said.

"He's willing to kill the human race," Outsider said.

"That's what Korkal said." Jim shifted in his chair. He couldn't help it. The interconnections were becoming plainer, more frightening.

"Is it a problem? It's hard to imagine that

Terra could be what the Packlord is so scared of."

"It's a problem," Outsider said.

"And . . . ?"

"What do you think? You're the only solution we have. I told you that you couldn't evade it. You have to come back into the arrays, take control again. Use the arrays to destroy Alba and Hunzza. Before they destroy us."

"That's murder on a scale I can't even begin to imagine."

"The Packlord can imagine it. And if you can't, you'd better start imagining something else."

"What's that?"

"Racial suicide. With your hand on the trigger."

"I can't—"

"You'd better," Outsider said.

CHAPTER EIGHT

1

Carlina Hansby logged the chairman's personal records into the main security database one by one. Part of her duties were to name each file, using a standard set of filing codes. She'd been in her present position, a high-trust classification rated CCS-10, for almost five years. After that much time, she could scan each record and apply the proper nomenclature after no more than a five-second viewing . . . usually.

Sometimes she watched longer. She paid particular attention to the chairman's personal records, those picked up by the microrecorder the chairman wore almost all the time. The chairman could key this unit with a subvocal voice command, since the embedded electronics were sensitive to the fine muscle movements of her throat. In any given day there were blank stretches, times when Serena Half Moon decided that whatever she was doing was too sensitive to be recorded.

And sometimes she forgot.

Carlina ran the snippet three times, her forehead wrinkled as she squinted at the monitor.

It was hard to make out—the light wasn't all that good. A lot of shadows . . . but the shape wasn't human. She saw it become clearer as the chairman walked toward it, and on the third viewing something clicked.

She pulled up some file holo and did a comparison. Yes, the shadowy figure was familiar. Korkal Emut Denai. The Alban spy.

Carlina wasn't sure whether there was any value in what she'd found, but she memorized it anyway. She possessed both verbal and visual eidetic memories, and aided them with her own very carefully embedded recording chip. The technology involved was more than state of the art, at least Terran state of the art, though Carlina didn't know that. She would have been horrified to discover that the microscopic bead buried in her skull had been manufactured in a highly classified laboratory under the direct control of the Security Office of the Packlord of Albagens. She thought she was working for a fusion group of radicals like herself, believers in a unified galaxy.

Carlina reported to a friend named Heidi Lamont, whom she'd known since her college days and their mutual involvement in the One Galaxy movement. She'd been more of an idealist then. Now, she didn't begrudge the substantial payments deposited into her encrypted account in the First Bank of Curaçao once a month. After all, it was in a good cause. Why shouldn't she get something for her labors?

It took three days for her latest report to reach Park Ling Mundel's monitor station aboard the

Albagens Pride. Mundel, nominally a specialist 6 in charge of correlating raw intelligence, stared at the transcript.

> CHAIRMAN: "That went well, don't you think?"
> KORKAL EMUT DENAI: "Time will tell."

It seemed like a reasonably harmless interchange, but Mundel logged it in, making careful note of the time and location of the exchange. This snippet of data was bundled with others and, six hours later, squirt-cast directly to Albagens. There it was evaluated more fully and time-matched against the Packlord's personal schedule.

This final correlation turned up an interesting and sensitive juxtaposition, which was highlighted on the morning intelligence report the Packlord read as he sipped his first cup of tea.

Serena Half Moon and Korkal Emut Denai had been together at precisely the time Korkal and the Packlord had their conversation about Jim Endicott, Leapers, and Serena Half Moon herself. Korkal, for reasons not explained, had betrayed Alba to the Terran leader.

The Packlord's expression didn't change as he realized this. But when he was done with his first cup of tea, he told the aide who replenished the cup to send in the commander of his personal security team.

His instructions to the commander were short, to the point, and brutal.

2

When Char turned to face the opening door, the beamer was back in her hand. Her features were still and set; if Harpy could have seen them, he would have ducked.

"No!" Jim said, freezing, then raising his hands. "It's okay."

She held for a moment, then slowly lowered the beamer. The door was polished steel; she saw her reflection waver in it as he pushed it wider, revealing the dark man hovering at his shoulder.

She shrugged. Then her hand was empty, a magic trick. "You're gonna get your head blown off one of these days."

He blinked as he realized how close it had been. "Jeez, Char . . ."

"What the hell do you expect? Snatch me off a street, dump me in a locked room, and you want what? Kisses when you don't bother to knock?"

The dark man pushed past him, moved further into the room, his own expression somber. "I'm sorry," he said. "I should have warned you."

"Damned right." She glanced at Harpy. "You okay?"

"I'm okay."

"You don't *look* okay."

He brushed her away. She nodded. "So. One big happy family. You, mystery meat, you owe me ten grand," she said to the dark man. "And who the hell are you, anyway?"

His long fingers flickered, an arpeggio of

dismissal. "It doesn't matter. Ten thousand? For what, exactly?"

The beamer suddenly dangled from her right hand again, not aimed at anything in particular, but there. "For not pulling the trigger on your boy when he came through that door."

The dark man grunted. "You didn't deliver otherwise, not on our deal."

"Pay her," Jim said. "Or I will. It's nothing."

The dark man shrugged, glanced at Char. "Okay. Ten thousand, digital gold, in your account in the Antilles."

"Just like that?"

"Yes. Just like that."

"I'll check on it anyway."

"Of course."

Jim had wandered further into the room. "Some furniture, Outsider?"

"Outsider?" Char said. "Is that his name?"

"It will do," Outsider said.

"Oh, goody. Are we gonna have a nice chat now, everybody friends, maybe a soothing cup of tea?"

"Sarcasm," Outsider said.

"You're observant," she told him.

Jim found a keypad, began to tap. The lights dialed up, and form furniture sprouted like mushrooms from the floor. "I don't know about tea," he said. "But it's probably time to talk."

Harpy plopped down, his sigh of relief like air slowly escaping from a balloon. "This is all very nerve-wracking," he said.

Outsider seated himself, his hands prim on his knees. "A nervous Hunzza."

Harpy blinked at him but didn't say anything. Char sat down and rubbed her forehead, trying to smooth away the sudden ache. She felt adrift, vulnerable. And she didn't like it.

"This is all crap," she said. "All this mystery. Jim the wonder boy, and you, what do you call yourself now? Outsider?" She sniffed. "Holocomic stuff. You got superpowers, too?"

Outsider's eyes sparked. "Think for a minute about how you got here," he said softly.

"Char, cool off. Gimme a chance to get this stuff untangled."

"It doesn't have anything to do with me," she said.

"That's right," Outsider murmured.

"It's got to do with all of us," Jim said. He found his own seat, rocked back, laced his fingers behind his head, and sighed. "God, I'm tired."

He stared into the silence, wondering where to go next, considering the four of them, mismatched, mysterious. Watching Char, he felt something twitch at the edge of his awareness, a sudden sense of familiarity.

I know something, but I don't know what it is . . .

"So," Char said. "What now?"

The room lurched. The lights went out.

Harpy screamed.

3

The eternal problem with spies is always the same: Who will watch the watchers? You set watchers to watch the watchers, and then you find more watchers to watch *them*. And you hope that out of the snarl somebody in the daisy chain will spot the treacheries that are always, inevitably there.

Hith Mun Alter, Packlord of the Albagens Empire, was so ringed with watchers that sometimes he could imagine himself as the focus of a million eyes. Once it had bothered him, but now he barely noticed it.

He told the commander of his personal security section what he wanted without burdening him with any restraints on how to accomplish those desires.

The Packlord's wishes were first transformed into spidery sketches, then gradually given flesh and bone as machines and teams of experts fed their knowledge into the webs. The results were issued as concrete commands in the security section of the *Albagens Pride*, and brought Park Ling Mundel's jaws together with a snap.

He stared at the codes for several seconds, not really believing what he saw. Lord Korkal Emut Denai had been his ideal, his secret hero, as long as he'd been a spy. So when he'd been recruited to spy on Korkal by a lean, shadowy character with an identity chip code that made Mundel's neck hairs stand on end, he'd been reluctant. It seemed somehow disloyal to spy on

his hero. But he did it because he had no
choice, because it was a way up, because he'd
been a spy long enough to know there was
nothing clean about it. Because he knew that
Korkal, in a similar position, would have done
the same. And as the shadowy emissary had
said, somebody did have to watch the watchers.

Mundel had recruited his own hidden command team, scattered throughout the crew of
the *Pride*. It was a smaller group than the large
organization Lord Denai ran like a finely tuned
machine, but it was, in its own way, effective.
And it was capable of more than simple effec-
tiveness, if called upon. Now it was called upon.

He examined the codes a final time, then
took a blank chip from his belt pack. He fed the
flat, matte black chip into his workstation. The
machine twittered to itself and spit the chip
back, no longer black but gold.

Mundel held the chip between thumb and
first claw, staring at it. So small to be so powerful. Just a bit of frozen glass, but when
threaded with the proper codes—as it now
was—it was a key to any door on the *Pride*.

A key . . . and a death sentence.

Mundel's hand trembled just a little as he
inserted the key into a different slot on his console. He plugged a thick cable into the cyberjack
set into his skull beneath his left ear. The codes
on the chip flooded into him, and out from him.
All over the *Pride* heads came up and eyes narrowed as a wave of orders flowed from Mundel's
workstation into their own varied means of
reception.

It took a surprising amount of time—not to transmit the orders, but to overcome the natural hesitancy and resistance to them. He felt his nerves going raw and shaky. Who would watch the watchers? Who was watching *him?*

He knew what he would do if he were Korkal Emut Denai. He would look around to see if anybody was watching him, and then he would watch *them.*

So it would be a race, and he had more than a passing interest in who got to the finish line first. Whoever that was would be the one who survived. Him or Korkal.

No matter what, though, Lord Korkal Emut Denai eventually would be one dead Alban. The Packlord himself had passed the death sentence.

4

In his quarters Korkal woke with a start, blinking sleep from his eyes, his ears twitching. Something was wrong . . .

He rolled out of bed and padded to his private console, ran his claws across the touchpad, waited. On the standard check, everything looked okay. Nothing was happening.

He thought about it, reached down, picked up a cable, and jacked in. He felt the usual momentary sense of dislocation as the mind-machine interface built up and patched him into the nervous system of the vast, semi-autonomous organism that was the *Albagens*

Pride. Without using an interforce helmet and a full link he couldn't be sure, but . . .

A chilly claw ran down his spine. There were entire sections he could no longer access. Some kind of breakdown? That didn't make any sense. With these kinds of lockouts, alarms should be going off all over the ship. But there was nothing.

Korkal raised his head and looked around uneasily. He pulled the jack from his socket, slipped on a robe, and headed for the door. He paused, went back to his desk, opened a drawer, took out a miniblaster, and dropped it into his pocket. The weight of it was comforting, but not very; if he had to use it, he was probably dead anyway.

5

A strip of emergency lighting along the top of the walls sputtered and began to cast a dim glow.

"What was that?" Char picked herself up off the floor, rubbing one elbow. Harpy was on all fours, quivering. She moved toward him.

Jim glanced at Outsider. "I thought you had control." Char had no idea where she was, but he did. The *Albagens Pride* was the size of a small moon. He knew you didn't just pick up a chunk of mass that size and toss it around like a baseball. Something was happening, something major.

"I did. There's some kind of universal override cutting in. I was using Denai's codes, but they're not running anymore." His eyes seemed to go unfocused. "I'm working on it . . ."

Another grinding lurch. Harpy squeaked. The main lights flickered on, went back off again. Jim looked back and forth between the three of them, then cocked his head. "You got a link?" he said.

"Yes," Outsider replied. He tapped his chest absently. "This is only a construct. Not me."

"Can you link me?"

Outsider faced him, eyes narrowing, intent. "Link to the arrays?"

"Yes."

Outsider nodded. "Let me . . ." He stepped close and put his hands on either side of Jim's head, like an old preacher getting ready to heal. "It won't be perfect, but it ought to work."

"Do it," Jim said. A moment later his eyes rolled back and his spine arched. Then he went limp, dangling like a sack of flour, held up only by Outsider's iron grip on his skull.

6

Korkal hurried down strangely empty corridors. The *Pride* was a huge vessel. It never slept. Yet it seemed vacant, ominous. He felt a momentary twinge of utter abandonment, of being cut off from all living things. He shivered and kept moving, but slowed as he approached the vast, arched dome of the central control deck.

Something was going on. . . .

He moved to the side of the wide corridor and

slipped into a small alcove, where he stood waiting and watching, his right hand inside his robe, touching the weapon.

The deck underneath him shuddered and rippled, sending him staggering. He caught himself and looked around, his eyes wide. *What in the Seven Cold Hells . . . ?*

The ambient light vanished, then came back on, but with an almost subliminal flickering. Some sort of override. Somebody was shifting the ship's core machines out of their usual routines, and not doing it gently. The cores were fighting back—and losing.

He leaned against the wall, trying to figure it out. Brute-force codes, some sort of takeover routine so powerful it was simply smashing down any encrypted barriers protecting the brains of the vessel.

He didn't realize that his jaw had tightened, exposing the white glint of fangs. He pressed tighter into the shadows as a squad of Alban marines trotted past, weapons at the ready. He watched them go, and made up his mind.

Whatever was happening, it was temporarily beyond his power to affect. Better to retreat and try to fight another day.

He poked his head out, checked the corridor, then half walked, half loped back the way he'd come. He turned, turned again, and reached a disk chamber. It took him a moment to jigger the controls so that his course wouldn't be immediately obvious—whoever was hijacking the ship would be able to track it down eventually, but if his luck was in, he'd be long gone.

He was moving toward the silver transmatter disk when he felt the pressure at the base of his skull. He froze.

"You may turn. But careful . . ."

Mundel.

"Mundel, what do you think you're doing?"

"I've already done it, Lord Denai." A full company of marines poured into the chamber. Rough clawed hands took Korkal, turned, patted, dipped, came up with his weapon. Mundel smiled. "Or should I call you Lord Traitor?"

"What are you talking about?"

"You know what I'm talking about."

Korkal stiffened and drew himself up. "I demand a private connection to the Packlord."

Mundel's own teeth showed, a menacing flicker. "That won't be necessary, Lord Denai."

"What do you mean?"

"Who do you think gave me my orders?"

Uh-oh, Korkal thought.

7

Flip. Click. Complete disorientation.

It was always like that when he went into the arrays. But this was the first time he'd ever linked without a full interforce helmet, or at least a heavy-duty cable and jack into the socket behind his ear. He wondered how Outsider was doing it with just his hands. Some kind of induction . . .

The inside of his skull felt like old-fashioned

television static, a mental white noise that expanded and contracted. And then he was there, in the patterns, the tiny hard points of light stretching out in ordered ranks from himself to infinity.

The feeling was different this time—somehow sharper, more immediate. He felt as if each one of those points was now a part of him, and he of each of them.

He could never describe what he did in this strange place, not to anybody who had never experienced it. Only Outsider knew the feeling, and even he didn't experience it as fully. Or so he said.

Now he . . . *reached* . . . out to those countless shining points. Each one was a human mind, or at least the excess capacity of that mind, roped by the new link programs into a seamless net. No psychosis, no damage. No guilt for him. He wasn't hurting anybody, not the way Delta had before the new linkages were built. He remembered the stench of burning bodies, the total terror of the first time he'd seen the Pleb Psychosis at work. Cat . . .

Maybe a billion minds out there, waiting. He reached out to them, still not really knowing how he did it, drawing on the power etched in his DNA, a brutal gift from his mother, all the more brutal because she'd known what she was doing to him when she did it.

The power came on him in a dark rush, a surprise, as always. The power, the force, the massed weight of a billion psyches suddenly under his control, lifting him up . . .

"I'm here," Outsider said.

The root of each hair on his skull felt as if it were tingling with continuous electrical charges. His mind was a bonfire, a white bonfire. "I see you," he said.

And he did. Outsider floated in the glittering dark like a darker stain, a black fire, a hole in the nothingness of the mind arrays.

"Here," Outsider said, and showed him. Jim saw the pattern, saw the override immediately, and let himself sink into it. Entering it made him feel fizzy, bloated with possibility. He manipulated the patterns, pushing, tugging, changing them. Felt the fizziness dissipate, the pressure lift.

"That's got it," he said.

Suddenly he felt bands of iron clamping his skull, and he was back in the room with Outsider holding his skull like a grape.

"Unh . . . hurts . . ."

Outsider released him, and he crumpled to the floor. Char scrambled over to him, knelt, touched his forehead. "What's wrong with him?"

Outsider looked down on her. "I unplugged him. It can be a shock."

She didn't understand. She had Jim's head in her lap. His eyes were closed, but faint nervous twitches, like tiny bugs, crawled across the skin of his face.

"What did you do?"

The Outside shrugged. "He took over this ship."

"What ship? What the hell are you talking about?"

"We're on a ship. An Alban vessel, the *Albagens Pride*. In deep system orbit."

"What?"

Outsider's lips quirked. "When we first met, you told me you were up for anything."

She stared at him, shook her head, and looked back down at Jim. Jim's eyelids flickered, then popped open. His eyes stared up at her like chips of blue-green ice, melting.

"Are you okay?"

His lips moved, but nothing came out.

"What?"

He tried again. "Okay . . ."

She realized he was smiling. And pushing his head harder against the soft swell of her belly. "You sonofabitch!"

She dumped him and stood up. He was grinning when he got to his feet.

"You're kinda comfortable, you know that?"

"Asshole!" Her cheeks were flaming.

Outsider moved between them, saying dryly, "Teenage romance. Delightful." He glanced at Jim. "I've got the pattern now. Everything's frozen."

Jim sobered, then nodded. "Okay. Let's go get Korkal." He closed his eyes. "What a mess."

Outsider said, "We've got it under control."

"What the *hell* are you two talking about?" Char said.

Jim moved toward the doorway. "It's easier to show you," he said. "Come on."

"Are you nuts?"

"I don't think so. At least not yet."

She glared at him. "This crap is gonna cost you extra."

"Huh. I thought you liked me."

"Maybe. But what the hell does that have to do with business?"

He realized she was honestly puzzled.

Women.

He would never figure them out.

8

Mundel felt it as a surge of dark static that seemed to rise from the bottom of his skull, a wave that overwhelmed his connection to his codes, to the ship's cores, to everything. For a moment he slipped into an endless vertigo, somehow separated even from himself. When he came back, he saw Korkal grinning at him.

"Something wrong?" Korkal asked.

He knows, Mundel thought. *He must have sensed it, or something. But what . . . how . . . ?*

He raised the blaster in his hand and pointed it at the center of Korkal's chest. "It doesn't make any difference to you. I still have my orders."

"Do your orders include suicide?" Korkal asked.

Mundel thought about it. "I suppose so. If necessary."

Korkal shook his head slowly. "I admire you, Mundel. I see what's happening and I don't blame you. Although I knew that somebody had to be watching me, I didn't know it was you. You're very good, you know."

Mundel's ears twitched.

"And you're very loyal. To the one you should be loyal to—the Packlord." Korkal paused. "It is him, isn't it?"

Mundel nodded. "And you betrayed him. Betrayed all of us." The barrel of Mundel's gun wavered. "Why, Lord Denai? *Why did you do it?*"

"Do you know what I did? You call me a traitor, but do you know why?"

"It doesn't matter. The Packlord wouldn't make a mistake."

"Even Hith Mun Alter, Packlord of the Albagens Empire, makes mistakes," Korkal said gently.

Mundel smiled at him. It was a sad, somehow touching expression. "Maybe you can question him, Lord Denai. But I'm not you, and I cannot."

"No, I suppose you can't." Korkal looked at the cable that ran from Mundel's skull to a pack on his back. "Are you here, Jim?"

Mundel blinked. "What . . . ?" He gave a sudden start. Then his eyes rolled back until nothing but white showed. His jaw worked. Saliva dropped in ropes from his suddenly clenched fangs.

"I'm here, Korkal." The voice was Jim's, but it came from Mundel's throat.

Korkal stepped forward and took the blaster from Mundel's nerveless fingers.

"Be gentle," he said. "It's not his fault."

CHAPTER NINE

1

Overhead arched the dome above Command Deck, the topmost level of Bridge Cluster. Jim shivered as he stepped out into the vast space. His memories of this place, both wonderful and terrifying, were suddenly overwhelming.

The golden orb of Drive Cluster appeared suspended directly overhead. In the distance, making up the other three points of a pentagram, were the red globe of Weapons Cluster, the silver Troops Cluster, and the purple sphere of Passenger Cluster. Each of these habitats was linked by a twisting necklace of transport tubes. The *Albagens Pride* was the largest vessel ever launched into space by any culture. At least any known culture. The sight of it was enough to set Jim's heart racing. It wasn't a monument to man, or even to Albagens. It was a triumph of intelligence and determination, a testament to the power of mind itself.

As he walked toward the raised structure of the captain's chair, Jim knew he could have been happy with nothing more than the command of this ship. Once that was all he'd desired out of life: a great white ship beneath his feet and the endless reaches of the galaxy before his face. But that was before, and this was now. He could never go back.

For a moment his thoughts drifted. That seemed the saddest thing, that he could never go back. He could never undo his own mistakes. He could never undo the things his real mother had done to him, or affect in the slightest what she had made of him. Time's arrow pointed always forward, and he was pinioned on its point. The only consolation was that the rest of the universe was also punctured by time, everything from quarks to quasars rushing from the past into the future. There was a certain poignant satisfaction in knowing that all life was embarked on an inescapable march from birth to grave and that the journey was irrevocably one-way.

"Jim? You still with us?"

Char's voice seemed to come from a long distance away. But it reached him and pulled him out of his reverie with a small tingle of shock. He shook his head.

"Yeah, I'm here."

He glanced at her. She was standing beside him, staring at him with a quizzical, faintly frightened expression. He reached out, took her hand, squeezed it, felt the answering pressure of her own thin, strong fingers. "It's gonna be okay. Really."

She nodded but didn't seem entirely soothed. She looked away from him. "Big," she murmured. "So big."

Understanding hit him so suddenly, with

such force, that he blinked. He'd grown accustomed to her toughness. To her implacable pragmatism, her ability to take whatever came her way on her own terms. But she had her limits, and now he realized he was seeing them.

The *Albagens Pride* was a vast ship even by the inhuman standards of Alba. In human terms it was nearly incomprehensible, a self-contained interlocking orbit of worldlets. And from Char's point of view, she had been standing on a Terra-side street only a short time earlier. Then, by means she couldn't understand, she'd been instantly transferred to a space vessel so huge it was almost impossible to encompass in any terms she'd ever understood.

Char was overwhelmed. He found it mildly unsettling to realize that she could be.

"It's a spaceship," he said gently.

"I *know* that," she replied, glaring at him. But he thought her outraged stare was only a protective mechanism, the anger she always raised to cover any penetration of her habitual self-possession. Events had rocked her. But she would rather die than reveal even the tiniest chink in her lifelong armor.

He found himself touched—and for one moment had the strongest desire to kiss her.

All about Command Deck faces were turning in their direction, like flowers finding the sun. From their rear suddenly sounded the soft collective thud of many boots.

"I thought I'd find you here," Korkal said, advancing at the head of a platoon of armed Alban troopers. At his side was another Alban, smaller and younger-looking, his gaze dazed and filmy.

The party tromped up and halted. Korkal tilted his head in a small, ironic bow. "That's one more," he said softly.

"One more what?"

"Time you've saved my life. I don't think I'm ever going to be able to catch up."

"I don't get it," Jim said.

"Think about it."

Jim stared at him. Korkal didn't understand what it was like to enter into the virtual space of the mind arrays. Nobody did, except for Outsider. But Korkal knew the arrays existed, and had listened to Jim speak of his experiences with them. More than almost any other person, Korkal had some idea of the breadth and depth of the capabilities that existed there.

Jim closed his eyes. Obligingly a sphere of memory bubbled up from the patterned storehouse of his own mind. He recalled the codes he'd overridden to take control of the ship. Compared to the patterns he'd manipulated to take control of Mundel, they were trivial. But the messages were there. Hith Mun Alter had sent orders to terminate Korkal. Mundel had been on an errand of execution when Jim had intervened. So he *had* saved Korkal's life again. From Mundel.

"Is that Mundel?" Jim asked.

Next to Korkal, the smaller Alban stirred at the mention of his name. He blinked slowly, his stare as wide and round as that of an infant still locked in primal incomprehension.

"Mundel . . . ?" Mundel said.

"Yes," Korkal said. He turned and peered into Mundel's stunned expression. "This is him. Are you still doing something to him? I already pulled his plug. He's harmless now, completely cut off from the ship's facilities."

Korkal passed his hand across Mundel's face. Mundel's eyes followed the movement, but a moment later, and slowly.

"No, I'm not—" Jim paused, then turned and looked over his shoulder. Directly behind him, Harpy was staring at him with an almost equally dazed expression. But nobody else was there. Outsider had vanished.

"Never mind," Jim said. "I didn't have time to be gentle. By the time you reminded me, it was already done. He may have been . . . damaged."

"Oh, Jim," Korkal said, "I hope not. He's not a bad sort at all, even if he did plan to kill me. He was just doing what he was told to do. I would have done the same if I'd been him."

Jim sighed. He tried to remember what he'd done, or maybe what Outsider had done. They'd both been busy. And Outsider possessed nothing that much resembled human scruples. Or mercy.

He could dig it out. But it would take time. And time, he now understood, was something in very short supply.

"The best thing is to keep him sedated," Jim said. "He may come out of it on his own. If not, I'll look into it more closely. But later, Korkal, later. Things have changed since I saw you last. I have to figure out what to do."

Korkal's eyes widened. "Figure out? What do you mean? There isn't anything to figure out. You've already done what's necessary."

"I have?"

Korkal's gaze slid away as it took in the wide sea of expectant faces watching them from every point of Bridge Deck.

"Of course. You've stolen the *Albagens Pride* from the Packlord. The only question now is, what are you going to do with it?"

2

As Harpy stood next to Char and watched Jim ascend the wide, raised platform that supported the captain's chair, he wished more than ever that he and his father had hit on some other plan years before, when they had made the decision to send him to Terra.

It was all he could do to keep himself upright and silent in the face of the dread that racked him now. How was it possible? He'd been told to seek nexus points, knots in causal space-time where the future was determined. But he'd had no idea that this boy would be as powerful a force as he was. Neither he nor his father had suspected the existence of a locus so incredibly powerful, so unimaginably dangerous.

It was plain now they had both made a terrible error. This young human was no minor flutter in the infinite flux of history, but a great font of determinism. Somehow Jim Endicott had taken into his unknowing hands—or been given—the most dangerous power it was possible for a living being to possess. Unless Harpy was misjudging the situation incredibly—and he didn't believe he was—Jim himself was a potential trigger for the greatest mystery in the galaxy: the unknown and perhaps unknowable process by which certain species made the leap into, if not godhood, then something so close it made no difference to those who were affected by it.

Harpy trembled with the knowledge he held close inside. If only his father were here to advise him, to guide him. But he wasn't, and there was no way to reach him. No way but one, and though he was more frightened than he'd ever been, Harpy wasn't quite ready to take that road. Not now, not yet.

But he was trapped—hoisted, as humans liked to say, by his own petard. It had been their mutual choice to send him here alone, the better to disguise his true mission. At the time it had seemed like a reasonable precaution. But now he found himself as helplessly ignorant as this monstrous boy in front of him, too weak and too young to handle the most horrifying event known to the universe: the first moments in the birth of a god.

But the thing that shattered him most deeply was a secret he could not reveal, could barely even think about—the suspicion that neither his father nor himself had made their decisions based upon their own free will. Harpy was who he was, and he knew it. And no Hunz-

za born and raised to the awful secrets of the Pit
of Souls could ever discount the possibility that
everything he did was utterly and completely
controlled by what Jim might *yet* make immanent in these strange, whimsical beings who
called themselves humans: the God itself.

Have I, Harpy wondered, *done the very thing
I feared the most?*

He didn't know. Worse, he had no idea how
to find out.

3

The object of Harpy's desperate yearnings
raised his ancient head in a silent room and
sniffed the air with the same delicate movements
his long-ago ancestors might have used as they
lay in mindless sprawls atop sun-baked stones.

Ikearos held still a moment, allowing awareness of his surroundings to slowly seep back
into his conscious mind. The simple room,
three bare white walls, a single hologram shimmering on the fourth. One window, now dialed
transparent to admit the weak rays of A'Kasha's
sun—A'Kasha, known to its inhabitants as the
Pit of Souls.

He lay upon a plain bed, beneath a light cov-
erlet. Across the room two chairs were pushed
neatly beneath a polished wooden table on
which was set a wooden bowl full of bright
fruits.

It was the chamber of an ascetic, consciously

stripped of the toys of advanced civilization.
Should one of his vanished ancestors somehow
step across the millennia to stand in the doorway, he would find almost nothing in the room
he couldn't understand.

The whimsical thought comforted Ikearos.
He liked to muse upon simpler times, when his
predecessors had no doubt thought the stars
were only lamps hung against the great roof of
the sky. When he was younger, such thoughts
had not held much fascination. Then, in his
pride, he had supposed those dreamlike forebears
helpless and ignorant, especially as compared
to his own high estate. Now he knew himself to
be helpless and ignorant also, though his knowledge was vastly greater. And because of that he
envied them for what they hadn't known. Doubt-
less the fathers of his race had supposed the
Hunzza chosen by God, just as some of his current brethren on other worlds also thought
today. So he was less ignorant than they, and
wished he wasn't.

He knew that the regard of gods could be a
deadly blessing.

His old bones creaked and his old muscles
ached as he sat himself up and put his feet onto
the floor. It had been a hundred years since he'd
done his duty in an egg chamber, and twenty
since young Harpalaos had reached his adulthood. He had outlived all but those few others of
the eldest who were stubborn—or stupid—
enough to cling to life with such tenacious sav-
agery. He knew his weakness. It was pride. He
knew his strength, too. It was pride also.

A hundred fifty years ago he'd first sensed the divine emanations. For some reason he was alone among his people except for Darod, the first of his line, to have been so honored. Or so burdened. Oh, he had been proud then, proud simply to have been selected. But now he felt a different, harder pride: that only he was strong enough to do what must be done. And even so, sitting all alone in this small white room, he quailed. For he knew the price he'd paid, was still paying, and would continue to pay. What he didn't know was the ultimate limit of that price, and whether his failing flesh would reach its own limits first.

He looked down at the plain woven rug on the smooth floorboards and grunted. Silly old fool.

It wasn't as if he had any *choice*, he thought as he lifted his eyes to the hologram on the wall. That strange picture had been near him since the very beginning of his long journey. He kept it to remind himself. Against a wide field of white stars gleamed a dark heart, a nothingness. A black hole punched through the fabric of space-time. Once that pit had eaten a tenth of all his people, and a great armada. Five thousand years after, nobody really understood how that had happened. But Ikearos thought he knew. It wasn't the hole itself, but what lived in it. Everything he knew of science said such a thing was impossible. But Ikearos wasn't a man of science. He was a man of God.

He rocked forward and came slowly to his feet. He felt a moment of dizziness and closed his eyes until it passed. Drifting in from beyond the doorway came the clovelike scent of something savory. The Younger Brothers who served him knew how finicky his diminished tastes had become as he aged, and they took great care to make his meals as enticing as possible.

They meant well, and he loved them for it. And because he loved them, he didn't tell them the truth—that almost everything had become ashes in his mouth, dusty and bitter.

He wondered if he would have to sacrifice his son. He wondered if he *could*.

4

A rush of cool air pushed against Jim's face as he settled into the climate-controlled environment of the captain's chair. He was dimly aware of the others gathered below, staring up at him, but he pushed away the fleeting, uncomfortable impression that they regarded him as some kind of idol, almost an object of worship.

Beneath him his seat shifted and flowed, molding itself to his body. Invisible sensors detected his skin temperature, his pulse, and a hundred other details of his current physical state and made ambient adjustments calculated to bring him into normal comfort ranges. After a moment he felt the ring that generated the interforce helmet settle softly on his shoulders.

"Engage," he murmured. The helmet, a perfect sphere of reflective force, sprang up, enclosing his head completely. From the outside, he knew it appeared as if a mirrored globe had replaced his skull, but from the interior, the only change he noticed was a momentary flickering in his vision that vanished as soon as the helmet's optics coordinated with his own sight algorithms.

The whole setup was designed to free him from body awareness while at the same time making the interface between his own brain and the ship minds as seamless as possible. At least that had been the original intention when the *Pride* was first built. It had been modified later, to take advantage of Jim's unique talents. Now the unimaginable processing power of the entire vessel could be devoted to one thing— strengthening and amplifying the link between Jim and the Terran mind arrays.

He took a breath. "Link," he whispered.

The world went away.

"I'm here," Outsider said, dark on dark within darkness.

I wonder what I look like to him, Jim thought.

"Like a pattern of lights, very small, very intense, rapidly changing," Outsider replied. His voice was cool, distant.

Jim felt an instant of chilly startlement. "You can read my mind?"

"I can read *our* mind. When you link with the arrays, you become a part of them. I'm already a part of them. We are one."

Jim thought about that. A slow wash of terror

filled him. Not at the thought that Outsider was privy to his thoughts, but that he might be equally able to access Outsider's thoughts. His memories. His knowledge of—

"You can't," Outsider said.

"Why?"

"Because I have taken steps to protect myself from you."

"How can you do that if we are now the same mind?"

"Can you consciously access your own subconscious?"

Jim considered. "No."

"Think of me as your subconscious, or at least a part of it. I can release what I wish. The rest remains hidden, even from you."

"How did you learn to do this? More important, why?"

"How is unimportant. Just say I've had more time—*much* more time—to learn about the mind arrays. Perhaps you will learn the techniques yourself. Why is easy. I don't trust you, Jim Endicott. I don't trust you at all."

Jim thought some more. "Because you fear me."

Outsider's reply was distant, fading, utterly cold. "No, Jim. I don't fear you. Or, at least, I don't fear you as much."

"As much as what?"

"As much as I'm afraid of what you might do when you encounter the thing I truly fear."

What *Outsider* truly feared? He tried to imagine what that might be. He failed.

"What is it? What are you afraid of?" he whispered.

But there was no answer. Outsider was gone, vanished into the heart of darkness, into the hidden subconscious of a billion linked minds.

5

"**W**hat happened?" Korkal asked later when they were all gathered in Korkal's suite over dinner. "You were pale as a ghost when you dropped the link. Was it . . . him?"

Korkal knew about Outsider. He didn't really know *what* Outsider was. Jim wasn't sure he did, either. Not anymore. But at least he could talk to Korkal. Harpy would no doubt be totally mystified. And Char would probably just laugh at him.

"In a way," he said.

Korkal shook his head. "What way? I don't trust him."

Jim laughed softly. "That's the whole thing, you see. He doesn't trust me, either."

"Is that important?"

Jim shrugged. "I don't know. It could be."

The door to Korkal's inner chamber slid aside, and Char entered, followed a moment later by Harpy. The Hunzzan youth still seemed shaken by all that had happened. His huge, round-eyed gaze slid to Jim, skittered, and slid away.

The room was large but spare, typical of a chamber that sprouted furnishings as needed. Large holographic screens filled the walls with views, everything from Terra as seen from the

Albagens Pride's orbit to rolling brown-green landscapes of a world Jim had never seen. He wondered if it was Korkal's home world.

Harpy lagged behind, but Char strutted right up to the small conversational grouping where they were seated, her stance taut with cockiness.

"Hey, the big brains," she said. She offered a single brittle grin, then flopped on another chair that had risen obligingly from the deck as she approached. Harpy, looking as if his skeleton had melted slightly, slumped with a long, whistling sigh onto another. His appearance was so sad, so beaten down, that after a moment what little conversation there was just petered out and left them all staring silently at each other.

It was a strange group, Jim thought. Korkal's people had been enemies of Harpy's people for millennia, yet the two of them seemed to feel quite comfortable with each other. Lord only knew what Char thought about them, though she seemed to like Harpy just fine. And yet all of them seemed to share a wariness about Jim, as if he were a being of a new and different breed, come into their midst for reasons unknown and purposes undefined. He realized he felt more alien, at least to himself, than either Korkal or Harpy. He felt alien within his own skin.

His mother had done that to him. His real mother. He suddenly realized he had no idea if he would ever be able to forgive her for that. What kind of woman must she have been to so coldly manipulate her own son, right down to the level of his molecules? She'd said she loved him. But if that was true, how could she have done what she did?

She had branded him with her own future. He'd never had one of his own. He'd thought he had, but he'd been wrong. And nobody remained for him to ask, or beg, or even hate. They were all gone now, Carl, Jonathan, Delta, Kate—all those who'd been there at the beginning. What had been done to him, the very shaping of his future, had first been dictated and decided by the relationships among those four. And he'd killed three of them.

For one shaking moment he wondered if it would ever be over, that awful Greek tragedy of a past. If there was to be absolution for him, a release from the simple guilt of being alive. If—

"You're doing it again," Char said.

He glanced up, startled. "Doing what?"

"Going away. Where do you go, Jim?"

He fluttered his fingers at her. "You don't want to know. It doesn't matter."

Something flicked across her features, visible for only an instant before it vanished. Something painful, he thought, and wondered what she found if she went into the same kind of place inside *her* that he sought inside himself. What was that place called? Memory? Soul? Regret?

The place of might-have-been and never-was. He thought that if he had to put a name to it, he would call it *longing*.

"Anyway," he continued, "we've got more important things to worry about than me being a dummy." He glanced at Korkal. "Don't we, old friend?"

Korkal nodded slowly. "Yes, I'm afraid we do."

Harpy seemed dead to the world, uninterested in anything they had to say, but Char was looking back and forth between them, irritation growing on her features.

"So give," she said. "Why don't you 'old friends' fill in your new buddies about these important things, okay?"

Korkal regarded her a moment, as if making up his mind about something. Then he nodded. "His race and mine," he said calmly as he inclined his head toward Harpy, "though we have been enemies for thousands of your years, have finally come to an agreement about something."

"Yeah? Like what?"

"The necessity of destroying humanity as utterly and completely as we can."

"Oh, boy," Char said. Suddenly her voice sounded small. She stared at Korkal's fur-ringed face but, having no way to interpret what she saw as truth or not, she looked down at her knees and bit at her lower lip.

Jim knew exactly how she felt.

6

On Hunzza, in the swarming heart of the Imperial Nest, a colonel turned his head slightly as his huge eyes widened. He had monitored this particular channel for nearly three years, and not once had he ever received a message beyond the periodic electronic throat clearings designed to test whether the link was still functioning perfectly.

Next to him the chief duty officer, a general despite commanding only this small group, stared back at him.

"Is it . . . ?" the general began.

The colonel blinked his eyes nervously, rapidly, the Hunzzan equivalent of uneasy laughter. "Uh . . . yes. It's real."

The general flashed several rows of white fangs, turned, and initiated a series of alarms. On a holoscreen before him appeared the visage of a much higher-ranking general.

"Yes?"

"We have a request to establish the hot link," the first general said.

The second general went silent, then tightened his jaw and nodded. "His Imperial Majesty will be notified of the request." He paused. A flash of darting pink showed at the edge of his suddenly exposed tooth line. "Who is calling?"

"The Packlord," the first general said. And though further identification was unnecessary, his nerves got the better of him and he added, "Of the Albagensian Empire."

7

Serena Half Moon was as close to rage as she ever allowed herself to get. Her skin was flushed dark, her eyes showed a hint of bloody spiderweb, and her harsh, raspy voice was dangerously low and controlled.

"I don't care," she instructed a male underling, a man named Horchow, whose face looked as if he'd been kicked in the balls but was trying to ignore the pain. "You find him. He can't just vanish. All of them. Endicott, the girl, the Hunzza. And Korkal Emut Denai. Find him, too. Find them all."

"Yes, Madame Chairman." Horchow knew better than to say anything else when she was in this kind of mood. He enjoyed his high and comfortable position. He hoped to maintain it, if he could survive this current fiasco.

She stared at him. "Use whatever it takes. You have any authority you need. But find them!"

"Yes, Chairman."

"Get out."

She watched as he turned and left her office. For a moment she was alone. Not really alone— she had never been *really* alone, not for one moment, since she took this office. Something or someone was always with her, watching, listening, sensing. But her human nervous system had evolved over thousands of years to react to physical presence, not the ghostly tendrils of the electronic fog that ceaselessly encased her in a cocoon of security. So she felt alone, even if she wasn't.

There was a thin streak of dust on the far right corner of her desk. It showed plainly in the afternoon sunlight slanting in from the window behind her. An incredibly expensive antique mantel clock ticked above the fireplace on the far wall. She listened to the sound, hoping her own pulse might respond by slowing to that softer, more regular cadence.

What did it mean? She had gone along with Korkal. She hadn't followed her own instincts, which had said—no, had screamed—for her to take the boy into protective custody.

And now everything had vanished. Korkal, the boy, the Hunzza, the odd little girl whose name wasn't really Char. Delta had warned her that the aliens were monsters, but she hadn't believed him. Now Delta was gone, too.

She sat silently in her chair, staring at the dust, and knew that even if a hundred people were in this room with her, she would still be alone.

For the first time since the explosion of his satellite had freed her to exercise the power she'd held only in name, she missed Delta. He'd been a monster. But now, more and more, she was coming to another conclusion: He'd also been right.

It took monsters to deal with monsters. She was afraid she might be too human to serve.

8

Harpy slowly lifted his head and stared at Korkal. "What? Albagens and Hunzza together? What are you talking about?"

"Shut up, Harpy," Char said.

But some fevered strength had come back into his voice. "No! What do you mean, Korkal?"

Korkal's gaze slid toward Jim. Jim nodded. He felt a growing sourness in the back of his throat. Harpy was terrified. He hated putting the screws to the Hunzza this way, but he had to know. Harpy had secrets, but secrets were a luxury Jim could no longer afford to allow—to himself, or to those around him.

"Tell him," Jim said.

A cone of red light appeared in the center of the room and began to flash. A bell chimed. A soft voice murmured, "The vessel is under attack. Alert. The vessel is under attack."

CHAPTER TEN

1

Heldun Und Rorg was a low-level navigation specialist, only recently promoted to a station on Command Deck. It was a minor station, hidden in a flock of a hundred similar interfaces, nearly a quarter mile from the crag of the captain's chair.

Rippling sheets of color were still flaring across the vast transparent dome covering Command Deck. The hooting of alarms had been turned off, but the warning colors remained as a reminder that the *Albagens Pride* was still under attack.

Rorg glanced up at the star fields that arched over the deck. The view was spectacular. The great glowing flag of the galaxy's lens, called by the locals the Milky Way, covered a good part of the visible sky. But coming in over that vast arch of stars were tiny flashing lights, barely visible.

The attackers were former allies, the escort left behind to help secure Sol System from Hunzzan attack until a larger blocking force could arrive from Alba. But their orders had changed, and now they flung themselves at the armored might of the *Pride*. Rorg knew they were doomed, except for one thing: Her orders had changed also.

She lowered her gaze from the dome to the party now making its way in the distance. It was a small group, but she recognized the familiar figure of the captain, Korkal Emut Denai, in the lead. Directly behind him were two humans and a Hunzza. A small group of guards made a screen around them as they walked. Rorg showed a flicker of fang as she stared at the Hunzza.

The group was about a third of the way in from the entrance to Command Deck, moving slowly in the general direction of the captain's chair. The captain was talking with the male human, and that one—she thought his name was Jim—was making a reply. He moved his hands as he spoke. She sensed his urgency, even if she didn't understand his gestures.

She reached up and unplugged the cable from her socket. She glanced around to see if anybody had noticed her disconnection from the navigation networks, but her supervisor was busy with her own station. She reached into a pocket of her jumper and felt the hard, molded lump there. It nestled in her hand as if it had been made to do so, which it had.

She did not know Park Ling Mundel at all. She had no idea of the immediate source of her orders. But they had come with all the proper activation codes, and so she had no choice about obeying them. Shortly after she'd received them something had happened. She was still not sure exactly what. But something had changed within the heart of the ship's controls. For a period of time it had almost seemed that something else had taken charge of the *Albagens Pride*. She felt a bit fuzzy about exactly what. Her own memories seemed to possess several blank spots.

But within a few minutes the situation had changed again. Now it appeared that the captain, Korkal Emut Denai, was once again firmly in control.

So her mission was still active. At least she thought it was her mission, though there was now an odd feeling of strangeness about her instructions. Her throat went dry and tight as she thought about that. When she'd been recruited, she had been given iron-bound proofs of the ultimate authority from where her orders came. Rorg was as loyal as the next Alban. If the Packlord told her to do something, she would do it. And she was sure her current instructions ultimately came from him. Where else could they have come from?

Slowly she stood up from her formchair. She glanced at her station and wondered if she would ever see it again. Her belly gave a shudder. She swayed a moment, then got a grip on herself. She began to walk toward the party. She took an angle that would intersect their path just before they reached the captain's chair.

The Terran boy. Jim. She wasn't a murderer, and so she felt a twinge of regret at what she must do. Not a murderer, no. But she would do her duty.

2

Char had remained mostly silent as Jim argued with Korkal. "I don't want to destroy Alban ships," Jim was saying. "They're only following orders."

"They're trying to destroy us," Korkal replied.

"Your own people, Korkal."

"It wouldn't be the first time my own have tried to murder me, Jim. Or I them. You can make the *Pride* fight better than anybody alive, when you link with . . ." He let that thought trail off unspoken. The less said about the Terran mind arrays, the better.

"Maybe I can just disable them. That would be enough, wouldn't it?"

Char had been listening. Now she grabbed Jim's elbow and squeezed hard. "Hey!"

He turned, blinking in surprise. "Char, not now."

"Now is exactly when. Are we under attack? Is somebody trying to kill us? To kill me?"

He stared at her, surprised at how her features were knotted, congested with cold rage.

"Well, uh . . ."

"Listen to me, you sonofabitch! If somebody's trying to kill us, then you kill *them!* Okay? None of that lame mercy bullshit. Just kill them! Do it now!"

In the darkness at the bottom of Jim's mind four words formed out of nothing:

Yes. Listen to her.

He could feel Outsider's pressure as a thin,

invisible membrane pushing up from his unconscious. *Shut up*, he thought. *Leave me alone, you bloodthirsty bastard.*

The darkness seemed to breathe inside his skull. Then it subsided, leaving behind the emotional equivalent of a bathtub ring, a feeling of scum stuck to the sides of his psyche. Sometimes Outsider made him feel dirty.

"Damn it, *listen* to me!"

"Char, don't panic . . ."

She was shouting now, her cheekbones tinged with a dull red flush. Her eyes gleamed with anger.

"God damn you, I'm not panicked! What the hell is the matter with you? Somebody is trying to kill us. Kill them first! What part of that doesn't make sense to you?"

Her anger, and the fear that lay beneath it, was like a fire burning on her face. She seemed to radiate heat—along with a scorn for his scruples so strong he felt compelled to defend himself.

"Look, Char, it's easy for you to say just kill them. But I—I'm the one who has to *do* it."

He reached out to take her hand, not noticing a minor stir at the periphery of their party. They had come to a halt as the arguments grew more heated. Now, out of the corner of his eye, he saw a young Alban tech trying to penetrate the screen of their guards.

It was an unwanted intrusion. For a moment he felt overwhelmed. Trying to deal with the attack, with Char's barely concealed terror, with Outsider's equally murderous desires—

"Korkal, what does she want?"

Korkal turned toward the technician, who had pushed her way between two guards and was approaching him, her right hand raised.

"Yes, what is it?" Korkal barked.

Her hand kept coming up, up, now swinging around, something in her hand—

The familiar pattern clicked. Jim saw it before anybody else, but he didn't see it in time. His human reflexes, even honed by youth and battle sense, weren't quick enough.

A sharp, ratcheting sound cut through the hush. Something heavy slammed into his chest. He saw a flare of light.

Char screamed. Suddenly the Alban tech was wreathed in a halo of fire.

Char's beamer, Jim thought crazily. Then the light died. He tried to raise one hand, but he was cold. Cold and falling. Falling into darkness.

"Char . . ."

Nothing.

3

Char stepped back, staring in horror at the smoking ruin lying twisted on the deck. Cooked tendons creaked. Charred fingers contracted, then suddenly relaxed. The needler that had been hidden in Rorg's hand fell to the deck with a small click.

"Oh, my God," Char whispered. Face pale, she lunged aside, crouched over, and vomited.

"Jim!" Korkal dropped to his knees beside Jim's fallen body, scooped up his head in the crook of his arm, cradled him. Blood dripped between his splayed fingers. "Medics! Get the machines!"

He glanced up at Char's bleached features. "I think he's dead," he said.

4

Machines hovered in the air above the party. Other machines sprouted from the floor, waving filaments like slow-moving deep-sea fronds. Jim lay unconscious on a floating gurney a few feet above the deck. Some of the filaments extended into his body. His face was white, his eyes closed. He was naked. His skin looked waxy. The slashes from the needler stood out like gouges in a candle.

With all the flurry, nobody had done anything about Rorg's scorched body. Char, trying to move closer to Jim, half stumbled over one outstretched limb.

"Jesus."

Korkal glanced over. "Somebody clear that away," he said. "Take it to the forensic pathology section. See if we can get a brain revival to last long enough to find out what she thought she was doing."

A cable now extended from Korkal's skull, snaking off toward the captain's chair. He raised his head. "We're still under attack."

Char stared around, her eyes wild. "Can't you do something?"

"I'm doing it." He began to move toward the high chair. "Look, there's nothing for you to do. Why don't you go to your cabin and wait? I'll try to keep you informed."

She shook her head. "No. I'll go with Jim." She wasn't sure what was happening. Maybe they were all about to die. But she remembered the ghostly memories from the time she'd been a part of the Great Linkage. Nothing specific. She didn't even know if Jim had had anything to do with that. But the feeling was growing that Jim was at the center of things. She wanted to be there, too.

"All right. We'll move him into the tanks now. We've got vital signs, assisted respiration. Some brain activity. He's not dead yet."

The gurney abruptly floated up a few more feet, then began to drift quickly toward the exit, escorted by a full company of hard-faced guards.

Char licked her lips. "He's alive?"

"Not on his own," Korkal said. "But we're still trying."

Overhead the alarm colors had increased in intensity. All across Command Deck, gleaming silver interforce shields were winking on. The *Albagens Pride* was girding herself, getting ready to go to war.

Harpy tugged at her elbow. "Char, we'd better go."

"I'm coming." Jim was vanishing through the main entrance. She turned, then turned back. "Korkal?"

"What?"

"If you lose, if we're going to die, I want to know. Before, understand? I don't want to be surprised."

He stared at her. "Of course."

She nodded, then headed for the entrance. Harpy trailed behind her, slumping, his skin a dusty gray-green.

That's one worried Hunzza, Korkal thought. The thought went away as he mounted the platform to the captain's chair. A moment later a full-body interforce shield sprang up around him and he vanished.

5

Rorg's shriveled corpse ended up on a steel table in a room that blazed with light. She'd lost most of her pelt in the flare of Char's beamer, and patches of skin as well. Her skull, however, was in decent shape. The pathologist, wearing a helmet whose front bristled with specialized viewing instruments, leaned over the table, examining the damage.

"We've got enough," the pathologist said. "Time?"

His assistant spoke softly. "Three hundred ten seconds since death. And counting."

Transparent tubes with glittering points whipped down from above, piercing Rorg's corpse in twenty places. The silvery bread-box shape of a portable laser surgery unit detached itself from the wall and floated over to hover above Rorg's chest. Bright green light lanced down. Skin and then bone were peeled back to expose an expanse of lung tissue. More tubes dived into the cavity. The lungs began to expand and contract, followed shortly by a pink shudder as Rorg's heart, stimulated by drugs and electricity, started beating again.

"Okay, that's good," the pathologist murmured. "Recorders on . . ."

The assistant went to work on Rorg's skull, peeling off the half-fried skin to expose naked white bone. When he was done, he mumbled into his own throat mike. Yet another apparatus trundled over, nosing against the table like a curious animal. After a moment the flat box on its top clicked sharply and extruded a thin black web that somewhat resembled a hair net. The assistant eased this around Rorg's skull and adjusted it until it made a smooth connection with the entire surface.

He glanced at the flickering data flows running across a screen atop this contraption. "Ready," he said.

"Do it," the pathologist replied.

Rorg's right leg twitched, then slowly bent at the knee. Her entire body shuddered, then quieted. Her jaw opened wide, and her pink tongue drooped out, then suddenly retracted. She uttered a long, liquid belch as her lungs pushed air through flabby throat muscles. Her left eye was a blistered pit, but her right eye, untouched, popped wide. Her eyeball began to traverse wildly back and forth.

"Urghhhkkk . . ." she growled softly.

"Percentages?" the pathologist said.

"Looks like maybe fifty percent short-term memory activation, but most of the midterm stuff is still viable. Call it ninety percent beyond five minutes. It won't hold long, though."

"Rorg, can you hear me?"

"Awwrkk . . . aghh . . . hear you . . ."

"That's good. Okay, we got to you in time. You'll be going into the tank shortly, but we think you'll be okay. You've been badly burned." It was a lie, of course. But it was hard to interview a person who knew she was irrevocably dead.

"Badly . . . burned. What happened?"

Rorg's voice was thick with phlegm as the machines struggled to keep the vocal passageways lubricated.

"Don't you remember? Tell me what you remember, Rorg. Why did you attack the captain?"

Synapses fired in small bursts. Rorg shuddered again. Her ears twitched. "Not captain. Captain traitor, but not him."

"You didn't try to shoot the captain?"

"Tried to . . . the Terrie. The boy."

The pathologist leaned closer. "Why, Rorg? Why did you try to kill the Terran boy?"

"Orders . . ."

"Orders from who? From Park Ling Mundel? Were you working for Mundel?"

"Don't . . . know who. Orders."

"Orders from *where*?"

"From the outside . . . from . . ."

Rorg's spinal muscles contracted, bending her backward like a suddenly drawn bow. Flesh cooked into a brittle carapace of deep-fried fat split in long, oozing tears. The pathologist winced. The pain must have been enormous.

"Outside? From the Packlord?" the pathologist whispered, repeating the question Korkal was whispering into his own comm systems.

"Packlord . . . outside . . ." Rorg groaned. "Aagghh . . . the *pain* . . . *help me!*"

"Rorg?"

"Unngghh . . ."

"We're losing her," the assistant said. "Short-term is under twenty percent, mid down below fifty now, and falling fast."

"Try stimulants."

"Won't do any good."

"Don't argue with me. Just do it."

A flood of high-powered neural activators roared into Rorg's bloodstream. Rorg's good eye bulged. Her fangs began to click together rapidly. Pink frothy drool bubbled from the side of her mouth.

"Aaieeeeee!"

"Told you so," the assistant said.

The pathologist was determined. But Rorg kept on screaming until they turned off the stimulants. Of course, she'd been brain-dead for a good hundred seconds before that.

6

Char followed the procession surrounding Jim's floating gurney into a chamber similar to the one Rorg had been taken to, but much larger. Instead of two technicians there were at least a dozen. As soon as the gurney arrived and settled onto a waiting pedestal, the small army got to work.

Char blinked, feeling her eyes water in the blazing glare of light from the ceiling. At her side, Harpy closed his eyes. When he opened them again, they were covered with a filmy blue membrane that filtered the harmful parts of the spectrum and protected his vision.

"Is he going to be all right?" Harpy asked.

She turned to look at him. The room was a hive of frantic activity. Nobody paid any attention to them. She didn't even know whom to ask.

"I don't know. I think without the machines he'd be dead now. Maybe he already is. Technically."

"Dead?" Harpy made a soft moaning sound. "Oh, no. He can't be dead."

Char glanced at what little she could see of Jim through the screen of technicians. The waxy pallor of his flesh was even more pronounced. He didn't seem to be breathing, either. More and more tubes were snaking into his body. The techs were speaking to each other in their own guttural language. She couldn't make anything of it.

"He looks dead," she said finally. She was

surprised at the sense of loss that admission brought. It made no sense. She hardly knew him. Why should his death make her feel as if something large and important had suddenly been shifted out from underneath her?

Gripped by that inexplicable sense of loss, she reached out and tapped one of the techs on the shoulder. "What's going on?" she said. But the tech only shook his head and hurried on past.

"Damn."

She felt Harpy push against her, as if he were seeking her warmth. Poor lizard. She knew how sensitive he was. He must be in even worse shape than she was. She put her arm across his shoulder and drew him closer.

"Come on. Let's get out of here. There's nothing we can do."

But when she tried to tug him back, he resisted. "No. I want to watch. He can't die. He can't."

Again the strange undertone of urgency and fear. But why was Harpy so concerned? That made no sense, either. He had even less connection to Jim than she did.

"Harpy, what's wrong? I mean, I know what's wrong. But why do you care so much? What's Jim to you? You don't even like him."

His blue-shuttered eyes blinked rapidly. He was laughing, but she knew him well enough to understand that it wasn't real laughter. Nerves, maybe.

"He . . . he's *important,* Char. I can't explain. But he is."

"What? How do you mean? Important to you? But he's just a Terrie kid, Harpy. How can he mean anything to you?"

He looked away. "I can't explain."

Curiosity surged in her. She welcomed it as a distraction from the dread gnawing at her. At least it was a puzzle she could try to comprehend. Not like the other. Every time she looked at Jim, she felt so helpless.

"Come on. Let's get out of here. I think we need to talk."

"No! We can talk here. Look. Over by that wall. They won't mind if we stay."

He was right. There was a space behind them, about ten feet away, where a clump of machines created a natural eddy in the traffic patterns.

"Okay." She walked over and slouched against the wall, waiting for him. After one long glance toward Jim, Harpy came over and joined her. She bent closer and lowered her voice. "What's this all about? What's the big mystery?"

His eyes were wide, glowing like sapphires behind their blue membranes. "I can't tell you, Char. Not won't, but *can't*. Because *I* don't know, either. But he's the most important human in your entire race. He's the reason I'm here."

"What? You came here for Jim?"

He nodded.

"But . . . I don't understand. Then who the hell are you?"

He took a deep breath, glanced around. "I'm my father's son."

"So who is your father?"

His reply was so soft she couldn't hear it. She leaned closer, till her ear almost touched the tip of his blunt snout. She could feel his agitated breath stutter warmly across the back of her neck.

"I couldn't hear you."

"My father is the voice of God," Harpy said.

7

As Korkal sank into the webs that controlled the *Pride*, he knew he had lost. He felt a profound sense of desolation. He had gambled, with Jim, with Serena Half Moon, with the Packlord, and with the survival of two, maybe three races. And he had gambled with himself. All lost now. All of his wagers were fading away as swiftly as Jim Endicott's vital signs.

With the aid of the *Pride*'s control system, he could partition his attention. He kept a small part of his awareness on the frantic efforts to keep Jim alive. But for now, he reserved the larger part of his attention on the battle shaping up around his ship.

He was no Jim Endicott, but maybe Jim wasn't necessary for something like this. He summoned a quick review of the tactical possibilities inherent in the hundred or so ships now rushing to englobe him. The mere fact that englobement was their strategy told him something. It limited some of their options while expanding others.

Weapons Cluster was on full battle alert now, the vast systems housed there locking on target after target. At the same time the *Pride*'s own massive defensive shields flickered into being: force fields, relativistic rail guns, mine fields, plasma beams, antimatter torpedoes. The *Pride* was by no means helpless.

After a time he came to that one prebattle moment when everything hung in the balance. When he must make some decision about what his own strategy would be. He saw two main options. The first was simple: Make an attempt to destroy every trace of the Alban fleet that remained in Sol System. The second seemed simple but was more complicated: Fight through the englobement, leave the attackers behind, and escape Terran space entirely.

The complications came from knowing that his decision would affect much more than the outcome of this single battle. He had gambled much, based on his own estimation of Jim's character and ability, even though he knew he didn't fully understand what Jim's ability *was*. But now Jim was—

He paused and examined Jim's situation more closely. The results were discouraging. Without the machines sustaining him, Jim would have been dead minutes ago. And even now, with all the force of Alban medical technology brought to bear on him, he was dying. They hadn't moved him into a tank. It would do no good. The tanks were mechanisms for regrowth and healing once the original crisis had been survived. But Jim was still in crisis, and his condition was growing worse by the moment. Korkal had an excellent idea of the limits of his ship's technology. Dispassionately he reviewed what he knew, and came to a conclusion. Jim had less than one chance in a hundred of living at all, and his chances of functioning at anything but vegetable level were even slimmer.

So there it was. The linchpin of his hopes was gone. It was back to him. The universe had chuckled at his presumption, and now he would pay for it.

He didn't mind the payment for himself. When he'd made his decision to betray the Packlord, he'd done so with the full knowledge that he would probably not survive that treachery. But his treason had been conceived in service to a higher loyalty: the survival of his own race, and of humans, and even of Hunzza. Now he thought all three might be in even greater danger. Jim had been his antidote to that danger, and now, with Jim gone, he had nothing.

Nothing . . . The word rattled around the emptiness of his despair, sapping his strength, draining his will. And for the first time he understood, in some small way, the sort of responsibilities Jim had labored with. Understood them because he now bore them himself. But he wasn't Jim.

He could always surrender. It would mean his death, but it might buy time. And if he were dead, the responsibility would fall on somebody else. *Lift this load,* he thought. *Oh, Gods, lift this load from me . . .*

"Stop your whining, Denai."

The voice came from within him, but it wasn't his own. And with it, rippling across all the various segmented visions of his own divided attention, came a sudden tear in the data flows. For a moment he saw a burning darkness, an emptiness superimposed on an infinite pattern of light. But only for a moment, before the darkness was inside his barriers, growing, overwhelming him.

"Outsider . . . ?"

"The boy just died," Outsider told him. "Now, listen to me, you fool, and I'll tell you what to do."

CHAPTER ELEVEN

1

Korkal stared into his inner screens and tried not to scream. It was strange. A nightmare. He could see his own mind at work, but it was as if he stood aside and watched someone else working the levers of his consciousness.

The partitioning effect of the interface continued. But the process was both faster and wider than he'd ever experienced. Instead of two or three foci of attention, there were hundreds. And these flickering moments came and went so quickly he caught only glimpses of them.

There was Jim, his face bleached and slack. There was a massive Alban battle cruiser, itself englobed in its own tactical group. Two of its outriders broke formation and turned their weapons on their leader. A moment later the cruiser exploded.

A pair of destroyers surged out of the line and raced inward toward the *Pride*. They charged heedlessly into range of the *Pride*'s plasma beams and were obliterated.

Then the entire mosaic of views abruptly shifted. Korkal's stomach lurched. The *Pride* had *jumped*!

That part of his brain still left to him analyzed it after a second or two. Outsider had hurled the vast bulk of the ship into a micro–hyper jump, deep within Sol's gravity well. It was a hideously dangerous move. Had he not just experienced it, Korkal would have said it was impossible. Even the *Pride*'s giant navigation computers didn't have the capacity or the speed to calculate something so perilously precise. Evidently Outsider could do it, though.

The arrays . . .

Now the *Pride* was positioned just beyond the englobement on the out-system edge. The Alban fleet was caught between her and Sol. Korkal caught a shimmering glimpse of a destroyer and a pair of tenders trying to escape. Their fields glimmered as they attempted to shift into hyperdrive. All three vanished in sudden, silent clouds of superheated metal.

As he watched, he saw a dozen similar incidents. Each moment came and went across his inner viewscreens with dreamlike intensity, an ever-changing montage of death. And he had nothing to do with it. He sat frozen in the captain's chair, his horrified features hidden behind the barrier of his interforce shield, his jaw twisted in a silent, paralyzed snarl.

The worst thing of all was that he could *feel* Outsider's dark power roaring through his synapses. It was a black, ravening force that used him as a key and conduit to the *Pride*'s systems but otherwise utterly denied him his consciousness, his conscience, his dignity as a living, thinking person. Outsider cared no more for him than he did for the ships he was using him to destroy.

Outsider. And Jim had had to cope with *that*, too? By the Seven Cold Hells, no wonder the boy had wanted nothing more than escape. This was awful. It was like having your brain peeled—layer upon layer stripped away with machine-like precision, until all personhood vanished beneath the force of the manipulations, and you became a thing, a switch, an *artifact*.

Outsider used him as carelessly as a glove, slipped on for an instant of use, then discarded. Korkal groaned as the full weight of that use penetrated and marked him. He tried to imagine the extent of his possession, but he failed. Outsider was beyond the understanding of living flesh. And Jim was *stronger* than Outsider?

That thought alone was terrifying. And as he thought it, a sharp, bleak bubble of humor rose in his awareness and burst there, a dark laughter.

"*Now* you understand!" Outsider said. "As much as a mortal can understand . . ."

"He's dead!" Korkal raged in reply. "If he's anything like you, I'm glad he is!"

"But he isn't, you idiot. And that makes all the difference."

Suddenly Korkal was back in his body, cut off from the ship's systems. He sagged in relief. He'd been too close to something he could not withstand. It had battered down his innermost walls. He felt raped, in the worst sense of the word. This was no fleshly invasion. Flesh could heal. No, it was his soul that had been ravished . . .

The stasis that had gripped him abruptly drained away. He felt the formchair beneath him shift, sag, then enfold him again. He began to shake. He raised one hand, stared at it, let it fall again. He was too weak.

It took nearly thirty seconds before he realized it was all over. There was nothing inside him. His mind was his own again.

He dropped the interforce shield and ripped the cable from his socket. As the shield vanished, he heard the sound of cheering. He blinked. All across Command Deck the techs were rising from their stations, clenched fists pumping, flush with victory.

He couldn't bear to jack in again. Not yet. He couldn't voluntarily open himself to the demon that had just possessed him. He brought up a rank of hard-wired holoscreens and surveyed the *Pride*'s battle status.

There was none. There was no battle. Not one Alban vessel except his own remained in all of Sol System. Not one. Only moments before there had been a hundred, with at least twenty thousand sailors, troopers, technicians.

Now gone. Every single one. He saw the faint streaks of expanding clouds of gamma rays, all that remained of a destruction so rapid and total he could barely imagine how it had happened.

And Jim was more powerful, he thought to himself. *More powerful than this . . .*

Monsters!

Now he understood for the first time the extent of the Packlord's fear. Maybe it was a good thing that Jim was dead after all.

2

Char felt rather than saw the traffic patterns in the trauma room change. And though the Albans were aliens, she also sensed the sudden relaxation in the focus of their concern. She raised her head, ignoring for the moment Harpy's startling (though at the moment meaningless) revelation, and looked at the group clustered around Jim.

Nothing appeared to have changed. Jim still lay motionless, his skin slack and pale, the marks of his wounds outlined in faint patches of blue and yellow. A faint chemical odor wafted from him.

As she watched, the various tubes and filaments began to withdraw, like fishing lines snapping back into their reels. The team that had been working on him were stepping back, pulling off gloves, dropping masks. The room throbbed with loss and defeat.

"No," she whispered.

An eerie sensation raised ripples of goose bumps on her forearms. For an instant she felt as if she *sensed* Jim's life leaving his body, leaving the room, released at last, drifting away to . . . wherever.

Her rational mind told her the feeling was only the sum total of observation—of the attitudes of the medical technicians, of the faint relaxation she thought she observed in the muscles of Jim's body. But still she shivered.

"What?" Harpy said. "What just happened?"

She turned back to him, grateful to have something immediate to deal with. Someone to soothe, so she could avoid the impossible task of her own consolation.

"I don't know. Wait a second."

A tech, his furry face blank with the sudden loss of tension, moved past her, heading slowly for the door. He tossed his gloves at a sterilizer disposal, which snagged them from the air and ate them with a soft, electrical snap.

"Excuse me," she said, touching his shoulder.

"Yes?"

She felt her usual confusion at the odd quality of the voice issuing from the translator speaker dangling on a chain around the tech's neck. There was the undertone of the tech's actual voice, speaking Alban, with a somewhat louder overlay of the same voice from the speaker, but talking in Terrie.

"What happened? Why is everybody leaving?"

She was not a good judge of Alban facial expressions. But even so, the tech looked depressed. "Why do you think? He's gone. You were a friend, yes?"

"Well . . ."

"I'm sorry. We did everything we could. But it wasn't enough. He's gone."

The tech paused, then patted her awkwardly on one shoulder. "I'm sorry," he said again, then dropped his gaze and continued on out the door.

•

"He's gone?" Harpy hissed. "What does that mean? Dead? The boy is *dead*?"

She sighed. "It looks that way."

"No!" His voice had a soft, moaning quality, a lament of unbearable loss. And that still didn't make any sense to her.

No matter. She would come back to it later. Now the room was emptying out. A couple of techs remained by the corpse, shutting down machines, reeling probes back into their housings. Somebody else touched her lightly as they passed, and she felt the sympathy expressed even across the barriers between species. Death was death. It meant something to all living things.

"Char . . ."

"Wait, Harpy."

She felt a curious mixture of reluctance and attraction as she began to walk toward the pedestal where Jim's body rested. Jim's *body*.

A necklace of memories suddenly appeared in her mind as she approached, each bead a moment, a specific recollection of him as she had known him.

Leaning toward her, a rueful, self-surprised grin twitching at the corner of his lips: "I would say yes. . . ."

The darkness that had twisted his expression as he'd pushed her away that first time in the Shawn Fan.

The pale white panic as well as the icy determination when he'd flung himself at her, intent on saving her life.

More.

A lot more, a surprising amount. She had paid attention without even realizing it. And now, as she came up to the side of the . . . bier? . . . she felt once again that odd sensation of connectedness to him. Of a link whose dimensions she could not fathom, but also whose existence she could no longer deny. This awareness frightened her. Who was he? What was he? What had he been *to her?*

And most important of all: why?

She touched his wrist. The flesh was already cooling. The two remaining techs eyed her but didn't speak as they continued with their dreary work.

Getting the corpse ready. *Oh, my God, the corpse.*

She remembered the blond woman with the wary, tired eyes who, armed only with an ashtray, had gone after a man with a shatter-blaster. To save her boy, her son.

Who would tell her? Who would bring her son's body back to her?

She quailed at the thought. She couldn't remember her own parents. They had vanished into some forgotten riot of Pleb Psychosis, leaving her to the tender mercies of a public crèche upbringing. Her childhood had not been evil. She hadn't wanted for food or any of the other basic amenities. And if love had been both general and impersonal, at least society had not utterly abandoned her. Nevertheless, she knew that if it were her lying cold and still on that pedestal, there would be no place for her flesh to go. No one would weep for her when she returned. She didn't even really have a place to go back to.

But he had, and did, and would, and somebody would have to take him there. The only thing she knew for certain was that it would not be her. She would not face that blond woman and her accusing eyes.

Was it only her imagination, or was the skin beneath her fingertips now noticeably cooler than a moment ago? Certain physical processes displayed themselves in her mind. She was neither stupid nor ignorant. The education programs at the crèche had been thorough and fundamental, if not far-reaching. The chemical equations that nominated the various forms of fleshly corruption mocked her with their inevitability. The wrist she touched was even now invisibly changing, dissolving.

This boy with the dancing blue-green eyes who had once smiled at her was rotting.

"Oh, Jimmy," she whispered.

"Is he dead?" Harpy whimpered.

"Yes. He's dead."

Harpy let out a low groan, but Char ignored him. Instead, slowly, she bent down and kissed Jim Endicott on the lips.

He didn't stir.

3

Korkal glanced up as the girl and the lizard entered the sitting room of his private quarters.

"Come on in. Just sit anywhere." He waved one hand vaguely at the formchairs and sofas scattered about. A light-duty data cable snaked from his socket, connected to a small processor floating near his elbow. Above the processor shimmered a holocube that Char glanced at as she seated herself across from him.

Korkal saw the glance and blanked the cube. He examined Harpy as the youthful Hunzza joined them. The lizard looked bedraggled. Korkal knew Hunzza a lot better than he might have liked. For him, it had been a survival tactic. But he had mastered that art well enough to survive even terrors like Thargos the Hunter, and he knew he was looking at something very rarely seen: a terrified, exhausted lizard.

He knew that to less discerning eyes most of the signals Harpy was sending out would be invisible. Which was why he'd summoned them. He thought there were perhaps members of his race who might know more about humans than he, and probably some few who knew more about the Hunzza, but he doubted anybody could surpass his understanding of both races together. Yet with all his experience and knowledge, he saw that he was missing something very large, very important. But what?

He had no certain idea, but he needed to know. He had to know, and he had to know soon. Because in a very short time he would have to make decisions. Things hung in the balance: Terra, Alba, Hunzza, himself. And these two, whoever and whatever they were.

The situation, as he saw it, was a tangled mess. He could see a strand here, a knot there, but he couldn't seem to find the one snippet that would unravel the whole thing for him. Once again he mourned Jim's death. He had always known the boy was important. He had even loved him as much as he could. But he'd never understood just how much he'd leaned on Jim's strange, inexplicable powers—his frightening ability to see patterns within patterns, and to somehow manipulate those patterns into shapes that *created* the results he wanted. By the Gods, he would give anything to have that with him now. But he didn't. So he would have to fall back on what had seen him through all those years before he'd come upon the strange, guilt-haunted Terran boy: his own brain, his own skill, his own luck.

But as he stared at Char and then Harpy, he wondered if any of that still remained to him, with Outsider living inside the mind of his ship. And inside his own mind, too? Now there was a thought. Gods, what if Outsider was somehow *inside* his mind? How would he know? How *could* he know?

A chill raised the hairs on his back and arms. What if he couldn't even trust *himself*?

"What the hell's the matter with you?" Char asked. "You just gonna sit there and stare at me?"

He pulled the data cable from his skull and watched it snap back into the processor, then watched the processor vanish into the deck. He was getting sloppy. Guarding his emotions had been second nature for him once. Now he displayed his shock for Terrie street urchins.

If that was what she was.

"I don't know what to do about you," he said finally. "You or . . . the Hunzza." He glanced at Harpalaos, but the Hunzza wouldn't meet his gaze.

"His name's Harpy. Call him by his name."

Korkal leaned back, regarding her silently. "Do you know where you are? Do you understand your position?"

She glared at him, but he continued to stare, and after a moment the expression faded from her features. "I'm on a ship. Your ship."

"That's right. You and he both. Have you considered the implications?"

She offered him another flare of anger, but he only waited her out. She was a smart woman. She knew. But he understood her well enough, or thought he did, that he wanted to hear her say it, admit her helplessness and his supremacy out loud, in front of both him and the Hunzza, so it was in the open. So it was real to all of them.

But she was too tough to capitulate so easily. "Implications? What implications? There aren't any *implications* for me, wolf man. None of this has anything to do with me. I'll even pass on the rest of my fee. We can end the contract now. Just send me and Harpy back—"

He shook his head slowly. "No, I can't do that."

"What the hell do you mean, you can't do it? Sure you can. And you will." That berserk glitter kindled in her black eyes again. Protective rage, to shield her from her own fear. But it was a sham, and he knew it.

"We can't get anywhere if you don't think, Char. Blind anger won't do any of us any good."

"To hell with you! I don't have anything to think about. He's . . . *dead,* damn it! And I'm *done* with it! With him, with you, with *all* of it!"

"No."

She came halfway out of her seat. "What do you mean, no?"

"What do you think? That you can just walk out of this now? You must have known there were risks involved. Yet you took my money. And you took other money, too, didn't you? From Jim, and from . . . *him.*"

For some reason he found it hard to say Outsider's name aloud. The same flicker of awe and custom that kept him from speaking the names of his own private gods to the world. But he didn't have to say the word. Char heard it clearly enough.

She settled back down and glanced around, plainly uneasy. "Where is he, by the way? I haven't seen him . . ."

"He's around."

She stared at him, then shrugged. A bit of her bravado returned. "It doesn't matter. None of it matters. So I took your money. So I took *his.* And Jim's, too. So what? You talk about risk. Well, you took your own risks when you paid me. It's not my fault he's dead. I gave you what you wanted when I could. Now I can't, 'cause Jim's dead. So that's it. Job's over. I was snatched off a street in Terraport, and nobody asked *me* about it. Well, unsnatch me. Send me back. None of this crap is my business. And I do have biz of my own that's probably going to hell right now."

She looked at Harpy. "Right, Harp? This crap doesn't have anything to do with us."

"But it does," Korkal said suddenly, as a very strange thought floated up into his conscious mind, floated up from . . . where, exactly? How did he know what Harpy had said? He'd never seen any tapes . . .

"It *doesn't!*" Harpy wailed suddenly.

"Really? Tell me something, Harpy. Which god, precisely, does your father speak for?"

Harpy let out a shriek, jumped from his seat, and tried to run from the room. But long before he reached the door it slid shut—though Korkal knew he had not activated any control—and Harpy bounced off the thick metal with a soft, solid thud.

He landed in a quivering heap on the floor. Korkal had never seen a member of that sharp, vicious, practical race so helplessly unraveled. It frightened him. Because he knew he was looking at a very un-Hunzzan display of terror. And he suspected that anything that so frightened a Hunzza should give him a few shivers as well. But what was it? What was Harpalaos so frightened of?

"Ask him, you fool!" The voice roared inside his mind, a tidal wave of power, then subsided.

Korkal's ears twitched. He stood up, walked to the wall opposite the door, and opened a panel. Inside was an old-fashioned metal switch. He opened it, breaking a crude circuit. Suddenly the room was dead quiet. All the lights went out. For a moment the space was dark as pitch. Then a few chemically activated light tubes, heretofore unnoticed along the tops of the walls, began to glow with a soft green radiance.

Harpy had curled himself into a quivering ball. Every few moments he grunted as if somebody were kicking him. Char crouched over him, her eyes snapping in the shadows, like some sort of mother animal guarding her young. Her left hand rested on one of Harpy's shoulders, gently kneading his taut muscles. Her other hand held her beamer. She aimed it at Korkal's face.

"Leave him alone, you bastard! I mean it, leave him alone!"

Korkal dropped his hand from the switch and stepped away from the wall, his head cocked, his gaze inwardly focused and intent. He waited, but nothing came.

Outsider?

There was no answer. He relaxed slightly. He knew he had no way of being sure. But he had just severed this room—and himself—from every possible electronic connection with the larger ship. If Outsider *was* still here, there were only three places he could be. There were only three "computers" in the room complicated enough to accommodate him. And all those processors were biological in nature, encased in bony skulls, driven by living chemical reactions.

The question was in which brain did he hide, if he did so at all. One? Two? All?

Korkal moved closer to the door, ignoring Char and her weapon as if neither existed.

"Harpy?" he said, trying to keep his voice gentle. "You know, don't you? You . . . understand. What it is we really face."

Harpy shuddered suddenly. Char's voice was absolutely level, absolutely deadly. "If you don't stop, wolf man, I am going to burn your face off. If you believe anything, believe that."

But Korkal only stared at her mildly as the full force of the knowledge slammed into his mind.

"You know, too, don't you? You know, too . . ."

Char pulled the trigger.

4

Hith Mun Alter, Packlord of the Albagensian Empire, missed his most trusted counselor greatly. Korkal Emut Denai had raised himself above a great mountain of courtiers during the past few years, particularly the last year. And it wasn't so much that he was gone, but the way of his departure. His treason shook the Packlord to his core, because it struck at the foundation of his own confidence. He had survived—yes, even thrived—for many years because his judgment of others was the sharpest he knew. He did not give his trust lightly. But he had given it to Lord Denai. And Lord Denai had betrayed him.

Worse, Lord Denai had not merely betrayed his lord. He had betrayed his people, his past, his own identity. In betraying Alba he had betrayed *himself*, and it made no sense. Hith Mun Alter could not bring himself to believe he had so completely misjudged things. Perhaps that was ego. And perhaps it wasn't.

So he needed to examine the options, check the links in the logical chains—try, in the only way he knew how, to decipher the reasons for the greatest error he'd made in his long, long memory.

Korkal Emut Denai. Why did you betray me?

He spent the next hour with all the records. Everything he did or said was recorded in some way or another. Only his thoughts remained his own, and not even them sometimes. But after looking at all the holovids and listening to all the transcripts, he finally switched everything off, leaned back in his chair, and closed his eyes.

If it was there, he couldn't see it. One moment Korkal had been loyal, the next he'd been talking to him while Serena Half Moon stood hidden in the room, listening.

So the first treachery anybody *knew about* was with the Terran leader. Had there been an earlier one? Hith considered the question and finally decided it didn't matter whether it had been Serena or Jim Endicott or—

Or the other one. The one Jim had called a harmless ghost. A fading reflection of a man once living who called himself Delta. What if that man somehow still lived? What would that mean?

Nobody had ever found a body, at least not that he knew. It was possible the discovery had been concealed. Serena Half Moon would have no compunction doing whatever she felt was necessary, not just for Terra but to cement her own power as well. He understood that. You needed power in order to rule. In order to get things done.

But Delta had once held the power that Serena had gathered into her own hands after his death. That had been the one thing that had convinced him of Delta's death in the first place. That suddenly Serena possessed real power. That she was no longer a puppet dangling on somebody else's strings.

Either Korkal had betrayed him consciously or Korkal had not betrayed him at all. Not knowingly so.

He replayed the most recent bulletins from Sol System about the disaster there. The entire Alban fleet destroyed by the *Pride*. For the moment Sol was both entirely unprotected and entirely uncontrolled—except by the power of the *Pride* herself, the strongest force still there. Which meant whoever controlled the *Pride* effectively controlled Terra.

So who controlled the *Pride*? Korkal—or somebody else?

The battle had been short and sharp. Too short, even given the *Pride*'s enormous capabilities. Lord Denai was a fine battle commander. By himself, he might well have managed to *defeat* the small fleet left behind—but not destroy it totally, and not as quickly as it had happened. That work was beyond him, beyond any commander Hith had ever heard of.

Except one.

So was Jim Endicott in command? Was Endicott actively taking a hand against Alba at last? Was Jim Endicott *controlling* Korkal Emut Denai?

He should have killed the boy when he had the chance. A soft bell chimed in the room. He glanced toward his desk and saw that a holocube had formed. On it was a familiar face.

The Packlord arranged his features into as blank an expression as he could manage. He had given the order for this meeting a good while before, but such things took a while to arrange. Heads of state didn't simply call each other up to chat. Especially not when their states were at war.

Well, that war is over. We can't agree on much, but we will agree on this.

"Good afternoon, Your Majesty," he said to the Hunzzan emperor.

Between the two of them, on full war footing, they might manage close to a million ships. The Packlord hoped it would be enough.

CHAPTER TWELVE

1

Korkal saw the flare of light explode from Char's beamer. Normally in these rooms his personal security system would protect him, his machines erecting a shield far faster than human reflexes could bring a weapon to bear. *But he had turned them off . . .*

The smell of charred ceiling tiles filled his nostrils. It took him a few stunned seconds to realize he wasn't dead. He ran his hands across his chest, half expecting cooked flesh to fall from his ribs like so much barbecue.

Nothing. Shaking, he raised his head. She crouched over Harpy, staring up at him, the beamer once again focused on his face.

"Warning shot," she said.

He drew in a shuddering breath. "You may . . . consider me warned," he whispered.

With the flash of the blast, Harpy had gone completely still. She slapped him on the shoulder she'd been massaging just a moment before.

"Wake up, boy," she said. "He'll leave you alone now." She glanced up. "Won't you, wolf man?"

Korkal nodded.

"Say it," she told him.

"Yes. Harpy . . . I won't . . ." He didn't know *what* he wouldn't do. He hadn't been sure what he *was* doing. Except driving in on whatever secret the Hunzza was protecting so fervently.

"Go sit down," Char said, and gestured with the beamer.

Korkal nodded. She waited until he was back in his seat, then stood up. The eerie green glow from the chemical light strips made her look haggard, far older than she really was. Her eyes were pits. Dark shadows dripped from her high cheekbones.

"Come on, Harpy. Get up. You're okay."

Slowly, reluctantly, Harpy began to unfold himself. First his head popped up, eyes wide and frightened, looking for Korkal, finding him, sliding away. Char poked him in the shoulder, and he looked up at her. She smiled at him.

"Come on, I won't let him hurt you. Or talk mean to you."

He stared searchingly at her, then finally nodded. She stepped back. Harpy came to his feet with that lizard quickness all Hunzza were capable of. For a moment Korkal remembered Thargos. He pushed that image away. This wasn't Thargos. Thargos was dead. And there had been *nothing* pacifistic about Thargos the Hunter.

Char and Harpy seated themselves on what formchairs remained. The seats didn't shapeshift to enfold them. They remained dead, frozen in whatever positions they'd held when Korkal disconnected the power.

Char glanced at her chair as she sat down. She folded her hands neatly in her lap, a prim gesture that didn't deceive Korkal for a moment.

"How come you turned off the power?" she asked.

It was a simple question, maybe even an innocuous question. But it opened the door to some very dark places. Korkal sighed, gathered his thoughts—if they *were* his thoughts—and walked on through it.

2

His Imperial Hunzzan Majesty Tharson, latest in a long line peripherally descended from Araxos (who had ignored his brother Darod and attacked a Leaper, and had, as a consequence, suffered the immolation of all his direct descendants) listened to Hith Mun Alter as the Packlord confessed his fears and what he'd done about them.

Tharson had to grit his teeth to keep his horror hidden. It was difficult. Hunzza, especially imperial Hunzza, weren't used to constraining their feelings. If he could have wrapped his jaws around the Alban's neck, he would have. But the Packlord was a hologram, his true flesh hidden safe behind thousands of light-years, and Tharson could not avail himself of the one thing that would have soothed his feelings: the hot rush of the Packlord's blood across his tongue.

Instead, he waited until the Packlord had

finished, all the while keeping a sharp eye on the various lie detection systems built into the communication linkage. Alter wasn't lying, or at least not much. Not in what he *said*. A more interesting question concerned lies of omission rather than commission, but since Tharson had no illusions about diplomatic conversations at his own level, he left all that aside—for the moment . . .

"What I should do, brother," he said when the Packlord had finally come to the end of his tale, "is redouble my efforts toward turning your miserable pesthole of a planet into interstellar gas. What kind of unholy, nest-exiled fool do you think you are? More to the point, what sort of fool do you think *I* am?"

He had the minimal satisfaction of watching the old wolf blink. No doubt it had been a while since anybody had spoken to Alter like that. Which was a shame. Somebody should have— before the Packlord embarked on this unbelievably dangerous enterprise.

"I beg your pardon?" Alter said. The lie detectors said he didn't, but that was to be expected.

"You tell me you've *knowingly* probed a possible Leaper culture? Not in ignorance, mind you. Not by accident. But in *full knowledge of what you were doing*? Then you are a fool, my friend. Worse, you threaten to bring my own people into your deadly idiocy. Are you insane?"

"I did what seemed necessary at the time. It was an accident, at least at first. You'd started a war against us. My own people were at peril. Still are, in fact. Unless you've withdrawn the two fleets we *know* are advancing once again toward Albagens Prime?"

Now it was the emperor's turn to click his teeth in startled surprise. The second of those fleets was a closely guarded secret, though evidently not guarded closely enough.

He ignored Alter's charge. He had larger birds to chew. All around him, holoscreens were popping up, feeding him visual data his advisors felt might relate to the situation. Other voices, soft and compelling, filled his ears.

"I miss Thargos," he said. "It's a pity. If he'd been successful, this might no longer be a concern to either of us. But he wasn't. Do you know how he died, Packlord? I never discovered the truth."

"As far as we know, he died when the ship he was hijacking exploded."

Tharson nodded. "As I said, a pity." He shifted in his seat, wondering how to fully communicate his feelings to the leader of the Alban Empire. It was a delicate question. Both he and Alter had not only their own pride—which was considerable—to think of, but also the official pride of their races and empires to maintain. Formal diplomacy was constructed to handle such things properly. But this was neither formal nor diplomacy. This was akin to a pair of savages huddled outside a cave, chattering in terror about the angry roars of the beast inside. The beast they'd stirred up with heedless—and needless—pokings of a very crude stick. What in the Seven Cold Hells had Alter been *thinking*?

"You say you've lost a small fleet already. A

hundred ships or so. And now you propose we end our war, combine our forces, and proceed to attack this tiny, insignificant system, this Sol, this Terra?" He wondered if the rage he felt was seeping through the link. If so, it would be an insult of large proportions, but at that moment Tharson didn't care. "Do you," he said slowly, "see any historical parallels to this situation, Packlord?"

And how much do you know, enemy mine?

The Packlord hesitated only a moment, but it was enough for Tharson to picture him equally surrounded with machines, advisors, and technological whisperers.

We two are all-powerful in name and office, Tharson thought, *but we are puppets anyway. I must be sure to keep that in mind.*

"Your race's first empire foundered on the stone of Gelden," the Packlord said at last. "Yes, I see the parallel. First you sent a small fleet, and the Gelden Leaper ate it. Then you sent a great fleet, and the Leaper ate your empire."

This wasn't entirely common knowledge—for obvious reasons. Simple policy dictated that the survivors write their history to their own purposes. Mighty Hunzza had no interest in broadcasting the details, or even the existence, of so shattering a defeat. It might give subject races— or great rivals like Alba, for that matter—ideas.

"You have done your research, Packlord," Tharson said.

Hith Mun Alter only nodded, a sparse acknowledgment.

"And do you think that excuses you? I say it

makes your madness all the worse. Because you *knew*! Because you had before you, plain and simple, the potential outcome of your insane meddling! And still you went ahead with it! I ask you once again: Have you lost your mind?"

Evidently the Packlord had had enough of being called a fool and a madman for one conversation, because his ears twitched upright and a line of white suddenly showed along his grizzled jawline.

About time, Tharson thought.

"Your Majesty, as you also do, I made what I thought were the best decisions at the time. Nobody knew—or even suspected—that Terra might be a Leaper culture. How could they? One insignificant planet, barely into its technological age. Surely no threat to ancient powers like ourselves."

"And you didn't think it strange that such a primitive civilization could offer you the means to defeat a culture so vastly more powerful than itself? A culture like . . . Hunzza?"

The Packlord winced. "The Terrans have a saying: Don't look a gift horse in the mouth." He paused. "A horse is—"

"I know what a horse is!" The emperor was staring at a picture of one as he spoke. Strange-looking thing. Looked edible, though. But then, so did these humans. He felt his own temper slipping, and took hold of it again. He sounded almost mild when he spoke again.

"I take your point. You were in danger—from me, obviously—and you took whatever help you could find. I might have done exactly the same thing. But later, Packlord. *Later*. When you saw what was happening. The signs are unmistakable! The rapid technologization of the home system. The amazing advances, coming faster and faster. How could you ignore that? Yet you remained there, meddling and manipulating, as if *you* could affect the outcome. And now you come to me and ask that I join you in your folly."

"It may not be folly—"

"*And I say it is!* Who better than I would know the *folly* of sending my fleets against a Leaper? Though many have forgotten the lessons of Gelden, I have not!"

"Your Majesty—"

"In fact," Tharson continued, overriding him, "if there is anything to be gained from this, perhaps it lies in continuing my attack on the doomed race that chooses to meddle with a Leaper. The enemy of my enemy is my friend. It seems to me that this might be my best course of action. Not this suicidal alliance you propose."

The Packlord stared at him. "Yes, I can see how you might reach that conclusion. Especially if you thought you were privy to the motivations of a Leaper culture, *after* it vanishes into its Leap. But you don't know them, do you, Majesty? No more than I do. So how can you be sure it's not already too late?

"Yes, I meddled. I had my reasons. But neither you nor I can say we know anything about why Leapers do the things they do. Five thousand years later, you don't have *any idea* why your empire was broken. Perhaps your fleets had nothing to do with it. Perhaps you were just in the way of something. Perhaps it was the Leaper equivalent of a sneeze. You just don't know!"

"No, I don't. And since I'm ignorant of the matter, as is everybody else, yourself included, it seems to me that the best course is not a duplicate of an earlier one that led to disaster. We Hunzza are often considered rash, Packlord. But I shiver in fear at the madness you propose."

He lifted his head. "I don't think we have any more to discuss, sir. Do you?"

The Packlord raised his head slightly as well. "Perhaps. Just one thing. A small thing. Why did you send a Hunzzan spy to shadow Jim Endicott, Emperor? A mere youth, a barely nested male named Harpalaos? You damn me for meddling, Majesty. And yet you send an untrained child to the very heart of the mystery. What were *you* thinking of?"

Tharson stared at him, his own thoughts as momentarily frozen as any block of ice. Harpalaos?

Now *there* was a name to conjure with.

But how did Hith Mun Alter know it, this nightmare name out of black legend, a name so dreadful that not one living Hunzza would ever dream of using it?

Bringer of the Deadly Dawn.

Harpalaos, son of Darod, maker of the First Fall, the ancient voice of doom himself?

That cursed name. What in the Seven Cold Hells was the Packlord talking about?

A spy?

3

Harpy flinched as Korkal stood up.

"Careful," Char said.

"Oh, put down your damned blaster," Korkal said. "I'm not going to hurt him and you know it. But we have to unravel this thing."

Char shook her head and stared about the room in mock amazement. "We? Why *we*? None of this mess has anything to do with me—or with Harpy. All *we* need to do is get back to Earth, back to our biz. You've got problems, solve them yourself. Don't make us a part of it."

Korkal whirled in frustration. "You asked why I turned off the lights. It was more than that. This whole room is disconnected from the ship. It is as impenetrable, as shielded, as I can make it. And I still don't know if it's enough."

"Enough to what?"

"To keep out . . ." Korkal shook his head. How much to say? It was a tightrope between explanation and terror. They just didn't know.

"You call him the 'dark man,'" he said, his voice hushed. And even as he spoke the name he flinched inwardly, waiting for a knowing chuckle to rise from the deepest part of his mind.

"The dark man? The one you and Jim—" She paused. "The one you call Outsider? What happened to him, anyway? One minute he was here, the next gone. Poof!"

"He's not gone. He's here. In the brains of my ship. And maybe in other brains as well."

"Other brains? What other brains?"

She glanced over at Harpy, who refused to meet her gaze. Korkal also sensed a sudden uneasiness on her part, just a flicker, but enough to convince him he had to go on. He groped for an analogy to make things clearer to her. He thought she was hiding something from herself. If so, only she could discover it. But he might be able to help.

"In certain Terran cultures there is a religious cult called voodoo. Or voudun, vodun—it has many other names. But the general outlines are the same. The religion has many gods, and these gods manifest themselves in their followers. Manifest themselves literally, I mean. They ride them. They take possession of them and ride their minds like horses. Those possessed become for a short time the gods themselves."

He was picking his way carefully. But even as he spoke he suddenly marveled at the aptness of the analogy. How strange that hundreds, even thousands of years before, humans could have constructed a faith that so perfectly mimicked what he'd felt happening to himself as Outsider rode him to the destruction of his enemies . . .

For a moment he felt himself glimmering on the edge of some greater understanding, and he paused. But the glimmer faded, then vanished.

"Possession? Gods, all that old spirit gook? It's only superstition, ignorance . . ."

"Is it? Are you sure, Char?"

Her uneasiness seemed to grow. "I . . . it's all gook, Korkal. And it doesn't have anything to do with us, anyway."

He caught her eye. "Really, Char? Are you *sure*?"

"This is *bullshit*!"

"You still don't understand, do you? Or if you do, you don't want to admit it. Even to yourself. But you felt it, didn't you? When Outsider took possession of me, of my brain and my body, and *used* me to destroy the Alban fleet."

It was a wild stab. While he'd been sitting in the chair, trapped in a horror Outsider completely ignored, she'd been with Jim, watching him die. But the stab hit home.

Her face was pale as a sheet, her eyes like charcoal smudges. Her hair looked limp, disheveled. She refused to look at him.

"Maybe . . . maybe I felt something . . ."

"What? What *did* you feel?"

"I don't know. Like a . . . something huge. Dark. You know, like a storm coming, or something. I was . . . afraid."

Ah!

"That was Outsider you felt. I'm sure of it."

She shook her head slowly. She looked slightly dazed. "I don't know."

"You sensed his power. Maybe even felt a small portion of it. Now, Char, imagine something strong enough, great enough, to smash that power. To control it, defeat it, shape it to his wishes. Imagine something like that."

He had her full attention now. Her wide dark eyes stared at his face. "I can't . . . I can't imagine that."

"Harpy can, though. Can't you, Harpy?"

"I told you to leave him alone!"

The beamer was in her hand. Korkal felt his life teetering on the moment.

"Are you going to let her kill me, Hunzza? My life for your fear? *Are you?*"

It was insane, betting his life on the mercy of a lizard, but it was all he had left.

"Damn you!" Char thrust the beamer forward and came halfway out of her chair, her features wild with—what? Terror, hate, disgust?

"No!"

Harpy's thin, hissing voice cut through the dread like a knife. Char froze. Korkal risked a slight movement.

"Go on, Harpy. Say it."

"Jim," he whispered miserably. "Jim Endicott. *He's* stronger." His shoulders began to shake. "But he's dead now, and *I don't know what to do!*"

Korkal felt his back muscles rippling with the release of tension. He moved toward the crumpled Hunzza and patted his tough, leathery hide. Odd thing. He'd never done something like that before. Hunzzan skin, touched gently, reminded him of the bark of certain trees he'd known as a child, dry and warm in the sunlight. "It's okay, Harpy. It's all right. I'll think of something. We'll all think of something."

He glanced at Char, who had lowered her beamer. She looked like one of those people you found standing in a puddle of blood after a bad accident, mentally examining themselves for missing parts.

"Won't we?" he said.

A dull, repetitive sound entered his awareness. Somebody was knocking on the door.

4

Tharson stared at the empty space where the Packlord had been only moments before. His primary eyelids were narrowed as he sat deep in thought. Around him his aides, knowing his mood, waited quietly. Finally he looked up.

"You have the pictures of this Hunzza. This Harpalaos. You have the results of the tests done on him by the Alban spy, Korkal Emut Denai. It should be more than enough. Find him. Find out who sent him, and why. Find out everything and tell me."

He thought he sounded entirely reasonable, but his assistants knew differently. Tharson didn't notice the faint ripples of tension that tightened muscles, softened movements, and sent slight color changes shimmering across Hunzzan flesh. Not that he would have cared, of course.

Nor did he notice similar responses on his own part. It was the sort of thing he couldn't admit even to himself. Fear was not allowed to the supreme Hunzza. Not ever. But he *was* afraid, and he had *been* afraid almost from the beginning of his meeting with Hith Mun Alter.

But he felt his fear as a kind of emotional blockage, a dark barrier that raised all the old instincts: fight, kick, burn, slash it down. Destroy it.

Almost nothing remained in the galaxy that Hunzza truly feared. What had been, they had obliterated. All except one thing.

The names remained, recalled by a very few.

Gelden, of course. And Harpalaos, the Death Speaker, whose name had been the last thing on the tongues of uncounted billions of dying Hunzza, five millennia ago.

Now both names had been spoken aloud in his presence for the first time. Perhaps for the first time in *anybody's* presence, at least for the past several thousand years.

It felt too much like an omen, a bad omen. Tharson didn't believe in omens. But something—or some*one*—of Hunzza was disturbing things far better left untouched.

As he watched his aides scurry silently toward their tasks, a stray thought wormed into his conscious mind: Maybe it *was* too late. Maybe Hunzza *would* be destroyed. Again.

5

Outsider glanced at Korkal, a sardonic expression on his face, as he stepped past him into the room.

"The dog that didn't bark," he said as he watched Korkal shut the door behind him.

"What?"

"The one place on this vessel that suddenly vanishes from the eyes of the machines. Everything else barked. But this room didn't. Did you think I wouldn't come?"

Korkal shrugged as he padded softly back to his chair. He began to sit, then shrugged again, went to the wall, and flipped the crude switch back the other way. The lights came back on, along with the silent but still discernible exhalations of the atmosphere system.

"I'm sure you can guess my reasons," Korkal said as he settled into his seat.

Outsider dropped into a formchair that rose from the floor to meet him. "I can do better than that. I listened."

Korkal eyed him. "How? There were no connections . . ."

"Even the faintest of vibrations has an effect. The sound of your voice moved the entire bulk of the *Pride*. None of your instruments is powerful enough to detect that movement, but I can. And I did."

Korkal nodded. Outsider didn't seem to realize he'd admitted one lack: He might have listened, but he hadn't been able to penetrate minds. Whatever Korkal had said or done in the past few minutes, it had been of his own volition.

"All right, you heard. And here you are. So, now what?"

"Now he sends me and Harpy back home!" Char broke in.

Outsider eyed her calmly. "I think not."

Char raised her beamer. "I don't care—"

"Enough of this silliness." Outsider waved one hand. Char let out a screech and dropped the beamer. The tiny weapon fell to the deck and began to smoke. And before Char could say or do anything further, both her and Harpy's formchairs suddenly extruded soft, ropelike tentacles. They snapped around her wrists, ankles, and waist, and bound Harpy in the same way.

Korkal blinked. Those chairs had no such capabilities built into them. At least they hadn't—before.

"Let me go!"

"Sit quietly or I'll start running graduated currents through your nervous system. I can assure you it will be quite painful. Would you like an example?"

Char opened her mouth, then gave a slight jerk.

"Ouch!"

"Again?"

She glared at him but said no more.

"Good. My concern isn't with you, anyway. Or if it is, only peripherally so. Harpalaos?"

Harpy kept his head down, his eyes focused on his bound wrists.

"You will talk to me, lizard." Now Harpy jerked, his breath spurting out in a sharp hiss of pain. But he shook his head and continued to ignore Outsider, who seemed unperturbed. "You say your father sent you here. And that your father is the voice of God. What, exactly, does that mean?"

"Nothing," Harpy replied, his eyes abruptly wide, filmed with a glaze of terror. "It doesn't mean anything."

Outsider nodded, his saturnine features expressionless. He continued, his tones calm as silk.

"I think it means a great deal. At one time my analysis of Terra's problems pointed toward the inevitable destruction of both Alba and Hunzza. With Jim Endicott dead, I now have some doubts about my ability to accomplish that on my own."

Outsider crossed his elegantly clad legs and examined the brilliant polish on his shoes. He sighed. "But even if Jim were still available, further investigation has revealed what appears to be an even more dangerous potential enemy. I might have ignored it, except that this enemy has already penetrated deep into my affairs. You, Harpalaos—whose name means 'Bringer of the Deadly Dawn'—you have penetrated."

Harpy squirmed, but the formchair held him fast.

"It's strange. You seem so weak to be an emissary of something so powerful. You are a riddle. But a riddle I propose to solve."

Outsider leaned forward, his dark green eyes suddenly hard and glittering.

"I think you'll make a fine hostage, Harpalaos. You've lost your way, and now it's time for you to go home. It's the least I can do, after all your troubles."

Harpy couldn't seem to turn away from Outsider's hypnotic stare. But a loose pink froth of bloody saliva began to leak from the sides of his jaw.

"Will they welcome you? Will your father, the voice of God, greet you willingly when I bring you back to him? Back to A'Kasha, the Pit of Souls?"

Harpy screamed.

CHAPTER THIRTEEN

1

Despite the best the antiaging processes had to offer, Hith Mun Alter entered his own private residence aching in every bone and muscle. His quarters were nowhere near as opulent as they might have been: a large, comfortably furnished sitting room, a study and office, an archive cabinet where his lovingly tended collection of Amafarian birth egg artifacts reposed, a sparsely furnished bedroom in which there was not a single electronic outlet, and a refresher room that was his one concession to lavishness.

He padded across the sitting room toward this chamber with a sigh of anticipation, shedding clothes as he went. Inside, the small pool was already steaming. The surface of the liquid shimmered and rippled from the powerful currents beneath. Sitting on a tray at the edge of the pool was a cooler with a bottle of chilled Terran cabernet sauvignon from the North American Federated Region. Korkal Emut Denai had introduced him to this pleasure, and he had added to his cellar over the years.

He slipped into the water, his sigh expanding into a soft groan of pure pleasure, as the liquid—

a mixture of water and certain skin-sensitive relaxing chemicals—began to knead exhaustion from his admittedly overused carcass.

I am, he thought, *getting too old for this.* It wasn't the first time the thought had arisen.

He lifted the glass of wine and trailed just the tip of his tongue across the cool surface. A particularly poignant cluster of flavor-sensing nerves was bunched there, and he used them to their fullest extent, separating out the thousand different tastes of a great bottle of wine.

With those sensations (far clearer than anything a Terrie could experience) washing through his brain, he was finally able to let go for a moment and relax.

But only for a moment.

The problems were far too pressing to be stayed for long, even by a perfectly chilled bottle of Shafer Hillside Select '26. And as the first shimmering sip of ruby wine washed delightfully down his parched throat, all the details of a day depressing even by his own exacting standards came rushing back.

He closed his eyes and leaned against the wall of the pool, wondering if he had finally overstepped himself. It was a sardonic thought. He, the master manipulator, finally outmaneuvered? Was it possible?

Of course it was. He sipped again. If nothing else, the law of averages had to catch up with him eventually. Even the greatest of leaders never achieved a perfect score. And he had never numbered himself in that kind of company, anyway.

Although, he thought, *if I find a way out of this, maybe I should.*

The wine, the sensual twists of the water against his hide, the chemicals now seeping through his skin into his bloodstream, and the blessed silence began to work their combined magic on his disordered thoughts. Now, in solitude, maybe he could untangle this seemingly intractable nest of secrets, conflicts, and treachery into something he could grasp. Something he could *use.*

I'd better, he thought. *I don't have much time. Hardly any time at all.*

But instead of an ordered and thoughtful recapitulation of the day's events, he was surprised to find that the first thing flooding into his thoughts was regret. That, and a powerful sense of loss. He was the lord of a great empire, and he had long ago come to terms with the fact that he could trust nobody. Nonetheless, with Korkal Emut Denai, he had come as close to trust as he could. And Korkal Emut Denai had betrayed him.

The thoughts that had plagued him before now returned to devil him again. *Why,* by the dead gods of Alberan? Why had he done it?

Hith Mun Alter knew the folds and turnings of treachery far better than most. Betrayal was, after all, one of his most intimate companions. *So think. Why do sentient beings betray each other?*

Greed was always a reason, but he couldn't see how that might apply. He had raised Korkal into a station where financial concerns would never trouble him again. Lust for power was another, but he couldn't see how that fitted the situation, either. In terms of real power, Korkal already had more than most, simply by his close association to the lord at the top of the heap. And he had thrown all that away with his treachery.

Fear? Yes, fear was a concern. And it might even apply to this situation. But fear of what? He pushed that notion aside for a moment and continued with his glum enumeration.

Friendship and its great sister, love? Yes, that might play a role as well. How strong were Korkal's feeling for Jim Endicott and, by extension, perhaps the whole human race? It wouldn't be the first time a trusted operative had gotten too close to his subject and been seduced away from duty. Though somehow he still couldn't quite make himself fit Lord Denai into that template, either.

He would have nearly bet his own life—in fact, would still do so—that Korkal would not, *could* not waver from his basic loyalty to his own people. To doubt that now, even in the face of Korkal's treachery, would call into question his own knowledge and understanding gained over two hundred years of being invariably right on such questions. If he'd misunderstood Korkal so badly, then his own judgment was perhaps so flawed that he was no longer fit to rule.

He considered that idea dispassionately for a long moment, then shoved it to the side. Maybe it was true, but he wasn't ready to accept it quite yet.

So his judgment was still functioning, which meant Korkal was still loyal to Alba. But he had disobeyed orders, had consorted with the enemy, and had betrayed his own lord's confidence to a different lord, a potentially hostile ruler. How could he fit those two things together?

He brought the glass to his lips and slurped again, letting the tastes and the questions roll around in his mind together. There was only one possible reconciliation, he decided finally. Korkal had not believed himself a traitor by his actions. He must have known he disobeyed, but must also have been certain he did not betray.

In another man, that might have seemed self-serving foolishness. But in this one, the Packlord had to wonder if it was not.

Very well, then. What possible situation might have convinced Korkal that disobedience, disobedience to the point that it might be mistaken for treachery, was the only course available to him? The Packlord chewed at it a good while as the level of wine in his bottle dropped lower.

It had to be some danger to the Alban Empire, something that in his own mind prevented him from confiding in his leader. But what might that be? He had already been aware of the Packlord's fears about the threat to Alba of a Terran Leaper. What greater threat than that could there be?

And surely Korkal could not have underestimated that threat. The Packlord had given Lord Denai access to the most secret files about earlier Leaps, in particular the most devastating one of recent history, which had shattered the Hunzzan Empire five millennia ago.

In searching those files, Korkal *must* have seen . . .

In searching those files . . .

The Packlord erupted from his bath, knocking over in his exit the remains of a perfectly good bottle of wine. Water streamed off him as he rushed naked out of the steamy room and hurried into his study.

"Get me the records of Lord Denai's recent searches into the privileged archives!" he snapped at the empty air.

A disembodied voice replied immediately: "Right away, sir. Are you receiving calls now?"

"I don't know. Who is it?"

"The Terran leader Serena Half Moon. The chairman of the—"

"I know *who* she is, you idiot! Put her through!" He paused as he realized he was standing in a rapidly cooling puddle of his own drippings. "No, wait a second. Let me get some clothes on."

He rushed out of his study, his thoughts whirling. What in the Seven Cold Hells did *she* want?

2

S erena Half Moon, tall, angular, dark, determined, stared at the hologram of Hith Mun

Alter. From her vantage point it appeared that the Packlord sat at his ease in a comfortable chair on the other side of her office. She was likewise seated in comfort, the lights dimmed, a glass of fine single-malt scotch on a table at her right hand. Not far away a fire glimmered and crackled in a brick-lined fireplace, casting a flickering wash of shadow across her hatchet-boned features.

It might have been a companionable chat, a cozy conversation about trivial things. But it wasn't. In the games the two of them pursued, nothing was trivial, and nothing was what it seemed.

I have to keep that in mind, she thought.

"Thank you for taking my call," she said, her voice a soft whiskey rasp. "My aides tell me you had retired for the evening."

The Packlord shifted slightly in his seat. A half-empty bottle of Terran wine sat on a stand nearby. He held a shining crystal goblet in his right hand, which he now raised to his muzzle. He sniffed appreciatively.

"Ahh. If I were to choose one thing out of the many that I have come to cherish your people for, Serena, it is this wonderful wine that you make. There's nothing like it, you know."

The chairman stared at him, masking her surge of irritation with the ease of long practice. She wasn't certain exactly how well the Packlord could read human expressions, but why take any chances? She knew she couldn't read him as well as she would have liked. She hoped the same was true for him, but there was no way of knowing.

She raised her own drink in a vague toast, wondering if he could sense the irony. She sipped, set it back down, and said, "Of the many things you cherish Terrans for, Packlord? Tell me, Hith. Do you still cherish us? I think you did once, but now I wonder."

"But why would you wonder, Serena? What have I done? What do you think I've done?"

"It is what I've seen, Packlord. I don't know if you had anything to do with it, but since it involved your own military forces in Sol System, and your own most trusted associates, you may forgive my curiosity. Or at least I hope so."

He stared at her for what seemed like a long time, then nodded abruptly. "And you refer to . . . ?"

"My own military people tell me that the *Albagens Pride* just engaged in a space battle with the rest of the Alban forces in-system. As far as they can tell, the *Pride* emerged unscathed. But the other ships were destroyed. None remain. And now, with yet another puzzling event, Sol System remains entirely unguarded, except for our own navy. Open to any attack from, say, Hunzza." She arched her black eyebrows in a question and waited for his reply.

His ears twitched. A small movement, but she saw it. Maybe she'd surprised him after all.

"Entirely unguarded, Serena? I would hardly call the *Pride* helpless. Especially if, as you say, the *Pride* destroyed the other Alban ships. Evidently the *Pride* alone is a potent defense. Especially if, as has been the case before, Jim Endicott is at her controls."

"Perhaps true, Hith. Except that ten minutes ago, the *Albagens Pride* slipped into hyperspace and vanished from Sol System. And other sources indicate that Jim Endicott and Korkal Emut Denai were aboard. Along with, oddly enough, two others whose role I don't clearly understand. A Terran girl named Char McCain, and a young male Hunzza of unknown provenance named Harpalaos. Since Korkal is your man, I wondered if perhaps you might not have some enlightenment to offer me on the matter."

Once again the Packlord fell silent, this time staring into his wineglass as if answers might be floating there. Finally he looked up.

"Let's not fence, Serena. I know about the battle. I haven't yet heard about the *Pride* leaving Sol System. And I know that the one you call 'my man,' Lord Denai, has betrayed me to you. You were there, in the room, listening to our private conversation. With his full consent and help, I must presume. Is it not so?"

Now it was Half Moon's turn to be startled. Her reaction was no more obvious than the twitch of the Packlord's ears had been: She blinked. But she thought he saw it, because he raised his head, his gaze boring into her own.

"Serena, if we are to help each other, we must be open. There is too much about what is happening that I don't understand. So tell me, if you will. What do you know? Of me, of these strange events?"

She repressed her own urge to flare at him.

He accused Korkal of treachery. But what of his own?

What of it, indeed? He wants knowledge? Very well, I shall give it to him. Perhaps in greater measure than he desires.

"What is Lord Denai's betrayal to yours, Hith? One treachery to another? You plot the destruction of the entire human race. Perhaps that is a crime so great even your own henchman cannot swallow it? Perhaps Korkal's betrayal is only a response to a much more monstrous crime, and not a betrayal at all?"

The Packlord heaved a long, soft sigh. "Well," he said. "So you know."

"About Leapers? Yes, Hith, Korkal told me. I find it hard to imagine that the leader of so great an empire, a vast swarm compared to which Terra is less powerful than the least of your worlds, could be so frightened of us. So willing to destroy us on nothing more than rumors of ancient disasters. I know about Hunzza, Packlord. *But that was five thousand years ago!* How can you condemn us based on a dusty legend?"

She watched the Packlord's gaze dart away from hers, staring at something in his quarters beyond the range of the holocube, invisible to her. A moment later he faced her again, and though it might have been only her imagination, she thought he was suddenly gravely upset about something.

"I had made no final decision, Serena. That was one of the things Lord Denai was *supposed* to help me with, by doing what he could to either confirm or deny my worries."

"And did he, Hith? Did he convince you *not* to murder us?"

"I'd think you would know better than I, Serena. He became your tool, did he not? How can I be sure anything he reported to me wasn't tainted by whatever arrangement he had with you?"

"Now you fence with me, Packlord. Surely you know that Korkal remained loyal to Alba. I'm no fool. Our interests may have coincided momentarily, but he never wavered in his real goal."

"And that was?"

"Your *survival.* Not mine, not *ours. Yours!*"

"Serena, forgive me. I will be as honest as I can be. If Lord Denai thought he was pursuing my interests, *Alba's* interest, he didn't see fit to inform me about it. I discovered his treachery by accident—"

"By spying, actually," Serena broke in, her tone sour.

"Yes, of course, spying," the Packlord agreed. "We need not tell ourselves children's tales. All leaders need their eyes and ears, even among their friends. You are no different than I."

The chairman nodded. Spurious indignation on her part wouldn't advance things. "Of course—though your spies seem to be more effective than mine."

"Except for Korkal Emut Denai," the Packlord replied. "What did he tell you, Serena?"

"That if you decided Terra was a Leaper culture, you would make an alliance with the Hunzzan Empire to destroy us before we could become a danger to you."

Spoken so baldly, it sounded like an unanswerable indictment. But the Packlord only nodded. "He had that much right, at least. But what else did he say? Did he tell you why he would reveal this to you?"

"Because he had to stop you," she replied. "That's what he said. He told me there were things you didn't understand, things that would panic you into something suicidal if you knew."

"Did he tell you what these things were?"

"No."

"Serena, think carefully, please. You know I fear your people. I fear Jim Endicott. I fear the sudden startling spiral in the level of your technology. I'm afraid you may become a deadly danger to my people. To the galaxy at large. Put yourself in my place. What would you do if you—"

"If I stumbled into a nest of vermin and discovered they weren't vermin after all?"

He stared directly into her eyes. "Yes. Exactly that."

Her own gaze didn't waver. After a moment she sighed. "I'd do exactly the same thing, I suppose."

"Survival is a terrible drive, isn't it, Serena?"

She lifted her drink and drained it in a single gulp. "Gelden," she said abruptly. "He said it all had to do with Gelden. But he wouldn't tell me more. Do you know what it means?"

Slowly the Packlord lifted his own glass and drained it. As far as she could tell, his expression was completely blank as he set down the glass and stared at her. His voice held no inflection she could discern. He sounded almost robotic.

"I have to go now, Serena. I'm sorry. Good-bye."

"Hith, wait. What did I say? You can't—"

But he was gone. She sat in a room completely empty but for her and her own suddenly disordered thoughts.

Have I just killed the human race? she wondered.

And then another thought: *What is Gelden?*

3

The Packlord stared at the space where, a moment before, Serena Half Moon had been sitting. Of course she hadn't been actually sitting there, but illusion was everything. Perhaps they were both illusions—at least to each other.

"Bring it," he said, turning his head to gaze at the screen she hadn't been able to see. The results of his request for Korkal's archive searches had come back. He was familiar with almost everything Korkal had examined, all except for one thing. Korkal had done something he had never done himself. There were actual physical artifacts in the archive as well, things so ancient, trivial, and dusty that the Packlord had never bothered to examine them. But Korkal had. And now an aide brought in a metal box, something incorruptible enough to survive five thousand years, yet still bearing the marks of age. The aide set it on the floor and opened it. He began to remove items, small things, one after the other.

"Stop!" the Packlord said. "That one. Give it to me."

The aide handed the object over. It was a bit larger than the Packlord's hand; rectangular, heavy, smooth, cool.

Some sort of holographic representation, but ancient, physically frozen in a clear plasticlike substance. Captured thus, a figure, immobile, mysterious, stared mildly across five thousand years into the Packlord's wondering eyes.

In all the files, all the archives and history, he had never seen anything like it. Gelden had vanished forever, and no one had any idea what sort of creatures had lived in that insignificant system before they Leaped.

Now Hith Mun Alter wondered what sort of power it had taken to erase *every single image* of those long-vanished people, erase them so thoroughly that only the single physical image he held in his trembling hand survived.

The eyes stared back at him, daring him to guess.

A native of Gelden. How old? How long ago?

As he stared in horror at the incorruptible physical artifact that had survived five millennia, the image wavered. It shimmered and faded. It vanished.

He held an empty plastic cube.

Every one of his hairs stood on end. He'd thought that Leaper dead fifty centuries now. But it wasn't. It was here. It was now.

It knew him.

4

Outsider and Korkal faced each other across the silent room. Char had led Harpy, still quivering, away to find his own cabin, offering the both of them a general glare of pure hate as she made her exit.

"That's an angry young woman," Korkal said.

"Just so you understand, I control this ship," Outsider said.

"Yes, I assumed as much. I couldn't do anything when we were fighting the fleet."

"Keep it in mind, then," Outsider said. "No use trying any tricks. They won't work."

"No, I didn't think they would. What else do you control?"

Outsider searched his face slowly. "Do I control you? Is that what you mean?" He paused. "What do you think?"

"I'm not sure," Korkal admitted. "You were in my mind when I was jacked into the ship's brain, but I didn't feel you there later. Or when I was in my cabin and shielded from the rest of the ship's systems."

"I'm not controlling you now," Outside said.

Korkal wandered toward a shelf on the far wall that held a few beautifully turned steel bottles. He touched one and it chilled over immediately, covered with a thick rime of frost. "Which is not the same thing as saying you *can't* control me."

Outsider said nothing to that. Korkal shrugged.

"Do you drink?" He twisted off the top of the bottle and poured a honey-golden liquid into a tall, clear glass. "It's a type of Terran mead. But I synthesize it here on the ship."

"This artifact I use can drink, certainly. It is in every way a human body. Just between us, I fail to see the point, though. It can drink, but it isn't me."

Korkal sipped, arching his bushy brows. "Not you. But you feel the artifact's sensations? If it did drink, you could taste the same tastes?"

"Certainly. I could even selectively sort, amplify, and order the various inputs so that I could directly experience a far wider and stronger range of tastes, better than the artifact itself could ever feel, even though it is the—for lack of a better word—receiver of them."

"Hm. Must be strange. I find it hard to imagine. Is all of you inside the artifact's skull—in the brain?"

Outsider shook his head as he watched Korkal sink into a formchair. "I think I will join you in a sip," he said, moving toward the sideboard. He fussed with bottle and glass, then turned.

"Am I here? No, of course not. The human brain can code about ten-to-the-seventeenth bits of information—that's a one followed by seventeen zeros, or one hundred petabits—and it operates at a speed of about ten trillion floating-point operations per second—ten teraflops. But I am a distributed entity lodging in a mechanical framework that administers approximately a billion brains, and that framework—what you call the array linkages—allows these brains to transfer information among themselves at a rate a thousand times faster than a single brain can transfer information *inside* itself—one petaflop. In other words, only an unimaginably small part of my entire thinking processes are here"—he tapped his skull gently with one finger—"at any given time."

Korkal tried to imagine what being Outsider must be like. He failed. All he could think of was something dark and unimaginably vast, like a great storm moving slowly across the face of the universe. A storm of ceaselessly churning information.

"And Jim can—could—do that, too?"

Outsider raised his glass, sipped, then chuckled harshly. "Jim? Compared to Jim, I'm as crude as a garden gate. I'm like a conductor waving my baton at the orchestra. Jim *becomes* the entire orchestra. I link the individual brains into the array. *He melds them into a single pattern, a single mind!*"

Korkal stared at him, then shook his head. "I guess I really can't understand, can I?"

"You? *I* can't understand. Nothing in this galaxy has the ability to understand what Jim Endicott becomes when he takes full control of the mind arrays. Nothing, except . . ."

"Except what?"

For the first time since Korkal had first met Outsider, he sensed uncertainty, thought he saw a flicker of uneasiness wash across his dark, ascetic features.

"There is something around A'Kasha, or maybe only touching A'Kasha—the place where Harpalaos comes from. I don't know what it is.

It is able to block me, shield itself from my investigations. Nothing should be able to do that."

Korkal blinked. "A'Kasha? But where is it? In the Hunzzan Empire?"

"Yes," Outsider replied. "In it, but not of it. I've been trying to learn about it for some time now—some time by my standards. But I've failed. So I have to try something else."

"Something else? Like what?"

Outsider drained the rest of his glass and set it on the sideboard. He shrugged. "What do you think, Korkal Emut Denai? I'm going there to take a look for myself. I'm going, and you're going, and the *Pride* is going."

"When?"

"We've already started. We left Sol System and entered hyperspace half an hour ago."

Korkal licked his dark, rubbery lips. "What are you going to do?"

Outsider moved to the door, opened it, then paused and looked back. "What I should have done in the first place with your people, and the Hunzza as well. I'm going to kill it. Then I'm going to kill the rest of you as well."

"Kill us? But Jim wouldn't—"

Outsider smiled. "Jim's dead. Remember?"

His smile grew wider as Korkal sank back. Then he was gone.

CHAPTER FOURTEEN

1

Iskander stood in the door of Ikearos's room, watching him in silence. Ikearos was just smoothing his robe, and Iskander stepped forward.

"Let me help with that, Egg Guardian," he said.

Ikearos waved him away. "I'm not entirely crippled yet, Nest Watcher." He gave himself a final pat. "And what of your watching is so important that I have to be awakened in the middle of the night?"

Iskander glanced about the room. There were no communications terminals in evidence. Strange that a leader who oversaw the business of an entire world could—or would—so isolate himself.

"We have visitors," he told Ikearos.

"Visitors? Make them comfortable and give them a place to sleep. Why disturb me?"

"No, you don't understand. They haven't come here. Not yet. It's a spacecraft, Egg Guardian. A huge vessel, bigger than anything we could imagine. It's just now entering the A'Kasha System."

Ikearos froze. His eyes went out of focus a moment, and he seemed to sway slightly. Iskander took his elbow.

"Are you all right, Ikearos?"

"Just a . . . a bit of dizziness. I'm all right, Iskander." He blinked a few times. "You're probably vexed with me and my poor room. No big screens, no instant communications. Very well. Let's go to the big screens."

"Yes, Egg Guardian. Right away, I think."

"Is this an emergency, then?"

"I think so. The ship is Alban. But it isn't responding to any of our messages."

"Well, what is it doing?"

"Maintaining course directly for A'Kasha. They're coming here, Ikearos. This isn't some accident. They know what they want."

Ikearos sighed. "We'll go see. Come with me." He moved toward the door, then paused. "Have you notified the rest of the Speaking Nest? Is the Circle gathered?"

"I've sent out messages. I doubt the Circle is gathered yet. It's only been a few moments."

Ikearos nodded and continued on through the doorway. In the larger chamber beyond, several Younger Brothers eyed him warily. He ignored them and let Iskander lead him toward the main entrance of his apartments. "An Alban vessel, you say? I wonder what they want."

"Nothing good," Iskander said. "I think we can be sure of that."

2

Korkal knew he wasn't himself. He remained hidden in his quarters, leaving the operations of the *Pride* to others, refusing to venture forth. Nobody tried to intrude on his solitude. Harpy was terrified of him, and Char despised him. The scattered gods alone knew what Outsider thought of him—not that it mattered. There was certainly nothing he could do about Outsider, anyway.

His unaccustomed lack of control had manifested as a deep, choking cloud of depression. He had all of his communications facilities activated, so that he could watch what was going on, though he never interfered and never responded to those few messages forwarded to him. Other people—and things that weren't really people at all, but virtual avatars wholly owned by Outsider—were running his ship. He reclined on his sofa, drank a great deal of wine, and watched them do it.

Jim. He'd gambled *everything* on his trust in the boy, and the boy had betrayed him. Betrayed him by dying. Why hadn't he included *that* possibility in all his intricate plans?

Stupid, stupid. He sighed, finished off the glass he was holding, and got up to pour himself a refill. But as he moved toward the sideboard and its cargo of alcohol, a bank of storage drawers set into the far wall caught his eye. The reason for everything he'd done was in one of those drawers. Suddenly he felt an overwhelming urge to look at the thing again, to remind himself that he hadn't been as foolish as it now seemed.

He opened one drawer and pushed aside some papers. The artifact rested on the bottom of the drawer. He lifted it out and stared at it. A thick rectangle, plastic, smooth and hard. Faintly cool. A replica of the original he'd found in archives so dusty and forgotten that he doubted if even the Packlord knew of it.

He turned it in the light, staring at the strange figure frozen inside. It was squat and powerfully built, with broad, sloping shoulders, a massive chest, a thick waist, and bulky muscled legs balanced on wide, flat feet. Its eyes peered at him from beneath a shelved brow that receded into a flat cranium that bulged at the rear.

He had done his research on Terra and found it readily. Where else could he have looked? Though it differed in many ways from the current breed, it was unmistakably human. Not the *Homo sapiens* with which he was familiar, but another—a long-dead branch of the human tree, vanished thirty thousand years now. The Terrans considered it a great mystery. But now he knew an even greater mystery.

Neanderthals had disappeared from Earth. But they had appeared somewhere else: a dim, indistinct backwater planet called Gelden. A world eventually to be populated by busy, chattering gadget makers of not much account in the greater galaxy. A planet whose people had Leaped five thousand years ago.

The culture that had nearly destroyed Hunzza had been human.

3

Against the larger reaches of the galaxy, the movements of troops, material, and vessels that Hith Mun Alter ordered were trivial. But to divert a force numbering nearly a hundred thousand warships was not a minor undertaking, even for a great empire already at war. It took nearly two days to generate new battle plans and to distribute the proper sets of orders necessary to weld so great a number into a single coordinated fighting force.

He was kept apprised of everything, and when it was done, he breathed a sigh of relief—though not unmixed with fear. In his decades as a leader he had thrown the dice many times—made decisions in accordance with the best data he could gather, and then awaited the inevitability of events, hoping their resolution would turn out as he desired.

So he did now. The news that Lord Denai had revealed the innermost secret—the existence of Gelden, *and what Gelden was*—to Serena Half Moon had made his actions inevitable. As he sipped tea in the silence of his sitting room, he toyed with the idea of talking to the Terran chairman again. But what good would it do?

The grizzled ruff of fur at the back of his neck rippled slightly as he thought about what he'd seen in the plastic cube that Lord Denai had discovered. Korkal *knew*. His own evidence had vanished when the contents of the cube had rippled and disappeared, but even that carried its own message. Korkal knew that the Gelden Leapers had been a human culture. An ancient race of humans, now vanished from their home world. Or perhaps it was the other way around— had Gelden seeded Terra even further in the dim history of the development of the race?

He wasn't sure it mattered. What did matter was the connection itself. That, and worse: the evidence, from his own eyes, of the mysterious and impossible force that had reached into his own superbly guarded quarters and somehow manipulated the holocube itself. The connection existed, and it was alive on both ends. Unless Jim Endicott had somehow been the force that had touched the ancient holocube . . .

He shook his head, his mind swirling with a dozen possible ramifications. But he was a leader, responsible for the survival of his people. He had to consider the worst cases first. And the most frightening case of all was that there now existed a direct connection between the Gelden Leapers and Terra, most likely through Jim Endicott and the vast power of the Terran mind arrays he controlled.

It didn't matter if Terra went into its own Leap, not if the Gelden Leapers were somehow involved. If that was the case, his initial fears about Terra Leaping were now magnified a thousandfold, for he faced Gelden itself. And Gelden had devastated Hunzza as casually as he himself might swat a fly. He had no way of understanding the motives of something that powerful. By his standards—by any standards—those who Leaped became gods. And not mystical, metaphysical, revelatory gods, either. No, these divinities wielded a terrifyingly observable, testable, *destructive* presence in the everyday world. Such gods were *real.*

If there was a link between Terra and Gelden, transmitted somehow through Jim Endicott and the mind arrays, then he could see only one possible weakness in it: the arrays themselves. Jim was beyond his reach—for the moment. But the arrays were not. Whatever their enormous, inexplicable power, they were still created by linking human minds. Terran minds. Should Terra vanish in a breath of destroying fire, the arrays would vanish also— and Jim Endicott would be only a boy again, the strange secrets locked in his DNA left with nothing on which to work their dark technological magic. The threat of a Terran Leap, at least, would vanish forever with Terra herself.

And what of Gelden? Its location was lost in time, and after his experience with the holocube, he was sure that was no accident. The Leaper was still concealing itself, and its reach and awareness were so far beyond his understanding that he finally subtracted it from his calculations. Gelden would do whatever it chose to do, and he could have no influence on, or even comprehension of, the acts and motives of a god.

Was that where the *Albagens Pride* was bound? To Gelden? Did Korkal, or Jim, or Outsider, or that oddball pacifist Hunzza, Harp-alaos, know where Gelden was? Were one, or all, now just tools in the plan of an entity he could never hope to understand?

He sighed. Circles. Everything went in circles, and the only way he could function at all was with the sword of action, hacking crudely through those incomprehensible loops. So he had set in motion the brutal stroke of sending the breath of fire to Terra, in the form of a hundred thousand warships—sun-poppers included. And another stroke was his recent message to Tharson, emperor of Hunzza, that the *Albagens Pride* was most likely seeking some destination in his empire, possibly even Gelden itself, and to be on watch for it. If he desired, of course, to do so—and it had turned out that Tharson desired it very much. His own spies told him so: Hunzza had mobilized fleets an order of magnitude larger than his Terran expedition, to the point that the assault against Alba itself had been put off.

That much, at least, was a relief.

So Hunzza was humming like a kicked-open wasps' nest, and Alba was reaching with a mailed fist toward Terra. He had judged his data and made his decisions, and now he would wait.

But he would have given everything he had—and nearly everything Alba had—to know what was happening aboard the *Albagens Pride* right now.

There had been no messages, no communications, no secret reports from the great vessel

since—and he'd checked to make sure—forty-
five Terran minutes before she'd vanished into
hyperspace. The messages he *had* received
indicated that a secondary intelligence layer,
under the control of his own security people,
had attempted a takeover of the ship. Given that
this had occurred *before* the *Pride* had destroyed
the small Alban fleet already in Sol System, and
that subsequent communications from the
Pride had been completely normal, with no
mention at all of the battle, he had to assume
the takeover had failed.

So the greatest warship his race had ever
built was loose in the galaxy, bound for—

Bound for *what?*

He raised his teacup with shaking fingers,
wondering if he—or his race—would survive
long enough to learn the answer.

4

Korkal stood with Char and Harpy at the
base of the captain's chair. The seat itself was
completely enclosed in its gleaming interforce
shield. Korkal presumed one of the pilots was
there, conning the ship. Or thinking he was
conning the ship. The newest version of that
shield had been designed to increase the interface between Jim and the mind arrays. So whoever was hidden behind the shield now was
nothing more than a wide-open channel for the
controller of the arrays—and that was Outsider.

Directly overhead, gleaming green and blue and white, floated the orb of A'Kasha, the Pit of Souls. Harpy was staring up at it, shivering slightly. His jaws hung open, and his tongue darted in and out with spastic regularity. Korkal had never seen a Hunzza so paralyzed by terror. It made him queasy to watch. He thought that if Thargos the Hunter had been alive to see it, he would have murdered Harpy on the spot—out of racial humiliation, if nothing else.

"Well, Harpy, home again, eh?" he said gently.

Harpy moaned softly but made no other reply. Char glared at Korkal, as if simply stating the obvious was an unpardonable offense.

"Home again, yes," Outsider said. "But I think we need to make ourselves known before the touching reunion. Harpalaos!"

Nobody had noticed Outsider's arrival. He might have distilled his "artifact," the body he wore as another dressed himself with clothes, out of thin air. Perhaps he had. But now Harpy flinched beneath the whiplash of Outsider's voice and turned to face him.

"No . . . please don't make me. I shouldn't be here at all. I'm not allowed . . ."

"Not allowed? Allowed to what? Return? See A'Kasha again? See your father again? Not allowed to do what, Hunzzan spratling?"

"Leave him alone!" Char said.

"He's not as fragile as you think he is," Outsider said. "He's just a coward. But terror won't kill him."

"You bastard."

"To be sure," Outsider said. "Harpalaos, we've opened contact with the A'Kashan authorities. They say we must speak to one whose title is Egg Guardian. Who is that?"

Harpy moaned again and closed his eyes. But then he hissed, "My father. My father is Egg Guardian."

"Well, then. He's in for a pleasant surprise, isn't he?"

Korkal had never noticed before how much like that of a Terran wolf's the expression on a human face could seem. *Do we look like that to them sometimes?* he wondered.

A large holoscreen abruptly shimmered into existence before them. Outsider moved to face it, his body partially shielding the rest of them from view.

The scene on the screen revealed a surprisingly primitive backdrop: what appeared to be an ancient room, or cave, walled with stone. In the distance, a number of Hunzza, their heads covered with hoods, sat in silence. Their eyes appeared to be closed.

This held for a moment, and then the head of another Hunzza moved in to dominate the screen. He stared out at them, his gaze wide-eyed and hard.

"I am Iskander," he said. "I am Nest Watcher. Who are you? Why do you come here with your great ship?"

"We come on an errand of mercy, Nest Watcher," Outsider replied. "We bring one who was lost back to his nest."

Iskander didn't hesitate. "This system is forbidden to any but our own. You must leave."

"I'm afraid not, Nest Watcher. Not, at least, before we complete our purpose in coming here."

"You must—"

Outsider raised one hand, halting him, then stepped aside and gestured at Harpalaos.

"See before you Harpalaos, the son of Ikearos, who is your Egg Guardian and the voice of God. The prodigal has returned, Nest Watcher. Summon his father so that all can share in his joy."

The filmy inner membranes of Iskander's eyes dropped slowly, then snapped wide. Korkal knew it was an expression of shock. But the Nest Watcher caught himself and concealed any other reaction that Korkal could see.

"This also is forbidden," Iskander said. "You must leave. You don't understand your danger. Go immediately. It is all that will save you."

"We will go," Outsider replied, "but not before I see the Egg Guardian himself. Bring him to me, or I will slice his son, who is also called 'Bringer of the Deadly Dawn,' into ribbons before your eyes."

Once again Iskander's ocular membrane drooped, then snapped. "You will not!"

"I have been under attack for the last three-point-eight seconds, Nest Watcher," Outsider said calmly. "As you can see, the attack has not been successful. Put the boy's father before me!"

Something jostled the screen. Iskander turned, glancing at something beyond the focus of the hologram. He turned halfway back, his mouth opening to speak. Then the screen went dark.

"What happened?" Korkal said. "Are you—are we still under attack?"

"Yes," Outsider replied.

"What is it?"

"I don't know. It is very powerful."

"Stronger than you?"

"Yes. Much."

Korkal noticed that a faint sheen of sweat had appeared on Outsider's high forehead. What an odd manifestation—his *artifact* reflected his stress.

"If it is so much stronger than you are, how are you able to resist?" Korkal asked.

"I have help," Outsider said.

"Help? Who is helping you?"

The interforce shield concealing the captain's seat suddenly vanished.

"I am," a voice replied. "I'm helping him. And I'm holding. But only barely. *God, it's strong . . .*"

5

In the chamber that housed the Speaking Nest, the heart of A'Kasha, pandemonium broke out. Ikearos had been standing beyond Iskander, who was facing a holoscreen as he spoke to the dark Terran aboard the stranger ship.

Ikearos had seen his son's face when the Terran stepped aside, and he uttered a low hiss of shock. Harpalaos returned! Brought back by Albans and Terrans. What did it mean?

But as he tried to grapple with the implications, his back suddenly went rigid, his eyes rolled up in his skull, and he began to Speak.

"The Bringer of the Deadly Dawn has returned against the will of the nest. He must pay the ultimate price."

As Ikearos Spoke, the members of the Speaking Nest also went rigid as some unknowable force suffused their minds and their bodies. And though Iskander was not seated in the Circle, he felt the backwash of that possession as the smallest edge of an enormous dark fire, licking at the limits of his consciousness. He staggered, nearly falling, but caught himself. The Egg Guardian was not so lucky. Ikearos fell to the stone floor and began to convulse.

Iskander broke the communications link to the stranger ship without a second thought and rushed to kneel by Ikearos's side.

"Get help, medications. Hurry!"

Though attendants and Younger Brothers were never allowed inside the Speaking Nest chamber, machines monitored the interior for emergencies. As Iskander put one arm beneath Ikearos's head and tried to lift him up, the door to the chamber opened wide and a robot gurney slid in.

"Help me with him!" Iskander hissed.

Some of the other Speaking Nest members were now recovering from their daze, while others still convulsed like their Speaker. Two of the least affected hurried to help Iskander lift Ikearos's heaving, twitching form onto the gurney. As soon as he was settled, gleaming tendrils launched themselves from either end of the mechanism and pierced Ikearos's skin in a dozen places. As this happened, the gurney began to slide toward the door.

Iskander followed, pausing only to glance at the other Nest members still flailing in their own convulsions.

"Call in attendants and Younger Brothers. Help them!" he said. Then he followed the Egg Guardian out the door, giving almost no thought to the fact that he'd just broken several millennia's worth of traditions.

Suddenly everything was in turmoil. He sensed a great shattering yet to come. In the face of that, what had once been of paramount importance was less than trivial.

As he passed rapidly through a communications chamber, he paused again. "Regain contact with the Alban ship. Tell them they may land, may speak with the Egg Guardian. A small party only, whomever they wish. But they must bring Harpalaos down."

One of the techs stared at the gurney vanishing through the far door. "The Egg Guardian appears to be dying," he said. "How can the strangers speak to him?"

Iskander ignored this. "Tell them," he snapped. "Tell them to bring his son. The God is angry. He demands a judgment and a price of them both. If they are to speak to each other, it may well be in one of the Seven Cold Hells. But that isn't your concern, is it? Do what I tell you! *Now!*"

With that he rushed on out of the room. Shaking his head at the strangeness of it all, the technician turned to obey his orders.

6

Char made a harsh choking sound. Korkal opened his own mouth, but his tongue seemed paralyzed. He stared, his eyes bulging, his brain yammering nonsense.

Only Outsider seemed unsurprised.

Finally Char managed something coherent: "Jim . . ." she whispered.

Korkal stared at the apparition now revealed behind the vanished interforce shield. It was Jim Endicott, yes. But different, strange, bizarre.

A sudden shudder ran through Jim's body. He sat bolt upright, then slumped back. "It's stopped," he said.

Outsider mounted the steps of the dais to the captain's chair. "Are you all right?" he said.

Jim closed his eyes, then opened them. "Yes. No damage. Not to the artifact or to the gestalt."

"What was it, do you think?" Outsider said. "Those lizards dirtside?"

"I don't think so. It was focused and transmitted *through* them, but it came from . . . somewhere else."

"Transmitted? I didn't sense that. It seemed to come from everywhere—and nowhere."

Jim sighed and began to climb out of the chair, rubbing one shoulder as if the muscles there were kinked. "There were larger patterns at work. It was trying to impose its own patterns on the ones I was weaving. And it was using the Hunzza on A'Kasha to do it. Which was a good thing, I think. It was using them as tools, and so could be no stronger than the tools it used. I think if it had come at me with its own undiluted power, it would have overwhelmed me."

Korkal shifted his gaze back and forth between the two men. He had no idea what they were talking about. In fact, he had no idea if they were even men.

Jim took a couple of steps, then paused at the top of the dais and looked down. "Hello, Korkal."

Korkal raised his head. He didn't know what to say, what to think. From the neck down, Jim looked as he had before the shooting—nothing visible remained of his terrible, deadly wounds. His face also seemed the same, though he looked more tired, drawn, older somehow. But there was something about that face—something too perfect, too composed. As if it were a mask.

"I'm . . . I'm fine, Jim. If you are . . . *are* you Jim?"

Jim took the first step down. "Yes, I am. In some sense, at least. And I've come back to you. For a time. Are you glad to see me?"

Korkal felt the usual obligatory words of welcome and agreement spring to his tongue, but he stifled them. He didn't want to lie to this . . . whatever it was. And even if it *was* Jim, he didn't know if he was glad to see him.

Not like this. Not a dead boy come back to life.

He thought of an old Terran joke that ended with an awful punch line: *if you call this living.*

CHAPTER FIFTEEN

1

"**W**hat is *it*?" Korkal asked.

They were gathered in his quarters, Jim, Char, Harpy, and himself. Outsider had vanished again as mysteriously as he had appeared. Korkal wondered what, exactly, was that "artifact" Outsider said he used to appear before them as a man. He wondered if Jim was using the same kind of thing now. Was it flesh and blood? Or was it just some sort of mass hallucination? He had no idea what Jim—or Outsider—was capable of. Some of the things he thought they *might* be capable of made his skin crawl when he considered them.

"It?" Jim stared at him.

"Yes. You said *it* was attacking you. What did you mean? The Hunzza on A'Kasha?"

Jim was seated in a formchair. The chair had extended a high, fitted neck rest, the better to support his head. Jim held a cold beer. He sipped it. "I'm not sure," he said finally. "A great force or power. I believe it was operating *through* the A'Kashan Hunzza. Maybe Harpy can tell me more. What about it, Harpy?"

The young Hunzza had lapsed into silence

after seeing Iskander on the holoscreen. He no longer seemed afraid. He looked as if he had sunk so deep into withdrawal that even fear could no longer pierce his numbness. His skin was dull and gray. His eyes were flat. If Korkal had not known better, he would have thought Harpy was blind.

Harpy didn't answer. He looked as if he hadn't even heard.

"Harpy?" Jim said again, but before he could reply, Char broke in.

"What are you?" she said. "You were dead. I saw it. Jim Endicott was *dead*. So what are *you*?"

Jim stared at her. "Do you really want to know?"

She glared back at him, nostrils flaring, head tilted, chin thrust out. "Damned right I do."

For a moment Jim didn't say anything. Then he sighed. "Life isn't what you think it is," he said softly. "You think life has something to do with bodies, and intelligence with brains. But it isn't like that, not at all."

"Bullshit!" Char said. "Mumbo jumbo."

"No, the truth. You know what life really is? In the greater scheme of things? It's something very simple. So simple, in fact, that hundreds of years ago a physicist named Frank Tipler described it exactly. He said it was 'any entity that codes information, with that information being preserved by natural selection.' And he was right. That's what life is. In this universe, at least."

She shook her head. "I don't understand."

"No, of course not. It sounds simple, but it is

an extremely complex idea. What it boils down to is this: Life isn't dependent on the substrate upon which it is coded. The substrate—think of it as the 'blackboard' on which the codes are written—could be carbon-based life forms like us. Or it could be a computer, with the information coded on the various storage and processing media. Or it could be a particular arrangement of metallic crystals that shifts and changes in response to input. That's the 'natural selection' part."

She closed her eyes, grappling with it. "Okay, I think. You're saying that a computer could be just as alive as we are."

"Not exactly. What I'm saying is that life is nothing more than a computer program. It doesn't matter if that program is called the 'mind' and runs on a carbon-based processor like we are, or if we call it an 'operating system' and it runs on a processor made of crystal, metal, and electronic switches. In the end, both are programs, and indistinguishable in function from each other. Life is the *process* of encoding information, and what is encoded changes in response to modifying input." He paused and idly scratched his forehead as he tried to think how to continue.

"It's not the substrate, the medium, the *container* that's important, Char. It's the *pattern*. And *pattern* is just another name for an arrangement of *information*. If something processes, modifies, and encodes information above a certain level of complexity, that is what we call life."

"Patterns," Korkal said. "You've said all

along that what you do in the mind arrays is manipulate patterns. Is that what you mean?"

Jim smiled. "Yes, sort of. The arrays link together human minds, just as a computer network links together individual computers. The human brain is not an overwhelmingly powerful processor, by the way. Even Terra has computers much more powerful than the brain. We had even begun to recognize certain extremely complex machines running artificial-intelligence-level programs as legally living entities—if they could pass the Turing test. And high-technology cultures like Alba and Hunzza have machines many orders of magnitude more powerful than anything Terra has."

"What's the Turing test?" Char said.

"Another deceptively simple concept, also advanced on Terra several centuries ago, by a mathematician and computer wizard named Alan Turing. He said that if you could talk with a computer, really *talk* with it, and you couldn't tell the difference between it and a normal, intelligent person, then it *was* a person. What counts for personhood is *behavior*." Jim paused, smiled sadly, then went on. "In other words, if it waddles like a duck and quacks like a duck, then it is a duck. That's all."

"Okay," Char said, "I think I understand. Sort of. Life—and intelligence—is some sort of computer program, and it runs on all kinds of computers, not just what we call living bodies. Is that right?"

"Pretty much," Jim agreed.

"So what does that mean for you? You were

dead, and now you're back. Or claim to be. Are you alive now? Did you come back from the dead?"

"I never died," Jim said. "My body did. But I didn't."

"What? I saw you. You were *dead!*"

"Do you remember when Outsider linked me to the arrays just by putting the hands of his artifact on either side of my head?"

"Yes."

"When he did that, he opened a gateway that allowed my patterns, the computer program that is *me*, to copy at least parts of itself—the controlling parts—into the mind arrays. But this time, when my physical body died, he opened a much wider gateway. I had no choice. I copied *all* of myself into the arrays. And so my body died, but me—the program, the mind, the soul, whatever you want to call it—just moved to a different kind of computer. Instead of my body and my brain, I'm in the mind arrays. So I never died. I'm alive, as alive as I ever was, but I'm in the arrays now. The mind arrays are my body."

"Then what is this sitting in a chair talking to us right now?"

Slowly Jim raised one hand and gently touched his skull. "It's a construct, an artifact, just like the manifestation of Outsider."

"But is it you? I mean, really *you?*"

Jim's smile was bleak. "Thanks to my *mother,* my DNA encodes plans for certain . . . additions to my physical brain. Those plans had already been activated and the changes begun. When I created this construct, I merely completed a process already started. I use this body to interface with certain things you think of as being in the real world. But the real me is spread out over a computer that consists of a billion brains and the high-bandwidth linkages that bind them together." He paused, and this time he stared at Korkal.

"Do *you* see the implications, Korkal?"

Korkal thought he did. He said slowly, "You're too big now to fit into a single brain, even this souped-up thing inside your skull."

"Yes," Jim said. "All this does is let me get a somewhat larger portion of me into this flesh computer. This body can do things my old one couldn't. But it still isn't me. It's just a tool."

"So what you're saying," Char said, "is that Outsider saved your life, but in such a way that you can't ever be what you were before."

"*Saved* my life?" Jim's voice was edged with bitterness. "Think about it. Think back to when I was shot. At that time, Outsider was in utter and complete control of the *Albagens Pride* and everything aboard. His mind works so much faster than a human brain that he actually lives thousands of years in the time a physical human experiences a few seconds. Do you think he couldn't have prevented the technician from shooting me if he'd wanted to?"

Finally Korkal saw it. "You mean he wanted your body to die. He wanted you to be forced out of your body and into the arrays."

"Yes," said Jim. "It's what he's always wanted. And if I didn't know there are other players in this game even more powerful than he is, Korkal, I would guess that every single thing that has happened to all of us since Delta's 'death' was arranged in advance by Outsider. Probably with a plan created a few minutes after he was first translated into the arrays in the destruction of Delta's satellite. That was nearly a year ago for us. But in terms of his time view, it was thousands of millennia ago. You can't understand what he is, Korkal. Nobody can."

"Can you?" Char said.

"Now I can. He's got me where he always wanted me. He said I shirked my responsibilities by running and hiding from the arrays. Now I can't do that. I *am* the arrays, and there is no going back."

During all of this, Harpy had been listening and slowly coming back to life. Now he raised his head and stared at Jim. "Then you are the God," he said. "But who Speaks for you?"

The question sounded completely nonsensical, but Jim only nodded, his expression sad.

"I didn't see it before," he said, "but I do now. Char Speaks for me." He turned and stared directly at her. "I'm sorry, Char, but you do."

2

Iskander stood beside the tank in which Ikearos lay silent and still while the powers of A'Kashan medical technology did their best to preserve his life. He glanced across the tank at the lead medic.

"Well? What is the prognosis?"

"We have him stabilized. I don't think he will

die. But we can't determine what the damage is yet. Certain parts of his brain don't seem to be functioning. But whether that's just a normal shutdown in the face of stress or something more permanent . . ." The medic shook her head. "It's just too soon to tell."

Iskander made a clicking sound of frustration. "All right. Keep me informed of any change. *Any* change, do you understand?"

"Of course."

"Good." Iskander spared one final glance for Ikearos's slack, gray features, then spun on his heel and stalked from the room. As soon as he was outside, a small flock of attendants, technicians, and Younger Brothers descended on him, all chattering at once.

"Silence!" he hissed, raising one hand as he walked through them. "You! What is the status of the comm link with the stranger ship?"

A technician bobbed his head and said, "The link has been reestablished, and the message you ordered to be conveyed has been."

"And has there been a reply?"

"Yes, Egg Guardian, there has been. The ship will be sending down a party. The estimated time of arrival is in three hours."

Iskander's eye membranes dropped slowly, then snapped up again. His momentary shock wasn't at the news of the impending arrival, but at what the technician had called him: Egg Guardian. In the chaos that had followed Ikearos's collapse and the breaking of the Circle, he hadn't stopped to think of all the implications. But A'Kasha *must* have an Egg Guardian, no matter what. And if the Egg Guardian was unable to function, then the next in the line of succession became the Egg Guardian as soon as the previous Egg Guardian was incapacitated. Ikearos might or might not regain his full functions. If he did recover them, then he would resume his position. But if he didn't, then the Nest Watcher would succeed him.

Had in fact already succeeded him, at least temporarily.

For a moment Iskander paused as the full weight of his responsibilities crashed down on him for the first time. A'Kasha faced the greatest crisis that had confronted it since the beginning, and it was his alone to face.

He'd often dreamed of the succession. But not like this. He tried not to betray his dismay as he strode along. Only a certain tightness in his long jaw betrayed the tension he felt as he spoke to the highest-ranking of the Younger Brothers trying to keep pace with him.

"You! What news of the other Circle members?"

"All but one seem entirely recovered, Egg Guardian," the Younger Brother replied. "And that one, while still a bit disoriented, is making excellent progress."

"Good. Summon all of them back to the Circle chamber. I must face the Nest before the arrival of the strangers." He paused. "Did they say they were sending down the Egg . . . Ikearos's son, Harpalaos?"

"Yes, Egg Guardian."

Iskander nodded and said no more. The Egg

Guardian was the heart and soul of A'Kasha, with responsibilities and duties impossible to number. But all of this was based on one thing, and one thing only: the Egg Guardian Spoke for the God.

Ikearos had tried to Speak, and the God had nearly killed him. What would happen when the new Egg Guardian tried to perform his one greatest duty?

Iskander didn't know. But he knew he was about to find out.

3

"**I** don't understand why Outsider isn't coming, and why you are," Korkal murmured to Jim. They were standing at a viewscreen disguised as a window, in the single passenger lounge of one of the *Pride*'s landers. The landing process was entirely automated, with the small craft being controlled by the *Pride*'s piloting systems—in effect, controlled by Outsider himself.

"I'm not coming either, Korkal," Jim replied. "Just this . . . thing I'm using. It's really no different than if you stayed aboard and sent a robot simulacrum down in your place."

Korkal nodded and turned back to the window, though Jim could clearly sense the Alban's discomfort. No surprise there—he himself felt uncomfortable in his new skin. There was no way Korkal—or any other being entirely of flesh and blood—could understand this weird new state in which he found himself. He remembered his own fear and repulsion when, as he'd manipulated a regeneration tank aboard the *Pride* in order to build himself a new body—he'd discovered the full import of what Kate, his real mother, had encoded in the patterns of his DNA.

"What is it?" he'd cried to Outsider. "What did she do to me?"

Outsider had examined the changes. "She's increased the number, complexity, and sensitivity of your brain's connectors. I imagine she thought it would help make you a better interface with the mind arrays. Of course, she couldn't have foreseen . . ."

"Foreseen that you would force my entire pattern into the arrays, where interfaces, brains, and bodies don't make any difference at all."

"You were bound to make the transition eventually, Jim. I just speeded things up a little."

"I never get a choice, do I? I never *had* a choice!"

"No, not really. Not after Kate made her decision to do what she thought had to be done."

Jim felt a sudden wash of humor from the incredibly complex web of patterns that was Outsider's true existence.

"Did you know how she decided, Jim? No, of course not. I reviewed archives and found strong hints. Bits of recorded conversation between her and Carl. Some of her own notes. Evidently she couldn't quite make up her mind whether to do it. To make such drastic alterations in her own child. So in the end she flipped a coin. That simple. Everything that has followed sprang from that one random act. A coin flip. Don't you find it hilarious?"

Jim didn't reply. He didn't find it funny. He found it horrifying.

"Anyway, at least your transition into the arrays was easier than mine. My technology was much cruder, and so were the arrays. I lost something when I was translated. I don't know if I miss it or not, but I'm aware it was once part of me, and now it's gone forever."

"What? What did you lose?"

"Call it emotions, call it soul, I don't know. I believe it is an essential part of what makes a human *human,* but I don't think it's really necessary to my own functioning."

Jim felt a ghost of something then, from Delta, a whiff of regret. But that couldn't be, could it? Regret would have been banished along with everything else. Delta really was gone, then. Only a part of him remained—the coldly thinking part that was closer to machine than human—but what remained was . . . was what? More than human? Less?

But it helped him decide what to do about the creation of his new body. Even though this new body would not and could not be everything he was now inside the arrays, he wanted to feel and experience as much as it might be capable of, out in the world of living beings. So he allowed the changes his mother had programmed into his genetic code to occur, because that was the only way he could think of to reinforce whatever humanity he still had left.

The lander was approaching the small field

that served A'Kasha in its isolation, a wide, dusty stretch guarded by a single control tower. Jim stared out at the tower as the lander settled onto the ground, flinching slightly as the vessel's power abruptly switched off. But there was no renewal of the attack he'd felt before, now that he was at the bottom of A'Kasha's gravity well. Whatever he'd fought against remained hidden. Waiting, watching?

He didn't know. He, whose true self had already, in its own subjective time in the arrays, lived for thousands of years, still knew nothing about the other power he'd felt. And that was why he'd come. Somehow the power was centered on, or emanated from, A'Kasha. If he had to make this part of himself bait in order to tempt it forth again, then he would.

I am the cheese in my own trap, Jim thought. *And the mouse has great, sharp teeth.*

A small party of Hunzza were leaving the tower and moving slowly toward the lander.

"Get Harpy ready," Jim said. "We'll go down to meet them."

Korkal glanced at him, his eyes sharp, but said nothing.

Come out, come out, Jim thought. *Wherever you are. Whatever you are.*

4

Korkal led them down the exit ladder, where they gathered in a small group before the Hunzza. Jim tried to stay in the background, but while the leader of the native group—a lean, harsh-looking lizard with an air of haughtiness notable even for his normally haughty race—spoke with Korkal, he stared at Jim. So did the rest of his party. It was as if they somehow understood where the true power lay. Or was it something else?

Gingerly Jim let one of the new senses that now existed in his body expand a bit. But when he touched the leader with this peculiar new perception, the leader went rigid.

"I am Iskander!" he hissed. "There are powerful weapons trained on you! Stop what you are doing, or you will all die! Stop it *now!*"

Jim stopped. Well, that answered one question. This Iskander was somehow aware of Jim's ability to initiate nonphysical linkages. He couldn't precisely *read* other minds, but he could feel the nature of the larger patterns without reading the smaller patterns that manifested as language.

Slowly Iskander relaxed. "Very well. There will be no further warnings. If you attempt something like that again, you will die."

Then, as if nothing had been said at all, Iskander turned to Harpy. "You have returned to the Pit of Souls, young Harpalaos. And you have brought these . . . others . . . with you. You understand what is necessary now?"

Harpy, who had been standing slumped, staring at the ground, now slowly raised his head. "You wear the cloak of many colors. Are you Egg Guardian now, Iskander?"

"I am."

Harpy's shoulders slumped even further. "Then my father is dead?"

"We will talk of that later. Answer my question! Do you understand?"

"Yes, Egg Guardian."

"And do you accept?"

"I do. This is all my—"

"Silence!" Iskander turned to the party with him. Two of them stepped forward and positioned themselves on either side of Harpy.

"Take him to the appointed place," Iskander said.

The two nodded. Each of them took one of Harpy's arms. They began to lead him away.

"Wait just one frigging minute!" Char flared. "Where the hell—"

"Char!" Korkal said quickly.

"No, he's my friend. I want to *know!*"

She stepped toward Iskander, who raised one hand. "Look around you," he said, his voice mild.

Squads of heavily armed Hunzza had appeared on every edge of the landing field. Now they began to converge toward the group, weapons raised.

"What is this?" Korkal said. "You gave us your guarantee of safe passage."

"I did," Iskander said with satisfaction. "But the God didn't. I am only an instrument. Your fate is with the God now."

"Damn you, what about Harpy?" Char yelled.

Iskander stared at her. "He violated the Prime Commandment. The God has already demanded his life."

"You're going to kill Harpy?"

"Not I. The God will."

Korkal shifted his stance. "Have you forgotten our ship?"

Jim stepped forward and touched his shoulder. "No, Korkal, don't. Let it go, at least for now."

"A wise choice," Iskander said.

"We'll see," Jim replied.

5

Jim decided that evidently Iskander meant to separate them by species, or perhaps had something special in mind for Korkal, because he found himself and Char in a cell together. The door clanged behind the departing guards with a long, echoing sound that felt depressingly final. Nor was the cell the sort of thing a prisoner on Terra might expect. This one had gray, pitted stone walls, a single crude refresher unit, and two cots pushed against the wall opposite the door. An eerie green glowstrip provided the only illumination, painting dark, hollow shadows on their faces.

Char was seething. She glared at the blank steel door, then whirled, stomped across the small room, and dropped herself with bouncing force onto one of the beds. "Well. Great job there, Jim. Mister All-Powerful Mind Master. You sure caved in real fast. Hell, if you'd let me bring down so much as a butter knife, I could have done a better job."

"Of what?" Jim asked, his tone mild. "Getting yourself—and the rest of us—killed by those squads of troopers?"

She gritted her teeth. "Damn you, what do you care? You in that Halloween costume of a body. If I understand you right, you can't even be killed. They can chew whatever is sharing this cell with me into little bits, spit out the pieces, and burn them. And it won't matter to you at all."

"It would matter, Char. It would matter to me. But yes, you're basically right. Harming this construct can't really harm me."

She stared at him, her features drawn, her eyes shrouded in pits of shadow. "God, I hate you. I don't know what you are. You're not human anymore. You're as much a monster as this . . . *thing* . . . you say is you. And even it isn't *you!*"

He moved toward her, one hand outstretched. "Oh, Char . . ."

"Stay away! Don't you touch me!"

He froze, then sighed, dropped his hand, and moved back. He sat on the other cot, folded his hands in his lap, and stared at the floor.

"Char, I'm not a monster. I don't feel like a monster. Everything I ever was, ever dreamed about, hoped for—everything I ever loved—all of that is still with me. It's just that there's more now, so much more . . ."

"And you can't explain it, can you? Not to me. I'm only *human*. So what does that make *you?*"

He couldn't answer. The silence lengthened.

"They're going to kill us, aren't they? First Harpy, then all the rest of us. And you won't do anything, will you?"

He raised his head. "No, they won't kill us. Not if you mean the Hunzza who live on this planet."

"That nasty one, Iskander. *He* said—"

Jim shook his head slowly. "No, he didn't. He said the God would. And he was right. It might."

She clicked her tongue against her teeth in frustration. "Gods. The God. There isn't any God. It's all mumbo jumbo. Their excuse for doing whatever they want to do."

"No," Jim said. "It exists. It's real."

"How do you know?"

"I felt it," he replied. "That was what attacked me earlier. Their God."

"But *why?* What does some backwater divinity, even if it does exist, have to do with *us?* It's not *our* God. It's *theirs.*"

He kneaded his fingers together, trying to find the words. Finally something came. "Char, we didn't have to land. We could have turned around and taken the *Pride* back out of the system. But we didn't."

"I know. What I can't understand is why. You walked into their trap. You didn't even put up the tiniest bit of fight, either."

"Because when I fought it, I learned something. I don't know if it was by accident or by the intention of whatever it was. But I caught it, just a hint. And I have to know more. I *have* to!"

She snorted softly. "Oh, yeah? What's so important that it's worth sacrificing all our lives?"

He raised his head and stared at her, his eyes blood-colored in the gloom. "I don't think it's their God," he said. "I think it's ours."

CHAPTER SIXTEEN

1

Harpy was aware of the two guards who flanked him, but only dimly. His attention was riveted on the circle of hooded Hunzza surrounding him and the single figure who stood facing him. He heard a faint whining sound. It took him several seconds to realize he was making the sound. He felt disconnected from his body, caged within it but no longer in control of even his most basic physical functions.

"Bringer of the Deadly Dawn," Iskander intoned, his gaze boring into Harpy's own. "You stand in the place of judgment. You have been summoned here by the God, who Spoke through the Egg Guardian. Do you understand all this?"

Distantly Harpy felt moist warmth along the lower edge of his jawline. He reached up and wiped away the drool leaking from the sides of his mouth. His own flesh felt numb and dead; it was like touching someone else. He shuddered and dropped his hand. It was hard to see Iskander. Something was wrong with his vision. Light seemed to flare inside his mind, casting everything in hard-edged, discrete flashes, like a stroboscope.

Iskander took a step forward. "Can you hear me?"

"Yes . . ."

"Do you understand me?"

"Yes."

Iskander paused, as if he doubted the truth of what he heard. He tilted his head slightly, then stepped back again. "Hold him," he said to the two guards. They moved closer and took Harpy's arms. Harpy ignored them. His gaze wandered away from Iskander's icy, frozen features toward the hooded figures ranged all around.

"Father . . ." he whispered.

The anguish in his tone was so strong even Iskander flinched. But only for an instant. Then he stepped further away, flipped his own hood up over his head, and sank to the ancient stone floor.

Harpy began to scream.

2

Char had fallen asleep sitting up, slumped across her cot against the back wall, her chin on her chest. Abruptly she blinked, then raised her head.

"Harpy," she said. "Something's wrong with Harpy . . . Jim!"

He was seated on the other cot, his face turned toward her, his eyes wide and staring. Yet she suddenly had the creepy feeling that he wasn't there, that there was nothing intelligent or aware behind those calm, vacant orbs. She might as well have been yelling at a corpse.

"*Jim!*"

His eyelids flickered. He shook his head slightly. "Eh, what? What's wrong?"

"It's Harpy. Something's happening . . . something bad. He's . . . he's screaming."

"Screaming? I don't hear anything. How can you tell?"

"It's not—he's inside my head. Screaming inside my mind . . ." She felt her cheeks grow warm. What a ridiculous thing to say . . . except it was true.

Jim came off his cot and settled beside her. He draped one arm across her shoulders and hugged her. "Screaming? Can you sense his thoughts? Is he saying anything?"

She closed her eyes. It was the damnedest sensation, like being in two places at once but unable to *see* the second place. She could only feel it—and yet the feeling was horrible. She could feel Harpy screaming but not hear him. And somehow his feelings were mixed in with her own. It was becoming harder and harder to separate the state of her own body from whatever was happening to him.

"Jim . . . it feels like something is growing inside me. Growing everywhere. Like a . . . I don't know, a *cancer*. Like I'm . . . splitting."

She turned in his arms and faced him, face pale, eyes shocked wide. "I'm . . . Jim, I'm *splitting! Help me, oh, God,* help *me!*"

3

It was almost over. The pain had been terrible, and it had seemed endless, but now it was subsiding.

Only a little bit of Harpy was left now. He clung to that part, clung to the final shreds of himself, and hoped that this much of what he had been would still remain with him.

Iskander had thrown back his hood and was staring at him in horror. The Egg Guardian looked strange, distorted. As if Harpy was seeing him with new eyes.

But I am, he thought. *Everything is new now. And old, of course. So very old.*

Agony continued to drain out of him. Now only the ghost of pain remained, leaving a feeling of cleansed weakness behind as the last of it faded away.

This was what he'd feared. And despite everything he'd done to prevent it, it had happened. The part of the old him that still remained contained much of his previous memory. He knew what they had all thought: that he was a coward, a Hunzzan freak, terrified of his own shadow. But it hadn't been *his* shadow that made his muscles go weak with panic. No, the shadow he'd feared was far darker and greater than anything they could imagine.

Another, colder part of him analyzed his current situation. Iskander and the Circle had summoned the power of the God. But of course the

God could not be summoned. It manifested itself as it desired, for it was immanent, never coming nor going, but abiding always. And it had chosen to touch him, to trigger the things hidden deep inside him that made him what he was.

And what was that?

What he'd feared he was, of course.

He was lying on his side, facing Iskander. The strangeness of his new eyes was becoming less burdensome. In a short while, he knew, it would seem as normal as his old vision had. But there was still some fogginess as he lifted his head.

"I am . . ." he said.

His voice was thick, turgid, no longer the clean, sharp hiss of his former existence.

He got his hands beneath him, and then his knees. He crouched there, staring at the strange new arms, the partially scaled skin, the tufts of hair. Fingernails but not claws.

He came to his knees.

"You called me . . ."

Iskander uttered a short, choking moan.

So slow, so heavy. Hard to stand. The balance was different. It would take some getting used to. But finally he managed to rise to his feet and stand facing them, swaying gently.

"I feared it, you know," he said. "I feared it more than you did. But I knew what it was. You didn't."

"You . . . you . . ." Iskander gasped. He had also come to his feet, but he held his hands before him in a warding-off gesture. His face was a mask of dread.

Harpy almost felt like smiling at him.

"And now that you have me," he said, "what will you do? He who was named is now among you. I am the Bringer of the Deadly Dawn. Are you happy with me?"

Iskander stared at the great, hulking, slope-browed, bandy-legged form before him, at its hide of skin and scales, some impossible mixture of Hunzzan and . . . *other*.

He hiked up his robes, turned, and ran.

4

In the armored heart of the Albagens Empire, Hith Mun Alter sat in the deceptive quiet of his rooms, contemplating what he had done. A single small holoscreen floated not far from where he sat and sipped his ever-present tea.

Sometimes the raw power of his position peeped out from behind the mental and emotional blinders he had constructed over the centuries, and he found himself overwhelmed by the naked actuality of it.

A word, a gesture, even a slightly changed expression on his part might call forth actions and events so powerful he could only barely comprehend them. What did the Terries say? Something about holding a tiger by the tail?

He had issued a few simple orders. Now, on his viewscreen, he watched the result of them. The distant recorders were focused on a single white dot of light. It was a star, a relatively minor star, nearly lost in the blinding fields that were its backdrop.

That was Terra's star. And now Terra was ringed by an armada greater than it could imagine, let alone resist. With another gesture or word, he could make that star, and everything in its system, vanish into interstellar gas.

The fleet was in place. The sun-poppers were ready, as well as a hundred other violent and deadly weapons. All it needed was his will, his decision, his action to make it happen.

The scene shimmered and vanished, replaced by the fat, aging features of Kallan Gro Thun, second highest of his military commanders.

"Lord," Thun said. "All is ready. What is your desire?"

The Packlord raised his cup. So homey. So comfortable and cozy. Such a wild dissonance between here and there. For a moment he felt a flash of dizziness. Raise a cup of tea, destroy a race, burn a sun.

"My desire is that you hold in place until I tell you otherwise," he said. "Maintain the highest state of readiness, but do nothing else."

"Yes, sir. You do understand that such a high level of preparedness will take its toll on the troops over time? That we can't maintain it indefinitely?"

"It won't be indefinitely, Admiral," Hith replied. "But for a time yet. Still for a time yet."

"Yes, Lord." Thun snapped off a brisk salute and vanished. The Packlord watched him go, and thought of tea, and Serena Half Moon.

And Jim Endicott.

5

"**W**hat did you do with . . . it?"

Iskander couldn't quite bring himself to speak Harpy's name. He justified this to himself by trying to believe that the monster (there was no other word for it) that had appeared to mold itself out of Harpy's flesh had nothing to do with the youth who had been the son of the former Egg Guardian. Which was impossible, of course, however consoling. He would consider it later.

"As you ordered, Egg Guardian," the commander of the Circle garrison replied. "We took him to a cell."

"Did he resist? Did he say or do anything?"

"No, Lord. He went peacefully, and he said nothing."

"What cell? Where?"

"The main block, Lord. He's near the rest of the captives from the Alban vessel."

Iskander was seated on a comfortable chair in the new offices he'd appropriated immediately on his ascent to the highest rank. Ikearos might have played with the image of ascetic purity, but Iskander had no such inclinations. His word was law for the entire planet, and he saw no reason to hide or soften that fact.

Moreover, in this office he enjoyed the benefits of the highest technology of which his people were capable. A'Kasha had stayed deliberately hidden from the galactic mainstream for millennia, but it had eyes and ears—and spies. What it could take for itself, it did. He might not have the very latest technologies practiced on Hunzza Prime at his disposal, but what he had was adequate for most tasks.

Including keeping a watchful eye on the cell block and its occupants. If this new Harpalaos tried anything odd, he would have warning.

"Very well," he said. "Leave him there for the time being. Don't let him speak to anybody. You understand? He speaks to no one but me."

"Yes, Lord." The colonel seemed entirely happy with that. It struck Iskander that even this tough military man had no desire to be close to whatever it was Harpalaos had become.

"Very well. And now, what about this Alban ship?"

There were banks of screens arranged on two walls. Beneath them were machines and operators. Pictures came and went on the screens, sometimes with dizzying rapidity. Iskander faced them and tried to make sense of what he saw. Anything was better than trying to decipher what had happened in the Circle chamber.

One of the central screens abruptly refocused, its field of view narrowing onto the great colored necklace of the *Albagens Pride*. Iskander stared. He hadn't really seen it up close before.

"It's huge, isn't it?"

"It's the largest space vessel I've ever heard of," the colonel replied. "Even Hunzza itself has nothing like it."

"Could it harm us? A whole world?"

"Easily, Lord. I suspect it could destroy our sun, and our entire system, if it wished to."

"By itself? And we couldn't do anything to stop it?"

"By ourselves? Our own military power? No. But we don't depend on that, do we? We have a greater force protecting us. Do we not?"

Iskander knew he spoke of the God. The God that had hidden and protected the Pit of Souls ever since Darod and his son, Harpalaos, had first recognized the God and worshiped it.

He shuddered inwardly as he thought about that. The prince who had established A'Kasha and his son had gone further than recognition and worship, hadn't they? They had *served*. Bringer of the Deadly Dawn had not been merely a name. It had been a function, too.

And now he had a monster locked in his prison. A monster created *by* the God, molded out of one who descended directly from the first and highest. What was in that blood?

"Lord?"

"Eh? Oh, pardon me, Colonel. My thoughts wandered."

"Yes, Lord. You know we also hold the Alban who claims to be the captain of that ship, as well as two Terrans, a boy and a girl. What are your orders?"

"I . . ." He'd barely given any thought yet to the other captives. The two Terrans were of interest, of course. Ikearos had erred grievously in sending his son to that accursed planet. All Iskander had to do was look at what had come of it—A'Kasha, shrouded and protected for five thousand years, now stood naked and revealed, with a vast Alban warship floating in orbit a few thousand miles overhead.

Intolerable! What *had* Ikearos been thinking? Perhaps he had gone mad? He was very old. It was possible . . .

But Ikearos would soon die. As Iskander considered that, he decided it was for the best. He *and* his hideously mutated offspring. Had that been the God's punishment for Ikearos's ill-fated schemes? He wasn't sure. He had felt the Presence within him, flowing *out* from him, when he'd initiated his first Circle as Egg Guardian. But though he'd watched the effects of that power on Harpy, he hadn't been privy to the content of it. He'd been merely a conduit. The God revealed itself only as it chose.

Perhaps it might be expedient to help the matter of the former Egg Guardian along a bit. There was no real need for Ikearos ever to rise from his sickbed, nor for his son ever to leave his cell. Not alive, at any rate. Unless the God willed it, of course. If that was the case, then whatever the God willed would happen. Which did leave room for at least a fatalistic version of free will on his own part . . .

Thinking on all this, Iskander drifted away again. He was Egg Guardian. So many responsibilities. And of course there was this Alban ship. Maybe some sort of deal could be made about that—if the one who claimed to be its captain was telling the truth about it being his ship.

He raised his head. "Colonel, I—" His eyes widened. "What's that?"

Several of the smaller screens were now flashing red.

The colonel whirled and stared. "Lord—" he gasped. He took several steps forward and leaned over the shoulder of one of the techs. They spoke for a few seconds. Then he came back.

"Egg Guardian, our distant warning systems have been tripped. There are vast disturbances in realspace all around A'Kasha System."

"Disturbances? What do you mean?"

"Something is approaching from hyperspace but is holding just before breakout."

"Something? Can't you be more specific? *What* is hiding out there?"

The colonel's expression was grim. "It's a fleet, Lord," he said. "What else could it be? It's too large to be anything else."

"A fleet?" *Damn* Ikearos. What had he brought down on A'Kasha now? "Whose fleet? From Albagens?"

The colonel turned away to watch as new data flowed quickly across half a dozen screens. He shook his head. "We have a few real-space translations now. And more coming. Picket ships, scout ships. They're not Alban."

"Don't toy with me! Do you know what they are?"

"Yes, Lord. They are Hunzza. That's the Imperial High Fleet out there."

Iskander came out of his chair. A'Kasha had kept itself as hidden from Hunzza as it had from every other race. He knew that as the empire rebuilt itself from the rubble, the legend of the

Pit of Souls, and the few who had escaped that doom, had slowly faded. Now it was nothing more than the ghost of a rumor, a tale told to frighten children.

Or it had been. He glanced at the central screen, which was still focused on the Alban ship. The five great globes that made up its necklace shape had begun to shift colors slightly. Suddenly they all flared in unison and became perfectly reflective silver.

"What is that ship doing?" he asked.

"It appears, Lord, that it is going out to meet the incoming fleet. It has raised its shields."

"One ship?" Iskander said, awed. "Against all of the imperial Hunzzan power?"

"It appears so," the colonel replied. "That's some ship."

6

"I can still feel it," Outsider said.

"Yes, I can, too," Jim replied.

"It worries me. Whatever it is, it is immensely strong. You say it is stronger than you are."

"I think so."

"What if it interferes while we use the *Pride* to attack that Hunzzan fleet?"

"I haven't decided yet whether to attack," Jim told him.

"What? Don't be ridiculous. There's only one possible reason for it to be here: us. Or at least what it thinks is us." Outsider paused. "I can see your logic, though. Even if they destroy the *Pride*, we can't be harmed. We're in the arrays, and the arrays are in Sol System."

"Which is now surrounded by a similar fleet from Alba," Jim said. "If Terra is destroyed, then so are the arrays. And so are we."

"You know that Alban fleet can't touch us. We could initiate the Leap spiral immediately. The singularity would take only moments to form. Nothing could touch us once the singularity exists."

"No," Jim said. "I'm not ready to do that yet."

"Then what *are* you ready to do? We have all the subjective time we need, of course. But events do continue on in proper time—and the real problem is still with us. That other."

"It's what the A'Kashans worship," Jim told him. "What Harpy called the God."

"There are no gods," Outsider said. "There are only patterns, information encoded by natural selection. Just like the patterns encoded in Harpalaos's DNA. You watched the process of activation. You know."

As a matter of course, Outsider had invaded and taken over all of the A'Kashan data-processing systems as soon as the *Pride* had entered A'Kasha System. While Jim's "body" sat in a cell, its arms holding Char, Jim had watched Harpalaos's transformation through the observation systems in the Circle chamber.

"I know," Jim replied. "That's the key to this whole thing, you understand. What Harpy became. Why he became it."

"Do you understand the key yet?"

"Only partially. It's almost as if something is revealing itself to me bit by bit. Maybe hoping not to shock me or frighten me. As an adult would teach a child an unpleasant truth. Or a truth too large for the child's mind to understand all at once."

"Neither you nor I are children."

"Maybe to something else we are."

Outsider snorted. "To what would we be like children?"

"To a god?" Jim said.

7

"**A**re you all right?" Jim said.

Char stirred in his arms. Her eyelids fluttered. "I think so. It's over. I can't feel him anymore." She stared up at him. "I think he's dead. Oh, Jim, it was *awful*. I've never felt anything like it. He was still screaming . . . at the end."

Jim sighed and released her. He stood up and slouched toward the door of the cell.

"I don't think he's dead," Jim said at last. "He's changed. Maybe a lot of what he used to be is gone, or altered so greatly it's no longer him, but Harpy still exists. Maybe what he is now is the real Harpy. And the one we knew was only a precursor."

"A precursor? What are you raving about? Harpy was Harpy. Either he's still alive or he isn't. Spare me the metaphysical bullshit, please."

He grinned. "Char the practical. Char the pragmatic. Let me touch it and feel it, and I'll tell you what it is."

She sat up straighter. "Don't you frigging condescend to me, you bastard. I am what I am. I've got a mind. My mind *exists*! And so does reality. There's nothing mystical about reality."

He was silent for a moment, then turned to face her. "You're right, of course. But there's room in reality for a lot of things that look mystical. You can trust what your mind tells you, Char—as long as you remember that you may not know everything about reality itself."

"And you do, I suppose?"

"I know more than you do. I know that the physical world encompasses far more than human brains and human thoughts."

"I really don't want to talk about it, Jim. I know you aren't—hell, I don't even know what you *are* anymore. But if Harpy is still alive, I want to do something about it. I want you to do something if you can. Can you?"

"I'm working on it," he said, though his tone was vague, dismissive.

"And what about all the rest of this crap? In case you haven't noticed, this is a cell we're sitting in. You're in contact with the *Pride* somehow, aren't you?"

He nodded.

"Well, how long are you going to let this crap continue? Everybody kept telling me how powerful the *Pride* is. So why hasn't somebody come down to get us out of this cage? And Korkal— what about him?"

"Korkal's fine. He's taking a nap at the moment. It isn't the first jail he's found himself in."

She stood up to face him, her movements jerky and restless. One by one she popped all her knuckles as Jim winced.

"God, don't do that," he said.

"A little knuckle cracking bothers the big bad mind machine guy?" she replied.

"I think it's somewhere in the basic codes." He grinned. "I'm still human, Char. It's hard to explain, but—" He paused. "But I can show you. Sit down again."

"Huh?"

"Go on, sit down."

She stared at him, then returned to her cot. He came to stand before her, facing her. "Hold still," he said as he reached out and placed his palms on either side of her skull.

"Hey, wait a minute! Is this like what Outsider did to you? I don't want any part of—"

"Hush," he said softly, and closed his eyes.

She gawped at him, suddenly silent, though her lips still moved. Then her eyes rolled back in her skull until only the whites showed. She began to quiver.

The cell door slid open with a soft humming sound. Two Hunzza Circle guardsmen stood beyond, flanking a small, wizened old Hunzza riding on a float-chair. The chair scooted through the doorway.

"Stop that!" Ikearos said. "It's not time yet, and you're only making matters worse."

Startled, Jim released Char, who stopped

shaking and collapsed limply onto the cot, then sat up again, dazed and blinking. He turned to face the ancient Egg Guardian.

"You're Harpy's father," he said. "Who Speaks for the God."

"There's another who would debate you about that, but as it turns out, he's wrong and you're right," Ikearos said tartly. "So you know who I am and what I am. But do you know who you are and what you are?"

Jim raised his head. The two guards eyed him, their weapons ready, but didn't move.

"I think so," he said finally. "Do you have any opinions on the question?"

"No. I have knowledge. You are He Who Changes. And as to *what* you are, I intend to tell you that shortly. But first, Changer, we need to undo some of the things you've already changed. Your ignorance is appalling. But it's not too late."

"Are you Speaking for your God now?"

Ikearos glanced at Char's huddled shape. "No more than that one is Speaking for you, Changer. At least she isn't yet. But there is much history, ancient history, and it's time you knew about it. Come!"

He turned and floated out of the cell. Jim started to follow, then paused. "What about her? What about your son and the Alban captain, Korkal Emut Denai?"

"Those are some of the things that need changing." He glared at Jim. "Well, are you coming or not?"

"I'm coming," Jim said.

CHAPTER SEVENTEEN

1

"**W**hat?" Jim could sense Outsider's agitation.

"The old Hunzza. What's he doing? I'm getting that feeling of blockage when I try to probe anything about him."

"Yes, he's being guarded, I think. By what he Speaks for."

"I don't like this. But I can't seem to do anything about it. Can you?"

"I don't want to. I think we're about to be shown something new. Another piece of the puzzle," Jim replied.

"Puzzles. You act like this is a game."

"No. Be patient. I see more of the patterns than you do."

"I know. That makes me nervous, too," Outsider said. "Where is he taking the girl and your construct?"

"I don't know. I can't penetrate whatever is guarding him, either."

"Jim, be careful."

"It's only a construct."

"It's a way into where *we* are. If something wants to take it . . ."

"I'm going to devote more attention to it. Can you handle the Hunzzan fleet?"

"Yes. For a while, at least. If we become fully engaged, I may need your help."

"All right."

"Watch yourself! If you feel the construct succumbing to an outside force, destroy it. Cut the links."

"Yes. I will."

"Remember, we—our real selves—could be at risk."

"We already are," Jim replied.

2

Jim and Char followed Ikearos's float-chair down long hallways, penetrating ever deeper into the center of the ancient structure that housed the Circle chamber at its heart. Finally they reached a small iron door. Ikearos withdrew a metal key from his robe and inserted it into a lock-slot on the door. Jim heard a soft click. The door opened inward, and Ikearos floated on through.

"Wait at the door," Ikearos told his two guards after Jim and Char had followed him in. As they penetrated further into the darkened chamber, lights began to come on, hard and yellow, casting harsh shadows. *Incandescent lights? An iron door?* Jim thought. *How old is this place?*

As if hearing his thoughts, Ikearos said, "This is the Old Library. It was built by Darod the First, brother of the ill-fated Emperor Araxos, who perished in the creation of the God. This room is over five thousand years old. Most of what it contains is stored on hard media that are not connected to any data net. These are artifacts, young Jim. There are even paper books here, preserved in rare gases."

Jim sniffed. The air smelled of must and dust. As the lights brightened further, he saw that the room was broad and high. All of the walls were covered with shelves and drawers and other cubbies. Several tables were stationed about, flanked by chairs suitable for scholars.

"What do you keep here?" Jim asked.

"Darod was my ancestor in the direct line. He took this world as a refuge from what he knew was to come. He had warned his brother against interfering with the nascent God, but Araxos wouldn't listen. So Darod knew that a great disaster approached for Hunzza as it was then, and he made the Pit of Souls as a warning and a memory—for he didn't know if even he and his own people would survive what he knew was coming. He set out to make an archive concerning everything he knew or suspected, in case others in the future might need such knowledge. We have added to that store for five millennia now, but this is the first. This is the oldest. Here are the deepest secrets."

Ikearos broke off and glided to the left-hand wall. He worked a crude-looking button pad. The door to a small compartment slid aside, and he reached into it. He took out a small object and brought it to the nearest table.

"Secrets like this," he said.

Jim and Char followed him to the table. Jim stared at the thing Ikearos had brought. "Can I touch it?" he said.

"Of course. It's old, but it isn't delicate."

Jim picked up the plastic holocube and turned it in the light. As he showed it to Char, whose eyebrows rose sharply as she looked at it, Ikearos returned to the cubby and dredged out more artifacts.

"It's a holo of an ancient human," Char said. "A cave man. What did they call them? Nee-under . . . under . . . ?"

"Neanderthal," Jim said. "A branch of the human tree that withered and died thirty thousand years ago, for reasons we still don't understand."

He glanced at Ikearos, who had piled his load onto the tabletop. "I've seen this before, or something like it. Korkal had a copy of one he'd found in old archives maintained on Albagens Prime. He thought that maybe even the Pack-lord didn't know about it. Do you know what it is? What it means?"

Ikearos nodded. "Yes. Do you?"

Jim closed his eyes for a moment, remembering. "It's at the heart of what is happening now, isn't it? Do you know what has happened to your son?"

Ikearos made a soft hissing sound. Then he reached into the jumble on the table and withdrew another old holocube. "Yes," he said, and handed it to Jim.

From the plastic a strange, hump-shouldered

figure, thick and broad, covered in skin and scales, stared calmly out from beneath a heavily ridged brow. Jim shivered. Those eyes were five thousand years dead, but it seemed to him they watched him still today. Somehow . . .

"This isn't Harpy, is it?"

Ikearos clicked his teeth. "Yes, it is. The first Harpalaos. Darod's son. The Bringer of the Deadly Dawn."

Jim showed it to Char, who winced. "Is this what Harpy's been turned into?" She looked away. "Oh, shit, that's *awful.*"

Jim said nothing, but continued to stare at the unmoving form. Finally he set it down. "How long ago did the gene pools mingle?"

Ikearos nodded, as if Jim's question satisfied him somehow. "Thirty thousand years ago, long before the first Hunzzan Empire existed, my people were in their first surge of exploration out from the home systems. One ship happened across a system where a single planet teemed with life. They investigated long enough to determine that the planet held little interest for Hunzza. It was quite primitive—the dominant species were primates, with several strains vying for dominance. They performed routine testing and discovered a curious thing. One of the two primary strains didn't communicate by speech. The other, a smaller, quicker, more vicious race, did use words."

Jim stared at him. "How did the first strain communicate?"

"Telepathy," Ikearos said. "But a primitive telepathic race will take much longer to develop a discrete language. They have no need, since they can communicate so easily in feelings and mind pictures. So they will be slower to develop a high technology, because they cannot bequeath permanent records. They will be dependent on the memories they pass down to each other. On the other hand, they will be able to understand each other better. The scientists on the Hunzzan expedition thought they saw an interesting possibility."

"Yes, they would," Jim said. "It's obvious. At their technological level, they must have known about genetic surgery."

"By our standards only crudely, but yes. Remember, Hunzza had not yet made her empire. Many worlds struggled against each other for dominance. This ship was not from Hunzza Prime, but from a colony world. They thought they saw a chance to give their own people an advantage over all the rest. They were already technological, and if this telepathic ability could somehow be inserted into their racial plasm, it would give them a great advantage against all the other Hunzzan worlds."

"So they took samples, didn't they?"

"Yes," Ikearos replied. "Enough to establish a breeding colony. And then, in order to make certain no rivals happened across this discovery, they released a virus tailored to certain distinctive features of this primate strain's DNA. By the time they left with their precious cargo, that race was already dying out."

"Wait a minute," Char broke in. "Are you saying it was *Terra* that Hunzzan ship visited? And it killed off these . . . Neanderthals?"

"Yes," Ikearos said. "It was your home world."

"What happened then?" Jim asked.

"The ship returned to its own cluster and began a larger experiment. A barren world was seeded with these captives, in order to provide a dependable source for their experiments. Over many years they tried to blend elements of the primate plasm into the Hunzzan genetic structure. They were only partly successful, and finally they gave up the effort. The seed colony was infected with the same viral killer that had destroyed its predecessors, and abandoned. Even its location was forgotten. Things continued on."

"The viral killer didn't work, did it?" Jim said slowly.

"No, but it would take another twenty-five thousand years to learn that," Ikearos replied. "I imagine it did kill most of the colony, but some must have survived and continued to breed. It took a very long time for these people to develop language and finally ascend the technological ladder to become a spacefaring race. By then, they were nothing more than a backwater planet on the fringes of the First Empire."

Jim tapped the holo of the blended Neanderthal-Hunzza, the first Harpalaos. "You said the Hunzza were only partially successful, and they eventually abandoned the project. But they were more successful than they knew, evidently."

"Much more. They did succeed in altering the Hunzzan DNA—but the alterations were subtle and not dominant. So over the centuries, and then the millennia, the descendants of that experiments gradually began to grow. Their power was the ability to create a gestalt, though they didn't know this consciously. They just knew they could somehow sense which way the racial wind was blowing. You have a word for it?"

"Yes," Jim said. "Zeitgeist. A general racial agreement. A shared understanding of what the world is. I can imagine that the ability to consciously tap into that would be an advantage."

"It was," Ikearos replied. "Because the trait was not dominant, it took a very long time to make its way throughout all the scattered Hunzza protoempires. But those who possessed it most strongly began to dominate those who didn't. Finally, when the First Empire was formed almost twenty thousand years later, the royal line possessed it in abundance. And it lay dormant in most of the rest of the race. Only about ten percent of the entire Hunzza strain did not have it. Of course, in most it didn't manifest as a conscious ability, but it did in some—particularly the imperial line."

He paused, then took another holo from the relics on the table. "There. That is Araxos and his younger brother, Darod. Darod had the reputation of having the gift of Foretelling. He was his brother's closest advisor, all the more valuable because Araxos evidently had no trace of the gift himself. That happened, even in the royal family."

"A recessive trait," Jim murmured.

"Which was too bad for Araxos. And much of the rest of Hunzza, too," Ikearos said. "When an obscure planetary system on the fringes of the empire suddenly began to show gross astronomical changes—*impossible* changes—he followed the other great Hunzzan trait, aggression. We have always been a race whose first instinct is to smash anything we can't understand."

"The planet was the colony seeded before, of course," Jim said. "A Neanderthal world. A world of beings capable of linking their minds together."

"A planet named Gelden," Ikearos said. "I don't know how they did it, or why, but something happened, and they became what we now call a Leaper. Their power suddenly spiraled and became enormous. Darod sensed it and warned Araxos of it, but Araxos wouldn't listen. Following his own deepest instincts—the Hunzzan urge toward violence and aggression—he tried to smash it instead."

"And it smashed him," Jim said softly, trying to imagine it.

"Yes. It was the God, and it smashed him. And a son was born to Darod, whom he named Harpalaos because the God told him to. Harpalaos grew to adulthood as a monster, a blend of the God-people and Hunzza. And one day all Hunzza woke to dawn with Harpalaos in their thoughts. For about one in ten of them, it was the last thing they *ever* thought. And so his name came to mean 'Bringer of the Deadly Dawn.' It was the last act of the God's vengeance. If vengeance was what it was."

"Why?" Jim asked. "Why one in ten? Why that?"

Ikearos sighed. "It is the God. I can never know. But I can guess. Those who died were like Araxos. They didn't possess the gene, even dormant. They were pure Hunzza, responding always to their primary survival trait—wild aggression. It was this trait that had tried to destroy the God as it was being born. So the God simply . . . eliminated . . . it from the race. And, of course, destroyed the First Empire in the process."

Jim wandered away from the table, then paused, his eyes closed, deep in thought. "But why, Ikearos? Why now? You keep talking about a God. Surely you don't mean it. It was a race—a branch of the human race."

"But I do mean it, Jim. Whatever it was once, it's a God now. And I don't know what it means, because it hasn't told me. Why do you think I sent my own son to Terra? Because I *knew* the connection. I *knew* that the ancestors of the God had come from somewhere; I just didn't know where. But as soon as news of Terra began to filter out from Alba, I knew what it was. And then my own spies began to report of the Packlord's worries. So I sent my son to find out what he could—breaking our own prime directive of pacifism."

"Why?" Jim said.

"Because the God *did* tell me to do it," he said. "Not why. Just what. Send my son."

He looked up from his chair, a film coming across his eyes. "And now my son is changed into a destroyer not seen for five thousand years. When I gave him his birth name, I didn't know how true it was. I thought it was my own choice. Obviously it wasn't."

"Harpy?" Char said. "Harpy is a *destroyer*? That's ridiculous."

Ikearos stared at her somberly. "Five thousand years ago, his direct ancestor destroyed one tenth of the Hunzzan race. Nearly a trillion beings. And did it in the space of a single dawn. Now that power has returned. It is among us. The destroyer is my son."

Jim said, "You know what it wants me to have, don't you? What your God wants?"

Ikearos nodded and withdrew a final small bit from the relics. He handed it to Jim. "It's an ancient chip, but I'm sure you'll be able to decode it."

Jim turned the small bit of plastic and metal in his hand. "Yes, since evidently everything about my life has been twisted to lead to this very moment. It would be a joke, wouldn't it, if I couldn't understand what your God wants me to know."

"What? What is it?" Char said.

Jim raised the chip so she could see. "These are the coordinates. The greatest secret in this galaxy."

"Yes," Ikearos said. "The location of Gelden. The home of the God."

A sudden commotion in the doorway caught their attention. They turned. A troop of guards poured into the room. A Hunzza wearing robes of shifting colors followed them in.

"Egg Guar—!" He paused, began again. "Ikearos," Iskander said.

"Nest Watcher," Ikearos replied.

"No longer. I am Egg Guardian now. You

have forfeited your office. Through treason, if nothing else. But it looks like madness to me. What are you doing? Our most ancient secrets, revealed to . . . to these . . ."

"Careful, Iskander. You don't know what you're meddling in."

For a moment they locked gazes. Then Iskander looked away. "Take them all!" he hissed. "Return the Terrans to their cell. And take Ikearos to the cell prepared for him."

Iskander turned back to Ikearos. "You've gone too far," he said. "You know the price."

Ikearos nodded as the guards came forward. "I know the price," he said. "But do you?"

Jim slipped the chip into his pocket as the guards led him away.

3

The door to their cell slid shut behind them. Char whirled. "Well, what now, genius? We got to see all that dusty old junk, and to meet Harpy's father. Who doesn't seem very nice, either. And now we're back here, and that head guy acts like he's real unhappy with us." She stopped and placed her hands on her hips. "Do you have any idea at all what you're doing?"

"A better one now than I did, Char." He moved over to one cot and sat down.

"That's it? That's all you're gonna say?" She seemed close to tears. Jim couldn't tell if it was sadness for Harpy or just anger over their situation. Char was volatile. Almost as volatile as . . .

He closed his eyes.

4

"**I** don't have any way to read the chip," Jim said. "My artifact isn't equipped."

Outsider said, "We're in position to initiate engagement with the Hunzzan fleet. Do you want me to handle that, or do you want to take over?"

"I don't want to engage at all. Are the modifications finished on the *Pride*'s transporters?"

"Yes."

"All right. Bring us all back."

"You're sure? You really want to do this?"

"Yes," Jim said. "I do."

5

Iskander was determined not to make the same mistake a second time. He had no idea how Ikearos had managed to elude the watch set on him and wander freely through the halls—and cells—of the building. This time he made sure there would be continuous observa-

tion on everybody concerned. A bank of holoscreens in his office remained constantly
focused on the Alban captain, as well as
Harpalaos, his father, and the two Terrans,
while he tried to make sense of what the Hunzzan fleet and the big Alban ship were doing. And
so he didn't notice the change in the cells until
a moment or so after it had begun. By then it
was too late.

"What's *that*?" he asked of nobody in particular.

He pointed at the holoscreens. In all the
cells, a dim white light, like a nimbus, had
appeared around each occupant. The Alban
was looking up at the ceiling of his cell, as if the
light came from there, but it didn't.

It was discrete, hovering around each form,
now growing stronger and brighter. Iskander
sucked in his breath. "The cells! Open them up
and get them out of there!"

But before his orders could be acted on, the
shapes of the prisoners began to waver, as if
underwater.

"Hurry!" he shouted.

But the guards managed to get only the door
to Ikearos's cell open. Iskander saw it, just as
he saw Ikearos himself fade away entirely. The
guards rushed in as the white light vanished.
They stood gaping, with puzzled looks on their
faces, staring at the spot where Ikearos had
been. But he was gone.

So were the others.

6

"**A**s you can see," Outsider said, "the Hunzza have us entirely englobed. In theory, we should be unable to escape into hyperspace."

Jim let himself flow entirely into the arrays, meshing each individual link together into the unimaginable power of the full gestalt of a billion brains.

"In theory only," he replied as he took full control of every system on the *Albagens Pride*.

7

"**I** don't know, Your Majesty," the grand admiral of the fleet said to Tharson when he reported his failure a short time later. "Once we had the Alban ship fully englobed, the disturbances created in hyperspace by our own drives and shielding should have prevented the vessel from escaping. But it didn't."

"Then you failed," Tharson said. His tone was unforgiving.

"Yes, Majesty. But so did everything we know about naval battle tactics. Whatever else the *Albagens Pride* did, it managed to rewrite pretty much everything we know about space and hyperspace. What they did should have been impossible. By the Seven Cold Hells, it *was* impossible."

The emperor, no scientist, was unimpressed.

"Obviously not impossible. They did it."

The grand admiral sighed and bowed his head. "Yes, Majesty, they did it."

8

Korkal was pleased to find himself back in his own quarters aboard the *Pride*. He'd been incarcerated for days, cut off from any knowledge of what was going on beyond his own cramped chamber. Then, suddenly, the white nimbus had appeared around him. He recognized the strange glow from having seen it before—on Terra, just before Harpalaos, Char, and Jim had mysteriously vanished from an otherwise empty Terraport street. And so he wasn't entirely surprised when his cell vanished from around him and, after a moment of twisting darkness, the familiar sight of his own rooms suddenly appeared.

A moment later he saw the shimmering shapes of Ikearos, some sort of monstrously mutated Hunzza, Char, and Jim coalesce out of thin air. When everything seemed entirely solid, he cleared his throat. "Welcome to the *Albagens Pride*," he said.

The door to the room slid open and Outsider strode through. "Yes," he said. "Welcome aboard." He turned to Korkal. "If you would make our new guests comfortable, we can get on with things."

Korkal offered an ironic half bow. "Things

that are, I suppose, beyond our poor mortal ken?"

Outsider stared at him. "I see. A joke."

Korkal restrained a grin.

"Sit down, everybody, please," Jim said. He saw Char staring at the thing Harpy had become, her expression nearly impossible to describe.

"Harpy?" she whispered.

Harpalaos nodded slightly. "Yes, I was the one you knew."

Char burst into tears.

Korkal glanced at Outsider. "Where are we now, exactly?"

"Thirty light-years from A'Kasha . . . and the Hunzzan fleet there."

"Fleet?" Korkal had heard nothing about any fleet. Well, if it was thirty light-years away, it wasn't an immediate problem.

"And where are we bound?" he continued.

"A place called Gelden. Or it was called that once."

Harpy made a soft, grunting sound, as if somebody had just kicked him in the belly. He turned to stare at his father. "You knew, didn't you, Father? You knew all along?"

Silently Ikearos nodded.

"Why didn't you lead the Circle? I'd have thought you would have wished to observe the final results of your . . ." He glanced down at his misshapen body. "Your handiwork."

"I would have," Iskander said, his voice barely a whisper. "But the God showed mercy. It was not for me to do."

"Mercy," Harpy said, his voice musing. "This is mercy?"

"I think," Ikearos replied, "it is as much mercy as the God will offer."

"Then the God is terrible," Harpy said.

"Yes," Iskander replied. "It is terrible. It is a god."

9

The reports from spies with the Hunzzan fleet poured into the Packlord's intelligence gathering systems, were evaluated, ranked, and passed directly on to him.

He sat in his rooms and sipped his tea, the comforting warmth of the spicy liquid only partially assuaging the sense of loss he felt.

The *Pride* had escaped the entire might of the Imperial Hunzzan Navy. Another impossibility, but there it was. It was all the proof he needed about whether Jim Endicott was in charge of the ship. He could imagine nobody else able to pull off that sort of apparently magical escape. And he didn't believe in magic.

Now he was completely at a loss. Where was the Endicott boy going? What did he and the mysterious Outsider plan to do? How might it affect Terra? Alba? The Leaper?

He didn't know. But he could take no more chances. He waited while the proper communications links were set up. Then he gave his orders.

He repeated them so that there could be no mistake.

"Do not attempt anything other than destruction. Use sun-poppers. If you begin immediately, how long before Terra's sun goes nova?"

The answer worried him. It seemed like a long time. He wondered what Jim could do with that much time. Nothing, he hoped.

Well, life was a gamble.

When Sol went nova in twelve hours, he would know whether he had won or lost. He raised his tea and sipped again.

Friendship is not a suicide pact, he reassured himself. But somehow that mantra didn't soothe him. Nothing did.

He thought about Serena Half Moon. And waited. Twelve hours to go. Poor Serena. Poor Terra. Poor him. Poor everybody.

10

When he had their attention again, Jim said, "Our estimated time of arrival in Gelden System is eleven hours from now."

CHAPTER EIGHTEEN

1

In the world of proper time, in the world of flesh and blood, the Gelden singularity was a twist of nothingness that tugged and pulled at vision. Jim watched it in two ways: through the eyes of his construct, and from inside the arrays, where it looked entirely different.

"Gelden," he said.

"Look at the patterns," Outsider replied.

Life. Information coded by natural selection. Inside the arrays, that was the kind of life he was. Patterns on patterns, form not separated from content, but form that *was* content in itself.

I code information, therefore I am, he thought.

From his vantage point in the arrays, the black hole that occupied the space where Gelden System had once been now appeared as spinning patterns that described the paths that light made as it tried, and just barely failed, to escape the pull of gravity. Where light stopped was the strange, shifting form of the singularity's event horizon.

Through the eyes of his construct, he saw a muddy, hazy blob, an area that first appeared darker than the space surrounding it—until his brain realized it wasn't simple darkness, but an utter absence of light.

To his human eyes, the singularity was impenetrable and unknowable. But with the inhuman awareness he possessed inside the arrays, he observed that the entire spinning surface of the thing was bubbling with a fine mist of particle-antiparticle pairs created in the empty space that coated the event horizon like the rind of an orange. The overall effect was as if the black hole was emitting radiation, gamma and X rays, though it really wasn't—only the space around it was.

"The Alban fleet around Terra has initiated an attempt to destroy Sol System," Outsider announced suddenly. "We are threatened, Jim. If the human minds that make up the arrays are destroyed, we will be, too."

"We have an hour of proper time before Sol goes nova," Jim said. "That's an enormous amount of our own subjective time."

"Nevertheless, the threat is real, and in proper time it will culminate quite shortly."

"What would you have me do?"

"Initiate the human singularity," Outsider said. "Just like here. Just like what Gelden did, five thousand years ago. It's inevitable, anyway. The fact that you and I exist as we do makes it inevitable."

Jim moved his patterns of his existence closer to the Gelden singularity. "No," he said at last. "This . . . God . . . wanted me here. I think it went to a great deal of trouble to arrange this moment. Perhaps my entire life was only a part of that arrangement. You know I've always felt that everything about me was being manipulated by something beyond my understanding. At first I thought it was you. Then I thought it was my real mother, Kate. But maybe it was this. If so, there must be a reason. I want to know what it is."

"How do you propose to find out?"

Jim felt his resolve growing. To know. At last, to *know*!

"I'm going into it. Through the event horizon. Into the singularity itself."

"You're *mad*! You can't ever get back."

"I think I can," Jim said.

2

Jim's construct slowly mounted the steps to the captain's chair. Overhead, disconcertingly visible through the great dome above Command Deck, the black hole covered half the space beyond. Those who stared at it too long began to feel queasy and disoriented. Minds using flesh and blood as their substrates were not built to gaze on true nothingness for very long.

"Come with me, Char," he said. "And you, Harpy." He gestured toward a pair of chairs that had been installed next to the captain's seat.

Harpy nodded and started up the steps, but Char balked. "Why? What do you need me for?"

"I may need you to Speak for me," he said.

"Oh, man, that is such *bullshit*," she said. "I have no idea what you're *talking* about."

"Then humor me." He stared down at her. "Char, I need your help."

Her lips tightened. "And that's reason enough, huh? You *need* it, so I have to *give* it. You don't understand me very well, do you, buddy?"

"We're talking about payment here, aren't we? A quid pro quo. Okay, how's this? Without your help, it's very likely that in less than an hour almost the entire human race—everybody in Sol System—will die. Except for those few humans scattered outside of the system, you'll be alone. You can't even count on me. I'm not really human, not the way you think of it, not anymore."

Her face went blank a moment. But then she said, "So? I've never been much of a crowd person. Pretty much a loner, in fact. And unlike you, altruism has never rung my bell. You're the one with the world-saver complex. That isn't me."

Harpy reached the top of the steps. "Which chair?" he rumbled.

"Take the right one," Jim told him. Harpy nodded, lumbered to it, seated himself, and rested his hands in his lap. Fatalistic acceptance whispered from every movement he made. *Of course,* Jim thought. *He is in the presence of his God. How else would he act?*

But Char wasn't in the presence of her God. Or at least she didn't think so.

"So I have to pay you," he said to her. "Very well. What's your price?"

She folded her arms across her chest. "What's my risk?"

There was a time when, for the greater good, for humanity, even for *her* own good, Jim might have lied to her. But he couldn't, not now. Tricking her into joining him would be as great a crime as dragging her by force, against her will, up onto the dais with him. He sighed.

"I don't know," he said. "Maybe nothing. Or maybe you die."

She nodded. "Then I can't say what my price is, can I?"

"I guess not."

Impasse. They stared at each other.

Finally he nodded. "Can I show you, then?"

"Show me what?"

"I started to, before. But Ikearos interrupted us."

"When you put your hands on my head?" She grimaced. "No, thanks. I didn't like that feeling at all. I passed out, didn't I? For a little while?"

"Just a few seconds," he said. "Before you translated fully. Before you saw what you were meant to see. Before you understood what you were meant to understand."

"*Meant?* More mystical bullshit, Jim. I'm not buying today. Sorry."

He took the first step down, his eyes locked on hers. "Not mystical. Real. What you were made for."

Her gaze narrowed warily, but she stood her ground. "People aren't made for anything, Jim. People are what they are. And that's all they are."

"True," he said, and took another step. "You are what you are. But what you think you are isn't what you really are. I warned you. I told you."

He took another step. She glared at him but remained icily still, though her back had gone rigid.

"I was made for something," he said softly. "My mother made me. We would not be here today, facing each other, if she had not made me into something different almost eighteen years ago."

He raised one hand. A holoscreen suddenly appeared in the air between them. He gestured again. Codes began to loop crazily across the screen. The motion was dizzying to watch. But after a moment it slowed, then stopped. Several lines were frozen across the top of the screen.

"A section of my altered DNA. Now, watch."

More codes appeared, spun, stopped. They were markedly different from the codes above. "Normal human DNA." He took the final step down and stopped, two paces from her, facing her. "And the third," he said.

When the final row of codes appeared, he said, "Look at them. My codes, normal codes, and . . . your codes."

He waved his hand. The middle codes vanished. The top and bottom codes slid over each other, meshing and merging. There was no discontinuity. They slipped together perfectly. They were identical.

"My mother made me, Char. But humanity itself—a billion years of evolution—made *you*."

Her features crumpled as she stared at the holoscreen. "It's a lie," she whispered.

"You know it isn't," he told her.

And in the space where he really existed, where only a small part of him observed the scene on the *Pride*'s Command Deck through the eyes of his construct, he felt Outsider's shock as a nearly tangible disturbance in his larger reality.

Eventually Outsider asked, "How long have you known?"

"Known? For sure? Not until this very moment, when I scanned her codes. But I've suspected for a good while. Ikearos did, too. He said she would Speak for me."

Outsider's dismay was like a palpable force, battering him. Jim braced himself against that gale and weathered it. "If only I had known," Outsider said.

"Which is why I didn't check on her. Not before. There was too much risk you would discover the truth. And I couldn't trust you. In your obsessive zeal to protect humanity, you've lost your own humanity. Unable to control me, you would have tried to force her. You would have dragged her into the arrays by main force. And you would have destroyed her, yourself, and the arrays as well."

"Ridiculous. I could have dominated her."

"No. Look at her codes. They're identical to mine. She would defeat you as easily as I can. But she would hate you as she did it, and she would destroy the arrays in order to destroy you. You are a fool, Outsider, though you think you aren't."

"I am a fool? And what are you?"

"I am a tool," Jim told him. "I was made before I was born, by a conscious act of will on the part of my mother. But Char? I don't know what she is."

Outsider's answering chuckle was cold with bitterness. "You don't see it? That's strange. It seems obvious enough to me. You even said it to her."

"I said what?"

"You told her she was the product of a billion years of evolution. But so are you. That same billion years produced your mother, and your mother's brain, and the mind that created the codes in your DNA. You both came from the same river and reached the same destination. Your methods of travel just differed a bit. But not enough to make any real difference. Free will, Jim, eh? What a joke that is. Eh? Eh?"

So it was with Outsider's wheezing, windy, heartless laughter roaring in his mind that Jim saw the final bit of the puzzle, the one that unlocked all the doors, that superimposed a great pattern on all the rest.

On the Command Deck, his construct took a final step and clamped his hands on either side of Char's head. "Don't you want to *know* what you are?" he said.

Her gaze darted from him to the holoscreen and back again. She tensed and screamed into his face: "Then I'm a puppet, just like you are. I hate it! And I hate you!"

He dropped his hands from her head and enfolded her in his arms. She went stiff, then suddenly relaxed, sobbing quietly. "I'm so . . . afraid," she whispered.

"I know . . . I know," he soothed. "But you don't have to be. I know what you fear. I used to fear it, too. But not any longer."

He put his cheek against hers, against her smooth skin. "But I can't tell you. I can only show you."

For a long time they stood like that, pressed against each other, *leaning* on each other, the only two humans of their kind in the whole universe.

Finally she moved her lips against his ear. "Will you show me?"

"Is that what you want? Truly want?"

"Yes . . ."

"Then I will."

He released her and slowly raised his palms until they cupped her skull again.

"It will be all right," he whispered.

They went away.

3

A black hole, defined by Stephen Hawking and Roger Penrose as a set of events from which it is not possible to escape to a large distance, is a function of mass. The greater the mass of the singularity, the larger the event horizon. The universe itself can be thought of as a gigantic black hole, with everything knowable existing inside it and nothing able to escape it. And if a black hole is very large, passing across its event horizon may be nearly unnoticeable—except that, once having crossed that horizon, one can never return back across it.

"Take my hands," Jim's construct said to Char and Harpy.

"How much time is left for Sol?" Jim asked Outsider, who was keeping track of such things so that Jim would not be distracted from his larger concerns.

"Twelve minutes of proper time," Outsider told him.

"I'm going into the singularity," Jim said. "Be ready to initiate the Terran Leap if I don't return in time."

"I'm ready. Even if you do return, I don't see how it will make any difference. The destruction of Terra is inevitable unless the Leap begins and humanity enters its own singularity."

"I know," Jim said.

"You've changed, Jim. You seem calm. Remote." Outsider paused. "Like me."

Jim thought of what he'd said to Char, that he really wasn't human anymore. The full import of understanding smashed into him then, as he contemplated what he really was: a vast web of patterns, of arrangements of information, spread throughout array space, which was really *mind* space. All of that information encoded as a result of the experience of his own—and a billion other—minds, each experience shaped by interaction with reality, but preserved in the patterns alone. The patterns that *survived*. Like natural selection.

I'm not human, he thought in dismay. *I'm alive, but I'm not human. Have I ever been human?*

Outsider was right.

His own patterns enveloped the denser, deeper patterns that made up the Gelden singularity, the God in the black hole. He became a fog of hope, breaking on a rock of knowledge.

Dimly he felt Char's fingers in his left hand and Harpy's larger, rougher fingers in his right. He drew their patterns, his own, and the vast pattern of the mind arrays tighter about the corpus of the God and sank them all past the singularity's event horizon, into the dark, unknown, unknowable heart of it all.

Humanity had ten minutes left to live.

3

Nothing made of matter can long endure the forces that hold sway in the heart of a black hole. At its very center lies the singularity, a single point where even the laws of space and time shatter and vanish into the quantum soup. But the patterns of the mind arrays weren't matter. They were merely shapes imprinted on the fabric of space-time, the way a bowling ball will leave an imprint on a bedspread even after the ball is taken away.

There was nothing that seemed either spectacular or final about their passage across the event horizon. One moment they were outside, and the next inside. But as they sank deeper within, they began to see new patterns all about: swirling, twisting lines all focused toward the center, the same sort of shapes water made as it swirled down a drain.

Deeper and deeper, then.

"Are you with me?" he said.

"I'm here," Harpy replied.

"Me too," Char said.

Jim thought she sounded subdued. Maybe she was. When he'd finally linked her to the arrays and she'd first understood her own ability to shape the patterns as he did, she'd recoiled in terror. But even in drawing back, she'd learned. She couldn't help it, being what she was.

And she'd picked up something even Jim had not considered, a knowledge perhaps implicit in her own existence as a Pleb.

"If you send mankind into the singularity, only those linked in the mind arrays will survive. Everything else—the sun, Sol System, Terra, all the other humans—will die. Only the linked ones will live."

Why hadn't he considered that? But it was too late now. "Yes," he said.

She'd decided then. "If there's another way, I want to find it. I didn't ask for this. But I have it now. My responsibility. Damn you!"

"I'm sorry . . ."

"I'm not that kind of murderer!"

He could still sense her rage, smoldering beneath her withdrawal. But she was here, with him. And so was Harpy. Just as it had been destined to be. Just as it had—

Where did that come from?

As they spun and swirled ever inward, he felt it first as a growing certainty. That everything was *all right*, that things had turned out *as they were supposed to turn out*.

At the same time, it suddenly seemed as if the power of the mind arrays was rapidly increasing. As if he was thinking faster, better, longer.

A great ripple of power suddenly flowed through him, through all of them. Straight ahead now, a prick of brilliant white light, growing, spreading—

Exploding!

4

They stood on an endless white plain made of white stone. There were faint glistening bits embedded in the stone. The stone stretched out in every direction until it vanished in a haze of distance.

Overheard was a vast expanse of glimmering darkness. He stared up in wonder. This was no night sky, no brilliant field of stars. It reminded him somehow of his first glimpse of array space, of the infinite stretch of glowing lights embedded in the actual material of space-time. But this was so much more complicated, so much denser than that.

Suddenly a series of rippling colors, red, blue, gold, purple, flashed across, just a flicker before vanishing. As he watched, it happened again. He realized it was some sort of continuous process, but many, many orders of magnitude more complex and powerful than the mind arrays.

"It is me," a soft voice said.

He looked down to see a figure approaching across the empty stone.

"Don't let go of my hands," he murmured. He felt Harpy's fingers twitch slightly, and Char's grip on his grew tighter.

The figure came up before them and halted three paces away. Broad, shorter than he, dressed in a simple white robe that couldn't disguise the powerful slope of his shoulders. Those dark brown eyes, regarding him with illimitable calm from beneath a heavy ridge of brow, seemed to glow with an inner light.

His face was broad, flat, punctuated by a wide nose with upturned nostrils. His chin receded somewhat, but not as much as his ancestors' chins had.

Neanderthal man. With thirty thousand years of evolution thrown into the mix.

Jim was surprised to discover he felt no fear, only curiosity. And at the same time he realized this, he could also sense his own powers increasing by leaps and bounds. Whatever process had begun after he entered the black hole was still going on.

"It goes on forever," the Neanderthal said. "It never stops. It is infinite. Infinity is the nature of the singularity."

Yes, Jim thought, sensing it for the first time. *That must be true.*

"Who are you?" Jim asked.

"I suppose, for lack of anything better, you may call me God."

Though a thousand questions bloomed in his mind, Jim decided not to ask them. There was only one question that mattered, after all.

"Why have you called me here?" Jim said.

"Do you know *what* I am?" God asked.

Jim stared at him, feeling his own knowledge expanding, expanding, growing without ceasing. Growing forevermore . . .

He realized that he did know.

"Yes. I do."

God inclined his head slightly. "You've attained enlightenment, then."

More and more knowledge filled him up as his understanding grew. The process wasn't painful. It was the most transcendent joy he'd ever experienced.

It was in his need to voice that joy, to sing a song of it, that he spoke what he knew.

"You will never stop. Just as I won't stop. I have become life itself, information coded on space-time by natural selection. I cannot be destroyed, even by the singularity. And as I grow closer to the singularity itself, my energy increases. I think faster and faster. The faster I think, the more time I experience from my own point of view. My subjective time. When I am close enough to the singularity, my subjective time will diverge to infinity. I will diverge to infinity. *Everything* will diverge to infinity."

God smiled gently. "Yes. You have attained enlightenment."

Revelation kept on bubbling up in him, a

never-ending geyser of joy and knowledge. "I am you. You are me. And we—"

He stopped, his head thrown back, staring at the sky.

"And we are . . . ?" God said, urging him on.

As he became a part of it, Jim saw it at last: the greatest pattern, the destiny of the universe, of life itself. For only as he reached his own infinite reach could he comprehend the infinity of the Omega Point.

"From the beginning to the end," he whispered. "Life will fill the universe and subsume the universe within itself. The universe itself will become life. And the universe is the greatest black hole. In the end it will collapse into its own singularity, taking all life with it, until all life becomes infinite. Infinite, immortal, omniscient, immanent—"

He looked at the creature before him. "Omega," he said. "And the Alpha, too, of course. And everything in between."

"Yes," God said. "The destiny of this living universe. Its destiny since the first quantum ripple in nothingness, the ripple that became the big bang. The end encompassed in that first uncertain seed."

But Jim was still growing, still expanding into the infinity that this Neanderthal, representative of a race that had leaped into the singularity and joined with the All five thousand years before, knew so well.

"It's bad, isn't it? My existence. I shouldn't have come into being at all. How could I have? How did my mother manage to do it?"

"Schrödinger's box. You understand. She flipped a coin. The result called you into being, and called me as well—thirty thousand years before she was born."

He saw it clearly then. "How long can you maintain this emulation?" he said.

A clock appeared at God's right hand. "Humanity will enter the singularity three minutes from now in proper time. Then it will end. I will end. You will end. The universe will end."

"I'd better hurry, then," Jim said.

"You have all the time in the universe," God replied.

5

They stood on the Command Deck of the *Albagens Pride*, blinking and staring at each other, still holding hands. Overhead, far away, the black hole sucked light into darkness.

Korkal stared at them. "What? Did something happen?"

Jim dropped his hands, stepped forward, and embraced the tough old Alban. "Korkal, I love you," he said.

"What? Yes, well . . . of course. I love you, too, Jim. But what . . . ?"

Jim released him and stepped away. He took Harpy and Char's hands again. "Be well, Korkal. And remember—it really *is* all for the best."

Korkal stepped forward, reaching toward them, but then he stopped. Before his foot had touched the deck again, they had vanished. He would never see any of them again.

As Jim let himself slip back into what he had become, what *all* of them had become, he knew he would never see Korkal again, either. If he failed in what he had to do, this universe would never have existed. And if he succeeded . . .

He didn't know. Only the Omega Point knew. Some infinities were infinitely larger than other infinities.

He said it again as he vanished forever from Korkal's sight. "Good-bye, old friend. Good-bye."

6

The three of them stood in a dingy hallway, gazing through a smudged glass window into the small laboratory beyond. In the lab, a large dark-haired man was standing in front of a small blond-haired woman. They seemed to be arguing about something. The woman was nervously tossing a bright silver coin back and forth between her hands.

Char stared at them.

"That's it?" she said.

"That's it," Jim replied. "Where it all began. Beginning and end. For me, for you, for Harpy. For everything."

"Explain it to me again," she said.

CHAPTER NINETEEN

1

"**I**s that your mother?" Char whispered as she watched the woman on the other side of the glass.

Jim stared, too. He couldn't help it. All he'd ever seen of her was the holotapes she'd made, when she'd sent her love to him across the long years after her death. She looked tired. But she still possessed a vivacity, a great charisma he could hardly bear to look at.

"Yes. Her name is Kate."

Harpy stirred. "Is this real?"

"Yes," Jim said. "Do you understand the principle of identity?"

"If two things are identical in *every* way, then they are the same thing," Harpy said.

"Yes. And when that occurs, one instance is an *emulation* of the other. They are the same, because they emulate identically."

"Like a computer program," Char said.

"Exactly. We don't think of a computer program as being different when it runs on two different machines. It is the same program."

"So what did you mean when you asked God how long he could maintain the emulation?" Char said. "Emulation of what?"

"Of our entire universe," Jim said. "What else would God emulate?"

"But there is only one universe."

"No, there are an enormous number of universes. But for us, and for God—the Omega Point—only one counts."

"An enormous number?"

"Yes. Every time there is a choice, anywhere in the universe, quantum mechanics dictates that the choice is made both ways. And each time that happens, a new universe is made. Physicists call this the many-worlds model. The total number of possible visible universes is very large, but a computer with a capacity of ten to the one-hundred-twenty-third power bits would be powerful enough to emulate every one of them—all at once!"

"So why are *we* here, Jim? At this time? In this place? We *are* in a different time than we were, aren't we?"

Jim nodded. "Yes. This is about eight months before I was born. My mother is carrying me at the moment. And trying to make a decision."

Harpy said, "But how does this affect us? The future? The universe?"

Jim touched the glass, still transfixed by the scene beyond. Kate was arguing with Carl. Carl, whom Jim knew he would kill in a firefight next to a burning cabin on Wolfbane seventeen years in the future from this moment. He remembered Carl bleeding, choking, gasping out his life and his love . . .

He closed his eyes for a moment.

"Albert Einstein hated quantum physics. He spent most of his life, after formulating his special and general relativity theories, trying to disprove it. But he failed. When he said, 'God doesn't play dice with the universe,' he had in mind a special example called Schrödinger's box."

"Yes, God mentioned that, too."

"It seems impossible to logic, but quantum physics isn't entirely logical. Schrödinger's box was a mind experiment: Imagine a box with a cat sealed inside. Imagine that the cat flips a coin. If the coin comes down tails, cyanide gas comes into the box and the cat dies. But if the coin comes down heads, no gas enters, and the cat lives. From the point of view of someone outside the box, without looking into the box, is the cat alive or dead?"

"Why, it's—" Char stopped. Started again. "Well, it is . . ." She shook her head. "I don't know."

Jim grinned. "One of the possibilities inherent in quantum physics says that the cat is neither dead nor alive. More accurately, it is *both* dead and alive. But in separate universes."

"And so?" Char said.

"This entire universe, the one we know, is a gigantic emulation maintained by the Gelden Leaper. The Neanderthal is a subset of the Omega Point, the life at the end of time. Of God, actually. Its computing power is more than enough to maintain a single universe. And it is doing so for a single reason: So that I can come here and try to change the outcome of the coin flip my mother is about to make."

"That silver one?"

"Yes. She altered my DNA, changed it and hid codes in it, to make me able to manipulate the patterns of the mind arrays the way I do. But it was a hard decision for her to make, and in the end she just flipped a coin. It came down tails, and she made the changes in me—in her womb, before I was born. *So because of her coin flip, this whole universe is a Schrödinger's box.*"

"But you said that there would be two universes, that the coin would come down *both* ways."

"Ordinarily that would be true. But not this time. You see, the Omega Point, God at the end of time, springs directly from the human race. From Terra. Eventually humans will fill the entire universe—along with many other races, of course, but humans will be first and greatest. The *mind* of the universe will be essentially human. So anything that tampers with that history is *final*, in a way that everything else can never be. The Omega Point exists on the main branch, the primary universe. All the other universes split from that main branch. Without the Omega Point, the main branch does not, cannot, exist. And it can't exist without Terra having been, and becoming, everything it has been and will be in the future."

"But no matter what, humanity won't die, Jim. Even if we fail here, Outsider will start a singularity just like Gelden's, and all the minds of the arrays will transfer inside it, safe from anything."

"Not exactly," Jim said. "What you say is true. It will, in fact, happen if we fail now. But if it happens, the primary universe will cease to exist, because humanity will never create the Omega Point. It won't be able to. It won't be able to escape the black hole until the universe itself collapses and absorbs all the black holes inside it. But that will be too late. Humanity will have been cut off and the Omega Point never created. So the universe won't exist, either."

Char shook her head. "So you're saying that if your mom hadn't changed your DNA, the mind arrays wouldn't have become powerful enough to let humanity go into the singularity . . ." She stared at him. "But what about me? I can do the same things you can."

"I know. I don't know what will happen, though. Maybe you won't be created at all. Maybe you'll do things differently. Or maybe you'll be the same, but the arrays won't become strong enough." He closed his eyes again. "All I know for *sure* is that I have to change this. Here and now. If I can, then it will be all right."

"All right?" Harpy asked softly. "And what about you? What will happen to you?"

"I don't know that, either. But we are here now, all of us. And that's because the Gelden Leaper emulated a universe to enclose this single event and provide a way to change it. We are that way."

Jim took a deep breath and stared through the glass. Kate had broken off her silent argument with Carl. Now she had her back to him, facing a workbench. She was no longer tossing the coin back and forth. Now it rested on the tip of her right thumb and the side of her forefinger.

For a moment Jim felt dizzy. Had a billion years of Terran evolution gone precisely the way it had so that mankind could end up with opposable thumbs? And that merely so Kate would be able to flip this coin?

"Are you ready?" he said.

They moved closer to him. Char took his left hand and Harpy his right.

Kate's hand jumped suddenly. Her thumb sprang back. The coin leaped into the air, spinning quickly, catching the overhead light. It reached the top of its arc and began to fall back down, toward the top of the bench.

"Now!" Jim said.

2

Into the moment rushed the processing power of a billion human brains, coordinated by Char as she handed them off to Jim from the linkages Outsider pushed to the very limit of capacity. That force was joined by the rawer, cruder, but much greater capacity of every living Hunzzan who possessed the Neanderthal DNA twists that allowed for linkage, the linkage that Harpy had been born to create with the same powers his distant ancestor had used to destroy. And Jim himself, drawing all of it together into one great pattern, focused all of it on one goal: the alteration of the randomly chaotic events that affected the result of a single coin toss.

In any other circumstance, it would have been a trivial exercise. He could have modeled a billion different universes, each one with a separate result. But this was the primary universe. Here was where it all began—and ended. It *could not* split, for if it did, it would cease to exist.

His teeth ground together. His face turned bright red. His eyes bulged. His hands knotted into stony fists within theirs as he worked at the tiniest of limits, the strange fluctuations that lived on the other side of the quantum barriers, where time and space and energy became one.

"Ungh . . ."

Blood sprang from his lip where his teeth cut cleanly through. Finally, as he bent backward like an overdrawn bow, screaming and vibrating, the skin of his skull split and blood began to ooze forth.

"Aieee . . . ahhh . . . *yes!*"

3

*C*link!

The coin—it was an old-fashioned quarter Kate had inherited as a good-luck piece— landed on the scarred bench top. She and Carl leaned closer, staring.

After a moment Kate straightened. "Heads," she said.

She looked up at him. He was smiling. "I'm glad," he said.

Her lips trembled. Then suddenly she smiled, too. "So am I," she whispered. She touched her flat belly. "I didn't really want to do it."

4

Outside the door, Jim turned to face Char and Harpy. Now tears mingled with the blood streaming down his face. He dropped their hands, reached out, and enfolded them both in a hug.

"Did we do it?" Char whispered.

"We did it," he said.

"What happens now?" Harpy asked.

Jim was grinning and weeping at the same time. "I don't know," he replied. "I only know one thing. The universe goes on as it was meant to go on. I don't think we do, though. We weren't meant to be as we are now. We are supposed to be something else."

"Why are we still here?" Char said.

"Maybe a mercy. Maybe a blessing. Maybe just to say good-bye." He paused. "You know I love you both, don't you?"

Char wiped a streak of blood off his forehead. Her eyes washed his with dark fire. "Information encoded by natural selection," she whispered. "Where is any room in that for love?"

Harpy leaned closer. "There's always room for love," he rumbled. "Always . . ."

And so they clung to each other as the darkness grew around them, and the eternal light also.

Behind them, the door opened. Kate and Carl stepped out into the hallway. Kate paused.

"Did you feel something?"

Carl shook his head.

She glanced down. "What's that spot?"

He went over, crouched, and touched the moist, gleaming dot. He brought up one red-smeared fingertip. "Blood," he said. "It's blood."

INTERLUDE

WOLFBANE SYSTEM:
ANOTHER TIME, AN OLDER PLACE

Nausea gagged in Jim's throat as he realized what had happened. It had been his *mom* attacking that big man—and he hadn't been able to pull the trigger, even to save her. What kind of a man was he? What did all his brave promises, his shining ideals, mean when he couldn't even save his own mother?

But before he could think any further, he heard his father's voice call softly, "Tab? Jim?"

He started to reply, but lightning rolled out of the forest beyond, blinding him. He heard his dad cry hoarsely, and tried to blink the mask from his vision, his own weapon waving wildly.

Something moved. He gasped, straightened, and pulled the trigger just as he'd been taught, a clean, snapping two-shot. Then raw panic clutched him and, convulsively, he emptied his entire magazine into the dazzling, star-shot night.

With that, everything went silent.

For a long moment, nothing. Jim felt numb. His brain didn't seem to want to work. Then, with disorienting clarity, the world burst back into his consciousness. His ears rang with the recent explosions, screams, cries.

His nose burned with the stench of explosive powders and laser-lit fires. His stomach was a cold and curdled knot of fear. Gradually his vision cleared. In the background, the cabin burned with a lively crackle, casting weird shadows.

The night throbbed with menace. He could feel his teeth chattering in his jawbone. And all he wanted to do was burst into tears, run to his father and mother, and have them hold him and tell him it was all right.

"Jim . . ."

"Dad?"

"Over here," came the choked reply.

In the ghastly light of the cabin's destruction, Jim knelt by his father, a few feet from Heck Campbell's mutilated corpse.

"Dad?"

Carl Endicott groaned, swiping blindly at the blood that leaked from his shoulder. "Help me up," he said.

Jim's heart pounded in his chest. "Are you okay?"

"Just a glancing blow," Carl said. "Take my hand. Careful."

Jim braced himself and hauled gently. Carl Endicott came to his feet. He took a deep breath.

For an instant the night seemed utterly motionless. Wincing slightly, Carl shielded his eyes against the burning cabin. "Where's your mom?" he said, turning.

"Over . . . over here . . ." came a faint cry.

Both men rushed toward the sound. They

found her crawling along the edge of the clearing, a few feet out from the bushes.

"Mom!" Jim shouted, rushing toward her.

"Tab!" Carl yelled, close behind.

Jim reached her first and helped her to stand. There was a big lump on her forehead, but she seemed okay. Jim turned to Carl, his face alight.

"Dad?"

"What, son?"

"Did we make it? Are we all right?"

Carl paused and glanced at one armored figure pinioned on a distant tree. Then he turned and went back to the lump prostrate on the ground where he'd taken his wound. That one was dead, too.

But the most dangerous one?

It took Carl a while to find her. When he did, he knelt to make sure before he called out softly, "Jim? Come here."

A moment later Jim ghosted in out of the shadows. He squatted down next to Carl. The light from the burning cabin cast leaping shadows across his smoke-streaked features.

"This was Steele," Carl whispered. "You can't tell now, but I know her." He paused, swallowing. "Knew her."

Jim stared down at the ruin before him, at the smoking emptiness where Steele's head had been. His stomach heaved, but there was nothing left inside. After a moment he regained control. He stared at Carl.

"I did that?"

"Yes. Only your .75 could do that kind of damage to an armored fighter."

Jim licked his lips. He'd never killed any-body before—and only moments before, he'd almost killed his father. Now this. It felt . . . it felt *awful*.

"Dad?"

Carl stood up. His knees made a popping sound. He reached down, took Jim's hand, and pulled him up. They stared at each other.

"Dad?" Jim said again. His lips quivered. Moisture gleamed suddenly in his eyes. Then Carl reached out and pulled him in, wrapping him in his strong arms and holding him as if he would never let him go.

After a while, though, he did. They stepped apart, even though Jim thought that they had never been so close. "We did make it, didn't we, Dad?"

Carl grinned a little. "Yeah, son, we did."

"So we've got another chance?"

"We always have another chance, Jim. Always. As long as we live."

Jim nodded. "I'm glad," he said.

Overhead the stars burned in a great bowl of light. As Tabitha came over to join them, Jim looked up at the Wolfbane night. He blinked. For one moment he thought he saw great bands of color, red, blue, gold, purple, flicker across those distant stars, almost too quickly to see. And something else flickered, a fading memory of a history that might have been, that *had* been— but somewhere else. Where *he* had been some-one else. Some other universe. Some other Jim.

He reached for it, but just like that, it faded and was gone. And with it a weight of guilt vanished into the mists of might-have been, a dark freight train that now passed him by.

He sighed, wondering what it was he had just lost, and wondering what he had gained in exchange.

"Dad? Did you just see something in the sky?"

Carl shook his head. "No."

"I did," Jim said.

BIBLIOGRAPHY

Step into Chaos takes Jim Endicott into the very strange, but very real world of high energy physics, and proposes a unique way of understanding the universe. Such understandings are called Theories of Everything (TOES), and are one of the main concerns of physicists seeking to know how the universe works, from the tiniest quantum particles to the largest galaxies.

Here are resources that will lead the reader into a greater knowledge of the scientific background of this book, as well as introducing the novice to the fascinating field of cosmology, the study of universe itself.

SCIENCE FICTION

A Fire Upon the Deep by Vernor Vinge. Paperback reprint edition (February 1993) Tor Books; ISBN: 0812515285.

An epic novel with an interesting cosmological twist: time, space, and light speed vary by distance from galactic cores. This book won the Hugo Award in 1993.

Distress by Greg Egan. (February 1998) HarperPrism; ISBN: 0061057274.

Contact by Carl Sagan. (July 1997) Pocket Books; ISBN: 0671004107.

A brilliant adventure by the master of the cosmos himself which describes a universe based on Sagan's understanding of the science of the physical universe.

SCIENCE FACT

The research for *Step into Chaos* encompassed a number of sources. Here are the main ones:

The basic cosmology in *Step into Chaos* was taken from the well-known physicist Frank J. Tipler's book, *The Physics of Immortality*. (September 1995) Anchor; ISBN: 0385467990.

Perfect Symmetry: The Search for the Beginning of Time by Heinz Pagels. (1985) Simon & Shuster; ISBN: 0553240005.

Hyperspace by Michio Kaku. (March 1995) Anchor; ISBN: 0385477058.

A Brief History of Time by Stephen Hawking. (September 1998) Bantam Doubleday Dell; ISBN: 0553380168.

The World Wide Web has many sites that discuss cosmology and the universe at large.

NASA offers a very good site with many links at: http://map.gsfc.nasa.gov/html/web_site.html

The *Cosmology Review* provides the "latest theories, technologies, and opinions in cosmology" along with an excellent bibliography for further reading at: http://www.unc.edu/~jgreene5/

For an excellent discussion of Frank Tipler's Omega Point theory, on which this book is based, as well as discussions of other cosmological theories: http://www.aleph.se/Trans/Global/Omega/

FURTHER REFERENCES

Jim Endicott is faced with an alien religion in *Step into Chaos*. In essence, all religions are attempts at creating a structure and history for the universe. Religions are, in some sense, cosmological theories. Here are a few books that explore the subject:

Beyond the Big Bang: Quantum Cosmologies and God by Willem B. Drees. (February, 1991) Open Court Publishing Company; ISBN: 0812691180.

Buddhist Cosmology: Philosophy and Origins by Akira Sadakata, Gaynor Sekimori (Translator), and Hajime Nakamura. (April 1997) Charles E. Tuttle Co.; ISBN: 4333016827.

Cosmic Beginnings and Human Ends: Where Science and Religion Meet by Clifford N. Matthews (Editor), Roy Abraham Varghese (Editor), and C. L. Matthews. (December 1994) Open Court Publishing Company; ISBN: 0812692705.

Here is an excerpt from

BEYOND
THE STARS

BY
WILLIAM
SHATNER

coming soon from HarperPrism

1

The wrecked cabin stank of charred wood. The sun, its morning light filtered by a scrim of trees, leaked through a drifting haze of smoke. Jim Endicott licked his lips. His mouth was dry. His head ached. He could feel his pulse pumping in his ears.

He squatted next to Carl Endicott, the man who, up until a few days ago, he had believed to be his father, and said quietly, "Can you stand?"

"I think so. I'll need a hand." Carl levered himself into a sitting position. He groaned as the crust of blood on his chest split open. "No. I can't –" He gritted his teeth and sank back. Suddenly he seemed to shrink.

Jim's mother, Tabitha, until that moment seemingly calm despite the terror she had just survived, suddenly gasped.

"Oh, my God!"

"Mom, don't look."

Tabitha knelt next to Carl. She patted his shoulders, his head, his chest, as if her frantic touch could somehow heal him. Her hands came away streaked with red.

"Mom. . . ."

"Tab, it's not as bad as it looks," Carl said. He glanced at Jim. "Son, help your mother."

Jim put his hand on Tab's shoulder. She wheeled and glared at him. "Don't touch me!"

Jim pulled his hand back. "Mom, I –"

"You shot him! It was you, wasn't it?"

"I didn't mean –"

"This is all your fault! If you'd obeyed your father in the first place –"

"Tabitha!" Carl's voice snapped like a breaking bone. She turned back to him, her lips moving silently, an expression of utter helplessness on her face. Jim's stomach heaved. If there had been anything inside, he would have puked it up on the spot.

"I . . . I'm sorry," he said. He couldn't think of anything else to say.

I did all this. I caused it. My fault my fault my fault. . . .

He glanced over at the armored shape of Commander Steele's headless corpse, then quickly looked away.

Carl saw the glance. "Jim, stop it. Look at me!"

"Dad, I'm so sorry."

Carl shook his head, as if the apology was trivial, and Jim winced. "I brought a portadoc," Carl said. "It's in the large bag. If the explosion didn't damage it, I need it." He paused. "As for blame, there's plenty of it to go around. We can talk about it later, maybe. But right now, I'm bleeding. . . ."

A harsh, bright light seemed to explode Jim's skull, cutting through the film of shock that had leached all color from his world. The hues suddenly screamed at him: the crimson blotch on Carl's chest appeared to vibrate.

Blood. Too *much* blood. . . .

He turned and ran, not noticing the tears that streaked silently down his smudged cheeks.

"Hurry!" Tabitha cried.

2

Jim lifted the compact square shape of the portadoc away from Carl's naked chest. Carl's eyes were closed, his face pale, but his breathing was steady. The wound stretched from just above Carl's right nipple almost to his shoulder, an angry red welt now closed beneath a glistening, transparent line of instant skin.

Tabitha had pulled all their bags and everything else she could salvage out of the shambles of the cabin and piled them on the front porch. Amazingly, the roof of the porch still stood, though the cabin itself was open to the sky. She looked up as Jim added the portadoc to the pile.

"Jim? I'm sorry. What I said before, I didn't mean –"

He realized his hands were shaking. He took a deep breath. "Mom, it's okay. We were all crazy. Everything was crazy."

Her face was as pale as Carl's, and now Jim noticed the livid purple and yellow bruise that began high on her forehead and extended up beneath her disheveled hairline.

He reached toward her head. She flinched away from him, her own fingers involuntarily flying toward the lump.

"It's nothing. That big man hit me. I'm okay."

"Let me look. At least let the portadoc –"

"We have more important things to worry about. Your father . . . he needs medical attention. Real medical attention. We have to go back. . . ."

As Jim listened to her, he felt something stir deep within his mind. Something cold, dispassionate, and hard. It seemed to operate like a computer, pulling up facts, examining them, weighing them, discarding some, and generating new facts from old ones.

"Mom. We can't go back."

She stared at him. "But we have to. Your father. . . ."

He glanced at the unconscious man. "We can't stay here either, but we can't go back. I don't know where we can go. Maybe he does. I'd better wake him."

"Don't you dare! He's hurt! He needs rest!"

He was shocked at her vehemence. Under ordinary circumstances he would have obeyed her without question. But that new, cold part of him wouldn't allow it. She was too close to hysteria, operating on the ragged edge of sanity, reacting to emotions he knew she was barely able to understand. He couldn't obey her, but it wouldn't do to push her over the edge, either. That would only create another problem he would have to deal with, and he had enough of those already.

"Mom," he said, keeping his voice as gentle and steady as he could, "I have to talk to dad. Unless he told you what he wanted to do next. Did he tell you?"

She was staring at Carl. "He'll be fine, just as soon as a doctor. . . ." Her voice trailed off. "What did you say?"

"Did dad tell you what he wanted to do next?"

"Next?"

"Where he wanted to go from here. He couldn't have planned just to stay here. If they found us. . . ."

Involuntarily, his gaze strayed to the three silent bodies arrayed in contorted positions around the clearing in front of the cabin. The one without a head, who his father had called "Steele." Another one, impaled on a jagged tree branch. The third one, the big man, was nearly hidden in the underbrush, only his feet protruding into the clearing.

Two of them were women. Did it make a difference?

No, that cold part of him decided, it did not. All three had been doing their damnedest to kill him and his family. Now they were dead. But they had come from somewhere, for some reason, and there would be more.

There was no point in asking Tabitha about any of it, not when the man who knew everything was sleeping not ten feet away. The man he'd called "father" all his life.

Even the cold part of him cringed away from that. Carl wasn't his father, and that was somehow tied in with his own betrayal, and with these dead killers. He didn't want to think about that. It was too complicated, too frightening.

They had managed to survive the first attack. But he knew it was only the first attack, and there would be more. So they didn't have a lot of time. Some, maybe, though he had no idea how much. But his strange and surprising father, who wasn't his father, and who had turned out to know a hell of a lot more about the arts of death than Jim had ever imagined possible, might very well know.

"Mom?"

At the sound of his voice she blinked, as if he'd startled her.

"Mom," he said again. He reached out and took her hand. Her fingers were cold and felt thin, like sticks coated with ice. He tugged her up. She came without protest, evidently happy to be led. He walked her away, walked her around the end of the cabin, found a soft hummock where the grisly remains of the dead were no longer visible, and sat her down. She looked up at him, suddenly trusting as a child. For the first time in his life, he realized their roles were reversed. He would have to take care of her, not the other way around.

The thought nearly scared him senseless.

"Jim . . . is everything going to be all right? It is, isn't it?"

He patted her hand. "Yes, it is. I promise."

That was the most heroic thing he did that day.

3

As he rounded the corner of the cabin, Jim glanced back and saw him mother sitting placidly on the grass, her expression blank and helpless and weirdly expectant. He felt a knot just above the center of his breastbone, half in his chest, half in his throat, a knot it took him a moment to identify as terror. It was odd: he had never thought of terror as being a physical thing, a cold, almost fleshy mass that choked him as he forced himself to swallow it.

He went to his father and kneeled down near Carl's head, then slipped his left arm beneath Carl's neck and lifted him a bit.

Carl moaned. His eyes came open. His gaze was disoriented at first, but sharpened quickly.

"Where's your mother?"

"I took her around the cabin and sat her down. Where she couldn't see. She's not in good shape."

Carl Endicott's gaze went unfocused for an instant. "Your mother is one of the strongest women I've ever known," he said softly. "But this is too much for her. Maybe that's what I can't forgive you for. Causing something that even she can't handle. That nobody should be expected to handle."

"As you told me, we can discuss it later," Jim said, after consulting that new, cold part of himself. "Right now, I need to know. And don't lie to me or hold anything back for my own good, because if we are going to get away from here, I'm going to have to do it. You're too sick to depend on."

He looked down at the wound on Carl's chest. The portadoc had done as well as it could, but Tabitha was right. Carl needed more and better treatment, and he needed it as soon as possible. How soon that would be, Jim had no idea. Out on the edge of his awareness lurked the unthinkable: Carl might die.

Carl stared up at him. "You don't know it," he said, "but you just surprised me. Maybe I didn't do as bad a job with you as I thought."

"And we can talk about that later, too. In the meantime, I have to make sure there is a later. What are the chances that more of these killers will come? You said you knew this Steele woman. She's dead, but she came from somewhere. If more are coming, how quickly?"

Carl closed his eyes. "Steele liked to do things on her own, but the man who sent her watches everything. If he doesn't know what happened already, he will soon. And he'll send others."

"Who sent her?"

Carl went on as if Jim hadn't spoken. "There will be a mother ship somewhere. It will take them a while to put together a new team and send it out. We can't go back to the tube station, and we certainly can't go back home. So we'll have to go ahead."

Jim nodded. "Yes, I thought so too. Where are we going?"

"Hanna Port."

Jim had to think a moment before he remembered. "That little place. On the other side of the mountains from here."

"That's right. We need to get there. I have friends." Carl suddenly gritted his teeth. "Jim. The portadoc gave me enough painkiller to work under normal circumstances, but this isn't normal. I need more, enough to let me move around now. But that will be too much for me to function mentally. I'll be groggy, no use for anything. I'll be dependent on you."

"I'd tell you not to worry, that I'll take care of everything, but that would be a lie. I don't know what will happen. But I'll do my best, dad."

Carl nodded. "Then let's hope your best is enough." He shifted his weight against Jim's arm. "Get me the painkiller. The quicker we get away from here and get into the trees, the safer we'll be."

4

Jim felt happy.

They walked along a narrow, rocky path, beneath an arch of bowed green pines that concealed the sky almost completely. The path was more an opening than a path, a trail for things with sure hooves or pads, and humans weren't meant for it.

He was burdened with bags strapped down his back. Carl's left arm lay heavily across his shoulder. Carl could not really walk, but moved along in a halting, looping stagger, his head lolling, his eyes glazed and empty from the drugs. Tabitha supported her husband on the other side, and was similarly encumbered. She'd quit talking long ago, and now her breathing sounded raspy and labored.

Jim was aware of all of this. He was aware of more: of the hopelessness of their position, of the danger of death, of the yawning inner abyss of his own betrayal. He was terrified, and numb with grief, and yet he felt happy. When he realized what he felt, he was amazed. Happiness? For a moment he wondered if he was going crazy.

The trail wound upwards, following some secret fold in the land the animals had sensed, but he couldn't. Now the trees pulled back a bit, exposing ground stony with loose, dark gray shale, and Carl's feet suddenly went out from under him. Tabitha let out a sharp cry as her ankle twisted. She stumbled and went to her knees. Jim listed toward her as Carl's bulk dragged him down.

"Whoa!" He barely managed to lower Carl to a loose sprawl on the hard ground, and then he reached for Tabitha.

"Mom!"

She was sitting, rubbing her left ankle with both hands. He scooted around Carl, who began to hum tunelessly as he stared from one side of the path to the other, and squatted next to her. "How bad is it?"

She looked up at him. For the first time he saw, magnified by exhaustion and pain, the fine wrinkles at the corners of her eyes. Had they always been there? How little he had observed, how much he had always taken for granted! And still that odd, buoyant feeling of happiness would not leave him, even in the face of new disaster.

"It's not broken," she said slowly. She didn't sound sure.

"Let me see." Gently, he pushed the bottom of her pants leg back, to reveal a streak of discolored skin about an inch wide that began near the base of her heel and extended up over her ankle bone. The patch was faintly blue, but darkening as he watched. Gingerly, he pushed at the spot where the knob of ankle protruded. Tabitha drew in a sharp breath.

"You're right, I don't think it's broken," he said. "But it's badly sprained, and you won't be able to walk on it."

Her lips began to quiver. Without thinking about it, he put his arm around her shoulder and pulled her close, suddenly realizing how *small* she was, this woman who had towered over his childhood.

"What are we going to do now?" she whispered.

She began to shake, and he squeezed her tighter, until the shaking stopped.

"The portadoc. I think we can get the

swelling down, and maybe make some kind of cast. Or I can tear up a shirt, make a splint with sticks if the machine can't do that. Maybe enough for you to walk." He thought about it. "But you won't be able to help with dad . . . with Carl."

He knew she noticed the way he changed what he said, but she didn't say anything about it. *That* still lay between them, the mystery of mutual betrayal, but it was either too soon or too late to say anything about it, and so he was grateful for her silence.